All rights reserved. No part of this publication may be reproduced in any form or by photocopying or by any electronic or mechanical means, including information storage or retrieval systems, without permission in writing from both the copyright owner and the publisher of this book.

Published by: Glädtex Press
Interior Design: J. V. Bolkan
Cover Design: Sharleen Nelson
ISBN-13: 978-1-961246-31-2
Library of Congress Control Number: 2023916543

While several into this book were inspired by or are that events, students of the Freedom Movement will no doubt recognize them. A few passages mention actual Freedom Movement staff workers and volunteers which are identified by their real names. What happened to them, as stated in those passages, was real. However the novel's fictional characters and activities are products of the author's imagination and do not depict any real event or any real persons thoughts or opinions, emotions, or actions.

The opening epigraph, T.S. Eliot's, "The Waste Land," is printed with permission granted by Faber and Faber, Ltd. All respect and rights reserved.

10 9 8 7 6 5 4 3 2 1

The interior body text is presented in Garamond Pro point for easy readability. Chapter titles and drop caps are Gil Sans MT.

© 2025 Randall Luce
Black & Tan Fantasy

All rights reserved. No part of this publication may be reproduced in any form, by photocopying or by any electronic or mechanical means, including information storage or retrieval systems, without permission in writing from both the copyright owner and the publisher of this book.

Published by: GladEye Press
Interior Design: J.V. Bolkan
Cover Design: Sharleen Nelson
ISBN-13: 978-1-951289-23-2
Library of Congress Control Number: 2025936543

Several scenes in this book were inspired by actual events. Students of the Freedom Movement will no doubt recognize them. A few passages mention actual Freedom Movement staff workers and volunteers, which are identified by their real names. What happened to them, as stated in those passages, was real.

However, the novel's fictional characters and activities are products of the author's imagination and do not depict any real event or any real person's thoughts or opinions, emotions, or actions.

The opening epigraph, T.S. Elliot's "The Waste Land" is printed with permission granted by Faber and Faber, Ltd. All respective rights reserved.

10 9 8 7 6 5 4 3 2 1

The interior body text is presented in Garamond 11 point for easy readability. Chapter titles and dropcaps are Gil Sans MT.

ADVANCE READER COPY

Black & Tan Fantasy

A NOVEL

RANDALL LUCE

GladEye Press
www.gladeyepress.com

Springfield, OR

Dedication

With my love, to Elaine, Aziz, and Aaron.

Geneva smiled and squeezed back. "No. I was too ashamed." She got up from the table and took a broom from the hall closet and walked upstairs.

The next day Geneva's father came over with a stack of papers. "These are my payments and expenses. Don't get any idea that I can't do them." Burnett set the papers on the kitchen table. He didn't sit down. "But I never liked this part of my job. And you need something to do. I want my daughter to be happy in life. I don't want her tied down with a mope. So here you go. I expect you'll do as good a job as I do. I can't pay you a going rate. I can't afford that. But I'll be fair."

Harry picked up some pages. "The money doesn't matter. Thank you." He extended his hand. Burnett looked at it for a moment before taking it. Then he was gone.

Harry hardly ever went outside. Maybe Browning was right. Maybe he should.

But the few times he did, it was too much mess, too many unfriendly looks, and some said it straight to his face: you'll never be a Negro because you can always turn back White. Someday—and there's no ifs about it they'd say—someday something will happen that will be beyond your bearing, and you won't have to bear it. You'll just turn back White. But we, they said, we have to bear it, or fall down beneath it, because there's no turning for us.

Harry would bite his tongue and hurry back to Mae and Pete's house. He'd sit on his bed, going a hundred miles an hour, breathless, burning, and thinking: *They don't know me, because there is no turning back. There's no turning back for me.* Then he'd get up, and look in the mirror with the flaw, and sway, just small stuff like sweeping out a store or shelving stock. Not like you, Mr. Harry. Not at all like you."

"If you showed yourself more, that might help, but I couldn't promise you. Hiring a White man ... what would the Klan think of that? Or even all those rich White bankers and such that we deal with. It'd be touch and go."

Browning laughed. "Maybe if you passed for Colored. In another town."

After he left, Harry sat back down. Burning, burning. As if he could pass for a Colored. He wouldn't know how. He always prided himself on not overthinking his life, of just doing what there was to be done. Well, what could he do now? Doing books had been his only idea.

He told Geneva about passing. She paused, and looked off beyond him. "Well, I left home once before for a man. Mr. Barrett's right. We'd have to move away. I told myself when I did, I didn't have any choice." She laughed, softly, briefly. "I was wrong, of course. It's always your choice."

They were sitting at the kitchen table. She looked over at the icebox, the cupboards. "Do you want something?" Harry shook his head no. Him passing? He couldn't believe she'd even consider it. Geneva shook her head too. "But I'm home now and I don't ever want to leave again. In Alabama, I always wanted to come back." She reached for his hand on the table and covered it with hers. "And I don't think you could do it."

Harry turned his hand to hold hers. "Why didn't you leave, then? Why did you wait?" He paused and squeezed her hand. "Was it because of me?"

Browning drew two cigars from his vest. "You want one?" Harry smiled and said no. Browning cocked his head. "No? Well, I'll leave this one here for Mr. Pete." Browning set one on the table in front of his chair and lit the other, rotating the cigar's foot close to the flame. He puffed, lightly, one two three times, then he flourished the cigar between his fingers. "Ah. One of life's honest pleasures."

He leaned back in the chair. "White folk's cheating just comes with the territory. There's nobody or nothing to stop them. You've just got to find one who won't cheat you all that much. They're not bound to respect a Colored man, but you can turn them around, sometimes, and make them respect you in spite of themselves. Where they won't even admit it, but they still do. So they don't cheat you so much." Browning leaned forward and tapped the table with his index finger. "And nothing you can find in my books is going to improve on what I'm already doing, or make that situation go away.

"You're in a fix, Mr. Harry. You want to work, and I respect that. No proper man wants to go without work. But you need us more than we need you." Browning stood up, and Harry did too. "No Negro is going to hire a strange White man." Browning put his hand up on Harry's shoulder. "Tell me, I don't see you much on the street. Do you ever go out much?"

Harry could feel his blush. "No ... Mr. Barrett. It's ... it's just easier not too."

"Well, don't judge us too harshly. Not too many White folks live amongst us. Most who do, well, they're loners I guess, maybe not much family, or none, and maybe a little vacant sometimes." He pointed to his head. "Up here. Harmless, and friendly enough, but maybe a little off. And if they work its out at the street, up and down it—that sea of Negro faces, it was always there. He watched Hiram walk away, and he thought about Big Mama Darling and Geneva. Harry shook his head. *I'm no sea captain.* He'd sink beneath these waves.

Harry had to do something. He had to work. He talked to Pete about bookkeeping. Pete brought over a shopkeeper he knew, a Mr. Barrett Browning. Harry told him what he could do. Browning leaned back in his chair and asked him, "Why would I need to do all that? I've been running my shop for fifteen years. I keep my books well enough. Why should I pay you for that?" Harry cleared his throat. "You've got White suppliers, don't you?" Browning nodded yes. "And your storefront, I bet you rent that too, from a White man."

"White woman," Browning said.

Harry stopped for a moment, and then he continued. "So, you can be sure they're cheating you."

Browning smiled. "They sure do."

"So, if I did your books, I could show you just how they're cheating you, and by how much."

Browning leaned forward and stifled a laugh. Then he looked right at Harry. "Excuse me, Mr. Harry, I don't mean you any disrespect. But suppose what you say is true, that you could show me in black and white exactly how I'm being cheated, more so than I already know." He sat back in his chair; he looked very comfortable. He smiled. "What, exactly, could I do about it? What could I change, in my business practices, to stop that cheating, or even just cut it back a little? I'd be showing my hand, you see. They'd know that *I* know. And then they'd retaliate. They'd put me out of business."

he'd used, he started laughing. It wasn't funny and it hurt, but he couldn't stop laughing.

Back at Pete's, Harry went right to the nearest mirror. He'd only glanced in the barbershop mirror; he'd been in such a hurry to leave. Now he studied his face. He didn't recognize himself at first. Maybe that was a good thing. Harry frowned at his image.

Two days later, Mr. Hiram paid him a call. He looked at Harry's hair and nodded his approval. Harry didn't say that he still didn't look like a Negro. He thought he looked like a Mexican.

"You tell everybody you meet I gave you that haircut."

Harry told him he didn't think he'd be a good advertisement for his business.

Hiram frowned and muttered something underneath his breath; he pointed his finger at Harry. "You won't be advertising me. I'll be advertising you. With my reputation, I don't need any man's business or any man's opinion—least of all yours. But you, son, you'll need every friend you can find. So, you treat me with respect. And speak of me to others with respect. I'm about the best friend in this town that you can have."

"But, won't you—won't you lose customers? You saw the ones that left."

Hiram smiled. "No Negro man leaves a good barber once he finds one. And I'm the best barber in town."

The bottom rail on top, Harry thought, but suddenly he realized that Hiram Walker had always been the top rail here, and always would be. Harry saw him to the door, and looked blocking it, and Harry didn't know what to do. He looked back at Pete, seated against the wall.

Hiram looked up and down the row of seated men. "Lots of talk about color today." "And we can't help it—all Aunt Hagar's children *have* to be color conscious. Those White folks been beating that into our heads the moment we first set foot on American soil. In Africa, there was only one color and it was good enough for everybody. But in America there's lots and lots of colors, and some are good and some are bad, but we can all agree that one's better than all the rest. You got a dollar, son?"

At first Harry didn't realize the barber was asking him. He hesitated, and then he took a dollar from his wallet.

The barber held it high. "Lord, he's got a dollar!" Everybody chuckled. Then he flourished a dollar of his own. "Nobody would call green a bad color. In fact, it's my favorite color of all. All these years I been preaching from my pulpit here," he touched his barber chair, "that green will be the color of our salvation. Of all the colors in America, can't we all agree that this one's the best? Let's see—," he held both dollars up to the light. "His color's the same as mine. Have a seat, son."

Everybody nodded their heads, but not everybody was smiling. Hiram began to heat a curling iron. "Good thing your hair's already straight. Lord help you if you had to have it conked." Harry wanted to ask him why, but he didn't say a word.

Afterwards Harry told Pete: he had to be honest, that even if nobody had said anything, sitting in that narrow room filled with Negro men, he'd almost jumped out of his skin. He stopped as soon as he'd said it, and then, realizing the words in their seats. Pete nodded to the oldest barber there, with the barber's chair farthest from the door. He nodded back and Pete navigated Harry through the shop to the closest empty seat. Harry resisted the urge to stare. So, this was *the* Mr. Hiram Walker, the best Negro barber in Chattanooga. Pete had told Harry—over and over, and Harry had wondered why—how lucky Harry was that Mr. Hiram had agreed to marcel his hair. Harry gave Pete a wry smile. "Pete," he said, "he's just a barber. It's just a haircut." Pete gave Harry that look—so familiar now to Harry—like he was a useless child. Geneva had to tell him: "You don't have to understand. Just do everything Pete tells you." But the more Pete talked, the more Harry told himself this barbering business couldn't be anything important.

Now, in the barber shop, Harry tried to remember what Pete had told him. These Black faces— Harry looked straight ahead. Pete had gone over it before they came: Don't talk, don't read, just smile—but just a little. Don't grin like an idiot. And listen. And bite your tongue if you have to. Everybody knows something about you, how you showed up out of nowhere with a Colored woman. Some people aren't taking that too well.

Now, several of the men started talking—about color: how the blackest berries were the sweetest, how white sugar couldn't compare to brown, paper-bag tests and other stuff that Harry didn't understand, and most of all, about the evilness of Whites, particularly how they rape Black mothers, sisters, and daughters.

Harry bit his tongue. His face was burning and he couldn't hide it.

When Hiram Walker turned to Harry, Pete had to nudge him up. Hiram was standing in front of his barber's chair,

Over time the image would darken and fade. He knew he would never see them again.

◆—◆

He couldn't navigate the streets outside. How do you conduct yourself when you don't know what you are? Not White, not Black; was he neither, was he in between? All he knew was, he wasn't any one thing. And if you're not one thing, you're nothing. Every day Harry could see that this was true. The men in Geneva's family, so gregarious with each other, were reserved with him. What, he thought, would they say to him? What could they say? He had to admit that he gave them little chance. Even at family gatherings, Harry kept mostly to himself. He told himself he lacked the most basic knowledge. He watched when Negroes visited; he watched them greet each other. What they called each other—"Gate," "Dipper"—what did that mean? He repeated what Geneva told him to say. He hardly knew what the words meant.

Pete talked to him the most. After supper, when the dishes were cleared and the women were in the kitchen, Pete would question him. "What do White folks really think of us?" "How much do they talk about us?" "What do they say?" Harry felt like an informant—and ignorant. All his life he'd been around Negroes, but he could only tell Pete it didn't matter what White people said, because they didn't know a thing. "All the Negroes I thought I knew? I've never met anybody like your people. Not at all. Which means I never knew those Negroes at all."

◆—◆

When Harry's hair grew out, Pete took him to the barbershop. It fell silent. Two men stood up and left. The others fidgeted think or second-guess, you just *do*; every day you do, and you never look back.

But there he was, at the mirror, wondering—

There was one mirror in particular, it was flawed and his image would pinch, then bulge, shrivel and swell—he'd move just so, a little bit back and forth, and watch his features roil. He was never one thing. It fascinated and repelled him. He believed he was turning vain.

Only Geneva and her children could take him away from himself. She told him to be her children's father. She gave him a free hand. Lilly was quiet and shy—at least, to him she was—and she always stayed close to her mother. Earley gave him the business from the get-go, but Harry could never be angry for long. Putting up with Earley, correcting Earley, kept Harry's mind off himself.

Geneva and her children—Charlotte and hers— Did Harry see the ghosts of those he'd lost in the faces of those he had? But they were nothing alike. Charlotte, Harry Jr., and Mary Ann—Harry had their snapshots in his wallet and took them out when he was alone. One time Geneva came in. Harry was holding one of his snaps, of Charlotte and her children posing on what had been his front porch; Harry Jr. and Mary Ann standing ramrod straight and serious, and Charlotte in between— Geneva put her hand on his. He barely felt it.

He looked up at her. "She probably hates me now. She has to. And I don't blame her. But I wonder ... that night ... did she already hate me then?"

Geneva took the picture from his hand and only then did he see his tears had wetted the surface. He'd marred the image, Charlotte's face forever blurred. He still kept the snapshot.

didn't know how to react. She'd never been playful with him before, not in this way. He didn't know how he looked to her. Too white—what was that? He'd always looked this way. Geneva reached for his hair again, this time not playing, and gently lifted a strand. "Too straight." She shook her head. "And too short. But it's dark enough. You've got to grow it out. We'll get it marcelled." She had to explain: "To make it look conked, like a Negro's hair. Marcelled—waved. At the barber shop." This strange language—Harry looked at her hands as she talked, as if they could translate. Geneva smiled, proud. "My daddy goes to the best barber in town." Harry smiled back and nodded his head, she was doing her best for him, but inside he was burning. His heart was racing. He gathered himself and sat very still.

It took a long time to grow his hair long. While it did, Harry rarely went out. After a few days, he and Geneva moved in with Geneva's cousin Mae and her husband Pete. Lilly and Earley slept at the home house, with Big Mama Darling. Harry almost objected, but he saw that Geneva didn't mind. She still got them their breakfast and took them to school. In truth, Harry realized, no matter where they slept, the children still spent most of their days at school and with Geneva. Harry grimaced and laughed. None of it made sense to him, but who was he to object. *Nothing, really; I'm nothing. No importance at all.*

Harry began to study himself in their mirrors. He thought about himself all the time. He didn't like that. He'd never done that before. That was for people who couldn't just do their lives; because that's how you should live your life; you don't

"Have? Had. I had."

"And you love them don't you. You still love them?"

Harry nodded his head.

"So, do you love Geneva as much as you love them?"

Harry stared at this man, questioning him so. What had he asked? What were his words? Finally, their meaning seeped in. Burnett was getting up from his chair, frowning, when Harry finally answered, "Yeah ... of course I do. But ... does it matter? She's all I've got now. So, yeah, of course I do."

Burnett didn't reply. He didn't even look at Harry. Standing now, he turned and left the room.

—◆—◆—

Later, Geneva told him, "He asked me that too: if I loved you. I said the same thing you did. 'Of course I do.' Then he asked me if I always loved you." She was standing in the middle of their bedroom; Harry was seated on the bed. "I told him I grew to love you." Geneva knelt down to look up at him, his face felt red. She softened her voice. "So many times, in my family or others, kids marry who their parents say. A boy and girl from one family might marry a girl and boy from another, lots of times. They weren't expected to love each other right off. I told my father that when you burst into that burning room I wasn't surprised—that it was *you* who came." She put her hand on his knee. "I thought about that a lot when we were driving here to Chattanooga."

—◆—◆—

He looked too white. After a few days in Chattanooga, Geneva told him that—she smiled and laughed and mussed his hair, "What're we going to do with you? You're just so white." He

He reached both hands out to the corners of the den. "Look around you. I've done well. And, like I said, I enjoy my work. I'm a damn good carpenter. But every time I think about having to consider a thing like keeping free from White people, that that was necessary to determine how I'd live my life—and this goes not just for me, but for any Colored man of dignity—I feel a rage inside," Burnett brought his fist up to his chest, "and it burns."

That burning, burning. Harry was careful not to respond, but yes, that burning, yes. How odd it seemed, hearing that from this man right now, but really, wasn't that life? Hadn't Harry learned that by now? *Only my burning isn't rage.*

Burnett relaxed his fist and lowered his hand. "So, when I'm here at home with my family, I don't like to think about people who look like you."

He hadn't once taken his eyes off Harry. "What do you think of that?"

"You don't like me, do you?"

"I don't know you. I just don't like your presence."

"Then why do you let me stay?"

"Because I love my daughter. And my wife. And my mother. They're women a man respects. Whatever they say carries a lot of weight with me."

Burnett leaned forward. "Here's what I want to know: do you love my daughter?"

"Of course, I do! I'm," Harry looked around the room, "I'm here! Of course, I do."

"How much?"

"How much? How do you measure—?"

Burnett shifted in his chair. "Okay. Let's put it this way. You have a wife and two children—"

and every self around him—were given air and savored, but they were all alien to Harry. He tried not to look at them.

And should he have known these "selves"? Would that have been appropriate? Harry considered this. He didn't think it would be. That sea of people outside the Burnetts' door—what right had he to know them? Or Burnett's family: He had burst in upon them unexpected and unbidden. Why should he know them as intimately as his own? The family he'd abandoned. *I never meant to.* That was all he could say.

What was he to do? Geneva was his only answer. He must stay close to her. She could guide him, tell him what to do, interpret what he saw and heard. She would hold the sheltering sail and, walking backwards, her eyes on only him, lead him on his way. She, alone, was his family now.

—◆—◆—

Malachi Burnett was a carpenter. He told Harry that. The two of them were sitting alone in Burnett's den. It was Harry's second evening there. Burnett liked working with his hands. He was good at it. But, also, as a carpenter he didn't need an office or a shop. He kept his tools in his car. People came by his house to hire him. "And that was important when I started out. It still is." Burnett looked right at Harry, into his eyes. "I wanted a way in life that freed me as much as possible from dealing with any White man. No shop, no office? No White landlord. I own all my tools. I own my car. There's still the bank, and the hardware store to deal with—I wish to God a Negro would start one, make a go of that—and anybody White who sees me on the street, I have to contend with them. And from time to time I'll do a job for a White man, but I try as much as I can to only work for the people of my race."

family's heroes, in the stories he was hearing now, would be the villains.

Harry was standing off to the side and surveying the room: smiles and laughter, a head tilted with a you've-got-to-be-kidding look, eyes serious and heads nodded silently. His mind began to wander. These last few days—they wouldn't make a family story at all, but one about the end of family. So, he thought, he did share one thing with these people: his newly acquired knowledge that life—in sudden happenstance—can upend your entire existence, and all you can do is put your head down and, one slow step at a time, trudge through each oncoming day. And this, he supposed, might well be common—as common as the knowledge of death. All flesh is grass, and all life is lived under that shadow. A truth that the comfortable hide. And joy is only possible through denial, or forgetfulness. That's what Harry thought. He smiled to himself. Such rumination! This wasn't like him at all.

He looked around at the gathering: he could find nothing else, no other common cause with these people he now found himself among.

Weeks later the family went to a park, crowded with Negroes, to listen to a Negro band. Harry went with them. He couldn't follow the music. Each horn had its own melody; each one unravelling from the others, each one dancing off in its own direction. But look at them, Geneva's folks, tapping toes and patting fingers, eyes closed and heads nodding. They understood this music. They heard a center, a focus, that Harry couldn't find. He sensed that other people nearby were staring at him. Some were frowning. And Harry thought he understood why. He was the only White person there, and that place was where Negro "selves"—the music's self, and each distracted. When she paused, Harry told her yes and thank you, to whatever it was she'd said.

So many Negro eyes today—looking right at him! That was all he could think of. Open faces—not ducked down, not hidden or closed—and yet each open face held a secret, a self that Harry didn't know. And he doubted he ever could.

Through the evening, Harry caught snatches of conversation—Geneva's family were telling each other their family stories. Harry nodded to himself. That, at least, was familiar. He had grown up listening to stories about his family. They'd never seemed remarkable to him—no more than the family resemblances of hair and facial features, height and weight and temperament. As he grew older, he'd detected an air of self-satisfaction in those stories, but he never tired of hearing them. Even as an adult. They were him—and his siblings, his parents, cousins, grandparents, uncles and aunts, nieces and nephews. His children. (Here, his throat caught, suddenly.) He didn't exist apart from these stories. They took lifetimes to create and lifetimes to tell—the simple acts of living through every shared day.

So here too; stories that, no doubt, were repeatedly told. Some about simple joys—picnics and courtship, funny things said, stories about this great aunt or that uncle—the generations all bled together—but also others, about floods and fires, nightriders; life-and-death stories about their burdens and horrors, not overcome and not always survived, but borne and endured and somehow outlasted, now told as evidence of resilience and strength. Had his family any such stories? Just a few. Hiding their silver from the Yankees ... and riding roughshod over upstart Negroes. Suddenly Harry realized: his

At her house, no less tidy and ordered than her son's, Big Mama Darling sat in the biggest chair; it was stuffed, tall, and she herself was small in it, but somehow not diminished. Harry could see the serenity in her nut-brown face, just as Geneva had said. Her whole family gathered there, each one solicitous, asking her if she wanted this and that; she attended to every one of them, giving each what they wanted most, her acknowledgment and acceptance of their gifts and solicitude.

A safe shore after stormy seas—watching her family gather around her, it came to Harry that she was the sea captain. Not those White men he'd seen that morning on the street, but this woman grown small with age; Big Mama Darling—she was the sea captain.

Geneva presented Harry to her. She pressed his hands together, between hers, and he looked into her eyes. Looking far, looking inward; looking right at him. Harry fought a sudden urge to flinch from her gaze. He could only guess at what she saw in him, but her hands covering his, sheltering them—he was relieved to think she found him good. She held his hands for a while, and Harry gradually became aware of the qualities of hers: the old callouses, the skin softened over time and thin with age. The nut-brown color accented with darker hues. He looked back up, at her face, her gray-white hair pulled tight to a knot at the nape of her neck, and the skin hardly wrinkled. Her relaxed, serene smile. Harry could well believe that, younger, she'd been beautiful.

She spoke to him, but Harry could only nod and smile, his hands between hers. Her words didn't quite register. He was hers." Geneva laid the dress out on the bed. "You can thank her you have a home here now."

Harry smiled. He so much wanted to smile. He hoped it wasn't too wan. "Your mother said I had you to thank."

Geneva smiled back. "All the women. You have all of us to thank."

She started taking off her clothes. "Born a slave. But she doesn't like that word. She says that never was her. She's had a long, hard, row to hoe, sometimes crooked, but she always made it as straight as she could. And ever since I was little, such a calm look on her face, she'll look like she's remembering something—a faraway look, or maybe far inside. Maybe both." Her church dress on, Geneva started looking through her hats. "It's like she was on a boat, and sailed through stormy seas, and now she's finally home, safe and dry." Geneva looked up from her hats at Harry. "If she were a preacher, she'd preach about family. Everything she ever did was for family." Geneva put on a blue hat—wide brimmed, a thing with feathers—and posed for Harry. "My father, you'll find out, is a very proud man. And the one thing he's proudest of, is that his mama has her own house where she's comfortable, she doesn't have to worry about having a roof and a bed, and she'll always have her family with her. Of course, my grandfather did all that, but my father's been able to keep it. Nothing would upset him more than losing what his father left him."

Geneva fetched a damp cloth and began to wipe Harry's face and coat, cleaning them of soot. "None of that in Big Mama's house." She paused, her hand on Harry's chest. "She's so glad I've come back home. I don't ever want to worry her again."

Later that day, Harry and Geneva were alone, together in the bedroom. Apparently, it used to be hers. She was looking through the clothes in the closet, holding dresses up against her shoulders, and looking in the mirror. "Church clothes," she explained, "the occasion demands church clothes." They were going to see Big Mama Darling. Geneva looked at him sitting on the bed and sighed. "Why didn't you bathe? And those dirty clothes. It's too late now. You'll just have to do. Oh, what's your suit size, your hat and shirt sizes? Daddy said he'd buy you some clothes."

"When?"

"I don't know. You don't have to go with him. I think … he'd prefer you not to." She shrugged. "A Negro buying a White man clothes? It'd be better if you stayed here."

Harry wanted to object. He didn't want anybody picking out and buying him clothes. But, looking at this strange room where Geneva looked so at home, Harry asked himself, where would he go to buy those clothes, and what money would he use? He didn't know. He tried to picture himself in a store picking out clothes, and a Colored man taking out his wallet and paying. Impossible. So, how could he object? He looked down at the floor between his feet. "I'll write them down." Geneva nodded and asked Harry, "What do you think of this?" She held out the skirt of a blue and white striped dress. Harry looked up at her. "You're beautiful," he said.

Geneva brushed the dress with her hands. "She was born a slave. Big Mama. She's seen more in her life than—" Geneva stopped brushing. Perhaps she had a particular scene in mind. "She could teach our race their whole history just by telling kitchen. You should know, you have Geneva to thank for your staying. You must know that showing up at Big Mama Darling's house in the middle of the night was quite a surprise for all of us. I'm glad to have you. I sincerely am. No offense, but you could've been turned away."

He nodded. "Yes ma'am, I understand. None taken. For a while, I thought I would be. I wouldn't have blamed—" He looked back at the plate. The grits were creamy white, with a light yellow pool melting from the slab of butter in the middle. Just the way he liked them. But he couldn't take a bite. "I'm sorry. I'm sure this is very good." He looked around. "Could you show me how to get back to the bedroom?"

Harry sat alone on the side of the bed. He had shut the door. He was tired, but he wasn't sleepy. Something in his life had burned away. This room, familiar yet strange: looking at it now, it told him something he couldn't yet put into words. Something was lost—a chair that's only yours to sit in; a table and a meal that are yours, and yours to share—*your* house hosting *your* company—he'd only have the appearance of those things now, if that. In the car last night, telling Geneva he had no other place else to go to—he hadn't counted on this.

He was the top rail on the bottom.

Harry took Geneva's pillow and held it to his face. He breathed in deep, over and over.

Geneva would be his lifeline. But right now, she was gone, off to her grandmother's—he still didn't understand why—and he didn't know when she'd be back. He thought about all those faces outside the front window. Geneva would keep him afloat, above that sea of faces, and yet she was as strange to him as they were.

Harry followed her into her kitchen and sat at her table. She stood by the stove, facing him, smiling. "I'm Mama Lou, Geneva's mother. Mrs. Burnett. This is my house, mine and Mr. Malachi's, Mr. Malachi Burnett, Geneva's father. I'll have something for you in a minute."

She served him a plate of grits. "I've been keeping this warm for you."

He asked her, "Where's Geneva? Where're the children?"

"They're at Big Mama Darling's."

Harry nodded. "That's the home house?"

She smiled and nodded yes.

"Well, what is that? Why are they there?"

Harry hadn't yet looked at his plate. Mama Lou gave him a glass of orange juice. "Well, that's where all the family stays, if they're from out of town and visiting. It's where we gather for the holidays. You'd be there too, but Malachi wanted Geneva and you here, for now. Geneva said y'all came here for good. We weren't expecting her." She sat down opposite of him, facing him, and smiled again. "Or you. So maybe Geneva and the children and you will end up staying here with us, or maybe you and Geneva will stay with her cousin Mae." Mama Lou smiled. "Big Mama Darling sure would love to keep those babies."

None of that made any sense to Harry. He looked around. The kitchen seemed fine. Old fashioned fixtures, but clean, well-scrubbed and tidy, each thing in its place. He looked down at the plate. It had been a long time since he'd eaten. But he had no appetite. He stood up. "Thank you, but I'm not hungry. I'm ... I'm still very tired."

Mama Lou looked at the plate and up at him. She said, still smiling, "We have a good home here. I'm quite proud of this

Harry felt drowsy. He wasn't sure he'd understood. "Why aren't your children here?"

"Mama Darling's the home house."

He smiled, bemused. "What do you mean? You're their mama, aren't you? Why don't you have them here?"

She shook her head at him, like she would to a useless child. "I don't have time to explain." She stopped dressing for a moment. "Listen, you're lucky to be here. Big Mama Darling spoke up for you last night. You better not get on her wrong side. You better not keep her from her babies."

Harry watched her dress. She was all clean. He was still grimy. After she left, he got up. He wondered, whose house was this? The furnishings were of a familiar type—the bed, the chifforobe, a chair, a window, curtains. But it was all different somehow ... and worn. Old things he'd replace if they were his, but well-cared for; he could smell the polishing oil. He heard noises, inside and outside—Negro voices, nobody White.

Harry put on his dirty clothes and ventured out of the bedroom. Down the hall, the living room was empty. He looked out the window and saw a sea of Negro faces—he stood there for a while, he'd never seen such a crowded street before—and, every once in a while, a White man parting them like a sea captain parts the waters. Never before had he consciously felt what it was to be White, but now—he choked on the irony.

He felt a presence behind him. It was an older Negro woman.

"Please ... sir ... if you will, please come away from the window." She hurried past him and drew the shades. Then she turned to him and smiled and said, "You must be hungry. Do you want some breakfast?"

The man's voice continued. "How's he supposed to get a job? He sure can't work for no White man. Would he work for a Negro? And who would have him? What Negro would tell a White man what to do? No, no, no—there's nothing for it."

And Harry had to admit it, that man was right. Burning, burning, burning—he wouldn't last the night, and he had nowhere else to go. He shuddered. Life was burning him inside out.

Then an old woman's voice: "That man saved our baby's life and her babies, too. So she could come home. That counts for something, son. To everything you said, yes son yes, but what he did counts for something too."

And then Geneva's voice, the only one he knew. He lifted his head and turned to face the closed kitchen door. He heard her. He heard her saying, "Daddy, I want him. He's mine. I want him."

The talking continued, but Harry sat back, relieved, not listening any more. After several minutes Geneva came out, took him up, and had him drive to another house, where they went to bed. Her children weren't with them, but he was too tired to ask her why.

———◆◆———

The next morning Harry woke up and looked around. Geneva was up and had commenced to dress. This room was new to him, but here ... here *she* was. Harry smiled at the sight of her. "What're you doing?"

"I'm getting the children. They're still at Big Mama Darling's. We'll have breakfast there, and then I'll enroll them in school." She looked at him, and then she added, "Big Mama Darling's my grandmamma. My daddy's mother."

declared to one and all: These were *his* people. They were as important to him as his wife and children. Maybe even more. No matter what he'd intended, that was what he'd done. He'd gone in that building White. He'd come out ... what? A Negro? He didn't know. He didn't think so. But he wasn't White, not anymore.

What am I going to do?

Two more feet of road, then another.

I'll need shoes ...

◆—— ——◆

Harry was sitting in a strange house, in a closed, dark room. Later he would know the room for what it was, the house for what it was, but that night everything was dark and smoky and he was still back in that burning house. His skin was still grimy. The soot still stung his eyes and he could feel the burning in every breath he took. And now he was gasping, his eyes wide. He hunched over, trying to catch his breath. He tried to place himself here, in this room, but he couldn't slow down. Inside he was going a hundred miles an hour. Burning, burning, burning, burning ...

It was after midnight. He could hear them through the closed door to the kitchen—Geneva's people. He wondered, when had they come in? He never saw them. Maybe they'd come through a back door.

He was thinking about how Negroes were deciding his fate—and all he wanted was Geneva; she was all he had left now. He heard them arguing. A man's voice, wanting to kick him out. A woman's voice saying, "That's callous." The man again, "It's no such thing. I'm no such thing. I'm cautious."

"When should I've told you, before we went to bed or after?"

Harry could feel the boy behind him—kick, kick, kick.

"I never saw anything belonging to a man."

"He didn't live with us. He lived with his aunt. He'd come by for breakfast. He'd carry the children to their school."

"Did he know when I'd be over? Did you have him stay away?"

He could feel her eyes, hard. He kept his on the road.

She turned away. "You can drop us off in Chattanooga and go wherever you want. Anywhere you want to go, you can go there."

"I can't do that."

"You can do anything you want to."

The same few feet of road, like a treadmill rolling toward him, then underneath his car.

"I can't do that. I've just left everything I've ever had. I've left who I was, my people, my wife and my children, my parents, my store ... so I'm all alone now, except for you, so if you're going to Chattanooga then I have to go to Chattanooga too, because I've got to be somebody and be from somewhere, and I can't do that if I'm all alone." He turned to her, ignoring the road. "You need to have people to do that, so y'all are my people now, and I don't even know ..."

The words stopped. His open mouth worked, his eyes bulged; like a fish in a boat, he couldn't breathe.

Geneva reached out and caressed the back of his neck. "It's okay, baby. It's okay."

Harry leaned his head against her hand, and breathed out, one slow breath. *My people.* That's what he'd done. Rescuing Geneva and her children in front of the whole town—he'd

But he was listening to hear if Geneva was crying. He couldn't tell.

After a while, her breathing calmed.

Two feet, three feet, that was all he could see.

Miles on, and Earley started kicking the back of Harry's seat. "Where're we going?"

Geneva turned back to him. "Be still." Her voice was cold and she raised her hand, but then she lowered it, and then she took a breath. "We're going to Chattanooga, honey. We're going to see Big Mama Darling, and your grandpa, and Mama Lou."

She glanced at Harry and he nodded.

Geneva smiled for her children.

Harry concentrated on the road. He tried to keep from thinking. Would they ever go to sleep? No, they were fidgeting again. Harry could hear Lilly's whimper, and Earley was kicking Harry's seat again.

Geneva reached over her seat and swatted at Earley's legs. "I told you to stop that, child."

"Where's Daddy? Why're we leaving Daddy?"

Geneva turned to face the boy. "Don't you mind about that now. This is just a trip, honey."

Harry tightened his grip on the steering wheel. "Their father's still around?" His voice was strange.

"Was ... 'til now."

"You're married?"

"Should it matter? I've got two children. You'd feel better if I wasn't?"

"You never told me."

"Would it have made any difference?" She paused for a moment. Harry kept his eyes on the road.

5 • The Drowned Man

Chattanooga, Tennessee

Burning, burning, burning, burning—They'd be driving all night: Geneva beside him, her children in back. The smell of smoke lingered on their bodies. At first, nobody spoke or moved. But once clear of town the children began to fidget and whine. Geneva shushed them and tried to make them lie down, but they were too tired to sleep. Theirs were the only sounds for Harry to hear. The road stretched only as far as his headlights could show.

He could only see two feet, three feet ahead.

"Mommy! Earley's hitting me."

"Tattletale!"

Geneva started shouting. "Stop that! Y'all stop that!" She turned her body to reach over the front seat and swatted at her children. "I won't stand for any more mess, y'all hear? Now stop it!"

Harry slowed and fumbled with his rearview mirror to see into the back seat. Earley and Lilly were scrunched against the doors out of Geneva's reach. She was on her knees and bent over the back of the front seat, reaching and swinging. Suddenly she stopped, turned, and looked at Harry. He looked back at the road. Geneva sat back down, breathing heavily, her arms crossed, and with her right hand she covered her eyes.

Harry kept his eyes forward. He felt himself burning and burning, and it was all he could do to calm himself, just enough to drive his car.

what they'd have you be. Aren't you tired of that shit? We can stand up for ourselves; we can fight back without ever throwing a fist. Their game is violence. AND WE DON'T HAVE TO PLAY IT!

That last is written just like that, in capital letters. Addressed to my weary soul. God, I'm so tired.

Very slowly, I rise up and pull one suitcase, my smallest one, out and onto the bed. I pack my razor, my toothbrush, and some clothes. Just as little as I'll need. I close it and walk out my door.

I don't even give Reggie back his gun. I just leave it on my bed. I don't even say goodbye to Vivian.

Anything, anything to get outside the violence and what I almost did.

But ... what Morgan said? To fight back without throwing a fist? I don't know if I can do that. It makes no sense to me.

hasn't shown, just this crazy old man. "You fuck with me—I'll kick you in the ass!" People are laughing at him. I stomp back to my room.

And suddenly I'm so tired. I drop Reggie's gun on my bed. I remember that jar and the fingers inside it. I remember that White man hitting my Papa Joe. I remember so many times—whole families disappearing, driven off by Whites, their too-good-for-Negroes houses abandoned. And what we do to ourselves: men getting knifed or beaten or shot, they end up dead or injured, they'd be limping or deaf, or no sense left. Women too, lots of them, beaten or cut or crazy. No siree, there ain't no night like a Saturday night. And the law doesn't mind. As long as you're back picking cotton on Monday, no White man minds—

—and what I just did. For a dollar and a quarter. I must've been crazy. But I don't feel like Stagger Lee. I try to think of something else, but it's no use. All I can manage is a cotton field in winter, the spent stalks broken and prone, and it's just me there, my leg's stabbed and bandaged, I can't leave; I'm exhausted and there's danger and I'm afraid if I feel one more thing ...

I think of my father.

I can't breathe. I sit down and gasp for air. I glance over to my desk—the letter Morgan Wright wrote. Morgan was a mentor for all us boys coming up in Drew. We called him "Uncle." Now he's writing to me: Come back to Mississippi and join the Movement. Come join me here in Williams Point. The work will be hard. It will even be dangerous. Whites will spit on you and curse you to your face. You could get beaten up. The police will harass you. And you'll have to take it. But what you won't have to take is staying in your place, and being

"What're you gonna do kid? You gonna shoot me?" I lean forward and I lower my voice. "Go ahead ... boy. I'd like to see you do it."

The kid doesn't know what to do. Suddenly he takes his hand out, but it's empty. He takes off past me and runs down the street, away from me and the man who sent him. I watch him run. There's nobody else to see.

Then I hear Vivian, who doesn't curse, but she's cussing me now; she's telling me I'm crazy and I could've got everybody killed. Somebody's crying. It must be Betty.

I ignore them. I look for that man up the street but he's gone. But I remember seeing him before, on a particular street corner. I tell Vivian I'm going back to my dorm.

"What about the freedom meeting?"

Then I remember: we were going to a freedom meeting. I tell them to go on without me.

I go back to my dorm. I knock on Reggie's door. He's got a gun. I ask him for it.

"What do you need a gun for?"

"Goddammit, give me your gun. It's none of your business what I need it for."

When you're crazy mad, Stagger Lee mad, people mind you. He gets me his gun.

I go to that street corner. People are walking by. A few men are hanging out, but the man I want isn't there. So I wait. I don't see the people around me, just the high white sky, the concrete curb, the sidewalk, and the white-washed walls. An old man shambles up. His clothes are rotten. He stinks of liquor, urine, and sweat. He starts in: "Fuck you. I'll kick you in the ass. You fuck with me—I'll fuck you!" He talks like that for fifteen minutes, to nobody, to everybody. The man I want up—all they want is a fucking hamburger. And you want to rob me? I'm not your enemy."

I'm sure Vivian and Betty are yelling at me, telling me to stop, but I don't hear a thing they're saying. They don't exist. Just two people exist—him and me. The rest of the world has gone white, like we're in high cotton.

His right hand's back at his side, but he opens his coat again. "Gimme your money," he says.

"Are you crazy? You think I care about that gun you have? You think that makes you some kind a man? You're just a punk. A Black-assed punk."

He shoots his right hand into his jacket but he leaves it there. And I know I'm this close to him pulling his gun and shooting. We're staring each other down and I'm wondering how many words I'm away from getting shot. If it's three words, I'll say two; if it's two words, I'll say one. I'm not giving him a goddamned thing.

I've got a dollar and a quarter, in change.

Vivian's got hold of my arm but I shake her off. "Go. Get out of here." I think that, just for a second, but I don't remember if I said it. Vivian and Betty stayed, so maybe I didn't. I don't take my eye off the kid.

He glances behind him and I look up the street to a man standing about twenty-five yards away. He's got his arms crossed. He's scowling and he takes a step. I remember: I saw them together before the boy approached. I yell at him. "You back off now. You sent this boy to do your job, so it's just him and me now. You stay away."

The kid jerks his right hand in his jacket, but he doesn't take the gun out. "Gimme your money."

front door close. *You bastard, you bastard.* I told myself my father ruined everything. I couldn't even cry for my grandfather.

It's years later, 1962, and I'm in college. At Morehouse. I'm walking down the street with my girlfriend Vivian—she's from Spelman—and her friend Betty. I see ahead of us a kid, maybe high school, coming toward us and he's got his eye on me. He looks real nervous. I immediately know what he's up to. I clinch my fists and stick out my chest. I don't say a thing to the girls. This is going to be none of their business.

I've got a dollar and a quarter, in change.

The kid stops. He's got on old jeans and an old ratty jacket. He pulls it open so I can see the gun in the waistband of his pants.

"Gimme all your money."

I don't answer him. I'm sizing him up. He's a light chocolate brown. His face is dirty. His hair is unkempt. He's got his mouth set tight and he's looking me right in the eye.

I spread my arms out, palms front. "What the fuck?"

He hisses, "Gimme your money." He puts his right hand up where his gun is under his jacket.

I point my finger at him. "Do you know how to read, boy?"

He doesn't answer but his hand doesn't move.

"Can you read a newspaper or a magazine? Do you ever listen to the radio or watch TV? Can you understand the English language, boy?"

His face is dark now, his eyes slits.

I take a step toward him. "There're little Negro kids walking through mobs to go to school. There're people getting beat know. I'll know. And nobody'll take that knowledge away from me. It will truly be mine." Then he stood, so tall. "And nobody else, about their life, can say any different."

He put a foot on the bottom step, reached, and took hold of my shoulder. He pointed at my chest. "You take that to heart, Little Man."

My father was the one who told us. He stood in the doorway to our kitchen. Mama and I were shelling peas at the table. A dull job but easily done. Then suddenly there was father at the doorway. "Papa Joe's dead." He said it straight out and flat, with no tears. "Last night, in his sleep." Mama looked up, she dropped her peas, she started sobbing; her body curled up and hunched over her bowl. My father hesitated, then he took a step into the kitchen, toward my mother. But I got to him first. I was bawling. There had been no look in his eye, no emotion at all, so I jumped up and dove right at him. I didn't wait for him to hit me first. Because he never did; he never would. I drove my fists into his chest, I got him in a clinch. I pressed my face into his chest and I was hitting his sides, his back, whatever I could reach. For a long moment he did nothing, he just suffered my puny fists, then he pried me loose and passed me to my mother, who held me, and she and I cried together. He didn't say a word.

He must have done it gently—there would be no bruises on my arms—but all I felt was the release, the separation, the total absence of his touch. No matter what I did, I could never make him ... grab hold, fight back, anything. Cradled in my mother's arms, I thought over and over, *you bastard, you bastard*, because now I wasn't crying for my grandfather, I was crying for myself. I heard, away from my mother's and my sobs, the a situation not to be proud of and, seeing my puzzlement, he said I'd understand when I got older.

So, growing up, guns made sense. My grandfather and father with their shotguns, all night on their porches, that made sense. And there was a man in town, coffee black but for a milk-colored scar from his left eye down to the corner of his mouth, who nobody messed with. We all called him crazy, but he was Stagger Lee crazy, which meant Colored folks respected him, even though they'd say he was bad. They'd say he was so crazy, even White people stayed out of his way. But my father didn't respect him, and he certainly didn't like him. "You hear me boy, you stay away from that man. He's no good and he's no-count." I'd nod my head, and say yes sir, but to me that bad, crazy, Stagger Lee made sense, like guns made sense, because that was what my stories told me.

I was twelve when my grandfather passed. We laid him down like a king. The church was full, the pews and the aisles, and more people were gathered outside, standing on the grass and gravel, pressing their faces to the windows for a look.

He always told me to live my life in such a way that I'd be commended at my funeral. The first time he said it, I wasn't sure I understood. I was sitting on the top step of his front porch. He was kneeling in his yard, his eyes straight across from mine. "Aleck," he said, "I've spent my lifetime building this house, clearing and farming my land. All as God intended. But all of that could be taken in a second." He snapped his fingers. "Just like that! The only thing that'll truly be mine will be my manner of living, right up to my last breath. Until that moment, I won't know my final worth. But when I die, I'll standing. He would've kept standing no matter what that White man did. The blood from his wound falls to my ears and hair and drips down my neck. Dust from the car billows around us. It gets in my eyes. My grandfather soaks his handkerchief in the creek and cleans my face and neck. We leave that nickel be.

When we get home, Papa Joe tells my parents what happened. He has to. He has to explain his bleeding face and my scalded hand. But he leaves out the part about me attacking that White man, so I tell it, crying, how what I did brought out that White man's gun, and got my grandfather hurt.

My father drives him home. When he comes back, I figure I'm due for a whipping. Provoking a White man like that is about the worse offense a boy can do. And I want him to. I want my father to smack me in the mouth, or use his belt on me ... so I can hit him back. I'll go right at him with both fists flying. Then he'll hit me so hard—hit me back so hard his fist will go right through me. He'll knock me out. That's what I want; I can see him doing it; I can almost feel it. But he doesn't. He never does. He just closes his eyes, like he's looking back into his own self, and I can see him shivering, if only so slightly, and for some reason that is something I think I shouldn't be seeing, so I duck my head and feel ashamed, and I wonder why my father never beats me. He doesn't touch me at all.

And he never tells me what's a little man to do.

I later find out that for the rest of the week my father sat out on our porch all night with his shotgun, and my grandfather did the same at his place. But that White man must have been passing through, so nothing more came of it. When I asked my father about his protecting us, all he said was it was uppity. You boy, what're you waiting for? Take that bucket and fill it."

By now my world has shrunk into a white tunnel and that White mans at the end of it. He's all I see. "You bastard!" I run at him and ram my shoulder into his hip and knock him into his car door, then I kick his shin with the heel of my foot. My grandfather pulls me off and hustles me away from the car.

He holds me close and whispers. "Hey Little Man, you've got to be careful. You can't do that to a White man. He's probably got a gun. They always have guns." And he does. When we turn back around he's holding it on us.

Papa Joe holds his cap in both hands and stretches them out to that man, begging. "Sir. Sir. He's just a child. Me ... his parents ... we'll deal with him. Sir, you can ask around, I've never caused any White man a lick of trouble."

That White man doesn't hear a word my grandfather says. He's panting, red faced, and he's pointing that gun right at me. He walks over to his bucket and kicks it at me. "Nigger, git!" I'm staring, right down that barrel, I can't take my eyes off it, and I pick up his bucket.

I get that radiator cap off, it takes some doing and I'm shaking from fear, from rage, and it does scald me. When I get the water, I'm spilling it all over, and it takes me four trips to finish. That White man's holding that gun on me the entire time. And he's shaking too, and the gun's cocked, and his finger's on the trigger. When I finish, he walks up to my grandfather, holding that pistol like a rock, and again hits my grandfather upside his head. Then he throws a nickel in the dirt and drives off.

I'm clutching my grandfather's shirt and bury my face below his chest. I'm crying. He never went down, he kept

"It's easy." He takes a rag from the bucket. "You put this rag over the cap, and give it a twist." He holds out the bucket and I take it. I look over my shoulder for my grandfather.

"Go on boy. I haven't got all day." I can see his smile is tightening.

Just then my grandfather comes back. He pulls his cap from his head. "Hello sir. Can I help you?"

"This boy's going to fill up my radiator. I'm giving him a nickel."

"That child is my grandson." Papa Joe smiles and puts his arm over my shoulder and takes the bucket from my hand. "I'll do that for you, sir. No need for the boy. I'd be obliged to do it. No need to pay anybody."

I still have my head down, I'm still watching that White man out from under my eyes. He's still smiling, but it's tight, real tight.

"No, I didn't tell you to do it. I told the boy."

"Yes sir. But he's young. I'm afraid he might scald his hand. And ... my family ... well sir, we don't make it a practice of the boy taking money from strangers. We see to his needs. We keep everything in the family. You understand, I'm sure, sir." His head is ducked, and he gives that White man his best smile. "The creek's right over there. I'll have your radiator filled in two shakes."

There's no more smile on that White man now. "Listen, nigger, I don't care what your family's *practice* is. If you want to raise this boy right, you teach him to mind his White folks." He snatches the bucket from my grandfather's hand and swings it, and hits my grandfather upside the head, and throws the bucket at my feet. "Christ, I didn't think Delta niggers were so house. And he'd tell me how proud he was of me, helping to keep our family together. His Little Man.

That was what he preached, how Colored people should be united, as independent as possible, and not beholden to any White man, even if he's honest, even if he has an open hand.

I'm nine now, three years older from the time I walked into that sorry White man's store.

Papa Joe and I are walking from his place, my little wagon loaded with vegetables and covered pails of buttermilk. It's late summer, it's high cotton, the fields on both sides of the road, and close by is a creek with a brake of sweet gum and sugarberry trees. Papa Joe tells me he needs to make water and I'm to wait for him right there, just off the road, and he walks over to the brake of trees.

And just at that moment, like it was summoned by principalities and powers, a car comes down the road, driven by a White man, two suitcases beside him, who pulls to a stop right by me. Its front is steaming; the White man gets out and smiles at me. "Hey boy," he points at the trees, "is there water over by those trees?"

I keep my eyes down, but I can still see his face from under my brow. "Yes, sir. There's a creek."

He lifts the hood of his car. "My radiator needs water. You go fill it with some of that creek water." He pulls a bucket out of the car's trunk. "I'll give you a nickel."

I just stand there. I'm not supposed to have any dealings with White men.

"You ever open a radiator before?"

I shake my head no. Then I remember to speak. "No, sir."

swipe—where it was damp. "You mind your father now, you hear?" I don't answer.

"He'll tell you everything you need to know, when he thinks you're ready."

"Yes ma'am." I go back outside. What my father tells me: it's hardly ever enough and I didn't know why.

Little Man. That's what my grandfather called me. "Aleck, my Little Man." One of my first memories is of me, close by his feet, playing in his yard. I look up and he's so tall against the Delta's low horizon. The sun's behind him. His height, his great black mass—at first I don't recognize who this person is. I gasp. And then that tall, massive presence bends down in front of me and I can make out his face—his beard and hair, his high cheeks and noble Indian nose—Papa Joe Hardaway. (His daughter, my mother, has the same cheeks and nose.) He's smiling at me and caresses my shoulder, and that's the first time I remember him saying, "Hey, how's my little man?"

His is the first figure I drew with my crayons. The paper could barely contain him. No matter how hard I pressed, my crayon was too paltry a measure of his force. I colored him as dark as I could.

He lived out in the rural. He had his own place there. Farming his own land, that's way up there for a Negro. Then and now. I'd walk out to his place with my little red wagon and we'd fill it with whatever fresh produce, milk, or meat he could spare. Then we'd walk back to town together and my mother would swap his farm goods for our store-bought, whatever my parents had set aside, and then we'd walk that back to his

I don't quite understand, and I don't dare look up. "No sir." I barely say it. I hope he hears me. If he doesn't, he'll get mad.

"He thought he was in high cotton, sonny. You know where he really was?"

"No sir." I'm at the door. I want to bolt.

"Neck deep in shit, sonny." He laughs, and I'm gone.

Home, I tell my father about it. He, my mother, and I are sitting at our kitchen table. He stands up.

"Where'd you see a thing like that?"

I tell him in that new White man's store.

"What'd you go in there for?"

I don't understand: why those fingers, why these questions? I ask myself, why did I go? To be the little man. That seems so stupid to me now. I can feel tears on my cheeks. "I wanted to buy some candy, sir."

"And did you?"

I try to remember. "No sir. I left. Daddy, why're those fingers ..."

"That's mess you don't need to know about." He points his finger at me. "You listen to me. You aren't allowed to go into that store unless you're with your momma or me." He's looking down at me and I'm looking up at him. Then he lifts his head and closes his eyes, but he's still seeing something. Then he opens them, and still keeps his head up—he's not looking at me. "You understand me?" He hardly calls me "Aleck" and he never calls me "son." He doesn't call me anything.

I wait for as long as I dare. "Yes sir."

My father doesn't move a peg. I refuse to wipe my cheeks. After he walks out, my mother studies my face. She reaches over and rubs her thumb gently along my cheek—one slow

4 • Aleck Sharpe, the Wounded Man

The Mississippi Delta and Atlanta, Georgia

Two fingers in brine; scum on the waterline. The glass is cloudy, and even with the sunlight you can hardly see through it. I hear a fly. It lights on the lid and then off it goes, it just disappears, but I can still hear it. It's 1947. Drew, Mississippi. I'm just a child, six years old. I'm in a sundry store.

The store is new, or rather, its owner. The old one died, and nobody knows this new White man. He's from out of town. He just showed up and closed down the store. Word was, in a few days he'd reopen it. I had three pennies in my pocket and every day I walked by that store, several times a day, because I wanted to be its first customer. I'd be the little man, everybody saying, "Hey Aleck, tell me about that new White man and his store."

The morning it's open I walk in and look it over. What I see is that mason jar, up on the counter. What's that in it? It draws me in like a moth to a flame. I have to look up to see it. Two fingers. Pale gray. I don't know why, but it just hits me—they were a Negro's. They tilt from their severed knuckles downwards to their tips. They're pointing right at me.

"You know what those are, sonny?"

That voice behind the counter: it has that false-friendly tone that White men like to use. But I can hardly hear it. I don't say a thing. I only nod my wide-eyed head. I'm backing out of there.

The voice stops me. "You know what that nigger thought he was in?"

He tried to relax. He watched the road: the concrete, the cracks filed with tar. He brought his hand to his eyes—useless. The smoke and soot—burning, burning. He could smell it in his nose. He could feel it in his throat. It was inside him now.

He'd always thought himself a respectable man, a respectful man. There were channels for behavior, there was place and predictability. This affair—it had been something peripheral, its illicitness not anything defining: that was what he'd always told himself. But look at him now. Harry wondered about himself. How much had he cared for her? He glanced over at her, for less than a second. She kept her eyes straight ahead. *More than I realized. Much more. And now, everybody knows it too.* His breath caught; he had to breathe in sharply. *What have I done?*

Suddenly, he wondered about Geneva, about Negroes: weren't they religious? Wasn't she? Why did they live, so many of them ... going from bed to bed? Well, so had he. So, no better than them. And wasn't he still the man he had thought himself to be?

Not anymore.

Stop it. Stop thinking. Watch the road.

All he could see was the next foot forward, the next second. *How much gas do we have? How much money?* He felt a sudden revulsion. When they got to Chattanooga, he could just as well take his wallet with his name and his address, and except for the money and his snapshots, he could throw it all away.

now? He employed a clerk and a stock boy. What would they do now?

That morning he had gone to work the same as usual. And it was his usual routine all through the morning, and then home to dinner, and back to work till suppertime. After supper he read his newspaper and Charlotte read her book. Just like every other day.

I'll need money. Could I wire my account? Harry put that out of his mind. It was their money now, not his. And they weren't his anymore. He had no right to anything from his old life anymore. He couldn't even call them family. He hadn't meant to betray them. Was that what he'd done?

His children had been playing with their toys. It was their bedtime but they were pleading, they weren't that tired, and Charlotte's stern face couldn't suppress her smile. Then, suddenly the siren, and the children sing-song chanting, "It's a fire! It's a fire! Can we see the fire?" Harry put his paper down. It slid off his knees and onto the floor as he stood up smiling—

He could have said no. It was the children's bedtime. Had he wondered if it was Geneva's house, even then, as he went for his keys and his hat and his coat, with his children dancing to his side?

Junior, Mary Ann ... I've abandoned them. They have no father now. What will it be like for them, growing up? Charlotte must hate me now. Harry thought about his children living in a house of hatred. That would be his doing. *I'll never see them again.* Harry's eyes blurred. He almost stopped the car. Didn't he have a photograph? Didn't he? Finally, he remembered the ones in his wallet.

3 • The Drowned Man

Driving to Chattanooga, Harry hunched over the wheel, as if that could help him see. He could see only a few feet ahead, just far enough to stop. But he couldn't stop. And he couldn't see anything more.

I'll need shoes. This pair is ruined, I bet. How many black? How many brown? I'll need new pants. I'll need all new clothes. How will I buy them?

At least it was quiet now. That damned boy of Geneva's had finally gone to sleep. Geneva hadn't, but she hadn't said a word for miles. She was staring at the road. Was she thinking the same thing: how many shoes, how many dresses, how many panties? She'd need all new clothes too. Wouldn't she?

What's her family like? What's their house like? Does she have clothes there?

How does this happen in life? Just that morning Harry had woken up next to his wife—Charlotte!—and he'd heard his children down the hall. *My hall, my house, my family!* It had all been so ordinary, and that seemed so strange to him now, that there had been no warning that he was waking to a day the likes he'd never seen before, or would ever see again.

Harry's eyes still stung. Wiping them had done no good.

I'll need new shirts. Which shall I buy? Business shirts? I have no business. Harry gasped for air, and his hands tightened on the wheel.

His store was—it had been—a good business. He was an honest man; a respectable man. Wasn't he? Who would run it his car. He had known them all his life. Now he couldn't place a single one. He didn't care to; he didn't even try. They were a nuisance, they weren't even real, shouting curses and shoving, but parting as he passed. Then he saw Charlotte, almost hidden in that unreal crowd. Their eyes caught. He tried to read hers, but she turned away, sharply, and then she disappeared. Harry stared at the space where she had been, and, with a start, he realized their children must be with her. He hadn't seen them. He stood where he was, he couldn't move. He felt a hand at his sleeve. This time it was Geneva. She was pointing to his car.

He opened a door and Geneva ushered her children in. They moved stiffly, slowly; he had them sit. They stared at the inside of the car and ran their hands along the leather seats. Wide-eyed, neither of them spoke. They looked ready to cry. Geneva slid into Charlotte's seat. Harry started the engine and looked at her, goggle-eyed. A few more rocks, and then the White crowd surrounded his car.

They were pushing at it; rocking it, and those in front heaved chunks of ice and frozen mud at the windshield. Harry put the car in gear and started slowly, the car still rocking. He honked his horn and gunned his engine; the car jumped and the people backed away. He nudged their way through the crowd and still people laid their hands on the car; it slid and then stayed steady. Harry slowly took up speed. Then he was past the frozen, muddy street, and on a concrete road that looked like dirty, hard-packed snow, and laced with tar-filled cracks. He looked at Geneva, his face a question, and she told him, "Turn west. My people live in Chattanooga." Harry drove as fast as he could. He didn't dare stop on the way. At the city limits, Geneva would tell him where to go.

He remembered where he was, surrounded by neighbors and family—cousins, nieces and nephews, aunts, uncles, his parents, his in-laws, and his wife and his children. And he could hear their cursing and catcalls and boos. "Nigger lover!" "Go away!" "Don't come back!"

The ground below him felt sharp and cold, it hurt, and he shivered and almost passed out. He realized he no longer belonged—suddenly bereft of all his family and friends, and of his store and possessions too. Geneva was standing now, her children clutching her legs and waist, and she reached down to help him stand. She looked around. He didn't know if she was looking at the Negroes or the Whites. Then she looked at him, close, and made him look at her. She had never done that before.

"Come on baby, let's go." She spoke so softly, he could barely hear her voice.

The tarp was on the ground, forgotten. He put his arm around her waist and his other, only slightly hesitating, around her two children, like his, an older boy and a younger girl. In his confusion, he couldn't recall their names. The Whites in the crowd began to throw stones, chunks of ice, and clumps of frozen mud. A stone hit Harry on his arm, and he drew the children closer to his body. When a rock struck Geneva, he looked at the crowd, furious, trying to find who threw it. "Stop that! Not her. Not her!" He began to walk, cautiously, holding Geneva and her children close, and somehow walked them through the crowd. "My car," he told them. "We'll be safe in my car."

The cursing grew louder; it was a burning, burning, burning, in his ears and in his head. Angry faces were all around him—surging, ebbing—as he pushed through them to

Harry stepped in front of him and held up the tarp until it was soaked with water, and then he ran into the house—the front room was incredibly small—folding the stiff tarp about him and over his head, inhaling the smoke, dry and sour, and feeling the heat from the floorboards up through his shoes and into the soles of his feet. The smoke billowed and flowed. It leaked through the floorboards and out of the walls and windows. Harry stepped quickly across the room and reached for a doorknob, but caught himself in the nick of time, and instead drove his tarp-covered shoulder into the door and broke through, and stepped over the bottom of the door that was still in its frame, and in the smoke and soot and heat they were there. Geneva was crouching on the floor, reaching up one hand to the shuttered window, the other attending to her children. They were face down on the floor, stiff as planks, and resistant to his touch. Geneva had to lift them to their feet. Harry grouped the three of them close together and put the tarp around them. He held its sides—it bulged behind them like a sail—and, walking backward, guided them to the sudden night air, all of them stumbling the last few steps and gulping smoke and coughing.

Her children started to cry. Harry sat down in front of the burning house and Geneva fell toward him and embraced him, and he saw the far stars smudged by the smoke. His skin felt gritty. He looked at his hands. They were covered in soot. He brushed it from his sleeves—it smeared. He could feel it prickle in his nostrils; his eyes stung; and then he felt it on her hand caressing his face. He took his handkerchief from his breast pocket and tried to clean himself and to clean her hands, but it too was covered in soot.

and ran, in waves, to and fro like on a playground. Charlotte waited for him to open her door and they stood across the street with the other Whites, watching the house spitting wood and bits of tar paper, the firelight yellow and pumpkin-orange. The Negroes stood far off to either side, ceding this, their street, to the Whites, huddling for warmth in their threadbare clothes. The firemen turned their hoses to the houses on either side. Was the burning one beyond saving?

Harry saw which house it was. He furtively scanned the Negroes on either side. They were huddled too close together, he couldn't tell them apart. If she was there, or one of her children, he couldn't see them.

Away from the fire, it was dark. Harry squinted. His eyes stung from the smoke. Ash whirled like snow. But he was staring now, the fire almost forgotten; he was trying just to find her, to see her. He no longer even cared what Charlotte must be thinking, him staring so openly at the Negroes.

He stepped from the grassy curb to the dirt street, and stumbled over the frozen mud, walking close to one group of Negroes and then to the other. It was noisy from the gushing water; the White adults and children shouting and laughing; the fire devouring the wood and tar; so maybe he shouted her name—he wasn't even aware if he did; he couldn't see her!—And there was no response. She must still be inside. He paused at that thought, shivering.

He turned and stared at the fire, the house a hideous bulk, black within the malignant flames, and the gray smoke wreathed and writhing up and fading into the night. He felt a hand at his sleeve. Did Charlotte speak his name? He started walking, then loping, over to the fire truck. He grabbed a canvas tarp. He looked for the closest man with a hose.

2 • Harry Wilbourne, the Drowned Man

A Small Town in Alabama: 1923

Negro streets are crazy. The Whites who built each new block and neighborhood took no care in how the streets were laid. The intersections weren't always aligned, so you have to dog-leg it to the right or left to find your way through. And there are gaps between address numbers, and the odds and evens switch from side to side. You have to be on your toes. But this time, you could just head for the glow. And Harry Wilbourne knew this neighborhood; he wouldn't get lost. He hoped Charlotte, sitting beside him, wouldn't notice. He had no business knowing these streets the way he did.

His son and daughter were in the back seat, their heads out of the windows like hounds, craning to see ahead, each wanting to be the first to see it. When a house goes up in the Colored part of town, everybody comes to watch it burn: all the Whites and Negroes, the rich and poor alike. And houses burn every winter. They're shacks. Their wood is dry and bare, and when a fireplace is unattended, even for a second, all it takes is a gust through a gap between the weathered, shrunken boards: a spark flicks out, it catches a rug or a rag—the air cracks and whoosh!—the flames crawl and tumble, they jump and dance and thread their way up table legs and walls, and the wooden shutters bulge and crack and burst. At night, you can see the glow all the way over on the White side of town. Or you can hear the siren. Either way, you're in your car and there.

Harry's children scrambled out and looked for playmates—neighbors and cousins tumbled from their cars. They shouted

1 • Isaac Mendelsson: the Hanged Man

Summer, 1963

Killed by the Klan. Those four words: they were the headline of every newspaper and the lead story on the six o'clock news. Isaac Mendelssohn's father came down from New York City to Mississippi. He clutched his son's casket and wept. He bore the body home by train and, even though he was White (or perhaps, because he was Jewish) he insisted on riding in the car for Negroes.

To every question asked he gave the same reply: "Killed by the Klan. My son was killed by the Klan." He released the morgue shot to the press: the three Ks carved in his dead son's chest. It became iconic.

O, yes,
I say it plain,
America never was America to me.
—**Langston Hughes, Let America Be America Again**

Madame Sosostris, famous clairvoyante,
Had a bad cold, nevertheless
Is known to be the wisest woman in Europe,
With a wicked pack of cards. Here, said she,
Is your card, the drowned Phoenician Sailor,
(Those are pearls that were his eyes. Look!)
Here is Belladonna, the Lady of the Rocks,
The lady of situations.
Here is the man with three staves, and here is the wheel,
And here is the one-eyed merchant, and this card,
Which is blank, is something he carries on his back,
Which I am forbidden to see. I do not find
The Hanged Man. Fear death by water.
—**T.S. Eliot,** *The Waste Land*

a touch; his eyes, his mouth, his nose, his Mexican hair; they'd bulge and pinch; they'd waver, ebb, and flow.

6 • The Wounded Man

Williams Point, Mississippi: Autumn, 1962

All the way from Morehouse I keep Morgan's letter in my shirt pocket. I take it out every so often to read it on the bus, to pass the time riding, west out of Georgia and through Alabama and into Mississippi, from one end of the Cotton Belt to the other, finally dropping down into the Delta. I'm almost home. But I don't go home. No, at 2:23 in the afternoon on October 14, 1962, I step from the Trailways bus down to the pavement below, and I'm in Williams Point, Mississippi, just two stones-throw from my hometown Drew, but Drew could be on the moon for the way I feel. I hesitate—one foot on the pavement, the other on the bus—and then I worry that I've been noticed and people are wondering, "What's with that boy?" I try to shrug it off. I step off the bus. I hold my suitcase tight against my chest. It feels as light as a matchbox, cradled in my hands.

I'm with SNCC now. I'm thinking, this better work. I take a look around, but I don't see Morgan. Should I go find him? No, I better not. It's better to wait. I wipe my brow. Its autumn cool but I wish it was hot because then nobody would notice my sweat. If there'd been snow to my knees I'd still be sweating, because I'm a partisan and an agent provocateur, and I'm behind enemy lines in an occupied country. I keep telling myself that nobody can know that, it's too soon—but I still don't feel safe.

How long will I be a secret here? The whole idea is: not for long, not at all.

"Aleck Sharpe."

I turn to the sound of my name, spoken so emphatically, as always, as always. Mr. Morgan Wright—Uncle Morgan—he's standing by the door just outside the terminal. He was always there for me in Drew, and now he's here in Williams Point. He's taking my suitcase and then my hand, he's shaking my hand, and I fall into the sound of his voice, as familiar as my father's. The words don't matter—they'll be repeated—I'm just grateful for that down-home sound.

Morgan drives me to his place that's hardly two rooms, up an outside stair. The first room has only a bed and a table and a chair. The room's so small, we can barely move around. There's only a hot plate and a basin in the other. It's smaller than the first. Morgan tells me that's our kitchen and our washroom. The privy's outside. A rear window looks out on a fence. Three days later that window will save our lives. But now we unfold a cot and try to fit it in the front room. We manage by putting one end through the doorway to the kitchen. "Head in the bedroom, feet in the hall." We sing it and laugh. Morgan tells me, "Hey, don't knock it. My first two weeks here, I slept in my car."

He sits on the bed. "First thing I'm going to tell you, we're not alone here. You know how our folks tried to register in 'forty-five, 'forty-six? Well, here, a man by the name of Chambliss, Mr. Courtland Chambliss, he tried to get our people here to register. Went door to door, just like I'm doing now. He's got himself a nice little café, people say he owns it outright, so the banks can't touch him. The first day I got here I went to see him. He was expecting me, and I had a letter from Ella Baker to introduce myself. He's the one who found me this place."

Morgan opened a box of papers. "What you'll be doing here, it's as simple as pie. Every day I go door to door to ask people about voting. I tell them I've got these registration forms they can practice on. I don't call Mr. Courtland's name; the situation's too hot here to call any undue attention to people like him. Most folks know what I'm about by now, and if they don't slam the door in my face, I figure I got a decent chance. First few days, a police car followed me everywhere I went. Can you imagine, folks open their door to some stranger and behind his shoulder, they see a police car?

"And—fool that I was—I was happy when those police stopped following me. I figured, now I can get someplace. But that was the day three peckerwoods tried to beat the hell out of me. See this?" He pulled down on his lip. "One caught me right here on my mouth. Then the next day, I had dodge a truck." He smiled. "I stumbled face-first in the dirt.

"Like I said, every day's simple. I try to talk to folks while the peckerwoods try to kill me. And starting tomorrow they'll try to kill you. I tell folks we're going to take them to the courthouse to register, and they know better than anybody the hell they're going to pay. But I pay hell too. You will too. And every day we'll be coming back, and the same folks'll be slamming their doors right in our faces. But every day we're still alive and knocking on their doors—our faces may be bruised, we might be barely walking—but every day, we'll still be coming back, because we hope—we know—that one day our people are going to get over.

"And call me Morgan, Aleck." (I've been calling him 'Mr. Wright.') "We're brothers now."

Brothers? Just for a moment, I don't know how to take that, he's so old. Like I said, he was like an uncle to me.

My first day out I wear overalls over a T-shirt and work boots. Morgan loans me the clothes. I've never looked so country, not even back in Drew. "Country's good," Morgan says. "These people are country people. Just like the ones back home."

He tells me what to do. "Don't start right in on voting. They don't know you and you don't know them. So draw them out a little; get to know them. Find out if they know anybody who knows your people. The politics will come."

Morgan shows me how it's done. A police car follows us. My skin is slick with sweat. I'm nervous as hell. The first house the woman doesn't even look at us, just at that police car that slows to a stop as she opens her door. Morgan tries to talk to her but I don't believe she hears a word. She looks sick with fear as she closes the door. The policeman turns on his siren, just for a few seconds, and door after door on that street, when we knock, nobody answers.

That police car follows us all morning. Not a single door stays open. Morgan says not to worry; some days that's what happens. We knock off for dinner.

We go back to our place. The police car follows, stops, then after a while it speeds away. After it's gone we walk over to Mr. Courtland's café. Morgan says to me, "You'll like it there. You'll like him. He knows your mother's people."

Like Morgan said, going door to door there's always cars. Sometimes it's the police; other times it's just crackers out for a good time—young men no older than me most times. They follow you, and they'll speed up, go right on by you—too close for comfort. And if you turn to see inside, you'll see two good ole boys—or maybe three with one in the back. One'll lift a shotgun off his lap for you and Jesus and the world to see. They don't hide anything. They don't have to.

With that one gesture, he's telling me he holds my life in his hands. He's reminding me that his buddy could slow that car, and he could squeeze that trigger with no further thought than if I was just a rabbit or a squirrel, and the only thing stopping him would be the noise, or maybe the shotgun's kick would push him back into his buddy driving. So he shows me that shotgun and grins because there's nothing else on God's green earth that keeps them from killing me right there, right then, right in broad daylight.

It makes you think you've misplaced your life, or that it belongs to somebody else now, or that it's been thrown away, crumbled into bread crumbs and cast upon the waters. But then another car pulls up behind you and the first one speeds away. It's like they're running shifts. And what seemed random, now you think is planned. And I breathe out a sigh. Those crackers are on a leash. They haven't killed me yet because they've been told "not yet." So, at least for those boys trading shifts on me, one of them isn't going to pull up beside me, and put his hand on his belly and say, "That sandwich just don't agree with me, so dammit, now I'm gonna kill me a nigger."

So I'm relieved, a little, not much, but enough. Barely enough. Whoever runs those crackers talks to the city, and the city talks to the FBI and the Justice Department, and we talk to Justice too. So I hope somebody's holding a leash. I clutch at straws. I have to. Because what I'm doing is makes no sense to me.

I wish I could say those crackers don't bother me. I wish I could say I don't let their hate dictate what I can or cannot do. But they scare the shit out of me. I don't have any grace under pressure. I need some reassurance that I'm not committing suicide out here. So I grab that straw. Hell, I make a whole straw man out of my bullshit rationalization that cooler heads prevail; that despite all the evidence to the contrary, even those who run those crackers by me have some interest in me living.

And every night in bed the fear returns because, thinking clearly, I can see how full of crap I am; because I can hear the cars drive by late into the night, slowing down and speeding up again, their horns blowing, and I even think I can hear their laughter, snickering really, but how can I hear them from that far away? But then I remember: I'm no more than a rabbit to them. So I've got a rabbit's ears. I can hear them snickering like they do when they follow me in the streets all day.

And then, in the morning, I grab hold of that same old, tired old straw. Because somehow, some way, I've got to get up, I've got to get dressed, and I've got to walk these streets, door-to-door, in broad daylight, and do my job. And to do that I can't let their hate dictate me.

Out on the street I tell myself I'm still alive. Sometimes I even smile—when my day is done and I'm all alone. And for that little while I'm Long John and I'm John Henry. I'm long gone and I'm still swimmin'! I'm a steel-driving man!

But at night I admit they know where I live. They see all and know all. They could come for us when we're fast asleep. So every night I lay in my bed and wonder, "Can I do this?" It makes no sense to me.

7 • The Wounded Man

It didn't take long—my third day here, we were climbing out our window. I try to remember because I want to tell it. If I'm telling it, I can survive. But doing it, there was no story to tell, there was no beginning or middle or end, there was just the fear in my sweat—the slipperiness of it on my skin—and everything was right there, what I saw and heard and touched and smelled, there and gone, and then the next thing, and the next. Everything was *now*.

But was it? Later, when it's quiet and I'm trying to make sense of it, I can't help but wonder: had I felt or seen or smelled anything at all ... at that time? Or were my senses frozen? The Klan was after Morgan and me, and I was so afraid—or was I? All I know is, there was only reaction, there was only flight, only the mechanics of it—up onto the chair and shimmying out the window, pivoting my elbows against the frame, reaching for and straddling the fence outside, and turning to give a hand to Morgan. His older body stuck in the window frame, that goddamned, tar-baby window frame. I'm holding onto his arm, and I'm pulling on it, jerking on it. How long were we there in that window and on that fence? It must have been only a second or two, but it seemed like an hour. What was memory and what was ... real? It's important for me to know.

From the time we heard that car drive by and heard them stop this time and the car doors slam and the White voices laughing (we saw them through our front window, we saw their rifles and their chains) and all through our escape (we'd had it planned: out the rear window and onto the fence and down the alley, to another street and another alley and under a house on risers; we'd huddle against the underside of its concrete steps)—from the sound of the car to the cold of the ground, was the danger so strong that it elbowed out the smell of my sweat and the beating of my heart and the sting of the skin I'd scraped? Did it even elbow out my fear? Had I been aware of any of those things at all, or were they driven underground? Did I feel them only after we came to rest and waited out the night?

Here's what I mean: had I been human all the way through it? Or did those White men rob me of that, while we were running for our lives? Did I have to recapture myself? That's an important fact to know if I'm going to do this.

Because maybe that's the only way I can: by shedding myself—gotta travel light sometimes—and then, afterwards, putting myself back on, because it wasn't until later, not even while I was under that house but when we crawled out to the morning light, that I felt my shame.

Because shame, while you're running, it might stop you. It might stop you cold.

We must've been quite a sight—absurd, really—crawling out from under that house, testing and stretching our arms and legs, trying our best to look natural in case anybody saw us. I couldn't look at Morgan. Did he feel it too? The absurdity, the shame? Shouldn't he? We ran like rabbits when those White men came. It was only when he touched my arm that I turned to face him. I tried to read his eyes.

But then I remembered him in that window and me pulling on his arm while the Klan broke down our door. And I remembered how important it was to not let go, that my only salvation, my only safety, had been in that arm I held and in his body coming through. It hadn't been courage or even loyalty; it had been an imperative … of survival, of …

I can't name it. I don't even know if that's what I experienced, or only what I remember. But I wanted at least to name it—so I could tell it as a story.

Because that's what I do to sleep at night and get out of my bed in the morning: I tell it. That's why I could crawl out from behind those steps and into the street, when I was so ashamed, and go back with Morgan to our place, with the door broke down and the two rooms tossed, and put our things back in order and go back to work.

This is what I've come to think: We've got to rescue ourselves from the pure, instinctual reactiveness of it. We may have run like rabbits, but we don't have to *be* rabbits. We can tell it, give it a moral. (Months later we could even riff it for laughs in our freedom meetings, and the audience riffs back: "—and thus, on the third day, we have risen—up on that chair and clean out the window!" And some people laugh and others smile and nod their heads. And that way we win. I'll be up there behind the podium like I'm saying, "Okay 'ofay,' what else can you show me?") And that way I can sleep when I'm weary, and get up to weary myself again.

I'd been here for three measly days. Those peckers sure don't give you much time to settle in. Three days and they're on my ass! But history is written by the swift, and the open window is mightier than the sword. Yeah, I'll be riffing: "Those dumb-ass peckers, they're coming in the front door, but Long John's going out the back!" But those peckers aren't so dumb, and I'm no Long John. By the end of the day I'm exhausted just from my jitters—from the cops, the passing cars, from opening my door to what's outside, or being out late at night. From living my life, so exposed. In bed, I listen to every car that passes.

That's why I've got to tell it and name it. Because that's the only way I'll believe ... that I can do this.

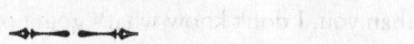

❖

All the neighborhoods look the same: No sidewalks. Dirt streets doglegged at their crossings and set in patchwork grids. Wooden houses perched on concrete blocks, their paint jobs thin, worn and peeling, their porches rough and slivery. The front doors are open and the screen doors are closed, their wire mesh is torn, patched, and sagging. Inside, the rooms are dark. You peer through a doorway, you might see old newspapers used for wallpaper, sealed with flour-water glue, and the window panes are yellow-brown waxed-paper. There's red dirt everywhere, in the streets and in the yards, rock-hard and dusty in the heat, slick and sticky in the rain. It's hard to wash from your clothes, it stains you so. Nothing grows in it except a bush or two, and patches of clumped, weedy, broadleafed grass, dark and gray-green, and long like wilted ribbons, with roots no deeper than a dime. And the air: when the wind doesn't blow there's a smell of urine and garbage and feces from the ditches out back. Stick around long enough, you finally won't notice it.

Old folks lounge in their front-porch shade, working their cardboard fans or snoozing, children run from house to house, and the grown women stay inside, cooking or cleaning and wishing for a breeze that just won't come. There's nothing to say about these neighborhoods; nothing to notice; nothing that anyone would remember. Neighborhoods like this are a dime a dozen all over the Delta—Morgan and I grew up in one little better. Can anything good come out of Nazareth?

The first few weeks are hard—closing doors, and faces that duck down as the door closes, ducking down like I was White. I don't like that. Look me in the eye—I'm no better than you. I don't know what's going on with that. Then I think: are they ashamed? I'm sitting in Mr. Courtland's café, sipping a coke. I'm tired, I'm waiting for Morgan, and I'm grateful that another day's done, and I can feel the edginess slowly rising to my skin and shivering free. I imagine it leaving my body and turning the air cold around me. I haven't eaten yet. I'm feeling giddy. I'm granting every ducked-down face absolution for their shame. Bless you, my children; bless you who close your doors on me in sin and shame. Receive now my blessing, for your sin is as the night before the dawning light of day. All sin passes, because every door shall be opened, and for every opened door history awaits. I giggle to myself. I almost spill my coke.

Today it's the cops' turn to dog me. There're two of them in a car. I cross a street. The driver pops his clutch, makes his car jump at me. I jump sideways, the cop car jumps again. I skitter out of the way. I'm trying to keep from dropping my fliers and pamphlets, my registration forms. I clutch them to my chest. I can hear their laughter. I mutter under my breath what I want to shout out loud.

One of them jumps out of the car. "Hey! You! Nigger! What's that you said?"

I stop and turn. I've got my head down. I really don't want him to see my face: I don't think I've got myself under control.

I shuffle my papers and shift my feet. "I didn't say nothing, mister."

He's right up in front of me. He's shorter than me. I think that makes him mad. I can see his face even though I'm ducking my head. He's all red. He's a really scrawny man. I'm thinking: I can take him. Even with his billy club and pistol, I can take this fool. He's yelling at me and I'm trying not to listen. If I listen I'll get mad. I figure my best chance is to say nothing.

"Answer me, nigger!" I've got to think of something to say.

He keeps yelling. "What do you think you're doing?"

"I was crossing the street."

"Don't you mess with me. What do you think you're doing?"

I'm destroying your world. "I'm just passing out papers. I'm just talking to some folks here ... Mister."

He takes the papers from my hand. He reads a few lines and drops them to the ground. He's got his billy club out. "You dropped your papers in the street. That's littering. You want to go to jail for littering?"

"No ... Mr. James." I'm finally able to read his name tag. That's his last name—he's Baynard James. I'll call him anything but "Mr. Baynard," and I'll never call him "Sir."

"Then you better pick them up."

I bend down to get them and he pokes his billy club in my side. I spread my feet to keep my balance and he pokes me again, harder, pushing, and I stumble to one knee.

He's shouting: "Get up nigger!" I stand up.

He's still shouting. "Get those papers."

I bend over. I know what's going to happen. The billy club again, hard, poking, pushing, and I fall over sideways. I know I could come up in a crouch and rush him, just like on a football field. I could put my shoulder in his stomach and knock him on his back. It's just him and me. There's nobody else. I'd be on him before he'd—

I hear the other policeman laughing. He's out of the car too, leaning on it. I see his hand on his holster. I remember what my Papa Joe said: they always have guns. I look at the houses on the street. I can see folks in their doorways, in their windows. This is all for their benefit. To see me humiliated in the street.

It's working. I stay on my knees and scoop up some papers. I shuffle over a bit, still on my knees and pick up the rest. Then I lean back on my heels. I'm not about to stand. I don't do anything but wait.

"You done, nigger?"

I steal a glance and he's got a grin on his face I'd like to wipe off. I keep my head down. "Yes ... Mr. James. I'm done."

"Then get up. Get on out of here. Go on home. Wherever you came from, go on home."

He's not so close to me now, so I stand. The cop car is sideways in the street, blocking it. One cop's at the rear bumper, and that Baynard James is at the front. To go where I was going, I'll have to go right by them. They both have their billy clubs out.

I'm just standing there. I don't know what to do. Those people in the doorways, in the windows—it's up to me what they're going to see, me turning tail or me getting beaten.

I turn as slowly as I can and walk away. I'm trying to keep some dignity here. But I don't think I do, because I'm turning tail ... like a rabbit.

Back at our place, I tell Morgan about it. He tells me I kept my cool, that I did the right thing. "That took real courage, Aleck." I remember what he wrote to me in his letter, so this is nothing I didn't know before I came. I'm thinking about all the words I heard in bull sessions and freedom meetings at Morehouse: violence isn't real power, it isn't real strength; real strength builds, it doesn't tear down. Nonviolence attacks the system that oppresses us, and that's our true enemy. Back then, there was no argument. How could there be? Back then, that whole scene was just us students and our ideas. Good ideas; very good ideas. But today, that "scene" was me humiliated in the middle of a street. (It'll only be later that I'll realize I should've been scared to shit, just like I should've been when I dared that kid to pull his gun on me.) But now, while I'm listening to Morgan, I still can't help but think: say me not taking on that cop was for the best, the best for the Movement, and say it took "real courage" for me not to—well, I still feel ashamed. (And dig this—that "courage" is supposed to boost my self-esteem!) Later, Morgan's gone and I'm alone. I see my suitcase in a corner. I put it on my cot and open it. It's so small. I've got a matchbox for my clothes. I've got nothing in this world. I slam it shut and throw it aside. I pick up the cot and throw that too. I look around for something else. But this room's so small, there's nothing else to throw. I start laughing. *Some Stagger Lee! I turned tail. Just like a rabbit!* I sit with a thud on Morgan's bed and my body's shaking. I can't get it out of my mind: I could've taken him. But he'll never know it—that scrawny cop with his big fat grin. It's a long time before I stand back up.

8 • The Wounded Man

We go to Mr. Courtland's café, and he feeds us and listens to us late at night in his kitchen in the back. He cuts on a light in the dining room, cuts the kitchen light off, and props the kitchen door open. Nobody on the street can see that anybody's here. Morgan pushes his food around with his fork. He wants to talk.

"What do you think? Are we too late? I mean organizing in the Delta here. I saw it in Drew. Fewer people in my store, fewer people I knew. And now I'm seeing it here. Our people don't know each other like they used to—there's too much moving around. We were a rural folk, a natural folk ... not so much anymore. 'Where's my milk cow gone?' 'If I was a bird, I'd be bird nest bound.' That's how we'd say things, wasn't it? A man would miss his woman. A man would miss his home. Anybody talk like that anymore? Anybody think like that anymore? Where'd all that go to? God knows, we never had much, but we ..."

He stops. He's looking at his plate. Then he looks up and sighs. You can hardly see the features of his face, but there's a glint in his eye from the doorway. He winces and looks away, the other way, to the backdoor. That whole side's black, but you can still make out the backdoor and the window and the wall. I look at it and feel like a mole underground.

Morgan starts up again, speaking slowly. "I think this would be easier, if we as a people were more hard-minded. People used to look out for each other; they used to know each other, be family even. But we're all strangers now. Are we a day too late, doing this?"

He falls silent. I don't say a thing. Mr. Courtland has hardly said a word. Mostly, he listens. He's a five-by-five, and he sits perched on his tall, skinny stool, sweating and breathing heavy. Morgan starts eating again and we listen to the night. Wind, leaves ... is that an animal, scuttering in the gutter? Is that a man's footfall? Mr. Courtland stops his wheezing and we try to catch the sound. There's so much in this world—what you hear, the noises in the night—that you just don't know.

When we're about to leave, Mr. Courtland takes his turn. "People here're closer to it than you think. They push back the hardest when y'almost got them. Now, y'all keep showing at their doors." Then he remembers what he wants to ask. "Y'all got a place to sleep yet?"

We've been sleeping in Morgan's car. After our place got tossed, our landlord had to put us out. Whites were going to charge him with bigamy. They got his first wife to sign a paper saying they're still married. He'd have lost his post office job. He did what he had to do.

Mr. Courtland shakes his head. "That's what I heard. I'll make some calls." He pauses to gather his breath. "And I'll just say this: People here—they're willing to support what you two are doing. Y'all got a lot of silent support. Taking all that shit," he shakes his head, "you two are a part of us now." Mr. Courtland looks into his dining room. "People whisper to me."

I take Morgan's plate and mine to the sink. Mr. Courtland sees me. "I'll get those, son. Now, as for a meeting place, I'm working on that too, with some of my Elks brothers. The Elks Hall here is the best place a Negro can get for a meeting. And I'm going to get it. Y'all just wait and see."

By Thanksgiving we've got a new place to sleep. We still don't have a meeting place, but we've found twenty-one people to register to vote. That should be our lucky number—three times seven, ain't nobody's business what they do. They gather in the evenings, crowding our new place, and we have some of the old heads who'd registered back in the 'forties tell them what kind of questions they'll be asked, and how Whites will try to trap them. Those twenty-one are old heads too. The youngest is over forty. The Rev. Lipscomb, he's seventy-five. Most live on federal checks, so the White people here can't touch them. And that's why they're with us.

Rev. Lipscomb showed up at *our* door. That first time, he told Morgan, "I've seen so many things, so many changes in my life, but the one thing that hasn't changed is me. I'm tired of being a second-class citizen. Yes sir, it's time *I* changed. Life ain't going to pass me by. No sir. I was afraid it would, so I'm so glad y'all came here. Y'all showed me what I can do. I'm going to register to vote."

Once we think they're ready, we take them to the courthouse, all together, four cars' worth, and inside the courthouse the Rev. Lipscomb is the first in line. On that, he insisted. He's a tall man, a burly man, with two large folds of skin at the back of his neck under a long bullet head, bristled and balding. He looks across the counter and down at the registrar.

"Mrs. Carraway? Now I've been knowing you all your life. I came down here to register to vote."

She smiles at him, the way you do to show you're in on the joke. "Now Bradley, you know that you can't read or write."

He points down at the counter, like there's a Bible there and he's pointing to a text to preach. "I know, I know, yes ma'am. But I'll be getting my check, my government check, every month, and I cash it every time. Now how do I do that, because I've got to sign for that check?"

Mrs. Carraway is not my idea of a Southern Belle. She's short and thick-set. Her head's shaped like an oatmeal carton, no neck, and she's thin-lipped; a severe looking woman, even when she smiles. And she isn't smiling now. "You sign with your X."

"That's right, Mrs. Carraway. So I'll sign my X right here and you'll know it's me. I've been studying this, I know you got to ask me a question, so ask me whatever you want, yes ma'am, just ask me and I'll answer it and it won't matter that I can't read or write."

Mrs. Carraway slams her palm on the counter. "What question could I ask you, that you'd know the answer?" She pauses for a second. "How many bubbles are in a bar of soap?"

Rev. Lipscomb steps back with one foot. He cranes his neck in his shirt collar and rubs the back of his bullet head. "Mrs. Carraway, I am sorry. I've been knowing you ... I can't say I know the answer. And if I can't answer your question I'm going to flunk this test, ain't I?"

She grins at him. "Yes, that's your question."

He looks down at the floor but he speaks distinctly. "Mrs. Carraway, I've been an ignorant man all my life. I expect you know that. But I hoped I'd at least be a first-class citizen before I died. My days are numbered, I got few left, yes ma'am. I don't want to die as ignorant as I am. So, ma'am, if you could help an old man you've been knowing all your life, please Mrs.

Carraway, now you tell me how many bubbles are in a bar of soap."

She slaps her palm on the counter again. Then she goes for her phone. She's so angry she doesn't know which way to turn, pivoting this way and that before she grabs it and shouts for the sheriff to come here from his office upstairs.

We see a group of Whites gathering behind us, outside the registrar's, out in the hall. They're crowding the doorway, our only way out. I can see the fear in our group's eyes. Morgan raises his hand and signals and we leave, edging our way through the crowd. Old women are trying to pass by young men who won't give way. When we've made it outside, in front of the courthouse and counting heads, the sheriff comes up to Morgan and spits in his face.

"Nigger." He pulls his pistol and shakes it at Morgan. "Let me tell you one goddamn thing. I don't want to see you here the next day, the next hour, the next minute or second. You and your buddy are going to pack your goddamn bags, and I want y'all to leave Horatio County right now."

We have those twenty-one people with us, and other folks, Negro and White, are gathering around us too. They're waiting on Morgan, to hear what he'll say. He pauses while he slowly takes his handkerchief from his hip pocket to wipe the spittle from his face.

"Sheriff, if you don't want to see me or my friend here the next day, or the next hour, the next minute, or the next second, then you're the one who'll have to pack his bags and leave, because we're going to stay right here. My name is Mr. Morgan Wright. That's 'Wright' with a 'w.' My friend here is Mr. Aleck Sharpe. That's with a 'ck' in 'Aleck' and an 'e' at the end of

'Sharpe'. You write them down. *Mister* Morgan Wright and *Mister* Aleck Sharpe."

The sheriff's too stunned to move. He almost drops his pistol. Morgan raises his hand and we all file through the crowd to our cars. We caravan back to Southeast Williams Point. We keep all four cars together for safety. The car I drive is filled with fear, funk, and exhilaration. Those old heads, they chatter like children, on and on about Morgan. "Didn't he take him down a peg!" They sound like a bunch of Br'er Rabbits back in their briar patch, but I can't help but wonder, "Who won?" Nobody filled out a registration form. The sheriff and his deputies follow us in their cars, and every time we stop at a house they write down the address. We drive a slow and winding route, turning down this street and that—what a comic parade for all of Southeast to see!

Rev. Lipscomb is what you'd call a jackleg preacher. For over fifty years he preached a gospel he could never read. He'd open his Bible and stick his finger on the page, and whatever he preached had nothing to do with the text at his finger. He knows Jesus and he knows Moses. I'm told he confuses them regularly. His wife collects the offering. She, at least, can count.

Any White who knows him surely thinks he's a fool. A lot of Colored people do too. They told us so. "He doesn't preach from knowledge." Well, SNCC doesn't either, or rather, we ignore it. We placed first in line an illiterate, in a state that requires a written literacy test. But Rev. Lipscomb's illiteracy is Mississippi's bastard child, so we decided Mississippi should be forced to claim it. People will say we're not being practical. We'll say, the way they do us in Mississippi, practicality be damned.

And Rev. Lipscomb himself, he knew. We'd told him he wouldn't pass and he understood. Yet he insisted that he go and be the first to face a woman he'd known since she was a child. He ran errands for her family. Did he think she might help him? Did he hope to show her, after all those years, that he was his own man? Her patronage, his self-respect—did he somehow hope for both?

And what of Mrs. Carraway and her bubbles in a soap? All she needed was to give him the form. She knew he couldn't fill it out. Even she didn't care about the law—that her side wrote. No, we're all actors, slapping counters and making gestures, in an allegory about power, exercised face-to-face. And the play *is the thing*!

I wish what we were doing was open and clean, but it's not. I wish we could put people in a line to register so they could vote, and the more we put up the more power their votes would have. That's what we tell them this is about. But it's not. It's a shadow play about intimidation and fear, and perseverance and courage. Maybe about heroism too. But voting? We're nowhere near voting. But that's not what we told those twenty-one.

When enough of our people are rejected, we'll record their depositions, like I recorded mine when the cops pushed me around, and we'll send them to the Justice Department, and maybe, just maybe, the government will support us and Williams Point will be just like Little Rock—where the streets were filled with federal troops—and then we can be open and clean and straightforward.

Until then, the play's the thing. But I can't help but wonder: our people know the good guys from the bad, but which side plays the fool? And I can't help but answer: if we can't register our people, we'll be the fool.

When I let Rev. Lipscomb out, he takes a few steps toward the sheriff's car behind us. "You don't scare me no more. No sir, you don't scare me no more." He shouts it for the whole neighborhood to hear. And then he opens the door to his home and walks on through.

❖— —❖

That was our first good moment. That was the first time I thought there's a new game in town. But the aftermath? Like I said, most of those we had to register live on federal checks. The Whites know where they live but they still can't touch them. Not directly. They can't stop those checks. But some of their relatives—their grown children and nieces and nephews—they lost their jobs on account of what we did.

One comes to our place. He holds his fists out, his clinched fingers up, like he's pleading with us and threatening us too, because he doesn't know what to do. He curses Morgan; he says he never wants to see him near his family again.

"You tell us we got to make ourselves a way. Not up North, but here. Here! Well how am I supposed to live here without no job? Where am I supposed to go? Where am I supposed to live? You tell me. Where?"

He leaves. Morgan didn't even have a chance to speak. I follow the man outside. I could catch up with him and have it out, but I don't. I just stand on the edge of the street and watch him walk away. He has three little children to support.

Morgan's still sitting behind our desk when I come back in, like he hasn't moved an inch since that man left. He's muttering to himself: "—stayed in the wilderness a day too long. Why can't they see it? How can I—?" He realizes I'm back. He turns to me scowling. "I'm not White. I'm not his boss. I didn't fire him. People need to get some sense. He needs to know who his real enemy is."

I sit down. I'm suddenly tired. I'm thinking I once used a similar logic on that kid who tried to rob me. I gesture to the street. "I expect he does. But he can't curse *that* man."

So, is the play still the thing? Is our act, our face-to-face defiance, is that worth any man's job? Going into Christmas, canvassing, people still close their doors when they see it's us. But now they don't duck their faces when they turn us away. They look at us straight on, their own faces hurt and wondering, even as they close their doors. And don't they take a little longer now? To close their doors? I don't know, but it seems to me they do. Is that enough? Does that balance a man's lost job? I tell myself it does—that someday it will. It's got to. That's what gets me up every morning.

But every day I'm troubled. Because of Morgan and me, our people—whether they follow us or not—our people are punished. They lose their jobs. They get pushed around. Beaten up. All for what the Movement does. For what I do. Doing my job.

That hurts, and I don't know if I can take it.

RANDALL LUCE

9 • The Drowned Man

Chattanooga, Tennessee: 1923

Sunday afternoon, the two of them at Pete's kitchen table: Uncle John said he could help him. Harry said he didn't know how. For some things, there was no helping. Uncle John just let that pass and spoke his piece. (To Harry, the whole family was like that—they'd look beyond what Harry was saying and keep on talking; they'd hoe their row, they'd make their point—as if they were teaching a child.) Uncle John had a proposition. "I can make it so you can show your face in our streets. I can put before you your best opportunity to prove yourself to our people by doing something for the Race." He said he'd tell him how, "If you have ears to hear."

And eyes to see: Uncle John was seriously churched—a deacon; reserved in his manner and moderate in his habits. He was also a Communist. Pictures of Jesus on his walls, his Bible by his bedside; and stacks of the *Daily Worker* under his floorboards, hidden in case the policemen came. He'd open his Bible to the Acts of the Apostles, his finger underlining the words, hoeing a row. See here, he'd say, the Saints shared all they had. That squared everything for him. If that was what they did in Acts, that was all that counted. "Acts," he'd always say, was his favorite title in the Bible. There was no need for any what-ifs. He was content to *do*, to move forward as best he could, deliberate and serious, clear-eyed and clean. Harry liked that. He'd think, *I was once like that, back before*—and he'd wince at the thought—*back when I was White*. Not so much anymore. Harry envied Uncle John.

Uncle John would visit on Sunday afternoons. Harry didn't care for the Communism, but still he listened. So now Harry leaned forward across the table. "Tell me your proposition."

Two White thugs were robbing Negroes on their paydays. Harry nodded, he'd heard about it.

"But have you heard this?" Uncle John pressed his Bible with both his hands. "Two days ago, a Negro fought back and a bunch of our fellows joined in, and the police drove up and beat up all those Negro men and carried them off to jail. They let the thugs go free." Uncle John paused and frowned, Harry nodded again, and then Uncle John jabbed his forefinger straight down on the table. "My comrades in the Party say those thugs are policemen themselves, off duty, and not just two, but any number of them. They take turns."

Harry believed him. Uncle John was the only Negro Harry knew who counted White men, fellow members the Party, among his friends. They would know these things.

"My White comrades found out where two of these men go after they rob our people, and where they drink, and for how long, and what time they go home. They go to a bar where my comrades go, it's a working-class place, and they overheard them, you see, bragging about what they just done.

"We're going to bring justice to those men—a Colored justice, a working man's justice. We're going to mess them up some, so they and their friends know not to mess with our people. We're going to that White part of town and grab them when they're going home. There're plenty of alleyways there where we can conduct our business.

"There's no other way. No other way, Harry."

His comrades had a car he could use, clean of ownership so it couldn't be traced, and one of them offered to drive it. "But I told them no on the driver. I said we'll use our own driver."

It was sunset. They were alone. Harry had the books for a storekeeper laid out on the table between them. Burnett had told the storekeeper about Harry, so he brought Harry his business. This storekeeper was a deacon, just like Uncle John. And he was an officer of a Negro civic club. The Colored people in Chattanooga were proud to know him. Young men trying to make their way came to him for advice. He'd loan them money. He kept his hand open to his people. He sold dry goods, and in the back of his store he ran numbers. He was not above selling goods that had fallen from a truck. He had two sets of books and they were very complex. He barely broke even with his dry goods business. His prices, Harry would tell him, were too low. He'd just smile and lean back in his chair. "I can afford it. You just scrub those other figures from my 'sidelines.'" Harry was thinking how most Negroes held an irreverent attitude toward the law.

But why not? Harry would've never thought like that before, but listening to Geneva's family's stories, so many were about the wrongs done to them by policemen. A law unto themselves and no punishment possible. But here: a Colored man's justice, a possible justice. Wasn't that wrong? But you just *do*, don't you? Shouldn't you?

Still, respectable men like that storekeeper, like Uncle John, should abide by the law—Harry had always taken that for granted. Harry once asked him about that. Uncle John had sat up straight—straighter than he usually did. "How can a respectable Colored man abide the White man's law? They use that law to cheat us—to beat and murder us. How do you abide oppression? How do you abide evil? You *avoid* that law, when you can, if you can. You never abide it."

Harry had no answer but it worried him, that Negroes would think that, even if, when hearing all those stories he could understand it, and he was thinking about that now while Uncle John told him about those thieving cops. Uncle John pressed his hands down on his Bible. He nearly rose out of his seat. "This is your moment of truth, Harry. I told my White comrades that this is our affair. I told them, 'With all due respect, I didn't want any White men involved.' I told them, 'It wasn't just the danger; it was the necessity of us protecting our own. It's our justice we're after, not any White man's.' They said I couldn't use a Colored man to drive, driving in that White part of town. The cops would stop him for sure." Here Uncle John smiled. "I told them they were right. I needed a White man who wasn't White."

Harry would remember how the last light of day, golden green, trickled through the leaves of the trees and through the open window, making spotted, swaying patterns on the cupboard and the walls.

Uncle John spoke slowly and barely above a whisper. "All you've got to do is drive that car and keep your eyes on the road. You won't have to do what the rest of us are going to be doing. You won't have to see what we do, and you won't even have to know what we do.

"I've got my men all picked out. Every one of them has had a loved one beaten or murdered by the police. They were happy to volunteer. So, you see, this goes far beyond those payday robberies. And it's the only justice we have at hand."

He reached for Harry's hand. Harry let him take it. "And after this—there'll still be people who won't know you helped us—but there'll be enough of us who will. They'll tell the others that you're okay. They won't have to say why. And people will believe them because they'll know these men—all good and upstanding.

"And once those men have had their say, our people," he nodded his head, "*our* people: some will respect you; more will accept you; and everybody else will leave you alone."

Harry turned his eyes from Uncle John's and looked up at the walls. The last of the green-gold light above him, it looked like they were underwater. You could see through water, and you could hide in water. Pillars of the community ran numbers, policemen were thieves and murderers, and Christians were Communists. There wasn't anything solid. Not that Harry could see—except, that here, yes, something had to be done.

As the day darkened, the patterns on the walls slowly disappeared, like water drying. When the lamps came on the last patterns would be gone. Harry licked his lips. He was thirsty. He told Uncle John yes, because Uncle John *did*, and Harry envied him for being so clear-eyed and clean.

◆━━◆━━◆

There were four Negroes—Uncle John was one of them—and there was Harry. Each took his own route to a place on the outskirts of town. Harry had never been there before. It was dark. There was one street light. There was a row of shabby buildings on a deserted road, laid with hard-packed dirt and oil, and a single large sedan, empty. When Harry got off the bus, the last bus, and stood under the street light, he couldn't see a thing. The night surrounded him, pitch-black, like a curtain. He took a few steps away from the light, and there, standing in the darkness, he could make out the shapes of the buildings and the sedan. It wasn't far away. He walked to it, the bus gone now, and then the four Negroes appeared, their dark forms emerging from the larger darkness of the buildings. They all got in the car. The keys were under the driver's seat. Harry drove. The four Negroes crouched below the seats, out of sight.

Harry drove to Farley Street, in the White part of town, and found the alleyway and backed into it, far enough so nobody passing on the sidewalk or the street would see them.

He kept the engine running, but he cut the lights. Across the street, two White men were standing under a street lamp. They each lit a cigarette as soon as Harry parked, and stood there smoking. They never once looked at the automobile facing them.

Harry said everything was okay and the other men got up, but sat hunched so they could just see over the top of the front seats and the dashboard. Uncle John said, "Those are our lookouts." Then they waited.

The two men across the street were talking to each other. Occasionally they laughed. They looked like they were a little drunk. A policeman walked by and asked them a question. One answered and the policeman walked on. It was well past midnight. Harry looked at his watch, but it was too dark to see.

Suddenly, just like that, the two men threw down their cigarettes and ground them with their shoes. They left in opposite directions. Moments later two men came staggering past the alley. Uncle John whispered, "That's them." Harry put the car in gear and the men with him crouched below the seats. Harry pulled out of the alley and turned right. The two men were about twenty yards ahead. Harry gave the car some gas. Another alley was ahead.

Harry caught up with the men at the alley. He jumped the car up on the sidewalk to cut them off. He kept his eyes ahead, but he could hear it and feel it—the two right side doors flying open and slamming shut, and the scuffle of feet and men. Harry cut the wheel back and drove back onto the street and around the block. He stopped again at the same alley, the second one. The doors opened and closed and Harry drove on, the four Negroes hot and sweating and breathing hard, and hunched below the seats again. Harry rolled down his window. The air smelled of sweat inside. He kept his eyes on the road.

Once out of town, the four men sat up. It was a dry, clear night, but the air in the sedan felt close and heavy, even with the window down, like a storm was on its way. The four men sat silent, as if a burden lifted still felt heavy. One poked his head out the window to catch the breeze and breathed in heavily. Harry asked them, "What'd y'all do to them?" He tried to sound casual. Nobody spoke until Uncle John finally answered. "We gave them justice. Justice too long denied." He reached from the backseat and grasped Harry's shoulder. "We gave them justice." Another said softly, "Yeah, justice." So, Harry figured he knew. The man beside him relaxed, and the atmosphere in the car lightened. Gradually, the men began to talk, small talk, with an occasional laugh. Harry concentrated on his driving.

He drove to another location he had never been before. There, on the side of the road, was Uncle John's car. Nobody, and nothing else, was in sight. They all got in it. Now Harry crouched on the floor, the Negroes sat, and Uncle John drove. Somebody passed around a bottle of rye.

Uncle John drove them to his house. They brought in the bottle. Uncle John had a small burlap bag, tied up into a bundle. Everybody sat around the dinner table. Uncle John got them glasses but politely declined to drink. He sat silent, he seemed at peace, but he watched each man in turn. One poured; he clapped the other two's backs, he clapped Harry's back, he called him 'brother.' Another fell silent holding his glass, staring at it, ignoring it. The third gulped his drink, and commandeered the bottle. Uncle John rose, he shook the hands of the two men drinking. He shook Harry's hand. Then he kneeled down beside the last man, one arm around his shoulders, and whispered in his ear. The man nodded in reply.

Uncle John left the room, carrying his burlap bag. He was gone for a while. The three Colored men talked in fits and starts. Somebody laughed. Harry nodded along, but he barely listened. He drank his drink but didn't take another. He had an idea how these men had lost so much to the police, and what their anger must be, even their hate, and that there had been no other way to exact any due measure of justice—either for themselves or for their loved ones. Tonight had been a point of honor for these men, and Harry knew that Whites, for their honor, often did far worse for far less cause. But … Harry couldn't remember these men's names. He realized, suddenly, that he didn't want to. He felt split in two—and neither half was him.

Later, Uncle John drove him home—Pete's home—and walked him to the door. He took Harry's arm and told him that soon he'd be able to walk anywhere he wanted and nobody would bother him again.

"You just wait a week. You've crossed over now. You're home now." Harry said nothing. Uncle John eyed him closely. "Are you alright? You look troubled."

This was not a man you lied to, not to such a man so serious. "I feel torn in two ..." Harry let those words be, his thought unfinished, and waited for Uncle John's reply.

"The word of God can be a terrible thing, Harry. 'And they utterly destroyed all that was in the city, both man and woman, young and old, and ox, and sheep, and ass, with the edge of the sword.' Those are the words of the Bible—Joshua. Some White people say that's their book. I say it's every man's." Uncle John gripped Harry's arm tighter. "Another prophet told us this: 'On the 12th of May, 1828, I heard a loud noise in the heavens, and the Spirit was loosened, and Christ had laid down the yoke he had borne for the sins of men, and that I should take it on and fight against the Serpent, for the time was fast approaching when the first should be last and the last should be first.'"

Harry would always remember Uncle John's gaze: serious, gentle, urging Harry to understand, to nod his head, to give any sign of agreement and solidarity. "Don't you see, Harry? Foolish men of mammon, for an hour's profit, printed and published that man's testimony, without any thought for the inevitable consequences of their actions. That was God's doing."

Harry shook his head. "I don't—Who? What do you mean?"

"Nat Turner, Harry. The preacher Nat Turner. One of God's judges for His people. Like the judges in the Old Testament. Nat Turner tried to set us free. He was a martyr for our freedom. It's been a hundred years, and we still celebrate his memory because his testimony was preserved ... by a slaver. By God. He stretched His hand into the house of mammon."

Looking at Harry, Uncle John sighed. Then he smiled and released Harry's arm. "You feel torn, I understand. But I wouldn't worry. All men should be humbled before the terrible justice of our Lord. Every man I chose for this mission has carried a burden that I hoped to ease. Including you, Harry. Including you. You can let that burden go now. Call it God's gift, if you choose to take it."

Uncle John clapped Harry's back and turned back to his car. Harry stood in the doorway and watched him go. While riding back with Uncle John, Harry had seen the sun as a thin milky line on the horizon. Now, it was hidden by the houses.

⊷⊷

There was nothing about the attack in the newspapers. But Harry heard rumors. One was that the police had received a package of four severed thumbs and a note saying this was what happened to thieving cops. Harry never asked Uncle John about that or any of the other rumors. Several he knew weren't true. But the one about the thumbs—he remembered the burlap bag Uncle John had carried that night—that one he believed.

10 • The Drowned Man

Harry was sitting with Big Mama Darling in her parlor. It was, he now knew, the room he'd sat in his first night in Chattanooga, waiting to hear his fate. So dark then; light and airy now. Geneva was with Lilly and Earley in the children's bedroom, readying them for school. Big Mama's chair was situated to catch the morning light through her window. Harry had opened the curtains of all the windows for her. Her skin glowed caramel. Above her was a picture of Lincoln, cut from a magazine and framed, and twin silhouettes, profiles, cut from black paper, a man and a woman facing each other. Harry guessed it was her and her husband, done when they were young. Or maybe her parents. He'd have to ask Geneva.

Not Big Mama. She intimidated him. Just a bit, but just enough. She wasn't foreboding—she sat quite still, her breathing audible, but steady and relaxed. She was *beyond*, as if she'd lived past everything life had thrown up against her. Harry thought of a towering tree, a valley's vista, a mountain, a river—*I've Got Peace Like a River*—her body's surface was small, but … it bespoke of a vast interior. He figured he didn't know her at all, just her presence; it seemed too good to be true. But maybe her imperfections had all been weathered away, maybe living to an old age did that to some people.

And she spoke so rarely. If Harry had asked her anything, he wasn't sure she'd respond.

Family portraits were everywhere. One, a young Big Mama and her husband, Lionel, sitting side-by-side in formal pose. Like in all photographs of that era, they stared straight ahead as if the other wasn't even there. But Lionel's right hand had strayed from his side and was resting on hers, nestled in her lap. The color was a faded sepia, their faces were ghost-like, and small brown spots surrounded them as if there had been a pox in the air. Lionel, faded though he was, was darker than Big Mama. Harry tried to imagine what color Lionel's skin had really been, but the faded sepia gave him no clue.

Other photographs—similarly faded and spotted, and some even water-marked or creased, populated her walls and tables. All of family groupings, large and small. One—Geneva had laughed with him about it—was a long rectangle, a photo of the entire extended family. The grouping was too wide for the photographer's lens, so he had taken three separate pictures from left to right, and merged them in the dark room. After the first picture was taken, two boys from the left side had run to the right for the third picture, and so were visible on both sides of the finished photograph. Serious and ramrod straight on the left; leaning and laughing on the right.

Harry sat quietly, waiting for Geneva and her children. It was the same cushioned chair he had sat in before, on that first night, listening to her family debating his fate. The soot from his clothes had smeared the chair's fabric; the family had had it cleaned. Harry couldn't help but compare the room with the ones he'd grown up in: here, everything was older—and cleaner. Everything in its place. That was Geneva's and her cousins' doing.

Big Mama Darling held her cane in front of her, upright, her hands on its knob, its tip in the carpet between her feet. She smiled at him and said, "Lost, but now she's found."

"Pardon?"

"My baby, my prodigal." Big Mama Darling leaned slightly forward and peered at Harry over her cane. "Geneva. Lost, but now she's found. Come home at last." Her mouth opened in a smile. "She brought you." She chuckled. "She's a pistol."

Harry didn't know what to say to that.

Big Mama Darling tilted her head just slightly to the side. "I wondered if I'd ever see her again, but she came back." Again, she leaned forward in her chair. "You wouldn't take her away, would you?"

Harry sat up straight. "Oh, no ... ma'am. She told me, she wants to stay. And I've no place to take her."

Big Mama Darling leaned back in her chair, closed her eyes, and smiled. "Show me your pictures—your White family."

Harry hesitated, then he brought out his wallet and his snapshots. He got up and placed them in her hands. Big Mama Darling traced the faces with her finger. "Charlotte, Harry Jr., and Mary Ann—Geneva told me." Her finger lingered over Charlotte's smudged face in the photograph marred by Harry's tears. She looked up at him. "Every night I pray for them. I pray for you too."

Harry nodded. "Thank you ... Big Mama Darling." He didn't know what else to say. Somehow, her request hadn't seemed intrusive; somehow, he was grateful for the chance to confess. Somehow, confessing seemed to be what he was doing—acknowledging both his love and their abandonment.

She held up the photographs and Harry took them back, put them in his wallet, and his wallet in his pocket. Her eyes held his, and he didn't turn around to sit. Rather, he backed up to his chair and then sat down.

She peered at him again. "Malachi, my son, he's Geneva's father. He's the one who stayed. He's my righteous son. He needs no forgiveness. There's nothing to repent. Geneva was the one who left."

Harry nodded yes. He could hear her breathing, slightly labored now from her exertion.

She looked to the window and blinked in its light. "When Geneva left, that hurt him deeply. It hurt ... his pride. I don't mean pride as a sin; I mean the virtue of pride. He loves his daughter. He's always loved her, so dearly, so dearly. But I don't think he's ever understood her. Not completely. Not yet, and maybe not ever.

"So, I pray for him too."

Big Mama Darling settled back in her chair and closed her eyes. Her body seemed to well up, to fill some void that surrounded her, to transverse the boundary between herself and the world. Maybe it was just her breathing, her chest moving out and in. Or maybe it was the calmness she displayed, her seeming projection of her inner self outwards, her poise.

Her face relaxed. Had she fallen asleep? Harry sat in his chair, looking at her with the morning light all about her, her skin's warm glow, her breathing steady, until Geneva came with Lilly and Earley in tow, behaving for their great-grandmother and all dressed up for school.

When Big Mama Darling was buried, Harry stood at the edge of the family gathering, Geneva and her children beside him. It was windy cold; the ground had been hard digging for her grave. Harry blinked repeatedly to keep the wind-sting from his eyes. Ever since her death, her family's web of being no longer seemed so tightly woven; her passing manifested itself physically in how each person navigated the spaces between them—there was an awkwardness, a recalibration of how close one stood, and how one passed by another, and gestured, and spoke. Mama Lou stood at the graveside the longest, even longer than her husband. She was the matriarch now.

Mae had come over one morning to clean. She had let herself in, called, and called, and found her Big Mama Darling still in her bed, at peace, impossibly still.

After Geneva became pregnant, Harry wished Big Mama had lived long enough to see her with another child. But later he was relieved to know she hadn't.

11 • The Wounded Man

Williams Point: Winter, 1962–1963

Now we have the kids. They just came. They hang around. They follow Morgan and me even with the cops around, even with those men sticking their hands out their car windows, pointing their fingers in the shape of a gun. These kids follow us and carry our fliers and pamphlets all over town.

Most are teenagers. One in particular, one of the first hanging around our office: she's a tall, broad, big-boned girl, but her features are delicate, even girlish—with stone-cold eyes and a mouth ready to frown, and smooth, milk chocolate skin. Somehow this all adds up to one person. Morgan notices her first and cues me in. "You see that girl? I talked to her mother—before you came—I knocked on her door and she brought me right in and sat me down in her parlor. I thought to myself, I finally got one."

He shakes his head. "They've got a sad house of trouble there. I don't know the ground of it."

He rubs his chin. "Donaldson. Deborah Donaldson. That's her. She's the daughter. I first saw her peeking around the corner of her house. When I was leaving. She was spying me."

I glance over at her now, standing in a corner of the office. "She looks like she's got a chip on her shoulder."

Morgan nods. "Uh huh."

I take another look. The office is full of teenagers, young ones. The boys are clowning for the girls, making out at being grown, what they'd do to a cracker. Deborah's standing quiet. I can barely see her through the crowd, over in the corner. I turn back to Morgan. "Maybe that's just what we need."

Morgan tells me: Eunice Donaldson's husband doesn't live much in Williams Point. They aren't divorced, they aren't even apart, but he travels because there're so few jobs here—he picks oranges in Florida and peaches in Georgia. Once he'd gone as far as Chicago, but he didn't stay. The jobs were good, he wanted his family to come, but Deborah refused and her mother wouldn't leave her. So he left Chicago. Morgan shakes his head at that. Even though he doesn't like people going North, he shakes his head. "The jobs were too good there, she told me her husband said that. If he stayed he'd have stayed for good. He would've lost his family."

Morgan's leaning to my ear. I'm the only one who hears him. "There I am, sitting in her parlor—the first time knocking on doors I've ever been invited in—and I never once had a chance to bring up the Movement. She steered everything back to her troubles—hard enough, I'll grant you that, but nothing different than so many of our women. But there was something else. I mean, it was real important to her that I know all this she was telling me, but I couldn't shake the feeling she was leaving something out. After I left, I was back on the street and I turned around and there she was, Deborah—she's their oldest—she ducked back around the corner of the house when she saw me look. I thought, whatever the trouble is, it's that girl right there." He's pointing over at her now, there in the corner. "*She* wouldn't go to Chicago. No girl should be ruling her family like that."

I follow his finger. She turns away, quick. Had she been looking at us the whole time?

I call her over. "Your name's Deborah, right? You want to help us?" I give her some handbills to distribute. Thirty minutes later she's back empty-handed. A policeman, she says, took all she had left and threw them in his car. "Then he pushed me down on the sidewalk." She lifts her left elbow to show me the scrape. "And here." She lifts her skirt to show me her knee. There were no tears in her eyes. I study her face. She hadn't cried at all.

"Do you want some more handbills?"

"Yes."

I give her a stack. "I'll come with you."

That night Morgan tells me to watch out. "Whatever ails that house, it starts with her."

The next day she has a copy of the *Community Lantern*. It's a news sheet put out by the Pax Christi Center—White women, lay, not nuns, followers of Dorothy Day—they do community service here, but they won't have anything to do with our Movement. But the *Community Lantern* is the only Black newspaper here. Mr. Courtland has it in his café. Deborah's holding it out to me. "Winter ... winter time is here."

"What?"

"It's winter time ... people are cold and hungry. The county usually distributes food. And the Center does too, but just for Christmas."

She makes me take the paper. "Read it. Here." She points at a headline. "The county commissioners decided they're not going to distribute any food this winter. They claim it's gotten too expensive. But you know the real reason. It's us. SNCC. You can read about it right here. We could pass out food and maybe clothing too. Otherwise, people will starve to death. SNCC could get us lots of clothes and food, couldn't it?"

That night Morgan frowns—he's considering the source. "I don't trust that girl." The source, I say, is the *Community Lantern*. He finally agrees. He calls Atlanta and we set it up.

◆━━◆ ◆━━◆

Folks mostly come on foot, they hitchhike or they walk. Some still have mules and ride them, or drive them pulling carts; a few have cars, old and dilapidated. We collected the food and clothing in Chicago and New York and trucked it here, to Mr. Courtland's church, Pilgrims' Chapel. This is our first day distributing and people are lined up to get whatever they can carry. They bring their children, their old folks. The line goes far and down the street. Clouds like dirty, combed cotton stretch low across the sky and the dirt street is rutted, icy hard, and coated with frost. Everybody has to walk slowly, flatfooted with short steps. They carry their youngest children swaddled in burlap. The older children wear just shirtsleeves and thin shiny pants or tattered, oversized coats and rolled, grown-up trousers cinched tight with a cord. They wear their fathers' old shoes, their feet wrapped in rags to fill them. They stick out like the shoes of woebegone clowns.

But they aren't the clowns. The planters are. They don't want 'their' Coloreds having anything to do with us. They drive up and down the street, their cars jostling in the ruts, and they study the faces in line. When they see one they remember, somebody they replaced with their machines, how many years ago, they honk their horns and offer that man a job and food if he'll leave our line. The people just stare ahead while the planters bid higher; they're auctioning something these people don't want anymore—because it had led them to this. Now they have nothing but their place in line and their worth as people, as citizens—second-class, third-class, whatever class they may be. Their citizenship is their only coin because our food isn't free. They have to buy it by joining our voter registration drive. We take down names and addresses, signatures and Xs, and all around us the planters' voices are rising higher, hollering names and shouting deals. Their horns, their engines, their words: they're jumbled all together and carried by the wind, they rise up in the air, past us and down the street to someplace far—where they finally fade away. Not a single person leaves our line.

◆—◆

That was in early February, in 1963. We fed plenty of people, but not nearly enough. The federal government started investigating the county. Newspapers from all over the country picked up the story. The county commissioners caved and started up their old program, but we're not stopping. Now we have a presence and an identity—SNCC is the group that moved the county. We're the people who aren't afraid.

But we are. Every day we are.

12 • The Wounded Man

We're one hundred and three hundred strong, marching to the courthouse. We've worked on this for weeks. Things are moving faster for us, now that we're giving out food and clothing. Now the national press is here. Today's our first Freedom Day. We're going to have a lot of them. We're going to show the world what we as a people can do, and what we put up with every day of our lives. Our one hundred are our volunteers—our block captains, our door knockers, the kids who pass out our flyers, the church mothers who're with us and vouch for us to their neighbors, kin, and congregants. Our three hundred are the ones who signed for food—names, Xs, we didn't care—they're going to stand in line to register whether they can read or write or not.

We circle the courthouse, our hundred strong. We clap. We sing. Our signs bob up and down. Our three hundred stretch from the front door of the courthouse, down its steps, past the confederate monument, past us, to the grass, the sidewalk, the street, and the intersection beyond. But they barely move. The sheriff's got his men at the door and they're letting in only one at a time. The city police are there too. They're standing next to our three hundred. The cops don't touch them; they don't talk to them; they face away from them toward the Whites on the sidewalks, who curse and shout and laugh and jeer. Our three hundred strong stand their ground. A second person is let through the courthouse door. The day draws on. A third person, a fourth ... .

It's cold. Our three hundred, most of them in thin, raggedy clothes, clutch their arms across their chests, or clap their forearms, jiggle their hands, anything to keep themselves warm. There's no food or water and no toilets. But not one of them has left that line. Morgan walks over to them. He asks one a question. A cop, standing near, pulls Morgan away.

"You can't talk to them."

Morgan jerks his arm free. "Why not? That man wants to find a toilet. Others do too. They've been in line all morning." He points to the courthouse door. "There's just a few they've let in."

The cop pulls his club and points it at the line. "Anybody leaves this line can't come back." Then he points his club at Morgan. "And you can't bother them. They're supposed to be left alone."

It's the agreement the city made with the Justice Department. Nobody is to mess with our people in line. Apparently, to the city, that even means us.

A reporter approaches Morgan. He's from the *New York Times*. "You see those men over there?" He points across the street. Two men, in black suits and thin black ties, are standing in front of a storefront, a lawyer's office—it belongs to the city's attorney. "Those two are FBI agents from Memphis."

Morgan walks over to them. "I understand you gentlemen are with the federal government."

"That's right. What's your name?"

"Mr. Morgan Wright, sir. Do those people in line have the right to use a public toilet, or get a drink of water, and not lose their place in line?"

"Yes, I believe they do."

"Will you tell the policemen over there that? Will you tell them that's not the agreement?"

"No, I won't. I won't do that. We're here to observe, that's all."

―――◆―◆―――

The day draws on. Our people stay in line—no lunch, no water, no toilets, no movement. We who circle the courthouse—we clap and sing, we hold our signs aloft. Church mothers bring us cardboard boxes filled with homemade sandwiches in wax paper and old soda bottles filled with water. One of us shouts, "Give them to those in line." There aren't enough for three hundred, but Morgan takes an armful, and Aunt Ertharin takes some too—she heads our block captains, and everybody calls her "Aunt." They walk to the line. Mayor Lott steps in their way.

Morgan motions to our three hundred. "Mayor, we'd like to give these people some food."

I walk up to get a better look.

Lott rings his thumbs in his belt. His stomach nearly covers them. "I made a promise to the federal government, under threat of federal occupation. Those people will not be molested in any way. Not by anybody."

Morgan holds out his boxes. "We don't want to molest them. We want to give them food. They'd like to use a toilet."

Lott pulls one hand from his belt and sticks his finger at Morgan's chest. "If you do, you'll be arrested. They will not be molested in any way and that includes talking to them."

Morgan and Aunt Ertharin walk back to our circle. He waves over the newsman who talked to him before. Aunt Ertharin holds up an armload of sandwiches. She speaks loud to be heard above our singing. "We want to see if 'molesting' means giving people food. Mayor Lott says it does. We want to see if he means it."

A couple more reporters and a photographer join them. Morgan tells me to stay back. "You're too young. They'll beat you for sure. Let us old folks do it. With all these reporters around, maybe they'll let us be." He picks up a box of sandwiches and turns to Aunt Ertharin. "Let's go." They walk over to the line. The reporters follow behind.

Lott shouts, "Get them!" and the cops are on them. One knocks the sandwiches from Aunt Ertharin's hands. Two police dogs are on Morgan. He drops his box and tries to fend them off. One rips his pants leg, the other goes for his backside. Cameras flash. A dog lunges at Morgan's chest. He falls to the ground and two policemen are on him with their clubs. He tries to ball himself up.

I don't move a peg. I'm frozen to the spot. I'm asking myself, why don't I do something? I stand there and I've got no answer. Then I turn my head. Deborah's there. She's holding her sign like a baseball bat. She's running past me to the cops beating Morgan. I lunge for her and catch her by her waist and shoulder. "Don't. You'll just get hurt."

The cops push the reporters away from the scene. A cop grabs for a camera—he doesn't get it—and rips the photographer's sleeve. I've still got hold of Deborah. She struggles to get free. Aunt Ertharin covers Morgan's body; she grabs at his shoulders, he scrambles to his feet, he stumbles, falls, gets up, and she takes his hand and runs to us. Deborah breaks free. She helps Aunt Ertharin rush Morgan past me to the side of the courthouse, to a grassy area inside our circle. The cops let them go. I'm standing there, looking at one of the cops. It's him, that Baynard James who knocked my papers to the street. He's looking at me. He's grinning.

The FBI are still standing across the street, under the awning of the city attorney's office. They're talking to a third man who laughs and goes inside. They didn't do a thing. We were hoping that after days like this, we'd get federal troops to protect us. But now I know. Our federal government won't do a goddamned thing.

I turn back to our people. Deborah's over by Morgan. He's sitting on the grass. She's looking at me. She holds my eyes, she's frowning, and then she turns back and bends down to Morgan. I'd go over but I'm afraid of what he'll say to me.

The day draws on. Twenty people have been allowed inside.

At four-thirty a sheriff's deputy closes the doors to the courthouse and locks them. Forty people of our three hundred had gotten inside. Every one of them tell us, the registrar had told them they'd failed. That was our Freedom Day. We mass together for the walk back home. We shuffle our women and children to the middle and put our men on the edges. The Whites crowd around us. The cops have gone. We're jostled and shoved. White men, and even some women, yell and curse us; they lay their hands and fists on us. Our sweat mingles with theirs. And late into the evening, White men prowl the Negro neighborhoods. Three Negro men are beaten.

When we finally get home, I follow Morgan up the stairs. This place is like our first place: an outside stair to a second-story door. I follow in case he stumbles or faints. He walks slowly, stiffly, his pants are torn to ribbons and I can see the back of his legs and the thin dried lines of blood. Inside, Morgan gingerly stretches his arms and slowly unbuttons his shirt. I help him take it off. He touches his stomach and winces in pain. I tell him he has purple bruises on his back. "Do you want to see a doctor?" He doesn't answer. He just puts his shirt back on.

I tell him, "Our people were heroes today. They should be given medals." I'm afraid to hear what he'll say about me.

He doesn't answer. I did nothing to help him and I still don't know why. We look out the window of our apartment to the street below, to the houses on it and behind it, to their low roofs copper-cast in the last light of day, and beyond them the alley and the sewage ditch. It's a Saturday but nobody's on the street.

I feel itchy and restless. Our people were heroes. I did nothing to help him. I clench and unclench my fists, over and over. I want to lash out and hit somebody. By God I want to … now. Now that it's over. I want Morgan to tell me he wants to hit somebody too.

He's still looking out the window. "We've got to do something, Aleck. These people—they're my people—they rely on me. 'Heroes,' yeah, that's what they are, and we ask them for it over and over again, with everything we tell them to do, and they give it and give it and give. And every time they give, they get it in the neck. And they'll take it because those White folks sure aren't finished dishing it." He turns and looks at me. "We're not going to stop, but don't you feel ashamed?"

The question feels like a slap. I deserve it. I tell him yes.

He nods his head. "I'm ashamed too. We're not asking them to do anything we aren't doing ourselves, but this can't go on. I've got to protect these people. I've got to do something."

It's only then I realize he's not talking about me.

13 • The Wounded Man

"Try knocking harder." We're out in the rural, in the middle of the night, at a cabin on some White man's place. Morgan stands next to me. He's scrunched up, stomping his feet and blowing on his hands. It's bitter cold. The air feels like razor blades. I knock harder, but not too hard. I'm afraid to make too much noise. The word's out that Whites are on patrol to stop us from bringing food to folks out here. Just like the paterollers did, like we were runaway slaves.

Lots of folks in town still have people in the rural. Carry some of that food to them, they say, they're the ones who need it the most. Those in town even come with us sometimes—at night, always at night. We'd be run off with shotguns if we came during the day.

This cabin, we visited with the woman here last week.

We don't want to barge in. "Let's go around to the side, see if a shutter's open." I follow Morgan. But it's too cold, so if a shutter's open, there'd be nothing to see, nobody would be home. We don't dare use our flashlight. Not out in the open. There's only a little bit of moon and the stars are so far away—they're pinpricks, really. There're so many of them, and they're too small to be counted.

And these cabins—they're shacks! Most of them are deserted. And at night, they all look empty to me. Rundown, wooden, no paint, they're cold to the touch, the color of iron in the dark and pewter close-up with a light, and the grain looks worn-down smooth. But when you do touch them, the wood almost crumbles. When we go alone in the dark, we follow our directions, but that can't be the place—just look at it—we must be lost. Then, sometimes a lantern winks through a window.

After we give out our food and clothing we talk about registering. The people there always offer us something, coffee or even just water, and we always accept. Mostly they're women, "widows" they're called. Their men are long gone: gone to Florida for the fruit, gone to Chicago for the factories.

There's only one room to these shacks. They smell of smoke and sweat, and pork and lard—busy smells—but underneath those there's another smell that's hollow, cleansed, and futile. People—for decades, right up to now—have died in these shacks. And that's what we smell under the smoke and the sweat. The smell of the dead. Will these women die here too? Their children, wide-eyed and pot-bellied with skinny legs and arms, they peek from behind the doorway or their mama's legs. Even in the dark their hair looks rusty. That means they're starving. Will these children die here too?

◆— —◆

The widow at this cabin, when we saw her last week she didn't look much older than me. She'd had a man, but he'd left when she was pregnant. "He's in Chicago now. And I can't blame him. What was he supposed to do? There's nothing to do here. Not for a strong man that wants to work." She brought us a tin cup of water. "You'll have to share it." She sat down. "There's but two men on this entire place. Working, able-bodied men, not the oldsters. They're the tractor drivers. They do all the work on this place, and don't they strut like they're the cocks-of-the-walk in a yard full of chickens."

We tried to talk about registering. She wasn't interested. "Registering won't bring my man back. It won't feed this child here. I appreciate the food y'all brought, but once it's gone …"

She just stopped. She needed to compose herself. "What we need y'all can't give us, because you're not White. All us widows here and our children, all we got is some itty-bitty jobs the White folks scatter our way. Nothing jobs. Don't pay shit because they ain't but shit. White folks here, I think they keep us widows here to keep their tractor drivers happy. Well, I'm too tired and hungry to make any man happy. And I'd walk from here to Chicago if I had two shoes to my name."

We looked down at her feet: wide, crusted, dirty and calloused. She and her boy are barefoot. Feet caked with mud; stuck in the mud; drinking muddy water from a hollow log—these people were here and gone, all at the same time.

She looked down at her feet too. "Tired all the time. I got hardly any work to do, still I'm tired all the time." She kneaded her stomach with her hand.

Morgan stood up. "We can get you some shoes, for you and your boy. We'll be back as soon as we can with some shoes and some socks. And when we get more food, we'll bring that too."

She didn't reply at first. But at the door, while closing it, she said, "Find me some boots, men's work boots."

Back in the car I was angry. "This is some movement. We're twenty years too late and a million jobs short."

Morgan ground the gears when he shifted. He didn't say a word. He just peered out into the darkness. We were on a dirt road, and we wouldn't use our headlights until we got to the highway.

I couldn't give it up. "She's right, you know, much as people here need the vote, they need jobs more."

"There are no jobs here."

"Yeah, well, maybe we should move—all of us. That'll be our 'movement.' Everybody, on the same day—we'll fill up all the buses and the train stations. No room for White folks. Everybody moves."

Morgan didn't answer. He just drove.

Now we're back at that same cabin. We have some shoes, some woolen socks, and a pair of work boots too. At the side of the shack, we find an open shutter. I lean in the window and turn my flashlight on. Nobody's there.

We know her people in Williams Point and they haven't said a word about her leaving. I sweep the light across the floor and up the walls. Deserted, but not disorderly, not left too suddenly. We go back to the door and open it and step inside. I open the chifferobe. It's empty. We're too late. I'm wondering: will we always be?

On the way back, Morgan drives, leaning forward, peering through the windshield. The bag of shoes is in the back seat. The highway's a chalky gray in our headlights. The world could crumble right beneath us.

A car drives by the opposite way. Minutes later, headlights come up behind us. The car honks and pulls up even. We're caught in the glare of one of those swivel headlamps fixed to the passenger door. I see a figure lean out his open window, he's right next to us and he's aiming. Morgan ducks. I push him down and lunge over him. The twin blasts, the burst and shower of the glass, the sting of the shot in my shoulders and back, my head down against Morgan's door—it happens all at

We tried to talk about registering. She wasn't interested. "Registering won't bring my man back. It won't feed this child here. I appreciate the food y'all brought, but once it's gone …"

She just stopped. She needed to compose herself. "What we need y'all can't give us, because you're not White. All us widows here and our children, all we got is some itty-bitty jobs the White folks scatter our way. Nothing jobs. Don't pay shit because they ain't but shit. White folks here, I think they keep us widows here to keep their tractor drivers happy. Well, I'm too tired and hungry to make any man happy. And I'd walk from here to Chicago if I had two shoes to my name."

We looked down at her feet: wide, crusted, dirty and calloused. She and her boy are barefoot. Feet caked with mud; stuck in the mud; drinking muddy water from a hollow log—these people were here and gone, all at the same time.

She looked down at her feet too. "Tired all the time. I got hardly any work to do, still I'm tired all the time." She kneaded her stomach with her hand.

Morgan stood up. "We can get you some shoes, for you and your boy. We'll be back as soon as we can with some shoes and some socks. And when we get more food, we'll bring that too."

She didn't reply at first. But at the door, while closing it, she said, "Find me some boots, men's work boots."

Back in the car I was angry. "This is some movement. We're twenty years too late and a million jobs short."

Morgan ground the gears when he shifted. He didn't say a word. He just peered out into the darkness. We were on a dirt road, and we wouldn't use our headlights until we got to the highway.

I couldn't give it up. "She's right, you know, much as people here need the vote, they need jobs more."

"There are no jobs here."

"Yeah, well, maybe we should move—all of us. That'll be our 'movement.' Everybody, on the same day—we'll fill up all the buses and the train stations. No room for White folks. Everybody moves."

Morgan didn't answer. He just drove.

Now we're back at that same cabin. We have some shoes, some woolen socks, and a pair of work boots too. At the side of the shack, we find an open shutter. I lean in the window and turn my flashlight on. Nobody's there.

We know her people in Williams Point and they haven't said a word about her leaving. I sweep the light across the floor and up the walls. Deserted, but not disorderly, not left too suddenly. We go back to the door and open it and step inside. I open the chifferobe. It's empty. We're too late. I'm wondering: will we always be?

On the way back, Morgan drives, leaning forward, peering through the windshield. The bag of shoes is in the back seat. The highway's a chalky gray in our headlights. The world could crumble right beneath us.

A car drives by the opposite way. Minutes later, headlights come up behind us. The car honks and pulls up even. We're caught in the glare of one of those swivel headlamps fixed to the passenger door. I see a figure lean out his open window, he's right next to us and he's aiming. Morgan ducks. I push him down and lunge over him. The twin blasts, the burst and shower of the glass, the sting of the shot in my shoulders and back, my head down against Morgan's door—it happens all at

Author's Notes

"Black and Tan Fantasy" is the title of a musical piece written by Duke Ellington and Bubber Miley in 1927, named for the after-hour clubs habituated by jazz musicians and their fans. These were integrated places, not considered respectable. The piece itself is composed of two contrasting melodic lines: the first Black, bluesy and somber, and the second a "sweet" example of White popular song. But, as the scholar David Metzer notes, the first melody is derived from a "spiritual" Miley's mother sang to him as a child, based on a well-known hymn written by a White man. And the second, "sweet" melody is original to Ellington. Thus, the music's origins undermine notions of Black and White as distinct and immutable categories.

Then the solos start. According to Metzer, the cornet and trombone solos "elicited considerable commentary" by White critics troubled and "spellbound" by the solos' "distortion" (the growling and smeared notes and the vocalized tone) of the "purity" of the "White" source material. As a poet might put it, the music was "changed utterly," and "[a] terrible beauty [was] born." If you haven't heard it, give it a listen.

The Student Nonviolent Coordinating Committee (SNCC, pronounced "snick") was born in 1960 out of local sit-in movements that attracted Black college students from throughout the American South. SNCC members became the "shock troops of the revolution" when they began working in rural communities that other movement organizations thought were too dangerous for public protest. SNCC's staff workers sought to work with and develop local leaders to build lasting African-American grass-root organizations.

SNCC came to the Mississippi Delta in the summer of 1962 to register Blacks to vote, and never really left. The local activism spurred by SNCC has endured in the political activities of Delta Blacks to this very day. During the summer months of 1964 more than 1,000 college students, mostly White and mostly from outside the South, joined with SNCC and other civil rights organizations for Mississippi's heroic "Freedom Summer," which captured the attention of our country's media. Those months are perhaps the most remembered episode, by the country at large, of SNCC's work in Mississippi. But the timeline for this book's narrative focuses on the fall of 1962 through the summer of 1963—before the college students came.

once, jumbled in a kaleidoscope. And then the still and quiet dark.

Is that the sky or just the ceiling of the car? Are we moving? Is Morgan talking? I can't tell.

14 • The Drowned Man

Chattanooga, Tennessee: 1923–1924

When Geneva got pregnant, Harry insisted they get a house of their own. She never called it "home." "Home" would always be the home house, just a few streets over, now the house where her parents lived. But Harry—he called their house "home." A large pond was close by and Harry and Geneva took to taking walks around it. One morning they found a body there, drowned. It was a White woman, middle-aged. She was near the shore, on her back. Her feet were on the gravel and her torso and head were under water. The water was clear, so they could see her face. Harry told Geneva to go call the police. She hesitated, and then he said no, let somebody else call them. Geneva wanted to leave, but Harry couldn't. He had to stay and look at the body, at its face, at each feature, under the water. She wasn't anybody he knew.

Later they heard that nobody knew her and nobody had seen her, either near the pond or in the neighborhood. White people never came to the Negro neighborhoods except to carry their domestics. Those White people were known. Nobody knew how this woman had got there, or why.

It was only an incident in Harry's life, but he never forgot it. He would remember her features, under the lapping water, wavering with its ebb and flow, like she wasn't even real.

15 • The Drowned Man

It was supposed to be their house, their hearth, their table. It was supposed to be their bed and their kitchen. It was supposed to be their life.

But now, even the children were gone. Earley—he'd been a handful. He'd gone to his grandparents long before. Geneva's cousin Mae took Lilly and Timothy. This was no big deal, Harry understood that now. No matter where they bedded, he saw them every day.

Once Timothy was weaned, he'd ask for him back. He'd demand it. Harry sat in his chair. He kept his door and windows closed, but he could still hear the noises from the street—the Negro sea outside his door. He remembered his first morning in Chattanooga, looking out the living room window.

Geneva. His last sea captain was dead.

At the funeral Harry had stayed close to Mama Lou. She'd taken him by his arm; she didn't let go. Lilly clung to her too, and Earley held his grandfather's hand. Mae held Timothy. It was going to be a hot day, too hot for funeral clothes, so they buried her early in the morning. When the grave was filled, and the prayers all said, the words and songs all done, the family lingered as the sun rose higher in the sky. When they finally left, Harry stayed behind, Lilly and Earley with him, standing in front of each of his legs, his hands across their collarbones, pressing them to him, and each of their hands hanging on to his. Mae had Timothy, Harry would see him later. The heat rose, became oppressive; Harry and children remained, next to the grave, quiet and still.

<hr>

Months went by. Timothy was weaned and Harry had him back. And then, one day, Harry's father came—into his life and back out again, in one afternoon.

Harry didn't ask how he'd found him. Harry just stood in his doorway, the door only half opened, his hand on the knob, his father on the porch.

"Is that your hair?"

Harry didn't answer.

"Get in my car."

Harry considered this. Then he nodded. "I'll have to bring Timothy."

"Timothy?"

"He's my baby boy."

His father grimaced. He looked back behind him, as if afraid his car was gone. Then he looked up and down the street. He was the only White man on it. He looked back at his son. "Can't you let that ... Colored woman watch it?"

"Geneva's dead." Harry hesitated. "She died a few weeks after ... the baby was only a few weeks old. He's weaned now." He paused, looking at his father. "This is my house. We ... her father bought it ... for us ... when she was pregnant."

His father frowned. He walked to his car. Then he looked back at his son. "You didn't marry her, did you?"

"No, sir, no. We didn't marry."

His father had his keys in his hand. He nodded. "Okay, bring him. But hurry up." He got in his car. Harry carried Timothy from his house and sat down beside his father.

Harry's father started the car. "He looks White. He looks like you. You say his mother's dead?" Harry nodded.

"Was she the one in the fire?"

"Yes, sir." Harry looked down at Timothy. "Where're we going?"

"You'll see." His father turned on to a main street. He headed south out of town. "Are her people here?"

"That's why we came here."

His father nodded. "Good. They can raise it."

Harry didn't reply. He looked out the window. His father had turned west toward the river and the foothills beyond. Harry saw him stealing glances at Timothy. His father saw that Harry noticed, and looked straight ahead.

"Why is it so White?"

"Geneva was a high yellow. Her whole family's light. Her father's the darkest and he's paper-bag brown."

His father nodded. He drove on in silence.

He drove them to the top of Lookout Mountain. They stopped at a viewpoint and walked to its edge. Below them was the looping river and the city to its east.

Harry made no attempt to have his father hold the child. His father made no attempt to take him.

"Look, son, look out as far as you can see." Harry's father swept his hand across the horizon. "You see the city down there? It's mine." He looked at his son. "What you see is a White man's world. So that town is mine." He pointed to the view again, and faced it, his back to Harry and the baby. "This could be my first time here in Chattanooga and it wouldn't matter, it'd still be mine. And it should be yours. I don't want to know why you did what you did. You know you have no wife anymore, no children. After today you'll have no mother or father either." He glanced back at Harry. "You'll never see me again. I'm not asking you to come home. Quite the contrary—you better not." He paused, and turned back to the view. "You know, you broke your mother's heart." Suddenly he turned and faced his son. "But I am asking you not to turn your back on your race. I want you to be a White man again. Somewhere—not here and not in Alabama—I want you to move somewhere and be White again."

He looked over his shoulder at his son. "You. Just you." He looked back down at the city. "I don't want you passing that ... that Colored boy for White. That would be an abomination. It might look White, but it's not, not like you. It should stay with its own kind.

"I have four hundred dollars for you. That should be more than enough for a new start. I put it in the Commercial Bank here, under your name and mine."

He turned back to face his son and stuffed a scrap of paper in his hand.

"That's the account number. After two weeks I'll come back here—I won't see you—and if the money's still there I'll take it out and close the account. Two weeks, starting today—you understand? I'll be at the bank just before it closes on the last day."

He looked at the baby in Harry's arms. "You agree with me, don't you son? When I came here, I didn't expect you'd have that—" He pointed at the baby. "But you agree? It's best raised by its own kind."

Harry looked down at his baby. "His name is Timothy."

They got in the car. Harry's father started the engine but kept it in neutral.

"Harry, you agree, don't you? It would be the best thing. He should be with his own kind. When you leave here, you've got to leave alone."

"The hell with your money."

His father clenched the steering wheel with both hands and looked out his side window, back toward the view, where the city lay below. He waited until his hands relaxed. "You think it over son. You've got two weeks to think it over. It's a White man's world, son. You know that." He was looking out the window, to the sky above the city.

His father drove them home; he never said another word, not in the car, and not after he parked. He didn't get out. Harry hadn't spoken either. He got out of his father's car and carried Timothy to his house. He never looked back. He heard the engine start as he opened his door. And he never saw his father again.

The evening couldn't come fast enough. After Timothy fell asleep, Harry got drunk. The next morning, he woke to the baby's crying.

◆━◆

Later, it would be enough to make him laugh whenever he got drunk: life's insistence at his punishment; to prove to him, over and over, his inability to hold onto his self. One house out of a hundred burns, and it had to be *that* house. And one night out of hundreds, Geneva's father knocks at his door, twelve days after his own father had come. Two more days and the money would've been gone, and it had never occurred to him to take it.

Malachi Burnett stood in the doorway. He walked past Harry and sat at the supper table. He didn't bother to take off his coat, but reached in a pocket and pulled out a bottle and gestured toward the cupboard. "Get yourself a glass."

Harry looked at him. "Aren't you drinking?"

"You ever seen me drunk? No. What I've got to say, you've got to know I'm sober. It'll be *me* talking, not the drink. You," he pointed at Harry, "you drink."

Harry sat down and poured himself a drink. Just one finger. It was good whiskey. He looked up at Burnett, who nodded and gestured at the bottle. Harry poured himself another one and drank it down.

The room was dark except for the lamp on the table between them. Burnett's face, without shadow, glowed a light brown. He didn't squint in the light; his eyes were wide open. One hand was on the table, knocking softly on its surface. The other was under the table, close to his side. Harry wondered, a little drunk now, if there was anything in Burnett's coat pocket.

Harry thought of taking another drink, but decided to get on with it. "Okay, what's on your mind?"

"Why'd you come here?"

Harry looked at him, not knowing what to say.

"Why didn't you leave Geneva here, and go your own way?" Burnett frowned at Harry's silence. "She told me what you said to her in your car, about needing to be from some place where you had people, and not just a woman and children, but a whole family—parents, grandparents, aunts and uncles, cousins." Burnett leaned forward. "And I understand that. The whole family, we all understood that. We thought well of you for that. That's how you're supposed to live, with family—for family."

Burnett sat back in his chair. "So why did you stay *here*?"

Harry blinked and gripped his empty glass. "Geneva."

Burnett frowned. "But that's not what you told her. You told her family!"

He paused, and looked around the room. "Haven't I treated you fair?" Harry looked at him, not knowing what to say. Burnett scowled. "I—we, the family—we let you stay; we put you up. I got you work." Burnett swept up his hand from the table. "I bought you and Geneva this house."

Harry poured himself another drink. Two fingers this time. He took a sip. "Yes ... sir ... you treated me fair."

"But you've never settled in."

"You never wanted me. You told me so yourself. It was Geneva, your wife, your mother. They wanted me."

"Yeah. Your first morning in my house. We'd given you a bed. You shared it with my daughter. That morning my wife brought you into her kitchen—you were filthy, covered in soot, she had to wash the sheets—and she sat you down at her table and gave you food." Burnett leaned forward and pointed his finger at Harry. "You didn't eat it. Couldn't—or wouldn't. That was good food! In a clean kitchen! You hadn't eaten all night. What kind of mess was that?"

"I was tired. I ... I don't know." Harry gulped his drink. "I don't remember. I was upset."

"From that first morning on, it's always been the same. You never tried ..."

"I couldn't. I couldn't. How can you become something you're not?"

"You couldn't." Burnett nodded, frowning. "Or didn't want to. It doesn't matter which. You couldn't even pretend. So, why do you stay? Why do you stay now? That's the question. I'll buy your house back. That'll give you enough money. Go, take your boy, find yourself a life."

"Go? I've never thought of going. Timothy's your grandchild."

Burnett rapped the table with his knuckles. Slow, then faster. He reached across the table with both hands, snatched the glass and bottle, poured himself a drink and gulped it down.

"You don't understand. I don't want you here. I don't want you or your boy."

He slid the bottle and glass back to Harry. "It's time you took him and left." He shut his eyes and shuddered; opened them again. "You raped my daughter."

Harry stared at him, as if from a distance. "Wha—? We loved each other."

Burnett leaned forward, his face bright in the lamp light and sweaty, both hands on the table but close to his chest, as if he were hiding cards. "Whatever she felt for you, she couldn't have felt it at first, the first time y'all were together." He moved the lamp over, away from between them. From there the light shadowed the left side of his face. To Harry it seemed to be welded to the darkness of the room beyond the two of them, as if, if Harry had reached for him, Burnett would be far beyond his hand.

Harry leaned forward, but he didn't reach. "I had feelings. I'd seen her enough. Around town, on the street. I asked her once, she said I could carry her home. She—" Harry stopped. He was suddenly afraid that Burnett might rise up, from that distance away, and hit him. "I had feelings for her."

"I don't care what you felt. Did she have feelings for you? That first time?"

Harry didn't answer. Burnett nodded. He sneered. "I thought so."

Harry finally answered. "I don't know." Burnett seemed so far away that Harry wanted to shout the words. But he was so tired. He repeated them—"I don't ... I don't"—but his voice tailed off before he could finish. He remembered what she herself had told him: *I grew to love you.* So, the first time, the first few times? Had he cared how she felt? The thought stabbed: could her father be right? He couldn't remember. He couldn't think. Sitting there, flat footed, he wanted to flee. It was his own house (finally! his!) and he wanted to flee.

Then he remembered: He'd had no money. Burnett had bought it.

Burnett stabbed the table with his finger. "You raped her. You didn't hold a gun to her—or a knife. But you did what you did whether she wanted it or not. You didn't care. You ... intruded." He stood; he swept his other hand wide. "All day long I take shit from every goddamned White I see. I take it because I have to, but when I come home and close that door behind me, and I'm inside my four walls—" Burnett looked around him as if these walls were his. (Harry panicked. They were!) "I'm a man and a husband and a father." Burnett splayed his hand upon his chest. "I protect what's mine. I'm *me* in my house—my home. Your kind aren't supposed to intrude upon my hearth and home. But that's what you did." He dropped down in his chair. "Maybe you were far off down in Alabama, but she was my daughter ... so you might as well have done it here in Chattanooga, in my front room."

No's filled Harry's head; he waved his hand in front of him. He wanted to stand. "It wasn't like that. I always had feelings for her. She had feelings for me."

"—and you saved her life and her babies' lives. Don't forget that. I'm not supposed to. But God help me, every time I saw the two of you together—and I saw how she would look at you; somehow, she came to love you after all—but God help me, all I could think was that the first time, and how many times after that, it was rape."

Burnett stood up again. His face was dim at the edge of the light. He shut his eyes, hard, and to Harry's vision, Burnett's face seemed to tremble from ... Harry searched for the word. Big Mama Darling had called her son righteous and she was certainly correct, but here, standing at the edge of the flickering light, Burnett's face showed Harry not so much righteousness as rightness, and also a burden that must be shared by both the righteous and the right, the despair when neither brings peace, or even consolation.

Harry stared at Burnett, he couldn't focus, he blinked. The moment passed. Rightness something, what was it? A wisp of understanding, faded and gone. Geneva. Rape. No. "I love her."

Burnett opened his eyes and scowled. "And then you got her pregnant and took her to that hell-hole of a hospital and killed her. You didn't use a gun. You didn't use a knife. But you killed her." Burnett pushed his chair to the table. "I'm sick to death of the sight of you. You and that boy of yours. He's got nothing of her looks, her skin. I want y'all to leave." He stuffed his hands in his coat pockets. Harry tensed; his hands drew into fists; but Burnett just turned to leave.

Harry watched him walk slowly out the door. Burnett left it open. Minutes passed before Harry got up to close it. Once he did, he turned back to the room. It looked strange to him. A small circle of light, a table, two chairs. He told himself he was drunk. He tried to think straight. Burnett had never liked him. But Geneva's mother—even after Geneva died—she still liked him. And Big Mama Darling, she had liked him too. He found his way to bed. He would have hell to pay in the morning.

He woke up hungover, got up, and slumped down at his table, the bottle and glass still there. Rape. That word: he couldn't let it go. Had Burnett always believed that? Harry's first night in Chattanooga, burning inside, waiting to hear his fate; Burnett hadn't wanted him. But Geneva had, her Mama Lou had, her Big Mama Darling had. So, had it been rape? No. Not ever? Harry wanted to cry out. He wanted to shout "NO!" But Burnett there ... he was right there in last night's chair ... wouldn't let him.

Harry slowly stood up and leaned over the table. He looked right at Burnett. *So what if you don't like me? Why should I care? A person doesn't just walk away. Hearth and home go deeper than like and dislike, even deeper than love and hate. Hearth and home go blood deep.* Harry stopped and sat back against his chair. Burnett was telling him, you don't have our blood. (Days later, Harry would think about Uncle John, what he had offered Harry: a miracle, he'd turn Harry's blood black. And maybe he did, but Harry didn't think so. He could never cross that threshold into blackness. He could never shed his hesitation, his wariness, or, he only could with Geneva (Geneva! He couldn't ask her to forgive him!) but not with anybody else, not even with her children. How could he? It tore him in two; he'd have to be both Negro and White, each one whole and simultaneous. But you can't be two things; you can't be two hundred percent. So, he wasn't anything at all. Not Black. Not White. He was zero percent.)

Harry looked around him. This room—the table he was at, the chair where Burnett had sat, glaring. Finally, he was gone. He'd just stopped Harry cold, demolished Harry's arguments and denials, and, finished with his work, finally disappeared. Harry's head was burning, heavy. He rested it in his hands, his elbows on the table. He felt sorry for himself, for everything. Geneva! He couldn't ask her to forgive him, because that would mean he'd have to admit— He couldn't even finish the thought. So, how could he ever think of her again? He rubbed his eyes and looked at the heels of his hands. They were wet. When had he started to cry?

He slowly sighed. *Hell.* It didn't matter what Burnett thought, or Mama Lou. It didn't matter what Big Mama Darling had thought. What mattered was, Geneva could no longer forgive him. Harry sat up straight. So, who was left for him here? Earley and Lilly were Burnetts—more Mama Lou's and Mae's, and Malachi's and Pete's, than ever his. Timothy, only Timothy. And he thought again about looking down from Lookout Mountain with his father, while he held his baby boy. Harry stood up from his table and looked at his front window, at the curtains and the glass, not through it. *Yes, he's right. It is a White man's world.* If he couldn't be White, why couldn't Timothy? *The hell with my father.* Timothy could pass; he wouldn't have to know he'd ever been a Negro.

Harry dressed. He would go to the bank. He'd kept that account number, even when he thought he had no reason. Now he knew better. He put the deed to the house on the table—he'd leave it there. This would be his second betrayal, and his third life. And little Timothy, sitting on the floor, choosing from his toys—it would be the only life he'd know.

16 • The Drowned Man

Atlanta, Georgia: 1924–1941

His father's money got him a house in Atlanta and an interest in a store. It would be an ordinary life. It would be an end to the burning, and he'd see a clear, sharp image in his mirror. No more thinking—just *do*, like he'd once done before. Get up in the morning and earn your daily bread and come home in the evening, to Timothy, to bed, and then the morning again—a third life much like the first. He bought a baby buggy. On the weekends, he carried his son all over town.

And Harry still thought about Geneva. He never delved into why he still could, but time passing had detached himself from shame.

As Timothy grew Harry told him, it was "Negro" or "Colored." "You don't call them anything else." He'd say, "You treat *all* your elders with respect." It was the same instruction he'd given Harry Jr., and Mary Ann. But then he'd kneel to Timothy's eye level and tell him more, as if in answer to his own father and to Malachi Burnett, about who and what Timothy was, or could be—and maybe, what he, himself, could be.

"You're not the color of your skin. You're something different all together. You're Timothy. You're *you*."

And Timothy would gaze into his father's eyes and nod his head. Not because he agreed or even understood—Harry knew that—but because these were the words his father spoke, and Timothy was too young for anybody else to tell him different.

And then Harry would tell him, "Your mother is dead. You had a sister and a brother. They're dead too. There was a fire."

He'd tell his son these lies, and then he'd look in the mirror and wonder who he was.

Timothy's playmates would talk about their families and Timothy would have nothing to say. So they teased him—they called him "orphan boy." And what could Harry tell him? That one grandfather rejected him because he was White, and the other because he was Black? And to both he was a bastard? Would "bastard" be any better than "orphan boy"? Harry thought not. So he told his son, your grandfathers are dead—and that was the truth for Harry because they both were dead to him.

No grandfathers or grandmothers ... no aunts or uncles, no cousins.

Timothy would ask him: "What's an orphan boy? Where's my mommy? What does dead mean?" Harry tried to explain. "Dead means nobody can see them anymore, and they can't see us."

"How did they get dead?"

"Your mother died in a fire, in Chattanooga, Tennessee. That's where you were born. You were just a little baby. Your brother and sister died in the fire too. I lost everybody but you. Our house caught fire—"

Harry fell silent, he couldn't continue.

"Did my grandpas and grandmas die in the fire? Did my aunts and uncles—"

"No, they were already dead. They got too old. That's why they died."

"Tell me about the fire."

Harry snapped, "It's nothing you need to know, it's nothing I want to remember. You'll understand when you're older—" Harry looked at his little boy and stopped himself. "You say the children tease you?" Timothy nodded. He looked like he was going to cry.

Harry knelt before his son. "Tell them you lost your family in a tragedy. Tell them a tragedy is when something awful bad happens to a good little boy. Something that wasn't his fault. Tell them that makes you special because nobody else you know has had a tragedy. Have any of your friends had a tragedy?" Timothy shook his head no. His eyes held questions. "Well, that makes you a special little boy. Do you understand that, Timothy?" After a moment, Timothy nodded. He looked as serious as he could. "Tell your friends that means you know things that they don't know. If they ask you what, you tell them they wouldn't understand if you told them, so you're not even going to try. And tell them it's not polite to ask special little boys about their tragedies. Tell them to ask their parents, and they'll say that's so."

"Just remember, you're you, Timothy. Just you. That's all you need to be."

Timothy nodded. He still had his very serious look, serious and self-possessed, and Harry knew he wouldn't cry.

Harry hoped that that would be enough. Because what was the truth of Timothy's life? That he was just a little Colored child; a half-breed? Harry couldn't tell him that. And he'd never have him live like that, not in a White man's world. So he wouldn't tell him anything—not one word more.

"What did my grandpas and grandmas look like? My friends say they have books of pictures of their grandpas and grandmas. Do we have a book of pictures?"

"No. It got burned up in the fire. I lost everything but you."

Harry hugged his little boy, but he didn't tell him one word more.

He tried not looking in his mirror too much—only when he had to in the morning, to brush his teeth, to shave, and comb his hair. He told himself, don't think, just do.

When the questions finally stopped, Harry thought he could set his mind at ease—until he noticed his desk drawer ajar, where he kept his snapshots of Charlotte and their children. Timothy was ten by then; that was when Harry first noticed. The photographs had been moved, ever so slightly. He said nothing to Timothy. Thank God he had no pictures of Geneva.

Harry waited for the questions again.

But they never came and Harry was thankful. He wanted to let it go, but he knew that Timothy hadn't. Harry could picture him, during those hours after school, alone, sneaking in, afraid that his father might come home early, and still he'd open the drawer, so slowly and scared, and take out the pictures. Did he cradle them in his palms? At first, did he only hold them? Later, would he place them on the desk, or lay them out on the bed? He'd never dare to take them from the room.

Here at his fingers were father and mother and sister and brother. Did it make him feel real, holding and fingering these faded snaps? Did he study them and dream them? Did he keep the curtains closed? Or had he grown bold enough to open them, to better see the pictures in the light?

Harry spent his days thinking and worrying about his son. He could see his boy growing quiet, fretful, and shy. Timothy was dwindling before his eyes.

One evening, with the dishes put away, Harry went into his room. He returned with the pictures. Timothy's eyes grew wide and he stiffened in his chair. Harry smiled and sat down next to him at their table, and spread the pictures out. "Timothy, look here. These pictures didn't get burned in the fire. They're the only ones I have." He picked one up. "This was your mother." He laid it down in front of the boy. "You can pick it up. You can hold it. And this one has your mother and your brother and your sister. I took it before you were born. And this one, do you recognize me?" And then he told Timothy all about Charlotte and Harry Jr., and Mary Ann.

"I've kept these all these years in my desk. I should've shown them to you earlier. Now what I'm going to do is put them back. Come with me and I'll show you. And if you ever want to look at them, or show them to your friends, you'll know where you can find them. And you can ask me all the questions you want."

The years passed. "Tell me a story about my mother. Tell me more about my brother and sister." Harry repeated his stories, but his telling became shorter and shorter. And then the questions dwindled, and then they finally ceased, but a check of the drawer always found the pictures moved.

Harry tried not to think. He tried just to do—up in the morning, to work, to home, to bed. Nothing more was said; but this slight movement of the pictures, was this a message from his son? Harry would look at the snapshots too, and touch them, and try to imagine a photograph he never had to keep Geneva's face in mind, and he would be torn in two. He took to rearranging them. Finished, he'd slowly close the drawer. This arranging and rearranging would take the place of words, it would be their secret code; shared, but never spoken.

Harry and his son explored the city together—more and more as Timothy grew older. Would he be enough for Timothy? Could he replace an entire family? Harry told himself he'd have to. But one time, at the movies, they saw a short film about the wild men of Borneo. And Borneo seemed so far away, on a different planet even. Harry nodded in the dark, silently, at the screen. *Yes, that's what it's like. That's what it's like for us.* As they left the theater Timothy asked him what was wrong.

"Nothing, son. Nothing's wrong. Why do you ask?"

"You're so quiet, Father."

Harry smiled to reassure him. But milling all around him were people who were *something*, White people who belonged in this city, who possessed the ground on which they walked. All over the world people were something, and that something was their color; they were Black or White or Red or Yellow. The way that people looked was who they were. And here, in America, being White gave you possession. It gave you permission. That was why, outwardly, Harry passed Timothy for White. But inwardly, he thought of themselves as neither White nor Black. After all, what were they? The father White, his boy child a Negro? And they both looked White to the naked eye? Compared to the people all around them, he and Timothy were aliens, like the wild men from Borneo. If all these people knew their story, there would be no doubt what they would say: No, you're either White or Black. And as mixed up as you both are, y'all can't be White. Harry's and Timothy's White skin would mean nothing. It would be a cheap disguise.

It meant he had to lie to his son about his family. Surely, they could be seen through and found out— He looked at

Timothy, at the concern in his son's eyes. Harry searched his mind. "I was trying to remember a joke." Then he told one, a silly one he used to tell when Timothy was small. "Do you know Arthur?"

"Arthur who?"

"Our thermometer!" Timothy laughed and Harry took him for ice cream.

They sat together in a booth. He knew Timothy had only laughed as if to say: don't worry Dad, whatever your problems are, you don't have to worry. He knew Timothy had done this because he loved his father. Harry told himself once more: don't think, just do. Be enough for Timothy.

But Harry had wanted a life just like his first one, and this was nothing like it.

◆—— ——◆

One evening, when Timothy was fifteen, Harry found that the pictures had not been moved—and the day after that, and the rest of that week, and that month and the next. So it was over. Harry was relieved, but he was also saddened.

Harry still looked at them, late when Timothy was asleep. It had become a habit. Grazing each image with his finger, he feared what his son's future might hold, if ever the truth came out. He put the pictures back and closed the drawer. *Don't think, just do.*

◆—— ——◆

The first girl Timothy brought home, Catherine, the first girl he'd even spoken of ... when Harry first met her—his son looked so much like him, and she, she was a dead ringer for

Charlotte, she had the same color hair, the same Madonna's face …

Harry found it hard to stand, to speak, but he had to do something. He smiled, he nodded, he held out his hand. Touching her, seeing her smile—finally he was able to speak. He was glad to meet her. He looked over at Timothy. His boy looked so proud; he'd never looked that way before. And Harry realized how desperate he must be to win this girl he'd found.

He was eighteen. She was seventeen. Harry couldn't help but think: *They're old enough to marry.*

One day Harry found the pictures gone, but back again the next. *He's shown them to her.* Harry felt an initial relief, followed by a pang. *I should be happy.* But, somehow, he felt violated. Their stories should've stayed private, they should've been theirs alone. Nobody else should be privy to the lies he'd told his son. Harry felt an inevitable dread.

One morning he woke up to Timothy in the kitchen, his breakfast made. Timothy was sitting at the table with a cup of coffee.

"Dad, Catherine and I are getting married." He paused and waited for his father to reply.

"I can't say I'm surprised." Harry sat down, his hands together on the table. "Congratulations."

"We haven't told her family yet—" Timothy hesitated, then he put a hand over one of his father's. "We're going to move away from here. We're going to move to California."

Harry didn't say a word. He was looking down at the table, at his son's hand over his. Then he looked his son in the eyes. He didn't say a word.

"I've wanted a family so much, Dad. It's not your fault I don't ... I've never felt at home here in Atlanta ... not without ..."

Harry was looking in Timothy's eyes. He saw the tears forming. Timothy looked down at their hands.

Harry put his other hand over Timothy's, the three hands stacked. "It's okay son. I understand."

"I've spent my entire life being the only one ... the tragic one—" Timothy shrugged his shoulders, an awkward gesture—one shoulder up, then the other as the first shoulder fell. "We figured we'd get a new start there, we'd be strangers in a place full of strangers." He smiled, weakly. "So ... I guess we wouldn't be strangers anymore ... out there, in California. We could start our own family there. It'd be a fresh start."

He looked down at their hands. The morning paper was on the table beside them. The Germans had occupied Paris. "Anyway, if we go to war ... I don't know ... I guess I'll enlist."

Harry patted his son's hand. "It's okay. I understand." He smiled for his son. "She must love you very much."

Timothy smiled back. "She does."

※

They got engaged. But her parents hired a detective. And later Harry would see it, he would see it clear, how he had doomed them from the beginning. His worst mistake was to pass Timothy for White. White wasn't better. Black wasn't better. What was better was to have a family, to be somebody from someplace and to have a history, a true one, because that's what lost his son and the girl he loved, having no family except his father, and a phony family history. That absence of family was what had made her family suspicious—not of race—but that something must be wrong. All those stories Harry had told his son, they had no real connection to the boy—there'd been no stories about the siblings playing with their baby brother; there were no pictures of the mother with her infant child. No pictures of grandparents, or of aunts and uncles. None of that seemed right. Harry had to admit it; he'd have been suspicious too.

Their detective was good. He went to Chattanooga and he pegged them. The girl's parents got more than they'd bargained for—their Madonna-faced girl was engaged to marry a Negro.

Timothy came home one night to tell him the marriage was off. "It's all a lie. Tell me it's a lie." He had his father by his shirt.

Harry sat him at the kitchen table and sat down next to him. They were almost touching, side by side. "No, son, it's not a lie. What they told you is true." He held his son by his arm. Timothy tried to pull away, but Harry wouldn't let him go. "*I* lied. I twisted everything I told you into a lie. Every time you asked me, I cut you off. It's like I told you 'no.' Now I'm telling you the truth." He told Timothy who Charlotte was, and Harry Jr., and Mary Ann. Then he told him about the fire.

"Your mother's name was Geneva. She was beautiful—very light skin. She died seventeen days after you were born. Your half-brother is named Earley. Your half-sister is Lilly. She's a very sweet girl. I don't have any pictures. I wish I did, I'd show them to you. They probably have families of their own by now. I can tell you all about them."

Timothy thrust his fists behind his head. He pressed his arms against his ears. "No! Don't tell me anything! You're a liar. I don't want to know."

Timothy leaned forward over the table, his elbows on it. He stared up at his father, gasping for air, his eyes wide. Harry said, "Let me tell you. Geneva would've loved you so much. She was a wonderful mother. She was very gentle, and she was very smart." Timothy stood and knocked over his chair. Harry said, "Listen to me, listen. Earley and Lilly are your siblings. Your real brother and sister. They played with you. They were so proud to have you for a brother. They loved you. They still do. Just like I do. I'd swear to it."

Timothy scrabbled at the back door. "You're lying. How can you say you love me? You've always lied." He scrabbled at the knob.

Right then, Harry loved him so, so much; his heart filled and he wanted to help him but he knew he couldn't. Harry couldn't even move. But for the first time, after all these years, he finally told Timothy who he and Harry were. Then Timothy was gone, and Harry knew he'd lost him forever.

That burning, burning, burning—now it had his boy and Harry knew how wrong he'd been. His pretenses had all vanished. All these years, Harry had told himself he only wanted Timothy to be his own person, nothing else and nothing less, and that he could only be that by passing for White, because this was a White man's world. That was why Harry had left Chattanooga; that was why he'd lied. But without a family, Timothy had never been himself. What was a life that was nothing but lies, of nothing but 'no'? And when Harry finally told him 'yes,' it was too late to save him from that world, and from his father's lies.

17 • The Drowned Man

Williams Point, Mississippi: 1959

Eighteen years ... look at me now. Sitting in Atlanta, alone, for five years, hating the house he was living in, hoping Timothy might write him a letter or give him a call. His business was declining. There were too many rumors: Where's your son? What happened to him? Then one morning, standing in his threshold and contemplating the coming day, Harry set himself adrift.

He moved from town to city to town. He would stay for a month, a season, a year. Whenever he thought life might tap him on his shoulder and intrude itself again, he'd pick up and move. He believed he was toxic, he wanted nobody else to be harmed because of him, but he also, finally, realized the burning inside him burned harder whenever he'd leave. There were also the letters: his letters to Earley, Catherine's letters to him. This random wandering from town to town—what if Catherine lost his new address? What if Earley moved, and didn't know how to tell him where?

He couldn't go on like this. Maybe, he thought, life in the North would be different. Maybe there, life wouldn't take him unawares and overwhelm him. Maybe there, he would be left alone.

But the North was too gritty, too cold. Harry went as far north as he'd dared—to Pittsburgh. He'd considered Cincinnati but it was too much South. Chicago, New York, Philadelphia—they'd never entered his mind. Pittsburgh would be just enough North for him.

It had three rivers and he liked to live near water. But it only took one winter in a city that big, alone, for him to realize it was a mistake to live outside the South. His first sight of its buildings, covered in soot, shocked him. It was like a personal rebuke, mocking him, and the water in the rivers, cold and iron-gray, feeling its way between the factories, the smoke stacks, the blackened tall buildings— He could drown down there and his body would disappear, never to be seen again. The thought was irrational, Harry knew that, but the burning, burning that he could never escape, he feared it would consume him there.

He returned to the South, and then drove west, as far as he'd dared, to the Mississippi Delta, to a town with its own rivers. People had told him it was easy living in the Delta. There were plenty of Negroes, they said, to mow your lawn and drive your car and cook your meals, and though the money came only once a year, when the cotton sold, it came plenty when it did, more than enough to buy you your Colored gardener, your chauffeur, your cook. Everybody White, except the trash, had themselves a Colored.

Harry nodded, he smiled; he kept his counsel. He didn't want Negro servants. He didn't think anyone was "trash." But he went anyway. Where else could he go?

So he drove up and down the Mississippi Hills and dropped into the Delta and stopped where he landed. The Negro who pumped his gas gave him directions to the Browning Hotel. And sure enough, over the Negro's shoulder Harry could see through the gas station window the White man's feet on his desk, his newspaper open, his pipe's smoke curling to the ceiling. In the Hills, White men had pumped his gas; here they read newspapers.

Harry frowned, but just for a moment. Then he turned back to the attendant. "How do you get to the river? Away from town."

He drove eastward and found the dirt road that the Negro had named, and drove down to a broken-down pier, it was just as the Negro described it. There was little left standing. Harry looked past it at the river. It was green from shore to shore and trees hung down over the water. He could smell it; he could feel it. And he couldn't see a current, it looked so still. Harry strolled back up the road to where he'd seen a clearing. The ruins of a wooden building littered the grass. Harry walked to it. Trees were all around him. The air, the cloudless sky, the leaves, everything was still. Even the sound, the insect drone, seemed still; like one musical chord, modulating but impossibly long, eternal. He liked that. After so many cities and towns … Harry counted them off, silently. He wondered what might lie west—the plains, the mountains, the ocean. He realized he didn't care and he was relieved. He returned to his car and drove back to town and the Browning Hotel. He found it nearly deserted. Visitors, he would learn, now stayed at the Holiday Inn, newly built on the bypass south of town.

People were friendly. On the streets, in Stanney's Café, in the Chamber of Commerce, everybody was dreaming big. They told him: Williams Point was the biggest inland market for cotton in the entire United States. There were plenty of opportunities here for a man with brains and gumption. Loans, they told him, had liberal terms; nobody was afraid of credit. After all, every planter lived on credit for six months of every year; and every banker was a planter's son. Harry listened, he smiled; he kept his counsel. These planters, he didn't think he'd like them.

But this was as far west as he dared go; and the river and the clearing had sold him.

◆——◆

That first night he lay in a strange bed, staring at the ceiling, and he told himself: *This is my home. This is my fourth life.* He stirred and settled, he tried to feel comfortable. He lay there, quiet, but he couldn't sleep.

He was thinking about his first life: Charlotte and Harry Jr. and Mary Ann, and all his family and in-laws; his childhood friends, his business, his town. And his second life: Geneva and Earley and Lilly; Big Mama Darling and Mama Lou; Pete and Mae and Uncle John. (What was that—two years?) And then his third: Timothy. His fourth? Nobody but him. From each life to the next he saw the progressive narrowing, the fire burning, his life hollowing. He wanted to beg forgiveness from each and every person, but then he'd tighten and tell himself no, it wasn't him, he'd done nothing wrong—every time he'd acted it was for the sake of one of them.

And what had come of it—ever? So, no more, no more.

That first night, the fire that started it all—he'd never meant to take a stand; he was no soldier, no hero, no crusader—what he'd done, wasn't that just a human thing, a decent thing? He'd saved a person he loved, a fellow human being, and her children. Must that turn his whole world upside down? Who made that rule? He'd just wanted to live his ordinary life. Why hadn't life let him?

He turned over on his side. By now he was exasperated, as usual. Why go over it? It was spilled milk. At this he'd shake his head, as usual: Why not? How could he forget it? He'd lost everything that night, and gained everything new—and then he'd lost that too, again and again.

Losing Timothy, that had been the worst; that had been his final straw. And that, no matter his intentions, had been his fault. Harry counted the cites and the towns between Atlanta and Pittsburg—too many, too many.

He was tired of this back-and-forth. It had to end somewhere. And he wanted that to be right here, on the Delta's eastern edge, close by the Hills. He realized he couldn't cross the Mississippi: it was a threshold, a point of no return, and westward on would be a flat country, sitting on a flat world and tilting down to its very edge, where the water fell. California: Catherine, Timothy's former fiancée, had found salvation there but Harry doubted one for him. She had shed her past, her family, she had stripped herself down to her very core and, thus unencumbered, she'd recreated herself. That's what happened out there. Harry shook his head. That wasn't him. He was burned out hollow. Stripped to his core, there'd be nothing there.

This here, he patted his bed, it was a strange bed but it would do for now. True, this Delta land was also flat, but it was enclosed—not so expansive—room just enough for a modest recreation. *This will be my fourth life. This will be my last life, and my least.* That was what he wanted, as little life as possible. *My letters to Earley. Catherine's letters to me. Nobody but me and two people on a page.* Harry turned back to face the ceiling.

He didn't mind it so much, lying awake. He didn't mind the ceiling. Maybe this was him saying goodbye. Lining them up, those past three lives, and calling them out, each and every person, just memories now, and sending them home—bye-bye,

bye-bye, bye-bye—he mouthed the words, like sheep jumping a fence, he mouthed them over and over until he slept.

The next day Harry rented a post office box and a safe-deposit box, and looked for a place to stay.

He no longer cared what kind of work he'd do. He expected to get on. But he didn't expect to get married, or raise another son.

18 • The Wounded Man

Drew, Mississippi: March, 1963

Morgan had sent me home to Drew. For weeks, I kept to my room, huddled under my blankets where I waited out the winter. But today is sunny, even though it's cold, and I want to feel the air on my skin. So I take to the front porch, shirtless, just me and my bandages. It feels good out here.

People pass by. Good country folks, they pause and wave and we exchange our greetings. I think of stars and sand, numberless and numbered, and I think of Abraham's children. Here in the Delta, our old folks know we're the numberless and numbered, we're the children of Abraham. I remember the last stars I saw on the night I was shot, too many and too small to be counted. So I start counting the people passing by, and then I think about my family and neighbors and count them, and then my friends, my teachers, my comrades—

My shoulders start to ache and I shift in my rocker. I stop counting. I want to situate myself. I want to make sense of who I am and what my life is. I want to name myself and own myself. I want to *move*. But I'm stuck here in Drew. And I'm dissatisfied. I've been dissatisfied for some time now. I've been a victim of violence, of circumstance, of that game that White people play so well, and I don't want to be a victim. I didn't join the Movement for that. No I didn't. And I'm tired of it, more tired now than when I joined. (But I still have Morgan's letter.) And I don't know but I have to know, so I've been thinking how I could let Morgan be beaten on one day, and then cover his body to save his life on another. I can't explain that to myself. So how can I know where I'll place my foot, the next time I step?

He's coming today. I'll have to tell him something.

I see the plume of dust, then the car. It slows and stops and I stand up. Morgan gets out. We shake hands. I wince; I still can't move too well.

Morgan notices. "How're you doing?"

I smile and work, just a bit, my bandaged shoulders. "It still hurts, but I'm getting better."

He takes a look at my bandages. "How long do you have to wear those?"

"I really don't know. Too long."

We sit down together. Morgan takes the rocker and I take the bench. We don't say much, and I enjoy the quiet. Voices drift through the front door screen. Morgan gets up. "I should go inside and announce myself."

I get up too. "No, let's go for a ride first. I want to show you something."

"And I've got something to show you." We go out to Morgan's car and he opens the right-side door. Hanging under the dash is a CB radio. "We have these in all our cars now. If you're not too far, you can reach the office. Get in. Take a look at it." Then he asks me, "Where are we going?"

Inside the car, Morgan drives and I give him directions. We pass by bare fields. Cotton stalks left out in the mud—gray and broken, bent and prone. Morgan asks me, "You ever see some of those old Civil War photographs—all the dead bodies in the battlefields? They never seemed real to me. The bodies look too extreme. They're all twisted up, there's too many of them, and they're all piled up, just like those cotton stalks." He glances at me while he's driving. "Now I know I'll never see them that way again. They'll look real to me now—those dead bodies. How many people died fighting over the question of our freedom? It's a very simple question—should we be free or not? At least, it should be simple. So I wonder, how many had to die, back then … and how many more will die, right now?"

He glances my way again. "You took that shotgun blast but it was meant for me. Killing will come. I know that now. Everybody in the Movement is living on borrowed time. I want you to be safe, Aleck."

I look out the window. "We can talk about that later. We're here. Pull over." I push open the door and try not to wince.

Ever since I was a boy I'd had myself a favorite spot I'd go to, just to be alone in, to think in—or not to think at all. I'd told Morgan about it, but I never told him where it was.

Morgan stands beside me at the side of the road. It's late afternoon. There's an apron of gravel where we parked and that's where we're standing. Just beyond is mud and farther out, the cotton fields. We're looking south. There's a slight roll to the fields here, they're brown and gray and burnished by the copper light. Low in the distance is a long stand of bare trees, an irregular ribbon of faded gray softened by its distance from the road, and the sky is a light blue-red with clouds scattered across it like daubs of paint, each one a rose color that fades, upwards, to an eggshell white. It isn't quite sunset, and it isn't quite spring.

"I know it's not much. I've seen lots of pictures of mountains and canyons and waterfalls—some spectacular and really beautiful stuff. But this place right here, at this time of day, no matter what season—to me it's the prettiest place on earth." I smile. "If I ever see any better, I'll probably be disappointed—that this wouldn't be tops anymore. But I don't expect that to happen. Pretty is from the heart." I turn to Morgan. "Shouldn't home be the prettiest place on earth?"

Morgan nods. "It would be prettier if it belonged to us. You know about this particular place?"

"Yeah, I do. Negroes used to own it, I believe, some forty years ago."

Morgan points. "Out over there. The Danby family. That was where their house was. Whites burned it down."

I look back at the ribbon of trees. "Well, I still think of it, all of this really, as home."

I'm feeling better. Coming here's worked. I was afraid it wouldn't.

I put my hand on Morgan's shoulder. "I don't know if you came here to ask me back or to tell me to quit. But I'll be coming back, just as soon as I can."

Morgan looks me over; he smiles. "Well, you're looking good, Aleck. Better than you have for a long time."

"I'm sleeping through the night again. I can relax now. *You* look like hell."

We laugh, and we stay, standing there till sunset. Driving back, I invite him for supper.

"Your father won't mind?"

"Nope. Mom insists."

"How're you and him getting along?"

"I try to stay out of his way. He leaves me alone. But it's a small house."

I'm thinking I should've told Morgan back there, how I let them beat him. Deborah tried to save him. I just froze and let it happen. I haven't told a soul.

Morgan doesn't look at me, but at the road ahead. "I always thought I was on your father's left side—'touchous,' that's the word—relations have always been touchous between us.

I could say my father was jealous, but I don't say anything—I don't say a mumbling word.

Morgan turns on his headlights. I'm studying his face in profile. He knows it and he doesn't move. He just keeps his eyes on the road. He never had any children of his own, but he was always available for me or any other boy coming up in Drew. He'd explain it to us: Negro fathers need to be strong in this White man's world. Failure in the least little thing comes at a high price for a Negro. The wrong look in the eye, the wrong word—just the wrong tone in your voice and White folks would turn you out! We all heard about Emmett Till. And there've been others—lots of others. So any father worth his salt just can't tolerate anything slipshod in how his children behave. A father has to be strict. He has to be super strict.

And sometimes a strong man's a distant man. Like the top of a mountain. Morgan would tell us a boy looks to that mountain top; he'll set his direction by it, his north and south. But it's distant. And a boy can't climb it, not yet. So, he'll call on a hilltop—it's closer, and it's easier to climb. And that's what I am, Morgan told us, you can come and ask me anything, and tell me anything—all those things you wouldn't chance with your father. Dumb things maybe, you might think they're dumb, but they're about how you should think and act as men. So we did—all us boys—we'd go to him. And when Morgan corrected us, well, he wasn't our father. The stakes weren't so high. He wouldn't beat us. All the other boys—their fathers would beat them. But my father never laid a hand on me.

Morgan pulls up to the house. It looks like a jack o' lantern with its lights in the windows and through the open door. My father appears. His silhouette, a black coal glowing outrageously, nearly fills the doorway. He makes his way down the steps with that slight limp he has, into the night, and cools into a blue-black human being. I'd heard rumors about my father since I was a little child, about him years ago in another town, about him in jail, about violence. He walks slowly to the car. He tells me to go on in. "I want to talk to Mr. Wright."

I step inside and turn back and leave the door ajar. It's too dark to see too much but I watch my father and Morgan, out there on the street. My father's bigger, taller—Morgan's just a middling sized man. They're facing each other and my father's leaning in on him. I see Morgan's fist clench, at his side, and then it relaxes. He nods, but his body's stiff. They don't shake hands or touch in any way. When they turn back to the house their figures merge into one. At the sight of that I gasp—for a second I'm a little boy—then I pull my head in and gently close the door.

"What did he say to you out here?" It's after supper and we're sitting in Morgan's car.

Morgan smiles. "He goddamned me. He blames me for you quitting school and joining the Movement."

I look toward the house. I don't say a word.

Morgan looks there too. "I told him he was right. I am responsible for you. He doesn't like his boy getting shot. Can you blame him for that?"

Neither of us speaks for a while. All along the street, faint voices from the houses are all we hear. It's the same old thing—Morgan always covered for him. Y'all will never know, he'd tell us boys, what your fathers go through—never, not until you're grown. But now I'm thinking, I am grown and I still don't know—because my father won't tell me.

"It was my choice." I almost whisper it.

Morgan lets it go. He's drumming his fingers on the steering wheel. "Listen Aleck, I've got to start back now. I've stayed longer than I should have. But ... before I go, I've got one thing I've got to say." Morgan wets his lips. "Folks back in Horatio County have had a lot to say about your shooting. I talk to our farmers—our landowners—anybody who's not in hock to the White man—and to some of our people in Atlanta. This isn't just about you, it's something that's been brewing. A lot of folks don't like us not being armed."

I don't say a word.

Morgan goes on. "Our farmers say they'll try to register, but they'll also protect their families and property. They say they're not SNCC. They never signed on to nonviolence. And they say they won't abide anybody telling them what they cannot do to protect their families. They've got guns and they say they'll use them if they have to. And they tell us we're fools if we don't have them."

I ask him, "What do you say?"

"I say this is a grassroots movement. It always has been. I tell them to do what they think's best. And that don't change a thing as far as I'm concerned. We're not going to start no war. We're not going to be armed when we canvass our neighborhoods, or when we march to the courthouse, or when people try to register. But that's not when we're in the greatest danger."

Morgan reaches over and opens the glove compartment of the car. He brings out two revolvers.

"These are loaded. I keep one in the glove compartment every time I drive somewhere. The other one's for you." He puts it in my lap. "You take this and keep it in your room here. And when you come back, you bring it with you, and whenever you drive somewhere you take it with you. Because you never know, your car might break down, or you might be late coming back. We're not supposed to drive at night now, and I'm taking a risk right now, visiting you for so long, because it's when we're on the road at night that we're in our greatest danger. So no matter where you're going, you always take this with you in your car. Otherwise, I won't sleep at night. You understand?"

By now I'm not listening. I don't hear a thing; I don't say a thing. I'm looking at that gun in my lap. It's the first one I've seen since my last day at Morehouse. I pick it up and hold it. It's all I see—it and that scrawny cop and his laughing grin, just we two. I'll wipe that grin right off ...

"Aleck. Aleck." Morgan nudges me in my side. I look at him and at the street beyond. Again I hear the voices from the houses. A radio's playing, it's one of those stations you get at night, from New York or Chicago or St. Louis—jazz and blues. The tune is an old one, the music stops and starts, a clarinet conducts, it swoops and glides and the trumpets punch. I know the people, they keep a window open so their neighbors can hear.

I think about all those White men, leaning out their cars and pointing their guns at me. In broad daylight while I was walking our streets. I think about all those people, good country people, passing my parents' porch today—every one of those couples, they all waved at me, and each man among them owns a gun. Each one would defend his home.

So this is my gun and I'm thinking, This here—this makes sense to me.

But there's that day in Morehouse, when I was so tired. Yes, I'll admit it: the possibility of violence, when it's always around, can be exhausting. I was sitting in my room, reading that letter—Morgan's letter—and he said violence was *their* game. Hadn't I read that right? So, carrying a gun, it makes sense, but what will it lead to?

Morgan asks me, "Okay?" He's been giving me the eye. I shift in my seat to pocket the gun, and I tell him okay.

Okay? To be armed in the Movement? Okay. This gun makes sense to me, but somehow, when I think about our Movement, I'm not so sure.

19 • The Wounded Man

Williams Point: Summer, 1963

When White people started coming to us, to SNCC, in places like Alabama—that was Bob Zellner, he was the first—we didn't know where to put them. We put Bob in a White community—Whites organizing poor Whites, that became our plan—but we had to get him out fast, before he got killed. Because, much as they hate us, a White "nigger lover" is worse. So we put our Whites with us, working side-by-side, organizing in Negro communities.

But not in the Delta: it was too dangerous here. And for Morgan and me, that was alright, because we wanted this, here, to be a real grassroots movement. We didn't want any outsiders coming in, and any White person, no matter how sympathetic—they would always be outsiders.

That wasn't our people's doing, that's what Whites imposed on us, and on themselves.

So now it's my first day back and Morgan's telling me the news. We're eating cereal sitting on our beds—we've got no table. He's telling me we've got two new staffers, two Whites, who moved here from SNCC headquarters in Atlanta: Isaac Mendelssohn and Johanna Burnham. I know them. I'd met them at SNCC retreats. But I'm asking Morgan, what the hell? And he's talking back, saying, what? you've got something against White people?

We both crack up at that one.

"You've met them, right?"

I tell him yes.

"And you know their fathers, who their fathers are. They're rich, and they know people, important people."

"But it's too dangerous here. You know that. You're bringing rich kids here?"

So he's telling me he's doing this precisely because it is too dangerous here. It's too dangerous for Whites, and it's too dangerous for Negroes. But if you've got a rich White man for a father, somebody who—when they yell people listen—if your father's that sort of man, then if something happens—

"You're telling me they'll be our sacrificial lambs."

Morgan shakes his head. "They won't do anything we don't do. Look, all these months we've both been here, we've been the sacrificial lambs—every Negro here is a sacrificial lamb. Except that nobody gives a shit what happens to us. What I'm saying is, now that their fathers know they're here, I don't expect as much violence as before."

I smile. "You think their fathers have a direct line to Justice?"

"I do. Yes, I do."

"And Justice has a direct line to the Klan? They tell the Klan what to do?"

Morgan just looks at me. I try to read his eyes. Then he nods: "To the mayor's office here, and the county commissioners—Justice has a direct line there." He looks down and away, and then back at me. "You don't know what it's like talking to the Justice Department, trying to get an investigation on who shot you. It never happened. Justice said it was a local case. They had no jurisdiction. They would've found some if you'd been White. Anyway ... nothing happened. But I'm supposed to respect the laws of the great state of Mississippi."

He looks like he wants to spit. "Damn Justice. I don't trust anybody anymore. I don't know what to think. I try not to."

We start walking to our office. Morgan's put on a pair of dark glasses—black. The light glints off his lenses.

"You can call them sacrificial lambs. You can call them whatever you like. I was responsible for bringing you here. And now, I'm responsible for everybody on this street, and that street, and the one beyond that one—all these streets. Because the rock was always here, with all the bad things under it, but I'm the one who kicked it over."

❖ ❖

I meet Isaac and Johanna in our office. It's small; the windows are broken and covered with plywood (people drove by and threw bricks and fake bombs through them); there's a card table for a desk, with a telephone and papers strewn, and a worn couch—its fabric's like burlap—and some old wooden chairs and a fan. Stuff so sorry even the poor could spare it. It felt crowded with only two people in it. Now we've got four.

The first thing Isaac does is tell us about his father, and what a great guy he is. "He's the greatest man I know." Isaac says he's generous to a fault, a real man of the people, he'll give you the shirt right off his back. I can tell he's sincere, but I don't want to listen. Then Johanna says the same thing about hers. I'm thinking maybe they know why Morgan brought them here, and I wonder how they feel about that. They're sitting on that ratty couch and I'm leaning against the opposite wall, and they look me right in the eye and I look right back at them. This isn't the first time I've looked White people in the eye, not since joining the Movement, so I've gotten used to it. But I'm not comfortable because their eyes are full of doubt and anxiety and fear, and they so want my approval for their being here, and Isaac, he wants even more—I can tell—he wants to be my friend. Close friend. Best friend. And all I can think is: This isn't fair. It isn't fair to me. I want to choose my own friends. Just because Isaac's in the Movement, that doesn't mean he qualifies. Maybe later. Maybe he'll grow on me. Beyond that I don't know what to think, or if I'm thinking of anything else at all.

I look over at Morgan. He's sitting behind the card table, smiling. He's still got his dark glasses on.

20 • The Wounded Man

We send Johanna out for some canvassing. Deborah takes her around to show her this street and that. A beat-up car follows them, two White men in T-shirts and baseball caps; they drive up and point a shotgun at Johanna's flyers. The man with the gun asks, "What's those, missy?" The man at the wheel chuckles. Then the other points his shotgun at Deborah, but he's still looking at Johanna. "You like these niggers, missy? She your girlfriend?" In that neighborhood—it's so old—the dirt streets are worn down two feet below the front yards, and there're no sidewalks, so they have to walk in the street and the car crawls behind them and sometimes the fender bumps up against the back of Johanna's knee. She keeps Deborah to her other side, away from the car. And it's nothing, nothing that hasn't happened to her before, in Atlanta, or to Deborah here, but now the hearing of it wearies me more than it ever did before.

And this is because of Johanna. It's not her fault. It's just that her first day here, Johanna told us her father wrote to tell her a famous professor—his name is Seymour Lipset, I've heard of him, I've read his book—he'd heard about her working for SNCC, and once she's done here he'd like to have her as a research assistant. This is big news for her because this will set her up for life, and she seems genuinely surprised. But I never had any doubt about her being set for life, because her father's on the board of trustees for the University of California and that's why we brought her here. But now she's going on and on about all the plans she has for her life, and I realize they'll be leaving, Isaac and her, so much sooner than I will, because it'll be before this job is done. And they'll resume their lives, and they'll have very successful lives. So now I'm thinking that someday I'll be leaving too. Won't I want to do something that's "successful"? And I *do* want to, I want to very much. I want my life. I want my due. So, I'll be leaving too, before this work is done.

So this is weariness: to think that nothing here has changed, and nothing ever will. Deborah tells me the Whites are worse now that Johanna's out there with her—so there'll be no "done" here, nothing will ever be done here, not even when I go—and now I can't imagine when that will ever be.

◆——◆

Isaac tells me he's read about the Delta, he's heard its music, and now that he's here he can't quite believe it, not yet. He tells me this is Eden, with the tree of life here, and the tree of good and evil.

He tells me this is where bluesmen made deals with the devil, always at midnight and at a crossroads, to sing their sky songs, and hellhounds dog their trails.

He tells me he knows I know all this, but he wants me to know how much he appreciates he's here—

He tells me this is where the rivers scraped out the old land, the clay land, and then filled it with loam to make a new land, obscenely rich when measured by money, and flood-haunted, and cotton-white, nightmare white, and soaked in sweat and sperm and skin. People fled the Hills for here, both Black and White for here. They left their small, insignificant farms for here. And some White men made their fortunes here, and sent their sons to Harvard and their wives to London and Paris and Rome. And the Negroes lie down at night here, and listen for train whistles, the farther away the better, and their hearts break every time one blows.

He tells me this and smiles—he's embarrassed. And what can I say? This is where I grew up, with ordinary stores and ordinary jars—inside were ordinary fingers—and ordinary cotton fields and ordinary radiators, and ordinary knives and ordinary booze, ordinary fights on Saturday nights; and ordinary churches, and ordinary kin. My mother's wonderful—and ordinary. The trees, the ones I showed Morgan, and the sky: those are the trees and sky I've always seen. The music's the music I've always heard. Sharp molasses and crackling bread, cool wading creek water pooled around my ankles … and my mother's hand touching my face, and lingering. None of it's the less for being mine. But it's all too grand the way Isaac tells it.

❖ ❖

He's in the office—he leans against the wall, this is his speech: Most evil doesn't come from bad people. Most evil comes from good people living good lives in good communities. Most evil comes from people's certainty of knowing what the good is; and the same certainty tells us that anything different must therefore be bad and must therefore be feared. Evil on a grand scale—Isaac gestures to the street, he means the evil here, all around us; it's the same evil as the Holocaust he says—it's what good people do to those they fear. It's a matter of love, the common love for one's own, and the fear that those who are different will hurt them. Hate comes from love and fear. If a man loves his wife and children enough, his father and mother enough, and his friends and his home; and he will know his own goodness, even when he hates and kills. So a good man will kill with no compunction.

Morgan asks him, when did you get to know all the White folks here? All those Klansmen, all those businessmen on the Citizens Councils, when did you sit down with them to supper? That's just a theory you've got. Morgan gets up to leave. Theories about racists, he says, are luxuries for liberal White folk. We Negroes don't have time for that. We're too busy trying to keep ourselves together. He leaves and I think, yeah, Morgan's right. But he's biased. I can tell, he doesn't like Isaac. Me? I can't say if I do or don't. I don't know him so I can't say. And with the way he brags about his father, I don't even want to think about him.

The church mothers, our block captains, they love them madly—Johanna and Isaac. These women have never seen such White people before; they're delighted with these outside Whites. Miss Avie, who puts Isaac up in a room out back of her house, she bustles over him like he was her son. To her, Isaac doesn't eat or sleep or sweat, he just exists in his innocence; polite at her table, quiet in her parlor, he accepts her house rules and hospitality as something that's as natural as the rain and the sunshine. And they are, they should be, but a White man's never taken them that way. For Miss Avie, Isaac's manna every morning. After years of careful watching, and walking a zig-zagged path to avoid a White woman's anger or a White man's lust, suddenly Isaac has made her way straight. She's thrilled and astonished; she needn't calculate or second-guess her behavior around him. She wants more of this brave new world, where the White folks come straight from Eden.

So of course, Miss Avie doesn't know a thing about Isaac. How could she?

Deborah doesn't like them. I ask her why. She brings up race: "It's not because they're White, it's because they're not Colored."

But they're here now, and we asked them to come.

Johanna wants to change how we organize our block captains. I ask her, "What do you know about it?"

"Well, quite a lot, actually. Last summer I flew to Chicago and I interviewed Saul Alinsky. I volunteered with one of his groups. In a Negro neighborhood. So, yes, I knew something about community organizing before I ever joined SNCC."

She leaves. I sit down. Isaac is looking at me so I look at him.

After a moment I ask him, "Is she always like this?"

Isaac smiles, "Only when she thinks she's right." We're in our office. We have our dinners, covered plates from a church mother. Isaac takes a bite. "The thing is—she's brilliant. Her ideas about the block captains are probably worth listening to. In fact, I'd bet on it." He takes another bite. "But that's not the point, is it?"

"No, it isn't."

"Well ... she means well."

I attend to my plate. "I'm sure she does. But this is a grassroots movement. She needs to listen to the local people, understand what they're doing and why, before bringing in any outside ideas."

Isaac just shakes his head. He takes a mouthful and chews; he pauses. He's got something to say.

"Why are we here? Look, I can see your point—grassroots, self-sufficiency. This isn't about integrating buses or restaurants; this is about ... well, raising your people up to where *they* have power. You and Morgan are from around here.

Johanna and I are outsiders. I get that. So why did you ask for us?"

I've been waiting for this. I know what to say.

"We were too successful. Things got too big. We needed more help."

"I heard you asked for White staffers, specifically."

"We didn't want to take experienced staff from the other offices. Most of you newcomers are White."

"Is that it? There wasn't any other reason?" He studies my face. I smile, but leave my eyes blank, which is the way Negroes in Mississippi always look, only with their eyes averted, whenever they deal with White people—their bosses, the police, and now Isaac, who's supposed to be my comrade and wants to be my friend.

I decide to go on offense. "Y'all slept together in Atlanta, didn't you?"

He blushes. He fumbles with his fork and puts it down. "That won't happen here."

"It better not. Look, I wouldn't care, but the people you're staying with, they're deacons and church mothers. Y'all would ruin their reputations."

Isaac looks down, away from me, and I don't have to worry about what my eyes might say.

21 • THE WOUNDED MAN

One night Johanna woke to the sound of men in her room. She tells us all about it in the morning. She just ups and says, "I had a visit from the Klan last night." She tries to keep her voice bright, but as she tells her story her eyes grow wide with fear and wonder. A group of men, she tells us, were leaning over her, all around her cot. Flashlights flooded her eyes. A voice behind one whispered, "You helping those niggers?" Johanna replied, "Negroes. I'm helping Negroes." She tells us she blinked her eyes and reached for a candle and matches. "I told them to turn those flashlights off." They obeyed her and Johanna lit her candle. There were five of them, their faces waxy white, wearing blue jeans and open-neck shirts, and she said they looked to be in their twenties and thirties, and their hands were behind their backs. Suddenly, she says, she knew they were Klan. "All I could think of, was, they know I'm here; right here. They followed us the very first day we came here. As soon as we crossed the state line over Alabama, a car pulled out from a side road and followed us. And when that one stopped another would take its place, and then another, all the way here. They knew when we were coming. And now, they know where I sleep."

She says one motioned the others out. He was the oldest. "He looked at me. He studied my face. He said, 'I don't want a ruckus. You just whisper. What's your name?' I didn't say a word. Then he hissed, 'Goddammit, you don't want to cross me! What's your name?' So I told him. Then he paused and peered at me and then he backed away from my bed. He asked me, 'Where're you from?' and I told him. He opened my rear door and looked up at the sky. He left it ajar and he crept back to my bed and blew out my candle. He told me to shush. 'You don't want me to call my boys back in.'

"I pulled my sheet up to my chin and he took a strand of my hair between his fingers. But then, nothing happened. I closed my eyes, he let loose of my hair, and when nothing else happened I opened my eyes again. It took me awhile to make him out. He was standing in the middle of my room. I think he was trembling. He stretched out his hand. He said, 'You've got to leave here, now. You've got to leave.' Then he was gone, out the back door. I got out of bed and looked.

"I could see them all, all five of them. They were walking in the moonlight, down the alley and around the corner. They were casual. They didn't care if anybody saw them.

"I saw the crowbars and ropes in their hands."

She tries to smile. She can barely do it. She's fighting back her tears.

"I ... I ... look at me. I can hardly talk. I was going to be so brave when I told you all about it. It's just that—I must've been in shock ... afterwards. I guess it's only hitting me now, the reality of what's around us here, I don't think I ever really realized until now." She tries again to smile. "You see, I've always believed that I was privileged for something great and important in my life. That's one reason why I came here—to prepare myself for that." She squeezes her eyes shut with her hands over them, and shakes her head. "But it's just hit me ... telling it to you ... I could die here, in some little shack, without having accomplished a thing. It never occurred to me, not even last night, not until right now, this morning."

She stops and stands stock-still, but just for a moment. Then she wipes her eyes with the back of her hands and picks up a stack of pamphlets. She goes out to work.

※

Days later I ask her, why did Atlanta choose her? She finishes my question. "—To come here?" She smiles. "I volunteered."

"Yeah, but, it's dangerous here. Just because you volunteered—why did they choose you?"

"Because I'm not a man? Is that what you mean?"

"Yeah, that's what I mean." I'm thinking about the Klan in her room. She must be too.

"Well, I wanted to come. And nobody else did: nobody but Isaac. And I kept after them. I reminded them I was the only other volunteer. Were they going to *make* somebody go—when I wanted to? I wore them down." She smiles again.

I smile too. "Do you always get what you want?"

She pauses, like she's thinking, 'what's wrong with getting what you want?' "Yes, I suppose I do." She's still smiling. "But that's because what I want is reasonable. I'm always reasonable."

"Do you still think this is reasonable—for you?"

She pauses. "If you mean, am I afraid, more afraid than when I came, well I am. But isn't everybody afraid? Shouldn't we be afraid? Aren't you? But *you* can't give in to them. So I shouldn't either."

I've got to admit it. I'm beginning to like her.

22 • The Wounded Man

I've begun to hate the telephone, the one we have in our office. And it isn't just me; we've all begun to hate it. Every day we let it ring longer, we stop working and look at it, but nobody wants to pick it up. After a while that just makes it worse.

We've learned that when you do, some fool might breathe into your ear and call you something vile and filthy, and you know that if he were right there with you he'd kill you on the spot and then go home and hug his children.

Even worse, it could be SNCC—somebody's lost, somebody's beaten, or somebody's dead, somebody you knew, even if for only one or two days at a retreat. In the Movement, even one afternoon together can be a lifetime. So maybe it's somebody you love, even if you'd only seen them once, only known them for a couple of hours and for all your lifetime to come.

All across the South: In Danville they pin us to cars and walls with fire hoses, and a cop holds a submachine gun to Jim Foreman's head. In Americus we stand dazed in jail cells, with bandaged heads and open cuts on our arms, and a gang of police break James Williams' leg and take a bat to his head. In Camilla they smack Mrs. Marion King, kick her from behind, and knock her to the ground. She's five months pregnant and her three-year-old daughter sees it all. We're hit with rocks and bricks, chains and saps; we're pistol-whipped and clubbed; we roll up like stink bugs to protect ourselves, we never fight back; and William Moore, a Mississippi White man, a mailman, is shot dead with a .22 caliber rifle in Alabama while walking alone from Tennessee to Mississippi. He'd written a letter urging decency; he was delivering it to our governor.

And here in Williams Point: Somebody throws a rock through Mr. Courtland's window. Whites run red lights trying to hit our cars. A boy is arrested and beaten by the police. An old man walking is run off the road. They aren't even ours. Whites nudge our legs with their cars when we're crossing a street and God help you if you drop your petitions, your flyers, and your forms. Bustled down the street by somebody's fender—somehow that's the most humiliating outrage of them all.

So, whenever that phone rings you always think the worst, feel the worst, almost wish it were the worst—you want to be done with it for good, just yank that telephone out by its cord and throw it in the street.

And who in this State of Mississippi, outside of our stringy web of telephone lines and shitty little offices, outside of our people—heroes that they are, but kept so low—who really cares if we live or die? Who in the FBI? Who in Justice? Who in this whole country? That's how I'm thinking—nobody who counts will ever care.

And later I'll tell myself that's wrong. I'll sit down in Mr. Courtland's café and hold a cold bottle of coke against my head and then drink a swallow slow. And for a while I'll believe that I'm overreacting and I'm wrong. But the next time in the office when that telephone rings I'll know it in my gut— nobody cares. George Lee. Lamar Smith. John Reese. Herbert Lee. Nobody's paid for their lives. The telephone's ring says it itself, grinding, over and over, so after letting it ring longer and longer, finally none of us can stand it and I pick it up quick, but I'll still be slow to bring it to my ear, and I'll hold my breath without even knowing it.

It told me about Medgar. Yesterday it told me he was murdered. In his own front yard.

◆—◆ ◆—◆

It's late night and I can't sleep. I get my gun out of its drawer. I sit on my cot and hold it in my hand, resting on my lap. Morgan's snoring just a few feet away. I think about how lucky it is he's not dead. I think about my grandfather and father, their shotguns in their laps. They'd have used them if they had to.

I think about how the Klan came busting through our door, and that shotgun aimed out of that car door window, and that cop who humiliated me in broad daylight just because he could. I'm seeing his face right now.

"If I had my way—" That's a gospel song. Back when we called ourselves Old Aunt Hagar's children, that's one of the songs we'd sing. So, I'm studying that gun in the palm of my hand, and all I see is the face of that one cop, sneering. He's down on the ground. He's looking up at me and he's sneering. "If I had my way"—now his face is bruised, it's bleeding, it's caved. I'm holding my gun like a rock and I'm beating him. I'm telling him nobody's ever going to recognize his face again—no no no—not anymore. "If I had my way, I'd tear this building down."

◆—◆ ◆—◆

Morgan's edgy. The summer's almost gone. And he's telling me we're just not getting it done. We put people in line at the courthouse to register, but so few get inside, so few get to take that literacy test; and nobody passes. And Justice tells him most of that's legal.

I'm listening and I'm thinking: *which side's the fool?* That's all I want to know, because our people don't have any time for fools, and a spectator who thinks he's a player is nothing but a fool. Right from Jump Street, when Rev. Lipscomb first took the lead in line to register, we said everybody votes. He's preached his Bible for fifty years and he can't read a line, but not for any lack of want or ability. For too many years this state schooled too many of our people to be like mules. So now we're stubborn like mules. Literate or illiterate, Mississippi's rules be damned, we say, "Everybody votes."

And because of us, Justice brought out a voting-rights suit against the county. But it covers only the literate Negroes who passed the state's test and still were failed, and that will cover only a fraction of the people in our lines. We want all our rights, for everybody, right now. But Justice says: Here's a little bit for a few. We say: We can't wait. Justice says: One step at a time. We say: We can't insinuate ourselves into systems that were built to oppress us. Justice says: We aren't interested in politics. We're only interested in the law. We say: We're interested in freedom.

We ask: Whose side are you on? Justice says: Nobody's. Justice says it's blind. Their solution to our problem is to take most of our people out of the game and make us spectators to our own movement.

I'm listening to Morgan and it's clear as day to me. Up against Justice we've been the fool.

Morgan went to a SNCC meeting in Atlanta. He took his vote and my proxy. Now he's back and he's telling me we're changing course for the summer and the fall. We're not going to take people to the courthouse to register anymore, not until November, after the election's done. So that means they won't go. They could, but unless we're there with them they won't. Instead, we're going to organize our own election with our own polling places this November—a "freedom election." We're going to create our own "Freedom Party." We'll run our own candidates against the real ones.

Morgan's sitting on his bed and I'm facing him, sitting on my cot. Our knees almost touch. He's looking at me, but he can't hold my eyes, so he keeps looking to the side, or up or down, anything to avoid looking at me; then he looks me in the eye again and then away again.

"We're probably the most uneducated Negroes in this whole damn country, here in this rich man's Delta. And the White folks here, up and down Main Street in those mansions, they're doctors and lawyers, Harvard graduates, and personal friends of their US senators. Do you really think our government is going to force a voting majority of poor Negroes on White people like that? But that's what we wanted that lawsuit to do. And it won't. It just won't. So … we've got to take a little detour for a while. We've got to show America what it should already know, that its Negro citizens want to vote, know how to vote, and know who to vote for."

I ask him, "Did you vote for this?"

"No. And neither did you." He's trying to smile. "Not at first. But majority rules, and then they had a second vote to make it unanimous."

So, after our months of prodding, our bodies on the line, plowing a straight line to the courthouse, we need this new thing, this "freedom election," just to stay in the game. I can't help but wonder what it will do.

Where is history made? That's the crux. We say it's made out in the street, by people from the bottom, boiling upward. But what if it's made in offices, two White men or four, suited, seated at a table or both sides of a desk, negotiating Negro issues from a White man's agenda, proposing White solutions for Negro problems? We say history is swarmed in broad daylight, but what if it's jimmied in the middle of the night? And what if it's directed by the point of a gun? Like my grandfather told me, White men have cornered that market for years.

We won't play the fool, we can't. But, really, it all depends—where is history made? I can't say I know anymore.

"And to run this election, we'll be bringing in a bunch of White college students from Stanford and Yale." Morgan shrivels, just a bit, his shoulders hunched. He seems to age before my eyes. He looks down at our feet again. "This was supposed to be a grassroots movement. This *was* a grassroots movement. But we had no protection. I couldn't lead lambs to the slaughter. So I brought in Isaac and Johanna. It was the best decision at the time. Now SNCC wants us to bring in more outsiders, more Whites, to help run this election, and well, that's probably a good decision too. But I can't help but think—there'll be too many Whites and they'll be coming in too fast. It won't be a grassroots movement anymore, not to me. This isn't what I'd signed up for. Who says we don't have the people here already who can run this election? And if we don't, then maybe this isn't what we should be doing."

Ever since Morgan brought them here, he's wanted Isaac and Johanna gone. He knows they have to be here, but he wishes they weren't. But that won't happen now.

I tell him, "Maybe, if this was a grassroots movement, we'd be protesting for jobs instead of votes." I'm also thinking, maybe we'd be fighting back. Violence for violence. But I don't say that. I don't even know if I want that.

Morgan nods. He stands up. He has to put his hand on my knee to do it. "Jobs. You're probably right. But who's going to give them to us, to our people? They don't want us Colored folk around here anymore. They've taken all the jobs away. Remember that woman who needed shoes? Her and her child, barefoot all winter? There was no job for her. Now she's gone, God knows where. It's like she fell through a hole in the world. You said every Negro in the South should move up North; everybody should start on the very same day. Well, the Whites around here would turn that day into a holiday. And the Whites up North would be crying."

I can't argue. I'm thinking about Justice. They just want us gone. And we've worked how many months now, and now we're changing course?

You try to do right. Sometimes, you just do wrong.

◆━◆━◆

"It's going too fast, it's getting too big; too fast and too slow, too far and not far enough." Morgan hesitates. He starts to turn away but then he stops. He starts pacing the room, looking out the window, looking at the door, and looking at me. "I'd never say I was naïve, but I've seen things here that I never saw in Drew, perched behind my counter in my store.

That woman and child in the rural—my God—no shoes in the winter."

He goes on: he describes children, listless, potbellied, legs and arms like sticks, their hair rusty and their faces smeared and vacant; he talks about women in tattered clothes, with so little to wear they can hardly cover themselves; and young men gone away while they're standing right in front of you, restless; they're fingering that bus ticket North in their pocket whether they've got it or not—they want to be potent and unencumbered.

And I can't blame them. I want those things too.

It's just like Morgan said: the slow's too slow and the fast is too fast. I've started to daydream and I usually don't. I daydream about college, the slow-fast of college; what stifled me then would soothe me now. I dream about the slow, humid days; I'd loll in their insignificance—it's a tidal rhythm, slow days and fast years, just fast enough, I see that now, not careening like this—not shot at and wounded, not threatened, not beaten and jailed, and not working check-to-jowl with strangers while death stares; good people, but not who I'd choose to die with. And we could, Isaac and me, we could die together on some dirt road, after dark, our car stopped. What if, that time when they shot Morgan and me, what if they'd aimed at our tires first? They do that now.

I daydream about kicking that cop's ass. It's always up close. It's always with my hands. I'm a blur—it goes by so fast—but it's just me and him. I daydream fast and slow.

◆—◆

You can't forget the things that are real, because I'm nothing but what I know, what I can remember and tell, so if I'm to be real I must remember well. After the hoses in Danville we crowd the city hall's steps, 250 strong, and stay the night. In Camilla and Selma, we fill their jails, more than 800 of us, singing. We send each other messages from cell to cell on toilet paper. And in Alabama ten volunteers take William Moore's place, starting right from where he fell.

Right here in Williams Point: Just outside of town, we've got a small community of farmers that own their own land—Browns' Haven. Three big families, all intermarried. The McGees, the Eversons, the Lowndes. I'll go out there sometimes just to get away. They're already with us. They were with us before we even got here. I don't have to convince nobody of nothing. I can just sit out front on Silas Lowndes' porch and talk for talk's sake, and kid around and laugh, all in plain sight, and I'm not in any way scared or wary—for that short time, while I'm there. I don't even think about the gun I'm carrying in my car, or the shotgun that Mr. Silas cradles, so casually, in his lap.

And the telephone isn't always bad news. I've talked on it to Movement people from all over the state, and I can go to just about any town in Mississippi and there'll be people I know, and even if I don't, they'll know *me*—they'll call me a "freedom rider," and even though I wasn't, that'll be their way of saying "you're ours, we'll feed you, put you up and protect you," because calling you a "freedom rider" is them saying you're the most badass Race Man a man can be. Maybe not to my face on the street in daylight, but at night, in their kitchen, telling me they're so proud of what I'm doing, while their cousins and uncles keep watch at their windows and doors.

And that's funny, because, first off, local folk called Morgan and me "freedom riders" to mark us off to avoid us.

Somewhere along the line that changed. Somewhere along the closing doors, the faces pleading and fearful, the police siren blast and nobody opens their doors to us; somewhere along that line, "freedom rider" changed from a dismissal to a praise.

Somewhere along the line: hanging out at Brown's Haven, shooting pool here in Williams Point on Saturdays, and going to church on Sundays; showing up at any place and any time, meeting our people on *their* ground and talking about what *they* want to talk about, júst like Mr. Courtland and his kind did back in the 'forties; and now our folk have begun to draw us into their lives—they call us "Freedom Riders" and their kids hang around our office, and the old heads like Rev. Lipscomb are becoming first-class citizens, him telling that sheriff, "Y'all can't scare me no more." Those stories put me to bed in the evening and raise me up in the morning. They're my only true weapons.

So something's being born. But goddamn, the labor's hard, and it's long, and for every good thought I have, I've got seven bad. Are we playing the fool? After so much hard work, after our people's bravery and sacrifice, how many have we registered? The lawsuit says not enough. And why are we changing course? Because the lawsuit's not enough. Why doesn't the government do more? The fact we've brought in White people, and will be bringing in more, answers that. So, everything is touch and go, we could fail, and our people here can't afford that. If we do, wouldn't it have been better if we never came?

But even with all that mess, there's something more; much, much more, close to the bone more: Me, that gun, that cop.

And me and my people here, whom I've come to live among and suffer for, *and they for me.*

In the light of day, I tell myself that freedom and progress come from self-discipline, and that your every act will shape the outcome you're striving for, so be sure your actions commend yourself. I repeat to myself these arguments for nonviolence.

But they mean less and less to me, and I'm afraid. How much have I ever believed them? Is singing in jail enough? I don't think so. Our stories end with sacrifice and community. The Whites' stories end with us dead.

Every night, I've taken to studying my gun, nestled in the palm of my hand. I tell myself I'm not afraid of the violence—I'm afraid for myself. What am I going to be like after this is over?

Here's the nitty-gritty: Now when I answer the telephone I mostly just listen. I nod and hang up. I write a note if a note's to be written. Any appeal for help, any threat, any crisis, I'll do my job. But I'm slowly turning into stone. I'd ask myself if I cared, if I cared to ask. But I'm scared. And I'm tired of being fucked with. I tell myself: this is how you survive, this is how you get through it, because some things hurt too much to hear. I know, I know—that won't get me up in the morning. But why get up to daydream?

Can I do this? I tell myself I am. I tell myself I think too much. Most people, after getting shot, they wouldn't stay. So … don't think, don't feel, just do your job. But I failed Morgan that day he was beaten. And now I've failed Deborah … because some things hurt too much to hear.

13 • The Wounded Man

We sent some of our local people to a training session in Charleston. It was two weeks in a big city—most of our people had never been out of state before—and they'd earned this trip. Morgan and I didn't go.

On the bus ride back, through the hills of Mississippi—regular bus, commercial bus—everybody'd been in good spirits up till then, but as soon as that bus hits those Mississippi hills— The very first stop our people get off to stretch their legs, use the restroom, get themselves a soda. Getting back on the driver keeps all the Negroes off until the Whites have boarded, so now our people have no place else but the back of the bus. Well, that wasn't going to keep *them* down. Deborah and Aunt Ertharin lead freedom songs and we—our people—they fill that bus with song. So the bus driver starts making telephone calls on each of his stops along the way. But nothing happens, not yet.

The last stop before Williams Point is in Winona, in the Hills, just east of here. The terminal's crawling with cops. So most of our people stay put, but four get off for the restroom and café—Aunt Ertharin and Deborah, and two other women—Annelle Branch and Euvester Raines.

That's all we know when the others get back and check in like they're supposed to. They tell us that those four never got back on. When it was time to go, they told the driver they were short four people. They say he didn't care. They say he didn't wait.

Morgan calls every police and sheriff's office from Williams Point to Winona. We know you have our people he tells them; we know you want to kill them. We know all about it. And the Justice Department knows, and the FBI knows. But it's a bluff. We don't know where they are. So we sit and wait for our lawyers in Jackson, for Justice, the FBI, for newspaper reporters—anybody who could tell us something—we wait for them to call. And bail money, we have to raise bail money. Johanna calls her father. Isaac calls his.

The telephone: we're staring at it. Or we turn away, walk around our shitty little office. Today that telephone's the biggest thing in it. For once we want it to ring.

But it doesn't.

When it rings Morgan grabs the phone. "Hello? Winona you say? What're the charges? What's the bail?"

Johanna calls her father again. He's to wire the money to our lawyers in Jackson. They'll take it to Winona and get our people out and drive them here. Johanna gives him their numbers. More waiting—

When the telephone rings, Morgan picks it up again. Isaac grabs some car keys from the table.

Morgan's still holding the receiver. It's our lawyers in Jackson. "They've got the bail money," Morgan says. "They're leaving now for Winona."

Isaac's almost to the door. "I'm going too. There's no reason they should bring our people all the way here and then drive back to Jackson. It'll be too dark by then. I'm going to be there when they arrive. I'll bring our people back."

Morgan glares at Isaac. "Aleck, you go."

Isaac shakes his head. "No. What does he do once he gets there? If he's there before our lawyers come, what's to keep him from being arrested too? But they won't mess with me. My father's rich. Isn't that what I'm here for?"

Johanna's at the office door. "I'm going with you."

I follow them out to the car and take Isaac aside. "Don't let them intimidate you. Don't be rude, but don't flinch. And this is important. There's a gas station just outside of town. Stop there. Fill up so you'll have plenty of gas to get back. And talk to the attendant, he'll be a White guy there in the Hills. Shake his hand, smile, and be polite. If he's older than you are, call him sir. Then tell him who you are and tell him you're meeting a lawyer in Winona to get some people out of jail. After you leave he'll call the police and they'll know you're coming and that a lawyer's coming too. And if you see a pay phone, call Justice and make sure they telephone the jail."

Johanna's taken the keys from Isaac's hand. The car's already running when he gets in.

⸻

Isaac and Johanna tell me when they get back: Aunt Ertharin, Deborah, Annelle Branch, and Euvester Raines—their clothes were bloody and torn, blood crusted in their hair, their faces bruised and swollen. Aunt Ertharin couldn't walk, her back was hurt so bad. She had to take Isaac's arm. He pretty much carried her to our car. Annelle and Euvester needed help too. Johanna helped Annelle get in the car and whispered to her, "You're safe now." Annelle, her eyes just stared vacant, but she whispered back, just one word—*freedom*.

Deborah was the last one out. Even though she staggered, and one eye was swollen and shut, she walked out of that jail alone, hobbling, bent to one side, but upright. She wouldn't let anybody touch her. She wouldn't let any White person have the satisfaction to see her needing anybody's help.

A couple of days later she asks for me, and I go to see her. She's finally out of bed, she's dressed and sitting in her chair facing the room. Her eye's still bad. I sit down on her bed. The room looks too small for her now, she shares it with her sister, and it's for little girls. That's how I see it, and Deborah isn't little anymore. We're the only ones in the house.

She says she wants to tell me "everything." "I've got to tell somebody ... you and Morgan are the only ones not from here and Morgan thinks I'm trouble ... so that leaves you."

I don't know what that means but I nod. "Go ahead." But now, looking back—well, there's a consequence to everything you hear.

So while she's telling me her story I realize: this is a mistake. Not hers. Mine. She's speaking slowly, in very measured tones, almost in a monotone. You'd almost think she was telling me something about a stranger, but no ... no. She's not. This is the only way she can say what she's saying and not start screaming. And everything she says cuts too close.

I stand up. I can't hear this. What's she's telling me ... I don't want to know it, how her people—our people—my people—can disappoint us so. Old Aunt Hagar's children. I've worked too long and hard for them. And I can't do any more than I have. But what she's telling me, she's telling it to change me, to make me do something more, to feel something more.

But some things hurt too much to hear.

I tell her to stop. "What do you want from me?" But I don't wait for an answer; I'm turning for the door. Deborah stands up; she's looking right at me. She's saying something but I don't hear it. She grabs my hand. I sling it free. Now she's shouting: "Listen to me!" She's blocking her door. I put my hands on her shoulders ... and very gently ... I move her aside. Her face is pleading with me. And mine is pleading with her.

I flee the room. I want to be dead inside, it hurts so much. While I was moving her aside I was asking her—silently—please don't struggle, please don't fight. I so desperately didn't want to grab and shove her. But only because I could only do the least I could. I didn't want to *deal* with her. Now, I can't help thinking about my father and me. All those years as a child I wanted my father to do something—anything—even if that meant he'd hit me. And all I ever got? It just never was enough.

That's just what Deborah got from me. So I figure: if she was me, if I look in the mirror—

I'll see who I'm becoming.

24 • The Drowned Man

Williams Point, Mississippi: 1959–1960

First Emily proposed. Then they began their courtship. Thinking back, Harry couldn't remember when they'd first met. She was part of the crowd he'd fallen with. They were younger than him but they'd accepted him anyway. Everyone had a nickname, so they called him "Stranger."

Harry marveled that he had any friends at all, in this new place, in his fourth life. There were supper parties and movies, jaunts to Greenville and Memphis, and for the men, late Friday nights in their favorite bar. To Harry, it was so easy to fall into these friendships, as easy as floating down a river. The current takes you and all is quiet and still. Even amid the laughter, the lights and the noise, it's just a lazy river.

He did wonder if, back in his first life, he would've liked them. Probably not. They cultivated a cool insolence, an easy superiority. He wouldn't have liked that. But now ... it was such a luxury to have them. And—this at least—like him, they didn't care for the planters, the older powers that be. *Those* people were a bunch of "Old Figs"—that's what this crowd called them. Those people thought they were always on a stick—that's what this crowd said. And Harry would think of how his father had bought him—had even expected too—for just a few hundred dollars: that high handedness, that's just like the planters here, and Harry would settle himself in the booth in the bar and cradle his drink on the table. Their Friday nights: four men, five men, sometimes there'd be six, huddled together in their dark corner table; Carl Perkins, Elvis, and Jerry Lee on the jukebox and all the voices in the room—slurred and male—as thick and dim as the cigarette smoke around their table, like they were outside on a close and foggy night—and sometimes a woman's laugh, a shriek like lightning. They had to whisper loud to be heard but not overheard, and Lloyd Grove would do most of the talking and reach out his hands to make a point, and somebody else would laugh, and another would nudge Harry in his side, and Harry would nod his head, and all their movements were slightly exaggerated, and the table was ringed and wet with water and ice, whiskey and beer.

This crowd, his crowd now, called themselves the "Turks." Lloyd's smile slowly opened and he explained to Harry. "We used to be the Young Turks. But we all got married, we all got kids. We're sure as hell not young anymore. So now we're just the Turks."

And, later, with a little more liquor Lloyd complained, "So if *we're* getting older, how come *they* aren't?" Lloyd leaned back and held out his hands, palms up. He was talking about the planters. "They don't seem to—how can it be?—once you reach a certain age, do you just stop aging? *They* just keep hanging on. They never die off." A slow shake of his head and then that smile. "What this town needs is a bunch of prominent funerals."

Harry wasn't sure what their beef was. He was told there'd been a tussle over bringing in industries, the planters were against that, and the last mayor, who was for it, whom the Turks had supported, had been voted out. "Those Old Figs, they called us a bunch of 'nigger lovers.' Can you believe that? That's how they voted us out. And our mayor now? Tommy Lott?" Lloyd rolled his eyes. But businesses still were coming in—*trickling* in, somebody else said—so maybe neither side won. Harry wasn't sure. But it little mattered. Old Figs, Young Turks, they all shared the same churches and clubs, the same businesses and kin. "This is the peace of money and blood," Lloyd told him. By now they were the last ones in the bar. The music and voices were gone; only the smoke remained. Lloyd was speaking so softly, Harry had to lean closer to hear. "One would think money and blood would stir people up. After all, all over the world money and blood have kept people stirred up from time immemorial. But here ... money and blood is the glue." Lloyd was staring into his glass. His lips barely moved. "And we're all stuck." Then he looked up and smiled. "Forget it. It's a fool thing. Come on Stranger, it's last call, let's buy ourselves another round."

"Peace"—peace like a river, that still and silent river—but over time Harry began to see it, to recognize it on people's faces: a weariness and wariness that once he saw, he knew had always been there, if only he'd have noticed it before.

One evening Harry's doorbell rang and Emily was there. She'd never called on him alone before. She had a wild look in her eyes; her mouth was slightly open. Had she been crying? Harry stared at her for a second before asking her in. She just stood there, looking at him, before finally coming in.

Emily. Black hair and a heart-shaped face, not so plain. At their movie nights and at their suppers, she always sat beside him. One night Harry realized—there she was again, she was always next to him. He hadn't thought much about it. Most everybody else were couples. She was a widow; he told them he was a widower. (In his heart, he believed that.) She had a little boy. He told them his boy was dead. (In a matter of speaking, he was.) So why not sit together? Truth be told, he liked her. But even then, he hadn't known her intentions, or had any of his own. And now, here she was at his doorstep, unannounced and unexpected.

He took her to his living room, just inside his front door. He sat her down in the first chair there. He brought her some water and stood in front of her to watch her drink. She held the glass in both her hands, leaning forward, her shoulders hunched, but looking straight up at him. Then she said the words, "Will you marry me?"

Harry stared. Her face—he was looking right at her but if he'd been asked what she looked like, her expression, he couldn't have answered. All he knew was that he couldn't refuse.

She went on. "I won't lie to you. My son needs a father. He needs one right away."

He thought back to all those times: her sitting beside him. How could he not have understood? He wanted to tell her—

She wouldn't stop. "What I mean to say is—," she turned her head away and then looked back at him, "—he needs a father *right now*. He needs somebody who can protect him from my mother." She clamped her mouth shut, as if saying, 'There, I said it,' and looked defiant, as if expecting to be slapped.

Harry took the glass from her hand. "It's alright. I don't mind." He held her hands. Could he love her? He thought he could. And how could he say it? Her boy would be his reason too.

The defiance was gone. Her eyes were wide and wild again. "I want to explain—"

Harry shook his head no.

"No. Wait. Please. You'll need to know this."

So he nodded yes.

"My mother's a horrible person. She's domineering, she thinks she knows what's best for everybody, and when you look at her house! I had to grow up there! You should see it. She's terrible to her Negroes, she's obsessed with the Negroes, and she's always tried to run my life—she thinks it's her right to run my life—and here I am, I'm a thirty-five-year-old woman, I'm a mother and a widow, and she still wants to run my life, and now she wants to run my child's life too."

She wrung her hands. "You've probably heard all that ... it's not news ... people have probably told you." She looked at him, pleading, like she thought he wasn't listening. "But you don't know this: she wants my boy in her house! I won't have it. That house! It's crazy. She's crazy ... living there! But family's first around here. You can't go against your mama—people think you're being disrespectful, but then, first thing when they're alone they'll say she's crazy too—they know! Everybody knows! But you're still not supposed to go against her. I can't stand up to her. I should, but I'm not allowed to ... and besides, I can't."

She was near tears. He'd been told she was the nervous type. It was said her whole family was of the nervous type. He watched her. She was trembling. Was it her nerves? Or was it the shame, or the mere effort, of her telling him this?

She smoothed out the skirt of her dress. "When Albert was alive, he would stand up to her. He could stand between her and our son. A man has prerogatives a woman hasn't. But ever since he died, Evy's been defenseless. He needs a father anyway—but he really needs a man who can protect him. He's such a good boy. You've seen him. He's well behaved. And I ... I've got a little money and I'll be easy to live with. I won't make any demands."

She stopped and caught her breath and now, suddenly, she was crying. Harry put his hand on her shoulder. Feeling her body underneath her clothes—what he felt wasn't just pity, and it was even more than empathy.

He had been a long time without a woman.

Thus began their courtship. In the days ahead she told him she was ashamed of her raising, of her parents and their house. When she was a child, she never had friends over—and the worst part about it? They never asked her why, because they knew why, because everybody in town knew why—that Del Ray and Ester Kimbrough were oddities, that Del Ray's Uncle Lamar was an oddity. Their blood was odd, it had gone wrong, and the living proof was their house, where Uncle Lamar had raised Del Ray in conditions scandalous after his father died. And nothing about that house ever changed, not after Uncle Lamar left it to Del Ray, and not after Ester married into it. And after Del Ray died, Ester stayed and still changed nothing.

And she, Emily—she knew people said this—she was a ticking time bomb because one day she'd show what she has always been, what with her odd blood: an eccentric, a "Crazy Kimbrough."

"I've had my friends, I 'came out,' but I've always wondered, why it took me so long to marry, and Albert, he came from out of town, like you—"

She told him all of this, many times. She would not have him under false pretenses.

She hated her mother. "She thinks she's superior. She thinks she's the last matron of a proud lineage—the great Kimbroughs! And she's not even their blood, she's not even from the South, she was born in Boston—and they haven't been 'great' since over fifty years ago when Del Ray's father lost his place."

"They," "Del Ray," but never "my family" and never "my father." Emily spoke as though they weren't her people. Only her mother, whom she hated most, her she called "my mother."

She described their house—which Harry had only seen in passing—outlandish stories he could scarcely believe—old boxes stacked high in every room, almost to the ceiling; piled newspapers over fifty-years old; fresh-caught fish thrown into desk drawers.

———

She didn't tell him everything. Others told him more. They told him that after losing his plantation, the next person to see Samuel Yerger Kimbrough was his brother Lamar when he found him in Samuel's bedroom. Samuel was in bed, sitting against the headboard alongside his wife, both in their Sunday best, and their bedding was stiff from their blood, which also formed two starbursts against the headboard and the wall, wreathed with flies. The double-barreled shotgun, cold now and spent, lay upon his belly and between his legs, where it had fallen from his grasp.

When they moved Samuel, they found he'd sat in his wife's own blood on the bedding before he aimed the second barrel at his head.

Nor did Emily tell him much about her father—only that Del Ray used to wear, every day, white shoes and a white hat. To humor him, people would always remark about his shoes and he'd say with a smile, "White is the best color there is. You can keep your black shoes—white's the only color for me." He wore those shoes, Emily explained, just so he could say that. To the ladies, and to all the little girls, he would bow low from his waist before he passed them, and he would doff his hat with a flourish.

He was long dead but the people Harry asked still remembered his little speech and how he'd doff his hat. On the street they'd smile and say, yeah, that's what we'd ask him and that's what he'd say. It was his harmless little joke. But privately they'd admit: he was crazy as a loon ... and dangerous. They'd drop their smiles and lower their voices; they'd tell Harry stories like this one: "One morning Del Ray was driving out on Route 8. He saw a Colored sleeping alongside the road. This Colored had a suitcase, Del Ray tells me, a nice one: too nice. So Del Ray pulls over. He says he just happened to have a hoe in his trunk—sharp hoe. So he takes out that hoe, and kicks the sole of that Colored boy's shoe to wake him up, so he'll see that hoe come down—Del Ray took off the top of that Colored boy's head. He'd tell that story himself."

And another one: "Del Ray hears about a Colored doctor living in Jackson; hears he was doing pretty good. Del Ray had never heard of him before, but he goes out to that Colored's house, hides in the bushes just beside his driveway—early in the morning, see?—and shoots him when he comes out for his car. He told us that. He'd say, 'I might not have done it, except when I got there I saw he had a driveway and a carport for his car. So I had to kill him.' He was always telling stories like that. It's hard to know what was true and what was bragging, but that man was crazy as a loon."

Those were the stories she didn't tell.

◆——◆

Harry asked around about Del Ray's house. "I hear it's a strange one, inside."

People told him yes, it was. People even told him about the fish in the drawers, but nobody had seen one. Nobody had even been in it, not for many years.

"Then how do you know it's strange?" Harry asked Lloyd this. They were in Lloyd's office, Harry in the client's chair and Lloyd behind his desk. Law books climbed to the ceiling behind him.

Lloyd smiled. "Harry, I know it just like I know most of what there is to know about this town. From the time I was in knee pants, and could understand what two words were when they were said together, people have talked about that house in my hearing, and what it's like inside." Now he frowned. "Nobody's said anything crossways from what I first heard. That house is a crazy house. It's no place to raise a child."

He leaned back in his chair, smiled again, and fixed his eyes on Harry. "So why are you marrying her, Harry? Is it Emily or the boy?"

⭆⭅

The boy was ten. He'd lost his father at seven. When they found themselves together, Harry and Evy didn't talk much. Evy would play and Harry would watch. Once, when Emily was in her house and they were alone in her backyard, Harry had asked him, casually, cautiously, did he miss his father? Evy didn't look up, he was hunched over his toy soldiers on the lawn, as if he hadn't heard—but wasn't there the slightest hesitation in his play? Harry was sure he'd seen it. Gently, softly, he told Evy: "I lost my little boy."

Evy waddled one tin soldier to another. "Mama told me." Then he looked up. "Mama says I remind you of him."

Harry, who was leaning on a nearby tree, now stood straight. He looked down at the boy. "That's right, Evy."

Evy hesitated. He stood; he looked straight up at Harry.

Harry knelt. He put his hand to Evy's head. "He was a sweet boy—just like you. His name was Timothy."

"And he's ... the same place ... my father is?"

"Yes, Evy ... yes. They're in heaven."

Neither said another word. Evy crouched back down to his toys. Harry regretted the exchange. He could never tell anybody, not even this boy, the truth about his children.

So how could he hold it against Emily, for the things she hadn't told him?

He couldn't even tell her everything he thought about her boy, because there was also Evy's playmate, a Negro boy named Lucius, the help's boy. He was the go-getter. You could see it when they played—Lucius thought up the games and always took the lead, and Evy happily tagged along and completed the scene. Lucius reminded Harry of Earley, his second boy lost. Harry Jr. had been his first. One little boy White, then one little boy Black, and then the third was Timothy, but the Timothy he'd lost had been a man.

Visiting, Harry would watch the two boys play, him at Emily's front window, them in the yard. He smiled—Evy and Lucius. That Lucius sure had spirit. Earley had spirit too. What was he doing now? Harry knew he was still alive: he accepted Harry's letters, though he hardly wrote a reply of his own. How long ago was his last? It had been years. Harry would have to look for it. Was he well? Was he married? Did he have children of his own? When he was a boy, Earley never had a

White playmate and Harry thought it had been better that way. Evy and Lucius—in time their friendship would have to stop. What would happen to Lucius when that time came? How would he take his banishment? And how would Evy take his role as banisher?

Then something happened: Evy paused and looked right at Harry through the window, and Harry thought his face was beautiful. Evy was telling him something, just by his look. He was saying: See this, Lucius and me playing? I love this. And there was more. Evy was saying that he knew, already, what Black and White meant and that he didn't care, because playing here with his go-getter friend was his only unalloyed joy.

So Harry knew. When the banishment comes, both boys will take it badly.

And that look of Evy's right through the window—Harry came to believe they understood each other. They were secret sharers, and what they shared they never told.

Turning from the window, Harry saw himself in a mirror—his image was a perfect reflection; the mirror's surface was unblemished. It struck him how he rarely noticed his reflection anymore, because now it was normal again, instead of flawed.

But what, exactly, was normal?

That question: a remnant from his second life. Here, he had begun to think himself one person again. No longer split in two. But ... was he?

Harry frowned into the mirror. Once they were married, and he moved in, he would have it moved. Just then Emily joined him—the two of them in the mirror. She gestured over to the window. "Would you believe it? My mother told me she doesn't want Evy to play with his little friend. What's that little boy supposed to do while Calpurnia cooks and cleans? Should they each be playing alone in the same house? They're children. Children! There's nothing wrong!"

Harry hadn't answered so Lloyd leaned forward and asked him again. "Is it Emily or the boy?"

Harry still didn't answer. He smiled instead.

"I'll take that as a yes." Lloyd rested his forearms on his desk. "I don't know if you understand what you're doing. Miss Ester wanted to institute power of attorney proceedings against her daughter." He placed a finger, point down, on his desk and tapped it after every phrase he spoke. "She was inquiring, about the possibility, of declaring Emily mentally incompetent, and taking custody of the child."

"What the hell?"

"Yes, what the hell—but now you're in the picture."

"Who told you this?"

"A little birdie. Does it matter? But now you're in the picture, and that's stopped her, so you better stay in it. After y'all get married, you better stay straight my friend, because Miss Ester will be watching you."

"But how?"

"How could she take the boy? Because there's no husband, no father anymore." Here Lloyd grinned, he looked wolfish. "But also because of the Kimbrough blood, which she doesn't have, but which courses though her daughter's veins. Miss Ester pointed out it tends to suicide. She overplayed her hand on that one. Some people still think well of the Kimbrough blood ... or, at least, they regret how it turned out. And when it comes down to it, Miss Ester's not from here, so who's she to say. That got the little birdies talking."

"But she's stopped all that now, because of me?"

"For now, yes, because of you and the little birdies. She made a mistake there, but she won't do that again. Like I said, you be sure you fly right—Stranger." Then he dropped his smile, "—because that house is no place to raise a child."

Harry had to see it for himself. One day, when he knew Miss Ester would be shopping with her maid, he drove over, checked out all the neighbors' windows, and walked up to her porch. He took one last look at her neighbors' windows, then he opened her door and walked on in. The air smelled of mildew, dust, and sweat. The windows were shut and the blinds were drawn. Harry paused to let his eyes adjust. The hall rug was worn, its edges unraveled, its pattern faded, and dingy brown down the middle. Harry crossed to the front room and there he saw the boxes Emily had spoken of, piled up high, the lower ones wooden, the upper ones cardboard. They leaned, this way and that, like trees in a forest seeking a sun. He stood on tip-toe and slid one off to look inside. He found broken shards of china plate, thick with dust that came off on his fingertips. On the table were newspapers and magazines, stacked to the ceiling, too high for Ester or her maid to have put them there. He stood up on a chair and reached for the highest one. It was a *Commercial-Appeal* from twenty years before. The next one was a *Clarion-Ledger*, from the same year, the same week. Newer editions littered the floor. It was a forest of paper, cardboard, and wood, with no wind to sway it and no light to filter through; it was musty and dust-choked, and anchored down as if by its own weight and mass. Harry did not wonder how it could have stood so long, or, indeed, if it could stand forever.

He went from room to room. They were all the same. In the study he found a rolltop desk, open, gorged with papers, magazines, and newspapers. A nib pen was nestled in between them. He moved a stack of papers aside to find the inkwell behind. Dust spewed into his face and he stepped back, sneezing. He opened the inkwell and found it dry. One drawer was stuck; it seemed too full to open. But the other did. Harry jerked back and grimaced. Inside was a fish, dead, flat, its skin brittle and black, its eye open as if in wonderment that this, such a strange fate, should befall it. So that story was true.

Going upstairs, Harry reached for the banister. It tilted away from his weight. Harry let go and kept to the wall as he ascended. He didn't dare go into Mrs. Kimbrough's bedroom—at least he thought it was hers; through the barely open door he saw the bed, imperious, and the clutter there as well. One room, however, was clear. It held a child's bed, a stool, a chifferobe, and a desk with a chipped porcelain bowl, filled with water. Harry stuck his finger in the water. The dust upon it eddied and curled. The bed cover was old and faded; pink, with flamingos. He opened the blind and tried the window. It was nailed shut. He pulled the blind back down and returned downstairs, rubbing his hands with his handkerchief as he walked. Near the hallway to the door, a glinting light caught his eye. The door to the den was open. It was separate from the other rooms and he had not yet gone in. There was no clutter of papers and boxes there. But crowded on the mantel, on the desk, on the bookshelves, were mason jars filled with water. But not ordinary water, the liquid was green and cloudy. Harry came closer. They were pickling jars, filled with brine. Inside—he picked up one to better see—inside was a human ear, dark and gray, unreal. Harry almost dropped the jar. He set it back down and rubbed his hand across his shirt. He couldn't believe—He was spinning around, at the mantel, desk and shelves. In every jar a human ear—if he were to count them all, he'd know the number of Del Ray's victims. Or were some of them Lamar's? Harry's hands flew to his face, his palms to his mouth, his fingers to his eyes. He fled from the room and ran to his car.

25 • The Drowned Man

They married in Emily's church. Her childhood friends, the Turks, her family—so many people, Harry felt crowded. But that night Emily confessed that she was so ashamed there were so few people she could invite.

They lived in Emily's house. Harry's was too small and Emily wanted Evy to keep his room. Harry kept his safe-deposit box in the bank for his snapshots and his letters. Emily knew nothing about them. He told her about the box—there was no use keeping it a secret, there were no secrets here, not in this town—but he lied about what was in it: his birth certificate, an insurance policy, old business records. She didn't seem to mind not knowing about his past. Harry understood; she was that desperate to have a father for her son.

Before they married Harry knew the Kimbrough house would always bother him. This was a family of murderers. But there was the boy and there was something else—

Before they married he once had asked her why she hadn't gone away. She told him if he wanted an answer she'd have to take him to the Hills. They drove to Carroll County, just east of Williams Point, to a cemetery outside of Carrollton. She let Evy run to play. He lost himself in the trees, zigzagging between them.

"He knows this place like the back of his hand."

Here in the Hills the land dipped and rolled. The church was old—it looked abandoned. A wrought iron fence, only inches high, marked the cemetery's boundary. Harry almost stumbled on it. He thought of a line of jacks set out by a child in an overgrown yard serenely ignorant of order ... his Timothy—and maybe Evy. Green ash and white elms stood nearby, and the branches of giant oaks curved out over the graves like a parent's indulgent and protective arms.

Emily led Harry to a spot. "This is our family's corner. They lived here in Carrollton before they moved to the Delta." Emily walked among the newer graves; then she took his hand. She knelt by two tombstones and Harry knelt with her. "This is my great-grandfather, James Bledsoe Kimbrough, and my Bigma—my great-grandmother, Elise Yerger Kimbrough. I have a picture of her I'll want to show you. You know I met her once. But I was too young to remember it. This is what I remember, these gravestones. They're my only ... my fondest memory ... of my family." She stood and pointed in turn. "There's Uncle Charles—great, great uncle, actually—with Aunt Clarice, and Grandfather Samuel." She paused for a moment.

"I'm sorry." She daubed her eye. "I didn't mean to cry." She walked over to Uncle Charles's grave. "Look, kneel down. See, you can't read it. It's almost worn smooth. Touch it, Harry.

"I never met him. And this gravestone's been worn down ever since I can remember. But I know it's his. Not by reading, but by its location. And Evy, he'll know too, because I've told him, over and over, and even though he probably doesn't care now, he'll still remember."

Emily sat down in the grass. Harry stood above her, looking down.

She looked up at him, shading her eyes with her hand. "It's these older graves I love the most. Do you know why? It's because I can't read them. I just know them, like I know that tree over there. I carved my name in it a long time ago. Someday I hope that wears smooth." She paused for a moment, looking at the tree, then back at Harry. "When I'm buried here, and you as well, our graves will be intrusions, like each of these were. But when enough years go by, we won't be intrusions anymore. Our tombstones will be worn smooth, they'll be just as natural here as Uncle Charley's grave, and that tree I carved my name on. Just stones and trees, scattered on the grass, that's all; we'll belong here as much as anything could. It'll be ours, and somebody will know this is where Great, Great Aunt Emily lies, long after my stone's worn smooth, and a little boy will have his run of the place, and he'll know too." She reached up her hand. "Help me up, Harry.

"Just look at me—the only ones I can abide are the dead ones." Standing, facing him close, she took hold of his hands. "I took Albert here when we were courting." She laughed. "Pretty romantic stuff, huh? But he was like you. He came from somewhere else too. He didn't have much family either. I told him, 'You do now, you have all this now.' And it worked. Do you know—he proposed to me the very next day."

Harry smiled. Was there any courtship like these? He asked her, "Where's his grave?"

Emily tightened her hold on his hands. "We'd been married such a short time. His sister came. She wanted the body. Mother let her have it. She said he was more his sister's family than ours. Really, I think it was Mother's idea to begin with. I wouldn't be surprised if she told his sister to come and carry him back with her." She put her hands to her face. "I'm sorry. I didn't come here to cry. I wanted to tell you, this is why I couldn't ever leave. I could never go far away. Do you understand that? And you, you won't die so soon. So you'll be here too. One of us ... in heaven ... one will wait for the other."

Back at Emily's house Evy sprung from the car to the back yard. "Lucius! Lucius!" Emily and Harry settled in her parlor and looked through her family album. The once black pages now were gray and the faded photographs were smudged and gray as well. Uncle Charles, Aunt Clarice, and Great Grandfather James, and the photo she wanted him particularly to see: three women, each of a different generation, and a baby on the oldest's knee. The youngest held a saxophone. Harry pointed to her.

"Who's the lady with the saxophone?"

Emily smiled. "That's Big. She's my aunt." She pointed out the others. "This is her mother, BaMa—she's my grandfather's sister—and her mother, Bigma—her's was one of the first graves I showed you, my great grandmother Elise—and she's holding Big's little girl, Sissie." Her finger went back to Big. "Have you ever heard of such a thing: a woman playing the saxophone?" Emily laughed. "I never even knew any man who played a saxophone—just a few boys in high school. And she could play that thing! She liked to play show tunes."

Harry looked back at the photograph. "She doesn't look big."

"Silly, her name was Sarah. She wasn't big. It was just, Bigma, BaMa, and Big. Even her husband called her Big. Don't you get it?"

Harry shrugged.

But that's it, right there, he thought. He didn't care particularly where he'd be buried. But a woman everybody calls Big, her mother BaMa, and a saxophone—in the Delta, White people could do what they damn well pleased, and nobody thought it odd. Your spinster aunt from Greenville could stay with you for three weeks, or four months, or five years, and one day she'll wake up and see it was sunny, and a fancy would take her: she'll pack her bags and your car will carry her home, clear across the Delta; and once home she'll send word to her help and send your car to pick up that woman too—and she, the help, will come, no matter who she's working for now, to air out the house and dust it. And each of those days, the leaving home and returning after years away, will be as serene and normal as can be.

Harry thought of his first day in Williams Point—the still and silent river.

Emily's relations: despite the Kimbrough name, few of them had been rich. Most were middling: store keepers or plantation managers, with modest homes, but with one maid for the upstairs and one for the down, and with a cook and a driver too. Their money dribbled to a stop every summer, only to burst back with the cotton, when everybody got paid, just in time for Christmas and the gala balls. Harry could see them in his mind's eye, going about their business, but always thinking about the cotton, maybe with a quiver of doubt, held private, if the weather'd been bad, so they'd drive to the biggest plantations and watch their cotton grow. *Their* cotton—they didn't own it, they didn't grow it—but in some ways it was their cotton, as well as the planters' too. And the rich planters were no different, their money ran out in the summer too. Rich or middling, everybody rowed the same boat, hoped for the same things, and when the living was good everything was serene, and easy, just like the river. At least, that was how things were supposed to be.

Somebody had told him, it must have been Lloyd: Cuban cigars taste best at their last inch, where the nicotine collects. And this Delta is the last inch of the southern Black Belt, before the country turns west, and it's saturated in its own kind of juices. When people here tell you what they're about, it's the heroes and the oddballs they talk about. That's why the Delta loves its own, even his awkward Emily. That's the ideal. And, Harry thought, it's real enough often enough—(Harry could hear the boys playing outside.)—Often enough to make himself a bet. So Harry put it all in the balance: Emily's mother and her house and the wariness he saw on people's faces, against this serene easiness and Emily herself, and against the boys, especially the boys. He put up his money and put down his bet.

Life. That sonofabitch. It had caught him out again.

26 • The Drowned Man

Drinking in the bar, Harry would settle back against the booth and enjoy the dim, shadowed light and listen to the Turks. They'd pass around a bottle. He'd ask them for their stories about Horatio County and Williams Point.

When he came, his reason for staying had been simple—a peaceful river had matched an image in his mind. As small a life as possible. That had been his only aspiration then. But now he had a family and these men, these friends, and the South was deeper than the surface of any river, so Harry never tired of hearing their stories. He wanted to learn more about this Delta where he'd stopped his traveling and left what was westward to itself.

There'd been a West here too, maybe the last frontier in the forty-eight states, saddling the turn of the century. In their wagons and on their horses, the country had rushed right past it, headlong westward, like a flood around an islet in a river; past its cane breaks and its cypress, its holly, ash and oak and gum; and underneath was the richest land in the country, right under the noses of the pioneers rushing westward like a fast river flooding.

Main Street was mud back then. Liquor was plenty and wives and mothers were scarce, sheltered in the neighboring Hills from the Delta's malarial air—Lloyd would feed his whiskey with water while he told his story—there were gunshots in the street and horses in the saloons. "This was in the 1890s—a man named Thomas had himself a new saloon, and he'd cut a pile of wood pole length and stacked it in a corner for firewood in the winter. Well, all the men in there—I won't call any names but even you, Stranger, you would know those names by now, those men were all high up back then, they ran things—and they were having too much fun drinking that night, so when Thomas called out closing time they got themselves a good idea. Just for fun. They took that wood and put it up log cabin style and put ole Mr. Thomas up over inside it. Then they brought in their horses. They rode around Mr. Thomas' establishment and practiced shooting the bottles off his bar and off the shelves behind it. The object was to shoot the bottles and miss the mirror behind them. They were as drunk as Cooter Brown, but for all that—I reckon they aimed okay. And did the liquor flow! They had themselves their own little flood amongst the bottle shards and mirror shards and the sawdust on the floor. Little rivers of whiskey that bunched the sawdust up like levees and sharecropper shacks out there in the fields. All through this Mr. Thomas just stayed put. Now maybe he could've gotten out and maybe he couldn't, but if he could his discretion saved his day. And when every bottle was either drunk dry or shot to pieces, those men said their fare-thee-wells—but the next day they returned and paid Mr. Thomas for his liquor and his mirror, and about twice over that for his forbearance and good cheer. They were all prominent men from around here, our first families—I'll tell you this, one went on to become the governor of this state, and then a United States senator—and they were good customers too.

"And those muddy streets. We had a mayor—he had a vision that these saloons and cotton factors and general stores could actually be a town. He'd tried to get Main Street paved, but you can't let your cattle loose on macadam, so that idea had to wait its time." Lloyd took a sip. "So the mayor got an ordinance passed prohibiting the free roaming of livestock on the city streets—such streets as they were."

Lloyd hunched his shoulders and leaned over the table, his long, horse-like face grinning. The air around the table was full of smoke and liquor and dust and water, like a universe where life first sprang, and maybe you could make your life here, you could fashion it out of the words of your own telling—it seemed to Harry to be such a privilege if that were so.

Lloyd went on. "Now this I find fascinating—as a lawyer and a student of the law I find this fascinating. When I was younger, I would wonder, how did he get that passed? It was very controversial. Hell, nobody wanted it but him. And nobody had any mind to obey it. And then I realized—that was why it passed! Why not? Nobody would enforce it.

"But the mayor did. He was underestimated, it seems. His name was Mr. Milton Carroll. Here's what happened: the county sheriff—he was Captain L.T. Beecham—he'd let his cattle out and Mr. Milton had them impounded. When Captain Beecham heard, he went straight over to the impounding pen and, wearing his badge to show that this was no law to respect, he turned them out and drove them home. And Mr. Milton Carroll arrested him, did it himself, and marched him over to the jail, the city jail, just long enough to scare up a judge, and had him tried and fined, and that was the end of that. There was no more free roaming on the city streets.

"Now notice here: the mayor arrested him. Not the chief of police. The mayor. Because the chief of police wouldn't have done it, and nor should he—it was the mayor's law, or should I say, it was Mr. Milton Carroll's law, because, really, him being mayor had nothing to do with him enforcing it.

"Now, like I said, this is fascinating. The law I learned in law school was no respecter of persons. You'd find it in a book, and you'd apply it, as a policeman or a judge, just as good any other cop or judge would. That law was its own authority. You, as a policeman or a judge, or a mayor or commissioner, you got your authority from the law—those words, written on paper, in a book. But here, back then, only Mr. Milton Carroll himself could enforce that law because it was *his* law, it was passed as his law, and it had no authority save what he could give it.

"So Mr. Milton Carroll had to face down ole Cap Beecham and make that man come with him and be locked up in jail, and once he'd done that the rest was a foregone conclusion, because—well, it gets down to this: Milton Carroll facing Captain Beecham, it didn't matter which one wore a badge and which one didn't, one of them had to think, 'This man facing me could kill me on the spot, and he couldn't care less, much less, than I would care killing him.' The man who thinks that first loses. That's what made a man here, the utter lack of concern about the consequences of his actions. He'd clear the ground he stood on.

"All that stuff about the law being something written. Not here. Here it was pride and honor, and force of will. If you had to rely on something written down in a book, or a parchment, stored in some building in Jackson, you'd never be looked to, or spoken of, or obeyed. I don't know when that ended. I don't know if it ever ended," he looked around at the others, "but it must've, right?" Lloyd grinned and spun his empty shot glass on the table like a top. "God damn! Those were men!"

Harry would listen, holding his drink, moving it from one hand to the other, and thinking, *I've seen that pride and honor. I drank with it. I drove the car for it.* He wondered if those long-ago planters, or Lloyd, or any of the other men at their table, would recognize it in Negroes. Planters: Harry still didn't like them. What they did for honor was just for themselves, to bend people to their will, like his father had, paying Harry off in money. Those Black men in that car? Harry felt a twinge every time he thought of them, but those men had wanted justice, as best as they could get it. *Uncle John's eyes! Looking at me. He tried to save me!* Justice had been the last thing on these planters' minds.

Harry smiled and put down his glass. "Is all that really true, Lloyd? Don't you exaggerate just a little bit?"

Lloyd shrugged. He tilted his head. "Hell, a story isn't worth telling if it isn't exaggerated. What's the point of telling it, if you don't stretch it some?" He poured himself another whiskey and drawled. "That don't mean it ain't true."

"And it was more than vigilantism, because, back then, after a planter had his place cleared out of the wilderness and set up a general store for his croppers, and brought in a railroad line, spur line, and various other White people began to show and cluster around his place—peddlers, poor relations, such like—the next thing he'd do was build a church and then a school. That would be about a ten-year project, to do all that. After ten years, suddenly you had a hamlet; after twenty a town. And the way folks saw it back then, that planter didn't just bring civilization, he *was* the civilization. You've heard of Big Byron Southworth"—suddenly Harry realized that Lloyd was telling *him* all this, not the others there, but him—"one time he loaned some White man—let's call him Louis—the money to do whatever. They were way out in the rural. Big Byron was on horseback and a long ride from his house and no money on him, so he took up a wood chip and some tar that Louis had and wrote him a check right then and there on that wood chip. And there was no doubt in Louis' mind he could take that wood chip to any bank and get it cashed—because, to him, *Big Byron was the bank.* He was law and money and religion too."

Harry was staring at his glass on the table—he felt he was an inch away from where his body was. It must be the drink—too much. He looked up. There was Lloyd. What was his point—to him, to Harry himself? He tried a joke. "Aren't you the sociologist—you should write a book."

Lloyd studied his drink. He must've liked what he saw. "Oh, it's been done—several times, it's been done. You know what we did to all those who wrote them?" He took a sip. "Nothing. Because we never even bothered to read them. We already knew everything we needed to know." He leaned forward and pointed his thumb back at Winslow next to him. "His Uncle Porter played the bugle every night he was drunk. His street woke up to "Taps" at midnight almost every night of the week. And Big Byron's daughter never stopped for a stop sign in her life—or, should I say, she always had her chauffeur drive right through them—and she never paid a red cent for anything she took from a store, and she cut the flowers from your garden for the vase on her table, and she could do all that because nobody's family was bigger and older than the Southworths. They got here first; and your," he pointed at Harry, "your aunt by marriage played the saxophone. And everybody called her Big. So you see, everybody has a story, Stranger."

Harry nodded. Milton Carroll and Big Byron. Winslow's Uncle Porter and Emily's Aunt Big. Big Byron's daughter. People described their communities by their heroes and their oddballs—Harry knew that.

Lloyd nodded back. "Read a book? Why bother? Big Byron's daughter never bought an acre of land in her life. She never bossed the Coloreds into clearing that land, or plowing or planting it, or picking the cotton on it, and she never paid out their shares or made herself her fortune. She didn't bring in a single railroad or start a single town. Her father did all that. Big Byron. But, by God, every time she ran a stop sign or picked a flower from your garden she cleared the ground she stood on, just like her father did. She never married, and everybody in town called her "Auntie Southworth," even those older than her.

"And crazy or not, that's what the Kimbroughs did—they cleared the ground they stood on."

Harry looked down at his drink. He didn't like Lloyd bringing up the Kimbroughs. "Well, if y'all like them so much—these Southworths and such—why are y'all against them? Why call them Old Figs?"

Lloyd leaned forward—his 'this is serious' pose. "Because this isn't a frontier anymore—and those are qualities to admire, but if you're the sole proprietor of civilization that stretches from where you stand to as far as you can see, then you'll naturally figure that the only thing civilization needs is what you deign to give it. And besides, those men are long dead—and their sons can't help it that there're no more towns to found, and no more churches or schools to build, so they've got the burden of having all the advantages and none of the hardships and responsibilities, so maybe now their community doesn't go past their own skin—or past the wallets in their pockets. If our planters nowadays don't need their labor anymore, what with all their tractors and cotton pickers, they don't see why we good folks—in their daddies' towns—should be sorry to see that labor go ... while we sit in our poor little empty stores." He smiled again, "Hell, the Old Figs all shop in Memphis."

"I'm not sorry to see that labor go. They're all nigrahs—good riddance," Winslow said. "But you can't have a town if you don't have people. If we had factories now, we'd have White people in them."

When they finished, Lloyd would put a dime in the pay phone. "We'd better warn the wives. Give them a chance to put away their liquor and their cards." And then the wink and slow smile, and Harry realized Lloyd was winking at him. He'd put his arm around Harry's shoulders and draw him to the phone. "Here Stranger, you tell my wife I'm serious—I don't want to see her mess when I get home, so she better put that all away. And come by and see me tomorrow, Stranger, we've got some business to discuss."

The business was adoption. They were in Lloyd's office. "Are you going to adopt that boy?"

"Evy?" Harry didn't know what to say. He couldn't explain. "I really haven't thought about it. This has all happened so fast."

"You could've shifted down to first anytime you wanted, Stranger. If you haven't thought of adopting that boy, I suggest you do so now."

Harry didn't reply. Adopt? He would have to tell too much. People would pry, they'd find out—

Lloyd looked him over. "If something happened to Emily, you'd have no legal claim. Her mother would take him. If you want to protect that boy, you've got to adopt him."

Still Harry said nothing. Lloyd leaned back in his chair and looked up at the ceiling and started talking.

"I want to tell you a story. You've heard of Ole Brownlee's letter? He'd show it to you if you asked. It's the envelope—that's what he saved, he threw the letter away. He got it back in '48, addressed to 'Colonel Brownly, Mississippi'—spelled "l-y" instead of "l-e-e." That's all: no street, no town. It was from a Colored boy he'd met at Fort Bragg in 1942. That boy didn't know anything about where Brownlee lived, he just wrote down 'Colonel'—and Brownlee wasn't even a colonel anymore. It went to the post office in Jackson." Lloyd leaned forward, and looked at Harry, and tapped his desk. "They knew who he was. They knew right where to send it."

Harry nodded his head. Then he looked down. He suddenly thought of his father: *he knew right where to find me.* Funny how that is—somebody shows up, right out of the blue, and tilts the table of your life.

"The point is, Stranger, that everybody knows everybody here, even in the entire state. You meet anybody on the street, in any town, and y'all start talking—you'll be talking about your people and his, and your friends and his, and most likely you'll find a connection. And you can't hide in a town like this, or even in a state like this. You might think you can because nobody knows you here, or anything about your family, but that's what makes you different. You're the only one here like that, Stranger. There's no hiding. You stick out like a fly in the batter."

Lloyd smiled. "You remember that. And remember what I told you last night, about clearing the ground you stand on."

Had his father come? Had he seen Lloyd? Could he still be alive? Harry doubted it. What did Lloyd know?

"I've done nothing wrong."

Lloyd leaned back in his chair; he studied Harry's face. Outside sounds came with the wind through the window. Loud male voices and automobiles. "I never said you did, Stranger—Well, that's all, you just think about adopting that boy."

27 • The Drowned Man

Harry's boss was Hiram Stout. People said he owned half the gas stations in North Mississippi. That was in the Hills, where the Whites were common and poor. "Every man a king at Crown Gas." Hiram had played the banjo for his customers, and kept a barrel full of toys for their children. "Close your eyes, reach in and grab one. It's yours for free. And if you don't like it, honey, just throw it back and reach in again."

"Half the gas stations"—Lloyd would say that exaggeration either commended or condemned Hiram, depending on who said it. Hiram bought himself two plantations after he moved to Horatio County, and claimed kin to a planter here, but most of the planters didn't like him. He was a Johnny-come-lately. His money came from Hill-country trash. And that rich relation? The planters said Hiram wasn't as closely related as he claimed.

Hiram owned his own building on Main Street. Just as he'd done to buy his place, Hiram bought the building from a planter family at a price so high they couldn't refuse him, just to show that planters didn't scorn his money when he offered it to them. He bought the building lock, stock, and barrel and the first thing he did, he backed up a moving truck to take away all its furnishings. Did it at noon, when the street was full of people. Glossy Naugahyde replaced the worn and cracked leather, and pressed board desks replaced the scratched and blemished wood—new-fangled stuff the likes of which Williams Point had never seen before. Hiram's desk was the only thing that wasn't new. It was the same desk—stained with grease and oil—that he'd bought used for his first Crown station. "Never be ashamed of your beginnings." He told this to all his hires, including Harry Wilbourne.

Lloyd liked to say that Hiram Stout "had us all beat." He was the original, the first Turk.

After Harry married, Hiram had him in. There, the storied desk, and in a corner his banjo and a barrel—was these the originals?—still full of children's toys. Hiram offered him a cigar and Harry accepted, and Hiram came around his desk to light it. He asked Harry how he liked living in Emily's house and Harry answered fine. Then Hiram got to the point. Your salary, he told him, can't support a wife and a child, and your job can't support a raise in pay, but here—and Hiram held out a business card—is something you could do on the side. "Have you ever done any newspaper work?"

Harry looked at the card: Mr. Debben Strain, *The Memphis Commercial Appeal*. "No I haven't. I wouldn't know the first thing." He gestured with the card. "Who is this guy?"

"He's an editor, Harry. He has one of the regional desks—Arkansas and Mississippi. He needs a reporter for the Delta."

Harry shrugged.

"It's not rocket science Harry. You go out to the Delta Council, you check in on the chambers of commerce here and in Greenville and Clarksdale and Yazoo City. If somebody has a big party, they'll telephone you the guest list. You put it in the paper. You've got a camera, don't you? You know how to take snaps."

Harry nodded yes.

"Well, the paper will buy you a better one. You'll get people's pictures in the newspaper, everybody will love you.

It's extra money, Harry." Stout smiled. "And when that boy of yours gets older, he'll say his step-daddy's name is always in the paper."

So Harry agreed. Here was something, he thought, maybe a way to hide in plain sight: the man behind the camera, the name on the byline. People would think they knew him.

The *Commercial Appeal* bought him an expensive camera and more, and Harry set up a dark room in his basement. His nickname changed from "Stranger" to "Newsy." And he marveled at his life here: how much of it there was, and how it was turning out so easy. Lloyd never spoke of adoption again, and even Miss Ester seemed appeased: just like floating on a lazy river—and too good to be true.

28 • The Wounded Man

The news comes rolling down the street, repeated over and over. It gathers a current of people coming from their front yards to the streets. First, they come out to hear it. Then they follow it. It rolls right to our office. Somebody with a shotgun, two blasts, had shot through Aunt Ertharin's door.

People are gathering out front, pooling in the street. Morgan and I step outside. I look at him. Then I turn to the crowd to speak, but Morgan puts a hand on my arm. "Give them more time. Let them all come."

People are angry and confused. Questions ripple through the crowd. "Was she injured?" "Is she dead?" And then, as Morgan and I stand before them, they begin to quiet down, and now they're looking at us. Their faces are asking us, "tell us our questions and tell us our answers too." And I don't know what I should say. All I'm thinking is, people like Aunt Ertharin should be immune to history, to violence, to senselessness. People like her—for such a person to be beaten and now threatened— She's never wronged a single soul in her entire life.

And then, Aunt Ertharin's marches up the street as best she can, hobbling, with another crowd behind her. She's parting the one in front of her. She makes her way through and stands with us and faces the growing crowd. People see her: she's okay, she's okay. But still there's a restlessness among them because something is coming, has to come, let it come—and the three of us standing under our hand-printed sign that says

"Freedom Now" above our office door, we'll be the ones to tell them what it is.

We could tell them to burn this whole town down and they would do it. We could stop this town's world right in its tracks. And I'm thinking: Why not? Why the hell not? I look at that crowd—somehow it seems the three of us are high above them—and I think: we could tell them anything—

Morgan steps up front.

" 'Go tell it on the mountain.' That's what we sing. That's one of *our* songs. 'Go tell it on the mountain.' Well, what are we going to tell? This is what we're going to tell: that we're sick and tired of being sick and tired. And we're mad, we're mad as hell. I ask y'all, all this violence and all this hate, what's it for? We're just trying to be first-class citizens. Why should we be beaten? Why should we be attacked? Why should we face what we face every damn day we live our lives down here? Why should we take it?"

There's a chorus of amens; there's clapping, shouting.

Morgan keeps going. "This is our home! We just want to live our lives! This is our home! So who're we going to tell? Who're we going to tell? Let's tell the mayor, let's tell the city commissioners, let's tell the chief of police, and then let's tell the county commissioners and the sheriff. We just want to live our lives. We just want to live our lives! Let's tell every White person who works and shops on Main Street. Let's climb that mountain, from City Hall to the county courthouse, and shout it loud and clear: 'Freedom Now, Freedom Now; we want our freedom now.' That's how we're going to live our lives. Let's tell them right now."

Morgan takes Aunt Ertharin's hand. The crowd parts to let them through. I see Isaac in the crowd. "Quick. Go find everybody who hasn't come in yet. Tell them to meet us at City Hall. Make sure somebody brings a camera."

―◆― ―◆―

It's only two in the afternoon but City Hall is locked up tight. We press up against it, up the steps and right to the double doors, and to the right and left under the first-floor windows. We sing our songs to the bricks. A frosted window on an upper floor opens and closes. Then, the double doors open outward, first moving slightly ajar and then harder, wider. Two lines of policemen push through, and push us down the steps, and then they spread out right and left. I hear a bullhorn from somewhere. Is it from that window upstairs? I look up and see it.

"Y'all go home, right now, or y'all will be arrested for disturbing the peace."

We start singing, "We shall not be moved. We shall not be moved." Nobody had to call the song. The bullhorn again—we ignore it.

Everything is noise and everything's teetering. We're on the sidewalk now, pushed and pushing, just below the steps, and there's no way forward. We're face to face with the cops. Then I look behind me, up over our people. For all the noise, I can't tell what I'm hearing, but now, suddenly, there're policemen and dogs behind us, and a bus pulled up behind them.

I point, and Morgan looks and Aunt Ertharin, and now everybody's turning around and looking. And what was noise is quiet now, and I can see the faces of every one of those cops, and they'll wait for us to study and remember them all, because they own all the time in the world; from time past to time forever, they own it all.

Morgan gathers me and Aunt Ertharin, and Isaac and Johanna, and we pass through our people to face those policemen and their dogs. Our protestors, they're women and children mostly, they're the remainders—the people left at the station after the train's done gone—how many remain now, after all those years of our people moving North? I remember Morgan and Mr. Courtland and me, late at night in his café, and Morgan's question: Are we too late?

But there's no time for thinking like that. I feel somebody's hand and I take it. I'm looking at those cops. We march forward. We're singing. A cop shoves Johanna, another takes a swing at Isaac's face. We keep singing. A dog takes half a leg off Morgan's pants. The police are shoving, clubbing, mostly at our hands to break us apart. Now I'm surrounded and the police are pushing me to the bus. I crane my neck and look around—who else have they got? Morgan, Aunt Ertharin, the cops are picking off all our leaders and they're knocking the others to the ground. A cop prods me in the ribs and I double over. The police shove me into the bus, then Morgan, Aunt Ertharin, Deborah, about twenty more. The door slams, and the bus squeals away from the rest of our people.

They take us off the bus and file us into jail. I'm the last one. My first step off, a cop asks my name. I tell him. He yells, "Call me 'sir,' nigger!"

It's that same scrawny cop. I tell him I only call my father sir.

He yells he'll beat me if I don't call him sir. I look him dead in the eye and I know I can kill him. I could put my hands on his throat and never let go. The other cops wouldn't be able to pull me off. It'd be the last thing I ever do. His face would be the last I'd ever see—his red face dying. I've pictured it so often. It would just be him and me. Nobody else.

I look over at the last of our people going through the doorway to the jail. I remember something my Papa Joe told me, about how to live your life preparing to die. I keep my hands at my sides and I don't say a word.

He has a thick leather strop. The other cops fetch a bench. It's low and it doesn't have a back. They lay me face down on it. Two cops hold my arms out wide. I try to count every blow: it's important that I do that, to bear witness to my story, but I lose track somewhere after twenty. By then the pain is constant—during or between each blow it doesn't matter, it hurts all the same.

They pull me up and I can barely stand. I try to concentrate on the pain—its exact sensation. It's important that I do that but I can't. I can't think straight and I can hardly see or hear … just the glare of the sun and that scrawny cop—a blur. He's right in front of me but his voice is too faint for me to hear. I feel a slap on my cheek. Now I hear him. "You call me 'sir!' You want another beating?"

I look down and around and my body wobbles. Ah, there's the bench. The pain feels eternal. This might be the last thing I ever do. I step to the bench, careful not to fall, and I bend to lay myself back down.

29 • The Drowned Man

Williams Point: February, 1963

He'd never meant to take a stand. That was never his intention.

Harry drove south down Main and crossed the bridge. There—the cross street ahead and the courthouse just beyond—he saw the two crowds, one White, roiling on the courthouse lawn and spilling to the street, and the other, a ring of Negroes close around the courthouse walls, their signs circling and bobbing. The Whites outnumbered them.

Harry frowned. The mayor, Tommy Lott, had told the Whites to stay away. But he hadn't meant these Whites. He told that to the north-of-the-river Whites: the lawyers and the bankers, the businessmen and doctors, the merchants, the strivers—they were the ones to stay away. This rough crowd here, in dungarees and overalls and T-shirts, Harry figured these were Tommy Lott's people. Poor Whites. Most of them lived in Lott's little houses on the eastern side of town, south of the river and north of the tracks, hard by the Negro districts. Some were newcomers from the Hill counties, east of the Delta, maybe some still lived there now. But they all lived east of Eden—truck farmers turned day-laborers who worked a Colored man's job, and used-to-be storekeepers, their country stores bankrupt and abandoned, their Negro customers long gone North. Like the Negroes, now they worked for rich men. Harry frowned again. These Whites—they'd see him and he didn't want to take a stand.

His was the only car on the road. A policeman stepped forward, furious, barking; he waved Harry to his left, away from the courthouse and onto Front Street, and then, seeing Harry behind the wheel, he smiled and tipped his hat.

Harry nodded back. Now he was neck deep. A month ago, reporters had come for the first demonstration, from as close as the Memphis *Commercial-Appeal*—Harry's paper—and as far as the *New York Times* and *Chicago Tribune*. They'd needed a place to gather so the *Commercial-Appeal* gave them Harry's name. He called his editor to complain.

"What's your problem Harry?" His editor didn't like his attitude. No, they couldn't stay at the Holiday Inn. It had no darkroom, no teletype. And no, not the local paper either. "They've got their own pictures to develop, Harry—society types, Linda Lou's party, big doings at the C of C—your kind of stuff. You think the biggest papers in the country, covering the biggest story of the day, are going to wait on Linda Lou?"

"It's not your beat, Harry. You won't be covering it. All you've got to do is have them over. You don't have to like them, and you don't have to like the story. They won't care. Nobody will care."

What's your problem Harry? What could Harry say? How could he explain his life to any man ... White man? His whole life here depended on him not saying anything at all. He could tell himself: likely this won't disturb my floating course downstream. But that lazy river of his—the water was roiled and muddy now, and the water was wide. He knew that.

But his editor had left him no choice. So he opened his home and locked up his whiskey, and Evy stood wide-eyed and rapt as the reporters developed their film in Harry's basement, and telephotoed their pictures and teletyped their words to newspapers all over the world. Then they flopped on Harry's chairs and sofa, and drank his Coca-Colas and took nips from their flasks and smoked their cigarettes, and, setting the bottles at their feet and filling Harry's ashtrays, they swapped stories and gossiped while Evy stood before them, teary-eyed and coughing from their smoke. Listening and not quite understanding, Evy gulped down every word.

Harry watched him, and wanted to shoo him away, and told himself: *It's just for a day. I'm just a host. That's all.* Because he didn't want to take a stand. He'd never wanted to take a stand.

But at that first demonstration, the UPI man hit pay dirt. His picture of a police dog tearing the pants of a Negro marcher had gone around the world, printed in every newspaper and shown on the nightly news. And in the world's view, that was Williams Point now: that picture, that sooner or later everyone in town would know had come from Harry's house. It worried him. And now, for this new demonstration, the reporters were back and their numbers had doubled.

Today they had come back early. It was too hot out there, they said. They meant the Whites, not the weather. They talked about the Ole Miss riots, and the reporter who'd been shot dead there—that kind of crowd they said. They converged on Harry and told him the *Tribune* reporter and his photographer were still out there. They pled with Harry to go find them.

Harry said no.

"Harry, that crowd out there—they shot one of those demonstrators in his car last month. That's the kind of people they are. And these two fellows ... you're the only one who can rescue them."

"Who says they need rescuing? Y'all got back okay. They'll be fine."

"No Harry, listen. We're getting beat up all over the South now, just for showing up at these things."

Harry shut his eyes and shook his head, but Emily was there and she told him he had to go. He opened his eyes to her arms akimbo and her decent, dead-set face. And what could Harry say to her and how could he explain?

So Harry, in his car, turned left on Front Street and took a right at Fulton and parked behind Hiram Stout's building. He walked back to the courthouse as fast as he could, sometimes breaking into a jog. As he neared, flecks of human sound reached him: indistinct at first, then growing in anger and taking the shapes of words, ebbing and flowing, like leaves swirling down a rocky stream, and when he was close enough to hear it, underneath was the melody of a song, a spiritual—he recognized it from his Negro days—and at first it surprised him, until he realized it was the marchers. He couldn't quite make out the words. They seemed to be different from the ones he remembered.

He was close to the courthouse now. It's bone white tower loomed against the slate-gray sky. Harry slowed his walk, passed clusters of Whites. He recognized some but not others, and tried not to let anybody get a good look at his face. He was searching for the tall, goose-necked reporter—that was the description—and a man—any man—with a professional's camera. He hoped they were together.

He was on the courthouse grounds—sidewalks, bushes and lawns—and immersed within the crowd. All these angry Whites, cursing at the top of their lungs. Well, he could be angry too. He could find those reporters and curse them and chase them out of here. Maybe that would work. There, amidst the shouted noise, Harry could no longer hear the Black protesters' song. He tried not to look too long their way.

Harry elbowed his way through. He saw a policeman, a member of his church. Harry was about to ask if he'd seen a long-necked reporter, but stopped himself—there, just ten yards beyond, was Gooseneck, hunched over, his pork-pie hat at his feet, one hand to his face, his handkerchief to his nose. Another policeman was but a couple of yards away.

Harry leaned over from behind the reporter's back. "Jonas? Are you Jonas? Are you okay?"

Jonas stared at him in astonishment; then he shook his head. His cheeks were bruised; one eye was shut. Blood leaked from his nose and mouth.

"Who did this to you?" Harry turned to get the policeman from his church. Jonas took hold of his sleeve.

"Don't." Jonas winced and he touched his jaw. "Or you'll get beaten too. And I'll probably get some more."

"Do you mean the police—?"

"I don't know." He cursed. "Somebody came up behind me; gave me a shot in the kidneys. I almost blacked out. Then they held me up while somebody worked on my face. All I could see were knuckles." Jonas looked around. "Have you seen Artie?"

"Is he your photographer?"

"Yeah. I've got to find him." Jonas started walking. Harry followed, but now he was aware of being seen. He tried to keep a little distance between himself and Jonas. He saw a man with a camera and started to shout, but recognized him just in time—it wasn't Artie. It was a plainclothes cop, his camera trained on the marchers. Harry stopped. He stepped back into the crowd and worked his way through it, still following Jonas, who seemed not to realize that, again, he was alone.

The crowd surged and took Harry with it. He lost sight of Jonas and struggled against the people around him; panicky, he hopped to see over their heads. The sky, its meager clouds, was pewter gray like a schoolboy's slate, its words written and erased, over and over, but never washed clean. Harry remembered what his plan would be.

He caught a glimpse—Gooseneck Jonas with his porkpie hat, kneeling over a cluster of bushes by a bend in the sidewalk, and another man with him, looking for something. Harry pushed clear of the crowd and jogged over to them. The other man had plucked a battered camera out from behind a bush. Its lens was bent and the glass smashed.

Jonas huddled close to hide the camera from the crowd. "Is the film still there? Wind it through."

Artie was clawing at the camera. "It's busted. I can't open it."

"Don't let them see you have it."

Artie's hands were shaking. They were pocked with the blood dripping from his face.

Harry asked, "Did somebody break your camera?" Neither man answered. "Who broke your camera?" Artie was cursing at it in his hands. Harry glanced back at the crowd; they were looking at him. He was suddenly aware, again, of their shouts and curses. The sound was overwhelming. He grabbed the camera and pushed Artie away. He cursed them both—Artie and Jonas—loudly and repeatedly, and smashed the camera against a lamp post again and again. He bruised his hand but didn't notice. The back finally flew open and Harry snatched the roll of film as the camera fell from his hand. He kicked it clattering down the sidewalk. Then he turned to Artie and pushed him down, their hands entangled in awkward combat.

When Artie had his film, Harry pulled him up and shoved him next to Jonas. Then, still yelling, he herded them through the crowd. People jostled; Harry tried to push their hands and fists away. Their faces: not real, not recognized, just smears of white and sunburned red. A hand tore at his shirt, a fist swung at his head. People clawed at his face and hands. No one stepped aside. A punch to his ribs, and an open hand to the side of his face. Harry almost fell and pushed at Jonas and Artie, and cursed them, and beat on their backs with his fists. But people still attacked him. Jonas tripped and fell and Harry reached down and grabbed him, and cursed and pushed him clear of the crowd. They crossed Main, away from the courthouse, and then they ran for it, Harry chasing with his fists held high. Nobody followed. Harry herded them down Front Street, and cursed them as they passed the cotton factors gathered at their doors. Then, a right on Fulton, and finally they were alone. The shouts of the crowd shrank back down to flecks; the spiritual was gone; and the silence felt strange, like an extra person that Harry couldn't see.

He couldn't believe what he'd just done. He looked down at his hands and discovered his blood, sticky, shimmering on his knuckles and streaked to his wrists; staining his cuffs. He stared at his cuffs. They'd need laundering. Jonas plucked at Harry's shirt. "It's torn. Look, right down the side."

They walked to Harry's office. The reporters flopped into his chairs. Harry slid down to the floor next to his desk, his back against it. He reached up behind him for his telephone and cradled it in his lap and telephoned Hiram Stout and then his wife.

He asked Hiram to call them a doctor, and told his wife not to worry—and please tell the others he had Jonas and the photographer.

When he finished, he found himself trembling. Had his voice quavered on the telephone? He hoped not. He gasped for air. His lungs burned.

"You got a drink?"

That was Jonas. Harry told him where to find the bottle and a glass. He rubbed his hands, they felt so sticky and clammy. He needed to wash them but, for now, he just wanted to sit. Jonas joined him on the floor with a bottle and two glasses, one full. Jonas' lip was split, his jaw was swollen. He had a black eye. He passed Harry the empty glass and took a deep, fast drink.

"I don't like being the goddamned bad guy. Hell, I'm not even the bad guy here." Jonas poured himself another drink. "Look, I know those Coloreds' game. They want us here. They wanted all this today to happen. And the last time too. Goddammit, there shouldn't even be any story here. Those people in line to register: they're illiterates. They don't even qualify. You all should be as polite as pie. You should herd them in and herd them out, as fast as you can. We wouldn't be here if you'd only acted smart."

Jonas spat blood on the floor between them and wiped his mouth with his sleeve. "You got a towel?"

Harry looked at Jonas' face and gasped. Harry couldn't breathe. He couldn't remember who this man was, or even his newspaper—where he was from. "I'm not from here." That was all Harry could say.

Jonas looked surprised. He was on his third drink. "I thought you ... we came from your house."

"I live here now, but I'm not from here." Harry's drink was in his hand, untouched. He tried to swallow. He could hardly do it. And his lungs were burning. Then he remembered: the *Tribune*—they're from Chicago.

"How's ... what's your photographer's name? How's he doing?"

Jonas tilted his head back and to his side. "Artie's okay. He's got himself a flask." Jonas poured himself another drink and pointed at Harry with the hand that held his drink. He nearly spilled it. He was getting drunk.

"Let me ask you a question. Why do they act the way they do? Last week I was in the courthouse and your wife was there and she asked me why I only interviewed that rough crowd—that's what she called them—'rough crowd'—she said they weren't even from here, they were from the Hills. She asked me why I didn't interview some sensible people. I said, 'Give me some names,' and she did, a bunch of businessmen, and you know what I told her? I'd already asked every one of those 'sensible people' for an interview and they wouldn't tell me a goddamn thing. Oh, they'd talk, but nothing on the record. They'd tell me—just like your wife knew they would—sensible stuff, like I was saying. They'd tell me: 'We should just ignore all this. Let them try to register. The good ones won't try. They've just got illiterates in line. The smart ones stay away.' But these 'sensible people'—they're too scared to say anything like that on the record. They're scared about what their friends and family and neighbors will think. People might think they're 'nigger lovers.' That's what they tell me. So that rough crowd wearing overalls, out on the street yelling 'nigger this' and 'nigger that,' that's all I'm left with. And here's the punch line: the sheriff walks up to me and your wife and he doesn't even look at me. He looks at your wife and points at me and says, 'What's he doing here writing about those coons?'

"Now why would he say that? Why stir the pot? He knows I've got to report something like that when I hear it. They've got to stop acting like that. Somebody here's got to tell them. I know the sheriff and he knows me. I check in every time I come to town. I interviewed him when those agitators brought in all that food and those clothes. He knows I'm fair, he knows I'm on a job, and if I had half an inch of cooperation and if they had half an ounce of brains—but they're all like that. Why're they like that?"

Where was Hiram? Harry wanted to get up. He wanted to clean up the blood on the floor between them. He wanted to get away but he stayed right where he was, like he was chained to the spot. "I don't know. I don't have any idea."

Jonas gripped Harry's shirt, just below his collar. Jonas' breath stank. Harry leaned away and put his hand up to stop him, but Jonas held tight. "I'm telling you I'm not the bad guy here. That rough crowd, they're happy to talk—big talk about what they're going do to those Negroes—but then, you saw what they tried to do to me and Artie. They don't like us reporting what they say? So don't talk then! Or don't make that big talk. But *I'm* supposed to be the bad guy?"

He let go of Harry's shirt and slumped further to the floor. "Well, you just let those Coloreds alone. They'll get tired of it and go on home."

Harry wasn't listening. He wished *he* was home. He wanted to look at every room and at his yard—front, back and all around. One last look, if it wasn't too late, at his house and his wife and her boy, before their lives would change. In his first life, and his second and his third, he hadn't had that chance before.

→←→←

Years before this day: Harry had come to think he could live a normal life, which meant White. There had been the river. There had been his image, perfect in his mirror.

He knew better now.

Months before this day: Lloyd had scoffed at it all. SNCC had been in town for months and they'd gotten nowhere, just a small group marching to the courthouse and not a single application filed—an aborted, silly affair, a sideshow. He'd say, "What we need are industries. We need new jobs that'll keep people from moving away. The Negroes have been moving to Chicago since the 'twenties. At least they've got someplace to go. But where are the White folks going to go? When they've got nobody shopping in their stores, where're they going to go? These demonstrations just give the Old Figs another excuse to bellow." Bellowing old bulls, Lloyd called them, the lot of them, and now, because of these agitators, people were listening again.

"They voted us out the last time because we wanted our Negroes to stay. And now these ... these agitators; they come in here shouting 'Freedom Now.' Since when in the history of the world has anybody ever gotten anything worth getting *Now?* It's just a pipedream. And all it does is, it just makes folks listen to those bellowing old bulls. They'll go on home. They'll get tired of marching and go on home."

After a while Harry stopped listening. Once he had tried to explain it to Lloyd, when SNCC gave away the food and clothing—but Lloyd had interrupted, "You mean that mess created for no good reason by our Old Fig commissioners." Harry persisted: "Well, whatever the commissioners did is beside the point. SNCC didn't leave before and they're not leaving now. And as long as they're here, the Colored folks will keep on marching."

Lloyd just shook his head no. So Harry didn't say anything more. He remembered the severed thumbs he'd never seen, collected in a bag, and Uncle John on Peter's porch in the early sunrise, trying, with the force of all his will, to make in Harry a new creation. All that pride and honor Lloyd liked to talk about, he'd never see it in a Negro. Even now, when Lloyd had seen it for himself—the marches, the lines to the courthouse— he couldn't recognize it. Harry remembered how that long ago night had split him in two. Negro anger, Negro rage, a rough justice for all we've done against them (Harry, thinking this, used that word—we). *Yeah, that threw me for a loop. It'd probably blow Lloyd to pieces.* So that story was something Harry knew he would never tell him.

The last time they'd talked, Lloyd hardly said a word about industries and jobs. Between the Old Figs and the agitators, had he abandoned his hopes? Or had he noticed that Harry had stopped listening?

Weeks before this day: Emily's girlfriends, gathered for their weekly game of bridge in her living room. Calpurnia would circle the table, refreshing their drinks, serving their sandwiches. They'd talk about anything—the movies, television, or, lately, their mayor and their Negroes.

"I told Tommy, I told him not to drive away our good Negroes. He smiled and said he'd do the best he could."

"I don't think he likes them at all."

"Who?"

"Our Negroes. Tommy. He doesn't like them at all. I've never heard him say a good thing about them."

"That's just ignorant if you ask me. You can't just bunch them up. You've got to take them one at a time, just like anybody else."

Harry retired alone to another room. He tried not to listen. The ladies kept talking.

"My best friend growing up was a little Negro girl. Her name was Teenie. That was her first name. She was our cook's little girl. One day she just didn't show up—neither her nor her mother. My mother told me they'd left for Chicago. One day here, the next day gone. I never saw her again."

"Lots of times it's their men who take them. I really can't blame them—their men. What kind of work is here for them anyway? There, I said it. I don't care. People won't stay anywhere there's no work. I told Carlton that last night and did he blow up at me. But I don't care. I say, you take them one at a time, just like anybody else."

"Well, lots of times, their men are long gone. They leave them here and go get themselves another woman in Chicago."

"Do you know anything about those agitators that came to town? Tommy says they're communist agitators. He says they're going to rile up our Negroes and then the good ones will leave us. Those agitators will scare them all away."

"Hah! To Tommy, there's no such thing as a good Negro."

"Tommy's ignorant. Communists here? What would they want with this little town? Compared to where they're from, this is just a speck on the map."

One shouted to Harry in the other room. "Newsy, what d'you say? Are those agitators communists?"

Harry lowered his newspaper and shouted out his answer. "I don't know." Whatever question they'd shout, he'd shout back he didn't know. He'd imagine them throwing up their hands: did he ever know anything?

When the reporters first came, those women fled before them, flushed out through the door like a covey of quail, scurrying across the lawn and off in their automobiles, each on a short flight, scattered. They never returned.

Days before this day: Harry had not yet gone to the courthouse and had not yet led anyone to safety, had not yet been seen doing it; but that UPI photograph, from the first demonstration, wired around the world: that photo condemned every White in town, indiscriminately, because no matter their thoughts or feelings or actions, and no matter their reserve or reputation, that split-second image—the policemen loosening their leashes, the Black man's legs spread and knees locked, and pants ripped open, and one German Shepherd lunging for his chest and another biting at his rear—that had been done on behalf of every White in town; and the photograph had come from within their midst, from inside Harry's house.

Hand bandaged and home at last, Harry slowly walked from room to room. His body ached all over. He still wore the shirt with the bloodied cuffs and the tear down its side. By now the house was quiet, still—how strange it seemed!—and empty of reporters. The furniture seemed smaller, the spaces between them larger, and the air felt heavy and smelled of cigarettes. Empty bottles, half-filled glasses, crumbs in dishes strewn— Where was Emily? Where was Evy? Harry found them standing together in the middle of the kitchen, so suddenly vast, with cigarettes stubbed on saucers and papers crumpled on the floor. Evy clutched the skirt of his mother's dress. Something he hadn't done in years. Emily picked up a saucer here, a wad of paper there, setting one down to pick up the other. When she saw Harry she stopped, and faced him, and dropped the paper from her hand. She put her hand to her face and tucked a strand of hair behind her ear. With her other hand, she cupped the side of Evy's face, and drew him closer to her. She blinked her eyes and pointed at her husband. "Harry, your shirt— How's your hand?"

The doctor must have called her and told her what he'd found.

Harry could see in Emily's face the knowledge that, yes, in their lives there'd been a 'before,' but this 'now' *was now*, and their lives would be different forever after. Harry nodded and she nodded back. He wanted to tell her how sorry he was, that it was all his fault, but he knew he could not speak about this new state of affairs, because she would deny everything her eyes were telling him.

They woke the next morning to garbage strewn over their lawn.

30 • The Drowned Man

Emily called the police. She had to invoke her family name. Two officers finally came, they wandered around the trash-strewn lawn—one toed an empty beer bottle and flipped it in the air. They shrugged their shoulders. "There's nothing we can do ma'am." Harry could see them smirking when they thought no one was looking. He couldn't help but stare at their thumbs. After they left he had the gardener clean everything up.

From that day on Lucius and Evy no longer played out front. And they no longer played together. Emily saw to that. Evy was to play in the backyard. Lucius was to stay inside with his mother. Emily gave him some of Evy's toys, old ones that Evy no longer used.

Harry took to watching him, out the windows of his bedroom, sitting on his bed. Evy wandered the yard picking up this toy or that, or a stick or a stone, and then he would drop it, absently, and occasionally look back to the house as if he were trying to see through the windows and into the rooms.

Suddenly Emily appeared in the doorway. Harry turned to face her. He patted the bed for her to sit beside him. She didn't. She wrung her hands. "They can't be seen together," she said. "People will talk. They'll think like my mother does. I don't like it." She crossed her arms like she was cold. "We've got enough trouble …" Her voice trailed off; she didn't finish.

Harry glanced out at Evy. "They could play inside together."

"No. Little boys need fresh air."

Harry didn't reply. She had made her speech—it didn't seem to matter to whom—and then she walked out of the room, one arm stiff at her side, the other hand holding it by the elbow.

◆—◆

Emily took to following her help around. Callie would clean and tidy, Emily and Lucius would follow: Lucius searching for toys he wanted to play with, gathering them up whenever his mother finished a task, and staying behind his mother's "Missus" as they moved to another room; Emily talking about how terrible the situation was, that it was all a misunderstanding gone horribly wrong.

On one day Callie leaned the Hoover against a wall. "Missus, you must be all tired. Let me sit you down."

The two followed her to the kitchen. She pulled a chair for Emily. Lucius scattered his toys like jacks on the linoleum. Callie poured Emily a glass of water and sat down with her. Emily ignored it, had probably not noticed it. Callie poured her own and one for Lucius, and set it on the floor. She took a sip from hers.

Emily asked her, "Why do our best let the worst ones speak?" She named off the best, the sensible people, pulling out a finger from her clenched fist for every name. "I know you understand, Callie, I know all the good Negroes understand. But even they—they let those outsiders, those agitators speak. Are y'all too scared to stop them?"

Callie shook her head. "All that mess you've been talking about, Missus, that's White folks' mess, and I just stay away from it. I won't know a thing about it. I just look after my own—my boy here, my family."

Emily looked up from her hands. "Your husband—"

"He's still in Chicago, Missus. He's got work but he says he's looking for better."

"You're not going to leave here?"

Callie shook her head. "Now don't you worry about what troubles tomorrow might bring, Missus, with all your troubles today. Don't ask the Lord for more than your daily share. I just go from sunup to sundown, and workday to Sunday. Everything else is for the Lord."

Emily's eyes widened. She took hold of Callie's hand, her palm over Callie's knuckles. "You don't know—how much I dread.

"Yesterday I was downtown and ran into our mayor. We had a nasty exchange. Why is it we always put forth our worst? So I was driving home, under those beautiful trees that line the street, and I thought what a beautiful town this is and it's being ruined by hatred. Our mayor doesn't want us to see those demonstrations. So I stay away. But I see them when I watch the news on TV. Those hateful Whites. They're trash! I see what the country must think of us. We're not all like that. You know that. We're not all Klan. But I was driving ... I couldn't help myself; I had to pull over to the side of the road. I have a good friend who moved away to Kansas. I tried to write to her but I couldn't. I had to throw away the letter. I fear what she thinks of us now. I just started crying. Right there in the car. I couldn't help myself. I couldn't see the road for my tears."

Then she fell silent until a sound diverted her. Lucius had settled on a toy, a miniature truck in his hand that he wheeled across the linoleum, his lips sputtering the engine noise. He was on his knees, nearly under the table. Emily reached down to touch his shoulder. "What a sweet little boy you are!" She looked up at Callie. "What's going to happen to all the sweet little children?"

She brought her hand to her face. She was crying. Callie, always with a handkerchief, held it out to her.

<hr />

Quiet days followed that last demonstration.

Then, on a Sunday morning, all the Whites who carried their Bibles while walking to their cars, saw the flyers on their lawns, the cheap, thin paper damp with dew—a strange manna, the mimeographed print was hard to read—a "Delta Discussion," "Number one of a Series" from a "local Civic group." Below this headline the word "NEVER," repeated in the horizontal and vertical, formed three crosses, and under each were the words "TO SOCIALISM" "TO INTEGRATION" "TO COMMUNISM." The local newspaper stood accused: "Why does it expound upon the virtues of the Citizens' Council? What is wrong with the good, simple, hard-working people of Horatio County binding themselves together, and along with thousands of other Mississippians, standing up like real men and simply saying, 'WE HAVE HAD ENOUGH'? Because we pure, God-fearing men realize that, in the battle for racial integrity, there is no halfway, no compromise, it is a battle for all or nothing."

To read it, Harry had laid it on the Bible in his hands. Now he stopped, and put his Bible under his arm, against his side, and pinned it there. He held the flyer tight and taut and his fingers, stained from the flyer's ink, now smudged the paper's margins. "Too many of our so-called leaders don't have the guts for a definite stand. The Police Commissioner, the Prosecuting Attorney, they're only weak puppets of those who control them. Our Mayor is a good man, but he can only do so much when his hands are tied."

It also listed names: the White prostitute who favors Coloreds; the hawk-nosed storekeeper whose custom is too black; and an outsider, a newcomer, who showed his thanks to the town that took him to its bosom by sheltering and supporting the Yankee Press and all its lies.

Emily looked up from the flyer she held, over at Harry. He had wadded his into a ball and had thrown it at his feet. The neighbors outside, in their front yards, read the flyers and stared at Harry, turned their heads away and then, some, looked back again. Fathers shooed their children to their cars. To Harry they hardly existed. There was only Emily, with Evy right beside her, standing in their dewy grass. Emily picked at the flyer in her hands. The paper stuck to her fingers and her palms, and the ink stained her fingers.

Harry brought them back inside and got a towel for Emily. She held out her hands for him to clean. He tried to dry them both, then one. "Don't rub it on your dress. Here, wipe them off." Harry handed her the towel, now flecked with bits of paper like a leper's scabs. She barely touched it. It fell to the floor.

Harry insisted they go to church. They sat through the service in their regular pew. Harry didn't hear a word. Afterward, outside, the conversations were brief. Nobody mentioned the flyer, but people were in a hurry to leave— Harry's proffered hand: the men hesitated, their handshakes brief. Everybody shielded their eyes from the sun; it seemed hot for the season and Harry's sweat trickled down his back. He tugged at his collar: "Yeah, okay, goodbye. See you. Don't be a stranger." He soon found himself alone with Emily and

Evy, standing by the curb in front of the church. The sounds of the leaving cars had faded and now there was silence—so still—he'd once had found that comforting.

※

Hiram Stout called Harry into his office on Monday morning. He had the flyer on his desk.

"I made a few calls. I don't think anybody will bother you."

Harry didn't say anything.

"Sit down, Harry." Hiram waited for him to sit. "I know some of these people." He gestured to the flyer on his desk. "They're from the Hills like I am. They remember me from when they were children, and I was the gas station guy. I'm the man who played the banjo for them. I'm the one who gave them gifts—cheap little toys—when they came with their daddies. 'Come on down to Crown Gas, where every man's a king.' Their daddies were poor but they made me rich."

"They kill people, Hiram. They tried to kill those Negroes. They shot into their car."

Hiram frowned. "Yes … yes, I know. But they're not going to kill you."

Harry said nothing.

Hiram Stout drummed his fingers on the flyer.

"You want my help?"

Harry nodded. "Yes sir. Yes, I do."

"Okay, okay. You've already got it. Relax, will you? You look like a board sitting there. These people," he tapped the flyer, "they talk about 'racial integrity' like it's some highfalutin' idea, but they don't care about ideas. You know what they respond to? They respond to me, or whoever it is who owns their home or pays their poll tax. It's 'yes, Mr. Tom' or 'you need anything Mr. Hiram?' It's personal, everything's personal."

"And who's Mr. Tom?"

Hiram grinned. "That would be our honorable mayor. They live in his little ole houses. He pays their poll tax for them." Hiram picked up the flyer. He frowned and put it back down. "There's only one thing 'Mr. Tom' and I have in common: we're about the only people of consequence who'll look those people in the eye without wanting to spit in it. Only, he uses them. For his own ends. I never did."

"So you fixed everything?"

"I made inquiries. And yes, I think so, yes."

Harry was facing his boss, his benefactor, and if asked he could truthfully say that he was grateful. But in Harry's inner vision, Hiram Stout had faded to soot and ash and ink, and flecks of thin, cheap paper. How could he tell this man anything about his lives—*all* his lives? How could he tell Hiram that any help would be—had to be!—too late and not enough to thwart the forces that worked against him. Harry shifted in his chair.

"Can I leave now?"

Hiram sighed. "Yeah, get back to your office. Or take the day off. I'd be spooked too." He threw the flyer in his wastebasket. "One thing: the head of this Klavern isn't from here. There never was much of a Klan here anyway. It's mostly some poor folks from the Hills. They moved here looking for some of that good life in the Delta: Everybody has help. Even the gas station attendant has a cook and two maids. But these people, they didn't stop to think. When the Coloreds started leaving that good life left too. They don't want the Negroes to stay but they don't like it when they go. I don't think they realize that." Stout paused. "Anyway, they've never pulled much weight around here. So this outsider's come in with a few of his bunch and he's trying to call the shots here. He's over at the Holiday Inn." Hiram leaned down and picked the flyer up out of his wastebasket. "*He's* the one who put this out. Heh, he talks like half of city hall is in the NAACP. I'm going to keep my ear to the ground about this guy, but if you'd ask me, that flyer was just a bunch of mouth-talk."

"Mouth-talk?"

"Malarkey."

31 • The Drowned Man

Williams Point: Summer, 1963

The sky was bright outside, a creamy blue, but inside the bar the light was dim, gray and yellow, the window shades were drawn and fans pushed the air across the room. They didn't help much, everyone inside was sweating. Lloyd was leaning back in their booth; the back of his shirt was stuck to the booth's cracked leather but he didn't seem to mind. He was looking at his outstretched hand fingering his glass of beer on the table. Harry was slumped over his, his hands cradling the glass.

"Miss Ester came over. You told me once, a long time ago, that she'd never give up. Well, she saw her chance with that flyer. She says our boy isn't safe living with us anymore. She's bound and determined to have him. My God! To think of him stuck in that house of hers. She and Emily argued for over an hour. I tried to say something and she looked right through me. Kept on arguing with Emily. Finally, I just left the room. I took Evy outside but he knew, he'd heard enough."

It had been months since they'd last met. First Harry told Lloyd how Emily had become so afraid. "I got some money from the UPI, for 'services rendered' in our house. Emily didn't want me to deposit the check in our bank. She said people would find out. She said people would think it was blood money for that newspaper picture. I had to cash it in Memphis and bring the money home. Emily hid it somewhere in the house. I don't even know where it is."

Then he told Lloyd what Hiram had said about the Klan, and then about Miss Ester.

Harry turned his glass around on the tabletop. He was trying to keep the ring of water formed by the bottom of the glass a perfect circle. He lifted it to see. The ring was misshapen, wider in some places and smeared. He took a sip of beer and set his glass back down.

Lloyd kept his eyes down, trained on the glass at his hand, like he was watching—studying—the bubbles. "You know Miss Ester's going to get her way."

Harry shrugged. He wished ... he wished he could shuck off his skin, his history, his world, with just that shrug of his shoulders. He wished Lloyd would look up at him once. "I don't see how. You're the lawyer, but I don't see how she has a legal leg to stand on."

"She doesn't—not by the letter of the law. But the law doesn't execute itself. People do that. A judge might see things her way. And besides, the way I see it, it's not a matter of law at all. It's a matter of will. Miss Ester has a mighty strong will. Emily has never stood up to her. Not once in her entire life." Now Lloyd looked up at Harry. "That leaves you, Stranger. And I can't picture anybody taking your side these days."

Lloyd finished the last of his beer. "I've got to go." He got up, stooping momentarily over the table. "You got this?"

Harry nodded. Lloyd headed for the door. Turning, he said one last thing. "Hiram was right. You and Emily and Evy should be okay. It's been months since those flyers came ... but, just in case, you better lock your doors."

Harry smiled wanly. "Nobody locks their doors here."

Lloyd frowned. "*You* better. You better be the exception."

Harry stayed behind, turning his glass of beer, looking at nothing.

Back when Emily and he were courting, when he had first asked Evy what he liked to do, the boy, head down, half hidden by his mother's skirts, had mumbled, "Fishing." So they went fishing, from the very first. Sitting on the river bank, they rarely spoke. Occasionally Harry would remark, "Look, there, watch out now. See? Your bobber's twitching." And Evy would laugh and shout when he caught a fish. But mostly they would watch each other. Evy had a look, the one Harry first had seen through the front window, watching Evy play with Lucius. To Harry, it seemed knowing. And, side by side on the river bank, Evy didn't look away when Harry caught his eye. Harry would think: "He doesn't know the facts about my life, but he knows the truth about it: that my face can change, it can ebb and flow; and that I can't just be one person anymore. He knows that. But he doesn't seem to care." At first, fishing, they'd sat some distance from each other. Now they sat close, together.

"You finished here?" It was the waitress, her mouth twisted to a sneer.

Harry frowned. He looked at his glass, nearly empty but untouched for minutes. He rooted for the money in his pocket. Then he left.

◆━━◆━━◆

He hadn't told Lloyd the half. Men would stop Harry on the street. They'd say, and not kindly, "You're just lucky Hiram Stout's your boss. Elsewise, you wouldn't have a job here." And his last check from the *Commercial-Appeal* came with a pink slip. Then a letter came, explaining: "Due to recent circumstances" his abilities "had been compromised." Debben Strain hand-wrote a postscript. He was sorry. And it wasn't he who gave Harry's number out to all those newspapers. Harry said nothing about it, but his next paycheck from Hiram included an unexpected raise. Harry studied the new figure. Hiram, the original, the first Turk in town.

The other Turks—Harry hadn't seen them in ages. Only Lloyd, just now in the bar. They hadn't called him, and he hadn't called them. He kept to himself to spare them the embarrassment of turning him away.

◆——◆

Back at his office Harry found Callie waiting in the vestibule. "I— Sir, I need to speak to you, Mr. Harry, about Missus."

Harry showed her through his door. He closed it so nobody would see or hear. He moved a chair to his desk and gestured, that she should sit down. Callie hesitated and then she sat. Harry sat behind his desk and smiled. "What was it you came for?"

Callie was looking down at the purse she held in her lap. She didn't answer at first. Harry could see her shoulders move from her breathing. Then, after a moment of absolute stillness, she spoke. "Missus, Miss Emily—she keeps following me around the house while I'm trying to clean. She breaks into tears and then she takes hold of Lucius and almost smothers him. I can't get my work done. I'm always late coming home. My aunt needs her supper on time. She's too old to—," she stopped for a moment. "He doesn't like it, that's really why I came here. Lucius doesn't like Miss Emily crying over him and putting her hands on him." Callie was gripping her purse, but here she reached out her hand to him. She almost looked him in the eye, but then she ducked her head and pulled back her hand. "Lucius minds his manners. He's a good boy. I've tried to raise him right, but he tells me after we get home, Miss Emily bothers him. He doesn't want to come with me anymore."

Harry smiled again. "Then don't bring him."

"I can't do that sir."

"Don't you have any people he could stay with? What about your aunt?"

"I have plenty of people. He could stay with my momma, or he could stay with my sister. My aunt's too old to keep up with him. But he could stay at the home house and any one of my people could watch him. But Mr. Harry, that's not the point: if he doesn't come I'd have to explain why to Miss Emily and I couldn't tell her the truth. I'm afraid she'd catch me in a lie."

Harry nodded. Callie nodded with him but didn't say another word. He knew, she was waiting on him. It wouldn't be her place, to tell him what to do.

"I could talk to her I suppose."

"Could you please, Mr. Harry? And could you tell her without calling my name?"

"I believe I could do that. Give me a few days."

Callie smiled and then she glanced at the doorway. Harry told her she could go. As she stood he said, "You really love that boy of yours, don't you?"

"Of course I do, Mr. Harry. Everything I do, I do it for that boy."

―――◆――◆―――

Home, Harry didn't lock his door. Nobody locked their doors. Besides, it was summer now and too hot, even at night, for a closed front door. But he remembered the thumbs. He remembered that they'd worked. The thieving had stopped. The Klan could do the same to him. So he took to staying up with a shotgun in the front room. He'd take a chair and place it in the middle of the room, facing the front door. But he would always fall asleep. He would wake just before dawn and shuffle to bed. He began to think about that: why he persisted when he'd only fall asleep. And why he didn't lock his doors. He remembered what Lloyd had said, that nobody would take his side. He thought of Emily and Evy, and how he was no use to them now. He didn't think any violence would happen to them: if there was any danger, it would only be for him. "Stranger": that's what Lloyd called him now. No more "Newsy." He tucked his chin. Emily and Evy: they'd be better off without him. And there was the burning, burning, burning deep in his chest. He was tired of feeling that way. What was this? His fourth life—or now his fifth? For the first time, he wanted to push his life right off the table.

He shifted in his chair and looked down at his shotgun balanced across his lap. He got up and put the gun away and sat back down again. He listened to the night sounds, seeping into his house, billowing in his room: of insects and leaves, an automobile, a window ... a footstep? No, it was nothing. He watched the darkness. He felt it, moist upon his skin. Then he grew drowsy and then he fell asleep.

The screen door opened with a quiet knocking. A man crept in and found Harry asleep in his chair. He took another and set it facing Harry's and, with his hat in his hands, he sat down and waited.

32 • The Drowned Man

Harry slept soundly in his chair. The dawn was coming. The man stood up and slowly approached. He laid his hand on Harry's shoulder, paused, and then he shook him gently. Harry stirred to a blurred dark image that came into focus—a Black man he'd never seen before. He started, but the Negro only smiled.

"Mr. Harry, sir, it's me. It's Earley."

Harry squinted in the dark. Where was he? His front room, in this chair; this strange man was in his house. Harry looked about him for his shotgun—it wasn't there, he'd put it away—and then back at the man leaning over him.

Earley stood straight, stepped back. "You saved my life sir, when I was a boy. You took me to Chattanooga. You write me letters now."

Harry got out of his chair. He clasped hold of Earley's arms, just below the shoulders. Suddenly the urge came to hug him. As they embraced, Harry whispered in his ear, "What are you doing here? How long have you been here?" Harry stood back to study his face. "I mean," Harry couldn't help it, he smiled, "in town, here in town."

"Only a few days. But I've come to tell you, you've got to do something. Timothy's here. Timothy your son is here. You've got to stop him, sir."

"What? Here? With you? Stop him what? What's he done?"

"He's not with me, sir. He's with the Klan. You've got to stop him. Make him go away. Make him leave the country. He's killing his own kind."

33 • Deborah Donaldson

Williams Point: Summer, 1963

Aleck. She sits and watches him, flat on his stomach on Morgan's bed. His eyes are always closed. Sometimes she thinks he's sleeping. Sometimes she doesn't. Sometimes her anger wells, and sometimes it simmers. But it's always there. He wouldn't let her speak. He—

Still, she's the one who watches him.

These are Deborah's stories—the ones she tried to tell him.

"Come on, child. Mr. Tom's up in his room."

Deborah followed Lott's sister up the stairs. This was five years ago, when she was ten. Deborah can never forget what Lott's sister looked like going up those stairs, like a slow-moving tapioca pudding, her dingy hair pinned in a sloppy bun, nearly come undone. This was the mayor's sister? But the house seemed right, oversized even for White people, surely a mayor's house. The stairs were endless and the light dimmed as they climbed. Then they were at the head of a dark hallway. Miss Lott faced her, wiping her tapioca hands on her tapioca apron. She nodded toward a door.

"He's in there, child. He'll give you your quarter."

Deborah stepped inside. But it wasn't right. The mayor was in his bed, the covers to his chin. Deborah wondered if he was hot. He seemed asleep, but then she saw the glint of his eyes, his face lit by a single dust-spangled beam from the curtained window, the only light in the room. Deborah slowly took it all in, trying to see into the room's farthest corners, and listening. But there was nothing to hear. Then, gradually, she heard his breathing and hers. Lott turned his head towards her, and under the single beam she saw the features of his face. He looked like—she thought it so strange—like a boy with his face pressed against a store window. Years later she learned the words to describe him—a pleading desire and a willed innocence. Without speaking he pulled the covers from his body as he rose, his legs sliding over the mattress, his feet resting on a small rug on the wooden floor, his naked body blocking the light, his hand reaching beneath his bulging belly.

Deborah didn't move except to reach for the door behind her. Her fingers scrambled blindly across it to finally feel the doorknob she knew would be locked. Later she would be running down the street and back across the bridge over the river, running for home; she would be crying; but in between she hardly remembered a thing. But she would always know.

―◆――◆―

What followed was worse. What he had done was to rip a hole in her life—ten minutes gone, maybe more—all she remembered was the heat of the sheets, sticky from his sweat, and some pain, the first tip of it—the rest she wouldn't remember.

But she remembered the look on her momma's face when she stood in the doorway to their kitchen. She followed her mamma's look down her dress and legs, the blood smeared to her socks—they were ruined. She remembered her momma taking her to the enclosed back porch where she stood Deborah, fully clothed, in the wash tub, and silently bade her not to move, and hurried back to the stove where she heated water in a kettle. Not a word was said. Deborah didn't even cry from the scratch of the rag, or the hot water, or the sting of the lye soap her momma used to scrub down Deborah's legs.

Then her momma asked her, "Was he White?" Deborah nodded her head.

Her momma put her to bed and told her: "You keep still. Dr. Sewell's coming." He was the Negro doctor. Her momma never asked her where she had been or who had done this to her. And when the doctor came, and pulled back the covers, and looked there, she suddenly panicked and started to scream.

All this, she would always remember, and the darkness of her room, for by now it was evening, and the absence of her sister in the bed they shared, so large without her and somehow accusing. She could hear whisperings from the front room, and she wanted to tell all the adults in her family—she knew they were there—who had done this to her. She wanted to be out there with them, surrounded by them; and she wanted their outrage and their anger. She trembled. She felt cold. She stayed put.

Her parents did nothing. She was told not to speak of it. Whenever she tried, they told her "Mind, your sister is here," or "Don't be punishing yourself," and finally, "Please, child, please!" And they resented her, she could tell, from the sharp look and the short tone of voice, first from her daddy and then, after he'd left, from her momma too.

Deborah stayed indoors, her books laid open in her hands, the pages scarcely turned. Her movements grew cautious. But then she began to notice she could do anything she pleased—not that she was ever wild—while her brother and sister always had to mind their p's and q's. Once, Deborah purposely didn't set the table. Her mother, walking by, went on into the kitchen. Deborah followed. Her mother turned to her.

"You feeling sick, baby?"

"No'm."

"Well, you've been acting sick all day. Like you've got no energy. You go on, lay down." She raised her voice, "Dorothy! Come here and set the table for me, baby."

Deborah crossed her arms. "Momma, why're you doing that?"

"Do what honey?"

"Why do you let me off for things you yell at Dorothy and Danny for?"

"Why, honey! I don't know what you're talking about."

"Right now! I didn't set the table and you tell Dorothy to do it."

"I told you, you've been acting sick all day. And why should that bother you, if I'm not so strict with you?"

Deborah stood there, her arms still crossed. Her mother wiped her hands on her apron. "Come on honey. You've got enough sense for two. I don't need to correct you like the others. It's like you're grown beyond your years."

Deborah wanted to ask: "Just what was it, that made me so grown? How'd I get to be this way? The way I've become?" But she didn't. She just watched her mother turn away, saying, "Go on now, go to your room." Deborah, suddenly tired, obeyed. But that evening she didn't come for supper.

Older, she would understand her mother's lenience—it was her way of asking Deborah forgiveness for doing nothing, for saying nothing. But Deborah couldn't accept that. *Why should she decide how she can ask for my forgiveness? Without saying a thing!*

Why can't I choose? Don't I have that right? My head's been shouting for so long but they won't let me speak.

When her daddy left for Florida, he and her momma said he could make some money there, picking oranges. "Negroes can't make anything here no more." That's what her daddy said. And he did send money home, and more than they'd had before. The family didn't join him. Momma said those migrant camps in Florida were no place for children. Still, Deborah knew: her daddy had left on her account; he couldn't look at her without seeing his own life breached.

I'll never see him again. He'll never come back as long as I'm here. As soon as I'm gone, Daddy will come back home again. Deborah believed that with all her heart. She could feel her body stiffen. *Right now, I'm staying. It's my right to have a home.*

◆━━◆━━◆

Deborah woke and sat up in bed. It was the morning of the first Freedom Day. She looked around and took it in, her room; she'd had no other her entire life. And she'd never done that before, just sitting and looking at her room. She'd spent a lot of time alone there, but never studied the walls and pictures, the bed, the desk, the chifferobe— Now she saw how the rectangle of light from her window bleached the blanket at the foot of her bed. There was nothing new or changed, but now after all these years, the room looked different, strange. She couldn't say how. But the furniture crowded the room in a way she hadn't noticed before. So little space to walk about! And the bed, the desk, the chifferobe: they were, somehow, witnesses to her life—and also her accusers. They told her: you don't fit in here. She thought they might be right. She didn't fit—not for a long time, not anymore. Those thoughts confused and scared her.

She sat for a while, taking in her room and frowning. She slowly emptied her mind. Then she sighed. "Might as well get up." She said this aloud, but only to herself. Her brother and sister were somewhere in the house, probably making a rumpus, but she didn't hear them. She wasn't listening for them, but only to the sounds within her room—her bare feet on the wooden floor, the creak of the boards. Deborah opened the chifferobe and took out her best school clothes. She concentrated on each piece of clothing as she put it on, rolling her socks up her calves, fitting her dress about her shoulders and arms, moving her hands and limbs slowly. Then she sat down at the desk—her desk, not her brother's and not her sister's, but hers. They never used it. This room was hers, not theirs, she's the one who spent her time in here. She wanted to tame it, reclaim it. Then the thought she was avoiding finally came. *I could die today. I could die.* She sat up straight and stiffened her body, an act of will to summon courage. But even as she did, she doubted her courage would ever come.

Now she listened to the sounds elsewhere in the house. Her mother was in the kitchen; she would be calling soon. Deborah exhaled. She hadn't even realized she'd been holding her breath. It would be a relief to leave her room for breakfast. Maybe her mother would try and talk her out of marching today. Then her resolve would harden. Any sound, any motion: eating her breakfast, listening to her brother and sister fight or complain, her mother's shushings, anything that could hijack her attention and allow the time to pass unnoticed, so the moment could sneak up on her, and then, once outside and marching, she'd be overwhelmed by the group, by their songs and their clapping and their bodies moving together, and by the rush and warming of her blood.

Deborah waited for her momma's voice.

Earlier that week she'd told her about the Freedom Day. Everybody in the Movement would be there, marching up Main Street, across the railroad tracks at U Street to the White part of town, past all the White folks' stores (and almost to the bridge—*that* bridge—that spanned the river) and to the courthouse and around it. Deborah told her: "We'll circle the courthouse—just like Joshua at Jericho—and we'll march around it as many times as it takes for our people to go in and register. And when they come out, we'll march back down Main Street to the tracks at U Street and come on home.

"We'll have no guns, no clubs, and no knives. We'll have nothing but our bodies."

Her momma bowed her head and shook it as she listened. "Deborah, Deborah, honey … listen to me honey." But Deborah wouldn't stop.

"We asked for a permit to march but we probably won't get it. The White folks know we'll be coming, and they'll be out there waiting for us."

"Deborah, honey …"

"We're not supposed to be there. We're not supposed to do this. The police won't stop any of the White folks there from doing what they will. We'll probably be beaten."

"Deborah, please, this … is this … you don't need to do this." Deborah saw her momma's face, mouth pressed shut, then grimacing, her tears lost in the wrinkles around her eyes. Deborah leaned her head closer to her momma's and took hold of her hands.

"Yes, momma, I do!" She brought her mouth up close to her momma's ear. "We've been taught how to cover up our bodies. We'll bring up our knees and legs to cover our chests and stomachs, and duck our heads down under our forearms, and only our shoulders and back and buttocks will show. We'll be like a ball."

"But that won't stop them, honey. They could break your backs, they could paralyze you. They could pry your legs away. They could shoot you."

"Listen momma. There's nothing you can say. I have to do this, no matter what happens."

Her momma shook her head and tried to pull her hands free. Deborah tightened her grip and leaned back to look at her, full in the face. "Listen to me, momma. I want to be able to tell what happened. All these years—listen to me momma, look at me—I've wanted to shout out to everybody …"

"No, honey, don't …"

"I wanted to scream. I wanted to be alive …"

"No, no, don't …"

"You can't stop me from doing this momma. This won't be in your house, Dorothy and Danny won't see, you can't tell me not to do this. This is what it's come to momma. This is how I'll tell. It's what I have to do."

And that had been her trump. Her momma's hands went limp in her own. Deborah stroked them. For the first time in so long she felt a tenderness inside.

"Deborah, honey! Breakfast, honey!"

Deborah started at the sound of her momma's voice, so sudden after the quiet, alone in her room. Things just happen, with no warning, and everything's changed. Would this march be like that? Would something, again, jump in front of her life and change it?

She stood up from her desk and her legs wobbled, she felt dizzy for a moment, and then she felt her fear, heavy in her body, willing her to sit. She sang softly to herself, barely a whisper, "Ain't gonna let nobody turn me round, turn me round, turn me round." She stood beside her desk and repeated that one line of the song, like a chant in a ritual.

"Deborah, honey! Breakfast is ready!"

She stopped her chanting. "Coming momma!"

Dorothy and Danny were at the kitchen table, clowning. Her momma shushed them, but Deborah said, "Let them clown momma." She reached over and swatted away Danny's hand from the bowl of grits. "You already got some, you little piggy. It's my turn." She spooned her some and poured gravy on them.

"You going marching today?" Dorothy leaned on her elbow perched on the table, her cheek to her fist, her spoon held up like a flag.

"That's right. We're going to show the White people here that Negroes want to vote just like they do."

"Y'all gonna be afraid?"

"No, Danny. We're going to sing."

"Huh? What's singing gonna do?"

"You two hush now. Y'all bothering your sister."

"It's okay momma. I don't mind."

But she did mind. She felt as if freezing water had filled her lungs. It wasn't Dorothy and Danny, it was the impending moment. *I could die today.* The thought replayed itself in her head, a skipping record, a school yard jeer. Then she sensed another fear—that she wouldn't move. That when Morgan knocked on the door and came in to collect her, she would not be able to stand from her chair. She would shake her head no, voiceless, while Dorothy and Danny watched, until Morgan left without her. And then there'd be no more need to move, not ever again, because there would be no more need *for her*. And life would be worse than even before. *I could die today*—from courage, or from fear.

But she didn't hear him knock. Morgan was right beside her before she even noticed.

"Look me in the eye. Don't worry, I won't tell." Lott smiled. "I never tell. You know that."

He had her brought up the back stairs, policemen at her side, into his office. Lott was sitting behind his desk and had nodded to them, and they had shut the door behind them.

Deborah stood before him, her eyes down. She hadn't taken a seat. She wouldn't lift her eyes. She wouldn't speak. But she could still see him, and the window's glare behind him, up from under her eyebrows. His balding head and fleshy jowls were dim from the glare, but she remembered his face ... that look of his, the kid at the store window, but now his look was mocking. She noticed nothing else of his office around him, she didn't look around. She didn't care.

Lott was tapping his pen on his desk, waiting. Then he stopped. "You remember me. I know you do." He grinned. "I sure remember you. I want you to tell me exactly what you think of me. I want you to look me in the eye and tell me. Let it out. I want to hear it.

"You don't have to worry. Nobody will hear but you and me. And I won't tell a soul. Tell me what you think of me.

Because I know you remember me. I know you remember what we did." He paused and slowly tapped his pen. "What—we—did." He grinned again. He stood up and walked around his desk to her.

"That won't happen here. If that's what you're worried about. You're safe. You're too old now." He reached for her chin, the side of his index finger curled under it, and he lifted her face to his. Deborah closed her eyes.

"I thought you'd turned uppity. I thought the new way was no more looking down or stepping out of the way. No more 'yes sir' or 'no sir,' and no more hats in hand and all that other bullshit y'all used to make us think y'all loved us. I thought the new way was to speak your mind. So speak it. Tell me how much you hate me."

Deborah twisted her face from his hand. She looked back down at the floor.

"So you can't look a White man in the eye. Is that it? Maybe we've been right about y'all all along. Born slaves." He forced a dry, hollow laugh. "No, y'all were never born slaves. Born savages, that's more like it. So you're scared." He grinned and turned away. He sat back down behind his desk. "That's almost as good as hatred."

He looked at Deborah for a few minutes, her head still down, her body still, before he sat back down. But she studied him, from under her brow. She wasn't trembling. He looked up at her and frowned.

"I saw you marching. I recognized you. I don't forget a face, and, if you'll remember, that first time I saw yours was real close." He grinned. "So I asked around. I know your name now. I know where you live, with your mama and her two other children. I even know your daddy's gone away and he's never coming back. He wants y'all to join him." She could see him studying her body. She willed her body still—not the slightest flinch or tremble. No motion at all.

"So what's stopping y'all?" Lott picked up his pen. He began tapping it again. For the moment, that tap, tap, tap and the drone of the fan were the only sounds in the room.

"Y'all don't like it here." He chuckled. "That's obvious. So why don't y'all leave?" He was still tapping his pen.

"You know y'all lost, don't you? Y'all lost before y'all began. Before that ... Morgan Wright, and then—what's his name? Aleck Sharpe. Before they even came here from Drew—yeah, we know all about them—before they even came here, y'all ready lost. Years ago. Years before your agitators, your Martin Luther Coons, y'all ready lost. We used to lynch more of you niggers back before the war than we do now. I know every lynching in this county since the Great Depression. I've made it my business to know. And with y'all so uppity now, just asking for it, we lynched more of y'all back in the 'thirties when y'all had nothing, and said 'massa,' and shuffled your feet and ducked your heads and tried so hard to be good niggers—Yeah, we lynched more y'all then, than we do now."

Lott paused. She could see—he'd never taken his eyes from her body. "Don't you think that's strange? But it's not strange at all. No. Not at all. Back then, there must've been about seven or eight niggers for every White. And y'all were popping out those babies." Lott smirked. "That's when a Colored vote would've meant something. That's why we lynched so many of y'all back then; we had no room for error." He spread his hands in a gesture of innocence. "We couldn't afford otherwise. We weren't trying to push y'all out back then, the planters wouldn't have it, so we had to keep y'all in line.

"But after the war? Then y'all started to leave, because the tractors came—you know I sell tractors?—and then the planters, to a man, they finally said, 'Good riddance; niggers never could do a lick of work.'" Lott laughed. "Before they bought my tractors, they'd take you to the hospital when y'all were sick—and fighting?—they'd tell the sheriff to mind his own business, 'Don't come on my place and arrest my people'—'my people'—like niggers were their kin, but when their first chance came, they said niggers couldn't do a lick." Lott paused and smiled.

All the while he spoke, she never moved a peg. Her arms never relaxed and her hands stayed clenched. Her jaw was set and her eyes were blank. Holding yourself so still will tire you out, and she'd been standing like that for a while now.

"I've been working to rid ourselves of you niggers before I was even mayor. Back in the 'fifties, I pushed out my share. And now, so many gone, there aren't that many of y'all left, and y'all are still leaving, even now. I'd say White folks pretty much have the majority sewed up here now. So, all you Coloreds trying to get your freedom through the vote, you're about twenty, twenty-five years too late." He pointed his pen at her. "Do you think y'all would've got this far if y'all still had a majority down here? There'd have been some hot times down here; y'all would've been run out of town. Y'all wouldn't be alive this far. And nobody would care. Nobody here, and nobody in Washington DC. Niggers in charge?" He laughed as he said the words. "So why don't the rest of y'all go? Go up to Chicago, y'all have the vote there already; kick your dust up there. Show those Yankees why we do what we do down here. Give them a good dose of nigger."

While he talked, Lott kept tapping his pen. Deborah gave her attention to that, and the fan. The drone and the tap, tap, tap, irregular, like a clock ticking with a warped spring—and she still hadn't moved, not a muscle relaxed, her head still down, and not a word said. Lott was doing all the talking, but that was only background noise to the tap, tap, tapping. But she could tell: he was talking faster. And the tap, tap, tapping was growing louder.

She could see that he never took his eyes off her, and he was frowning.

"Why stay where you're not wanted? Why don't you leave with the rest of them, the smart ones?" Suddenly he stood and came around his desk. "Because now, all y'all got is me. There's nobody else. Not the Piercys, not the Southworths, none of those blue-blooded planters that called y'all 'their people', you've just got me." He poked her in the shoulder. "Me and you, you and me—that's it! And I never had no scruples, not like those planters had. I never had them at all. So why don't you get out? Planters used to boss everybody in this county. Now all they boss are their tractors—the ones I sold them. They used to want y'all here, and I did my share to push y'all out, so between them and me I won. I won and by God this town is going to be the way I want it. I pushed out my share, goddammit, while they just beat it to that country club of theirs. They tell me to come out there, they tell me to clean up this mess of theirs like I'm their janitor; they never admit they lost they never admit they're not in charge and you're too stupid to see y'all lost—y'all both lost, so leave! Get out! Dammit. Get out!"

She never moved, but two policemen barged in. They grabbed at her and she collapsed into a ball and they clubbed her, her hands covering her head. One drove his billy club into her side and her arms came down and they pulled her up and dragged her out. All the while she heard screaming. It wasn't her, it was Lott—he'd been screaming the whole time.

The police didn't beat her. They drove her north on Main Street, past the marble county courthouse and over the bridge and through North Williams Point, under the arching oaks—their branches bare but budding. She saw the long, broad lawns, yellowed now; and two grand houses, close by and on the same side of the street, each had a giant flag draped high on the balconies above their doors—one confederate, the other American. The police drove her over the last bridge in town and out from under the oaks and into the glassy white sun. Bare brown cotton fields lay quiet on either side of the road. They drove her ten miles north, and stopped at no place in particular. There they let her out, and turned around for home.

In Winona, the cops took them into the station and up to a desk. The cop behind it frowned at Deborah. "What's your name girl?"

Deborah told him.

"I want to hear you say, 'Yes, sir,' nigger."

"I don't know you that well."

"You say 'Yes sir' to me."

"Why is it so important to you?"

"You show me proper respect. God, you're an African-looking nigger."

"Why do you want respect from the likes of me?"

The cop at the desk stared at Deborah's face. She stared back. She could sense somebody crowding close up behind her: one, maybe two, maybe three. The cop at the desk wrote a note on his tablet.

"Where're y'all going?"

"Williams Point. We're going home. On the bus outside."

"Where're y'all been?"

"Charleston, South Carolina. We're going home now. On the bus, outside."

"What were you doing in Charleston?"

"We were on a vacation."

"The whole bunch of you on vacation? You're with those agitators—y'all were disrupting that bus. Are you one of those Freedom Riders?"

"No."

"Yes you are. You think you're some uppity nigger, don't you? You won't call me 'sir.' "

Someone behind Deborah punched her behind her ear. Deborah staggered but regained her balance. Behind her, she heard Aunt Ertharin shout. Then the man punched Deborah in the kidney. She fell and curled up on the floor.

"Get up. We got a cell for you."

Deborah tried to stand. "Please, let the others go."

"What?"

"Let them go." Deborah winced. "Let them go home."

The cop laughed. "Too bad you didn't say 'sir.' "

He and another man grabbed Deborah by her arms and dragged her to the cell. They pushed her through the door and Deborah stumbled and fell to the foot of a cot. Two strange Negroes stood on either side. Deborah found herself, inches away, staring at a pair of worn out, dirty shoes. Then she turned over and around to see the men who'd shoved her in.

The uniformed cop drew out a long, wide blackjack from his pocket and tossed it to one of the Negroes. The Negro stared at it in his hands.

The cop told him, "Use it or you know what I'll use on you."

They laid Deborah face down on the cot. Somebody pushed her face into the canvas. It smelled of lye soap and urine. Two hands held down her legs and another two her arms, stretched past her head.

The Negro laid into her. After ten blows the beating stopped. Deborah turned her head up over her arm to see. The cop was standing right there beside her, shaking his head. "Not hard enough." He turned and left, she couldn't see him anymore, so she turned her head back down. Then his voice, he must've been talking to the Negro. "Drink this. It'll get you going. Come on, take a couple of slugs."

After his drink, the Negro whipped the blackjack faster.

Deborah screamed and writhed. The men holding her legs and arms pulled them harder. Another man yelped and pummeled her head with his fists while the Negro beat her back and legs. And then the blows slowed, and then they finally stopped. Deborah turned her head up over her arms again. That hurt, and all she saw were blurs. Then, the voice again.

"Your turn now."

The beating began again, the blackjack harder and faster.

Deborah screamed, over and over, but after a while she couldn't hear. She couldn't feel the hands holding her down. She couldn't see. The world shrank—or did she swell?—and now her body filled the entire world and every inch was pain.

And then, finally, she couldn't even feel.

Her hearing came first. Screaming. Is that me? Deborah couldn't make out the words. She couldn't tell if it was her or somebody else. She lifted her head, just a bit; she tried to focus her eyes. All she could see was the color white—the cot's canvas, stained and frayed. Was she alone? The screams kept coming. It must be somebody else. She tried to remember who. Annelle Branch. Euvester Raines. Aunt Ertharin. One of them was screaming. Deborah squeezed her eyes shut. She buried her face. Everything went blank.

―――

Deborah heard a low-pitched moan, droning, constant. Her body felt hard and stiff. Her back, legs, and head ached. She was lying on her stomach, her arms dangling off the canvas cot, her head turned to the side. She opened her eyes and put her forearms underneath her chest and raised up her head. Above her stood a White woman. She was middle-aged, plain, her apron balled in her hands. Deborah couldn't tell where the moan was coming from—maybe outside the cell, or maybe inside her head. Maybe this woman heard it too, because she turned to look behind her. Then she turned back to Deborah. "I'm the jailer's wife."

Deborah tried to lick her lips. "Cold water." She could barely form the words. She wondered if the woman understood.

The woman turned and left. When she came back she knelt and held a cup to Deborah's lips. "My husband's out." The water spilled as Deborah drank. When she was done, the woman stood. Her face was flushed; her features were hard.

Deborah thought for a moment the woman would hit her. But she just stood there, beside the cot, and took her apron in her hands again, wringing it and wrapping it around the cup. "I try to live a Christian life."

Deborah closed her eyes. She didn't know what day it was. Perhaps she should ask her. But the woman had left and Deborah would never see her again. The canvas stank but Deborah couldn't move. The moaning didn't stop.

Deborah sits and watches. Aleck is flat on his stomach, his back exposed, bandaged, his head turned toward her. Underneath those bandages, she knows—his back's a bloody field plowed crazy. Sometimes his eyes are open; sometimes they're closed. Either way, she doesn't think he sees.

They gave him Morgan's bed. Morgan's gone off somewhere. She and Aleck are the only ones here. She'll sit as long as it takes. She still feels the pain from her own beating, but she's the one who's watching. He's the one in bed.

Sometimes she thinks he's sleeping. Sometimes she doesn't.

Sometimes her anger wells; her throat closes and her mouth tastes bitter. He wouldn't let her tell her stories. Because he knew: they're like gospel. You can't know these stories and do nothing about them.

She hasn't forgiven them—any of them.

34 • The Drowned Man

Earley and Harry stood together in Harry's living room, in an intimate pose, each clasping the other's arms. Earley was trying to explain, but Harry wasn't listening. He was looking out his window at the sky. It was gray, but soon it would be gold and cream, and Earley couldn't be seen here, in this house, or even on the streets here. He was a strange Negro for whom no account could be given.

"You've got to leave—now. You can't let anybody see you. What are you talking about? Timothy? The Klan? No. No."

"Let me show you his picture, sir. I know all about him, but only you can prove it's him. He's got a new identity. Only you can expose him. You've got to tell the world he's Colored."

"I don't want to see any picture. I don't believe you." Harry shook him. He pointed to the sky. "It's almost dawn. You can't be seen here. It's not safe for you here. Surely you know that."

Earley turned and looked out the window.

"Come on," Harry said. You've got to go."

"Okay. But please, sir, take a look at this." Earley took a picture from his coat's breast pocket and held it out. Harry wouldn't take it. Earley put it on a nearby table.

Harry grabbed the picture and, without looking at it, shoved it back in Earley's hands. Earley looked down at it, and then back at Harry. "You've got to do this."

He slid the picture back in his breast pocket. "I'll be back, sir. Your son is killing my people … his people. Only you can stop him."

Harry said nothing to that, and Earley looked about the room. "Where's your back door, sir?"

Harry led him through the house to the kitchen door, and stood in its threshold as he watched Earley creeping through the backyard, pausing every few feet and looking about and suddenly disappearing through the bushes without a sound. Harry stayed and listened for any shout of surprise from his neighbors, or any bark from a dog, but he only heard the early birds and insects, and the sound of his own breathing, heavy, but finally slowing and calming, until he allowed himself to shut the door.

He stood there thinking—too many thoughts. He tried to clear his mind. If Timothy was here, what would that mean? What would he do? What has he done? *What should I do?*

Harry went back to his study, trembling. He opened the drawer to his desk and shifted through its contents. There it was, the key. He picked it up and slowly closed the drawer. For almost a minute he stood, facing the window behind the desk. Then he looked around for the clock. How long before eight o'clock? Should he go to the bank as soon as it opened? No. He'd go at noon, at dinnertime, like he always did. He sat down at his desk and looked at the key in the palm of his hands. Why should he be worried? Even if Timothy was here, how could he know about the safe-deposit box? Still, he was worried, for Catherine's sake, and maybe, for her daughter's sake as well. Earley's and Catherine's letters— Harry kept them with his pictures.

Her first letter had come to him his last week in Atlanta. He kept it and wrote back after he moved. Thereafter, it was one or two a year, sometimes three, sometimes with a picture, catching him from town to town, in Pittsburgh, and finally in Williams Point. In each town he'd set up a post office box. It wasn't for his privacy so much, not until he'd married, but for the anticipation, the walk over to see if one had come. He wouldn't read it there. He'd walk it back to work. If he was alone he'd read it there. If not, he'd keep it in the inside pocket of his suit, where it's presence teased his mind, and if he could he'd go directly home and sit down and read it, over and over, and then he'd spread the pages and the picture on his table to gaze at them. After he married he read them in the bank, in the private room where you'd open your safe-deposit box, two chairs and a table in a small windowless cell.

That first letter: Harry could scarcely believe it was real. Just the fact of it, there in his hand, a letter from Catherine who'd been Timothy's girl—the possibility of such a letter had never crossed his mind. And the letter itself: it was like a fairy tale. She'd found herself pregnant. She'd had the baby—she'd had to leave home to have it, her family had wanted it stopped. But she told herself she'd have it, would take one look at it, and then she'd give it up. She was surprised when she saw it wasn't Black. It was a beautiful, White-skinned baby girl. So her parents had lied to her. Timothy wasn't a Negro. She kept her baby. She never wrote her parents, or called them on the telephone, or ever saw them again.

She moved west, as far as she could move, until she ran out of country. She wrote that she'd sit on the beach at sunset, and well into the evening, cradling her baby in her lap or nursing it, a blanket draped over her shoulder and breast, and she'd watch and listen to the waves and think about Timothy, who was the father of this child, who would never see this child, but who would always be a presence in its life, just like the sea at her feet, churning but calming. She wrote that the ocean's churn had told her there was something out there for her, for her and her child. "It's foolish, I know, but I can't help but believe that there will be great things in store for my child."

Harry had read the letter over and over. Here, perhaps, was redemption. Let it be so. The letter thrilled and frightened him.

Do you know where Timothy is? Would he ever want to see me again, or speak to me again, after what I believed about him? Timothy didn't know I was pregnant. Please, would you tell Timothy he has a child?

Harry wrote back to her. He told her he didn't know where Timothy was. Harry didn't describe their parting, but wrote only that Timothy had left. Then Harry wrote about his own circumstances. He wrote that she should forgive her parents and let them be a part of her life, if only they would.

Months passed and the letters continued, with pictures of the baby. Harry always answered them, and when he moved he'd send her his new address. He wrote her long letters about Timothy's childhood, but he could tell her nothing about his whereabouts, and her questions about him gradually ceased. She went to secretarial school. Harry encouraged her. She found a job and a young man who loved her, her boss, an up-and-comer, and when they were married he took her child as his own. She was very grateful. Over the years he became a wealthy man.

Harry was happy to hear this. Her new life, her own story, and a beautiful baby girl. And no Timothy. Harry felt guilty for his happiness.

Once married, she asked that he never write to her again—except to tell her when he moved. She would still write to him. Her husband knew of their correspondence and allowed it, but she knew he didn't like it. And Catherine was afraid that if Harry ever heard from Timothy, and told him, she would be caught out in a lie.

Please forgive me for asking you, but I can't risk any possibility that my husband might learn the truth, that it was I who abandoned Timothy. That I betrayed him. I told my husband that Timothy was dead. That we had married and then he died. We told my daughter too. But you deserve to know about the granddaughter you'll never see. If you ever hear from Timothy, please don't tell him I carried his child, please don't tell him he has a beautiful little girl. He must never know about her. Or of me.

But still, I find myself hoping that somehow, he will. About his little girl. I can't help it. Every time I look at her I think of Timothy. I feel so ashamed. Even though I think of him often, I can hardly picture his face anymore or remember the sound of his voice. I'm losing him to life, the life I've made for myself and my daughter. I tell her she can be anything she wants to be. I've encouraged her to become a great person. Oh, if only you could meet her, see her, talk to her! So I daydream. She'll grow up to do wonderful things, and one day Timothy will see her on the television or hear her on the radio, or see her picture in a magazine, and he'll know, somehow, that she is his. Because she looks so much like me. And he'd be so proud. He won't even have to meet her, but still, he'll be so proud.

It's a fantasy, I know. And one I shouldn't hope for. But I was the cause of his misfortune, and I can't help but hope that our daughter, unknowingly because she can never know him, will soothe his heart and maybe, if need be, also bind his wounds.

And Harry nodded his head. Of course. Of course. I understand exactly.

Now it was a letter every year, sometimes two if there was special news, and another picture. Letter by letter, he had followed his granddaughter's childhood, the news always late and from clear across the country, but he was in on every triumph. With every accolade—the honor society, the debate team, prom and homecoming queen—Harry allowed himself to think, "Yes, maybe somehow ... our redemption." This precious girl with the Madonna-like face: she looked just like her mother, who looked like his Charlotte.

◆——◆

Harry sat at his desk. He had lost himself in recollection. But Timothy. What if what Earley said was true? A small part of him hoped it was. His son, his son was here?

But the Klan? Timothy in the Klan? The safe-deposit box. If Timothy was Klan, he mustn't know about it.

Finally, just before seven, Harry heard his family waking up. He answered his wife's shouted question, "Harry, are you up? Where are you?" He showered and dressed, and ate his breakfast, trying not to eat too fast, or be too tense, too quiet; and he wondered if his wife or Evy had any inkling of his unease. He really couldn't tell. Emily did give him a look when he didn't finish his eggs. He watched her put the dishes in the sink—he saw nothing that wasn't normal—so he fled, and went to work.

He waited till dinner time. All morning he kept telling himself: there's no need to worry. Relax, he said, you're making something out of nothing. At noon sharp he walked, hurriedly, to the bank, and wiped his face with his handkerchief, and stepped inside, and asked to see his box.

He sat down and looked inside. The picture of him and Charlotte and their two children was torn to bits. And one picture was missing, the graduation picture of Catherine's daughter—Timothy's daughter—the most recent one that Harry had. He shifted through Catherine's letters. Earley's too. They were all there, but they must've been read. Harry was certain of that. Just the two pictures, nothing else seemed to be disturbed. He closed the box but then reopened it, took everything out and stuffed his pockets full. Then he closed it shut again and locked it, and then he sat there for a moment, thinking what to do and breathing slowly, and then he went back to the lobby. "Thank you. You've been most kind." He told them that and then he left. The next thing he knew, he was in his office. He usually went home for dinner. This time he didn't.

Harry couldn't work. He found an empty box and put his letters and pictures inside it. The last thing to go, the torn-up picture, first he taped it back together. Face down on his desk; pieces pushed together like a jigsaw puzzle; Scotch tape crisscrossed across it. Then he turned it over. Tears welled and Harry wiped them from his eyes. He closed the box and put it in his safe. *My pictures. He'd know that I'd still keep them. But where ... how could Timothy have known? Had he searched my office? Had he searched my home? How did he know about the bank? Somebody there must've told him.* Harry wondered—which one there, or how many, were members of the Klan? He sat down in the chair next to the safe and tried to calm his breathing.

The how's didn't matter. The why's did. For so many years, the touching and moving of Harry's old pictures had been his and Timothy's unspoken code. To find them ... maybe this had been his way of making certain, without the risk of meeting, that the Harry Wilbourne here in town was indeed his father. Timothy had always known his father was soft on Coloreds. But now he knew so much more. He knew he had a daughter, and he had her graduation picture, and he must have read Catherine's latest letter, how her daughter had gone far away from home, to Atlanta, Georgia, to be a Freedom Rider, and how Catherine feared for her, but was proud for her too, because she, Catherine, hated people like the Klan and their pernicious beliefs that had taken Timothy away from her, and from their bright and shining child.

Harry sat there thinking. These photographs and letters: voiceless communications, held at arm's length. But precious to him all the same. Now ripped to pieces and stolen. That was Timothy's message to him. Suddenly the realization gave him a start—this was the first he'd heard from Timothy in years.

―――◆―◆―――

Harry knew Earley would be back. He waited up, in the same chair as the night before. Again he listened to the night. He wondered if his house was being watched. He was afraid for Earley. If he was seen, caught—

There was a soft knocking at his front door. Harry opened it, just enough for Earley to slip in. There, just inside the door, Harry asked to see the picture. Earley took it, and a paper, from his pocket. "His name is different here, sir; he calls himself Wilbur Thomas, but it's Timothy all right."

Harry led Earley into the room, turned on a lamp, and studied the picture. He nodded his head—"Okay, okay"—and pressed it back in Earley's hands, not caring if he creased it. He pointed at the paper Earley held. "What's that?" Earley said nothing, but he handed it to Harry.

Harry sat down to read it, and motioned Earley to sit in the chair beside him. It was a history of Thomas's movements, running back in time, from one Klavern to another, back to his enlisted time in the army, in the years after World War II. "No. No. No." Harry slapped it down on the table beside his chair. "This can't be my son."

Earley explained. "He joined the Klan right after the army. Before he enlisted, we have no record of his life at all. He has his army papers, and his social security number, but you know as well as I do that this Wilbur Thomas didn't exist before he enlisted in the army. Before then he was Timothy Wilbourne, but only you can prove that."

Harry shook his head. "I don't get it. What's this paper? Where'd you get it? Who's this 'we'? What do you do? There've been no letters. It's been so long."

"I work for the N-double-A-C-P. When I moved to New York City I got myself a job with them. As soon as I saw this picture—he looks just like you. And what you'd been telling me in your letters, all about what happened to your boy." Earley took the paper and folded it away. "I don't like this at all, sir. He's my brother too. But he's come in here with his own group of people, and he's running the Klan here. He put out that flyer that had your name in it. And he kills people. He shot that young man here, just a few months ago, in that car. That young man could've died. I know he's your son, but you've got to stop him, sir. You're the only one who can prove he's Timothy Wilbourne, and show folks who he really is.

"I'm thinking you can expose him, with those letters from Catherine you wrote to me about, and if you warned him beforehand he could run away. Because the Klan will want to kill him. You tell him to leave the country and make himself a new identity, and stay away from any Klan. Then he'll be safe, and he'll also stop his killing."

As he spoke Harry wondered at him, this dark presence, sitting in the chair next over, the one lamp lit behind him. He could've been a ghost, a night shade; Harry had last seen him as a child. The tenor voice was new, but that tilt of the head, that gesture with his hands; Harry remembered. He felt a stirring, a need to keep this man near him. And yet Earley was from the same past that had come once again to claim him. Harry reached out a hand, but hesitated.

He drew it back. The words had only now seeped in. *Timothy kills people.* Harry spoke. "He knows I'm here. He wants me to leave town. He put my name in that flyer. He broke into my secret things. And now he knows ... it's really me."

"You need to stop him, sir."

"Maybe I should go. I could take Emily and Evy. We could go someplace—"

Harry stopped, suddenly exhausted. He could barely speak. "She'd never leave. And besides, the past is everywhere. I can't escape it." He looked about him. He looked at Earley. "You can't ask me to do this. You can't ask me to betray my son. I've already betrayed him once. I can't do it again."

"All you did was, you told him the truth."

"I betrayed him when I took him away from Chattanooga. And I abandoned you and your sister. I did all of that, all at once."

Harry stood, but had to steady himself with a hand on his chair. "You can't ask me to do this, Earley. You can't ask me to do this." He turned and walked from the room, his feet barely lifting from the floor. "Please leave. Please, leave this town. Leave me be, Earley." He heard no door opening or closing, and he didn't look back.

He'd never felt so heavy, lying down to bed. *My son has read my letters. He knows everything now. Oh baby, baby, our son is a killer. I've betrayed everybody now.*

He turned from one side to another. This wouldn't do, his restlessness would wake Emily. He got up, fumbled for some blankets, and shuffled to the sofa in the den.

He buried his face in a pillow there—embroidered trees and "Natchez Trace—1952." That burning, burning, burning, begun so long ago, was back inside again.

◆—◆—◆

At work the secretary gave him a message. A Colored man was waiting. It was about a job.

"Send him away. He's already bothered me at home."

Later, Harry stood by his office window, off to its side so he couldn't be seen, and looked down to the street. Cars were driving by; people were walking; life looked so normal Harry could hardly believe it real. He studied each Negro on the street. He thought he saw him, Earley, stopping at a corner, stepping aside for a White woman, his head down but looking, quickly, once she passed, up at the window where Harry stood.

At home for dinner, Harry could not keep his eyes from the window to his yard. There was his yard boy. But had there been another Negro there? Had they been speaking? After his meal Harry went out and asked him.

"No sir. Nobody's been here but me. I didn't talk to a soul."

Harry wanted to believe him, but he couldn't.

On the street, doing his afternoon errands, Harry was certain he was followed. But he wasn't sure by whom.

After supper Emily called Callie into the dining room. "While I carry y'all home, we can make our plans for tomorrow. There's the shopping, and the cleaning ..."

Callie coughed and Harry remembered.

That night he broached the subject. He was watching television when Emily came in. He turned it off and sat back down. "Emily, do you think it's wise to be hanging on Calpurnia so?"

Emily was at her chair but she didn't sit. She put her purse on it instead. "'Hanging on'? What do you mean, 'hanging on'?"

"I've noticed it, Emily—when I'm at home. These past few weeks, you follow her around the house and you go with her for the shopping. You never used to do that. You'd spend your free time with your friends."

"My 'friends'?" Emily looked around. She picked up a pillow and threw it down at her feet. "You've taken care of my friends."

"I'm just saying, people might think it's unseemly of you. They might talk."

"They already talk! After that Klan flyer? After that picture that you allowed to come out of our house? After you put up all those reporters?"

"You were for that."

"Not for what happened. I never was."

She began to cry. "You don't know what it's like Harry. You haven't needed—you didn't grow up here. You don't see people you've known your entire life cut you in public. And it's worse when they do say something." She picked up her purse and searched for a handkerchief. She daubed her eyes. "Margery, my best friend, who moved away to Kansas? I can't write to her anymore. I can't call her on the telephone. I turn on the evening news and I see my town engulfed in hatred. Those Coloreds marching in the streets and those Whites cursing them—how Margery must think of us now; how she must think of me! I write one line in a letter and I start to cry. I've thrown them all away. So I've got nobody left except you and Evy and y'all are away at work and school all day."

Harry rose from his chair to approach her. She stepped back. "Don't you come near me! Calpurnia is my solace; my only solace. She's the only one I've got who's here with me through the day; who I can count on to listen to me, and who understands what's going on here and wishes that the good folks here—the good Negroes, the good Whites!—wishes they could lift themselves above this hatred and put things right the way they used to be."

She turned to leave the room, but whirled back round to face him. "I'm about to go crazy but I don't see you concerned about it, or you even noticing me. How could you ask me to give up the one friend I have left to comfort me? And her boy, her sweet little boy. I can't turn my back on him."

"Emily, you forbid him to play with Evy."

Emily screamed and ran from the room. Later Harry saw her lugging her bedclothes to the sofa in the den. She had her pillow. Harry followed her in, and without a word he gathered them back to their bedroom. He took his pillow from their bed and two sheets from the closet and moved them there instead. "You keep the bed. I'll sleep in the den."

She followed him but kept her distance. He knew she wouldn't let him touch her.

35 • The Drowned Man

That night Harry wanted his bed, but there was nothing he could do—nothing but to wait, because *he* would be here. Harry didn't even know who this he might be—Timothy or Earley: both Black, both his. He couldn't lock either of them out. *Let him do what he'll do to me, tell me what he'll tell me. Just so Emily and Evy are spared. They would do that for me.* He believed that. So he stayed up late, in the den, waiting.

Harry rubbed his eyes. Timothy was a killer. He now knew everything that had been kept from him. He now knew the depth of his father's betrayal.

The light barely registered on the walls from the moon outside. Harry took in the room—pictures of Emily and Evy, even one of Miss Ester and one of Del Ray; a painted plate from New Orleans, a porcelain doll from Natchez, and seashells from the coast; the trifles and glitter of Emily's life, her birthright, so much of which she valued less than a bowl of pottage. Crazy as it was, he envied her for it, because there was nothing of him in the room. And how could there be? He felt as insubstantial as Earley had looked the night before, a shadow posing as a memory. What was there of his life but letters hidden, and a near-forgotten code now revived, of pictures moved and finally torn to pieces? His son was a killer.

The wind picked up, and tapped a tree against the window, like a finger tapping at his head. A decision beckoned. Shadows bunched and spread against the wall, obscuring this picture and that, and the plate, the doll, and all the knickknacks on the shelves. He would listen once again to Earley, and he would tell him "no" for the very reason that he would listen, for the very reason he'd written him and saved his responses, and the ones from Catherine too—to capture and hold whatever of those lives he could, whatever cords or cables that joined him to his long-lost families, and to never throw another human being away, or betray them.

When Earley came, Harry led him through the kitchen and out to a far corner of the yard, where a bench was sheltered by a willow and hidden by a lilac. The stars were clouded, the moon wasn't much. The lilac blossoms absorbed the meager light and left the heart-shaped leaves dark and gray. The air was sweet, close, and heavy. Harry was struck how Earley's smooth face favored Geneva's. In the dark it made this seem, too much, like an assignation. Assignation, assassination—the words flitted through his mind. His son was a killer and he, Harry, realized he'd be afraid for himself even if he did nothing. But he'd never meant to take a stand. He clung to that. He peered at Earley's face and again saw Geneva's. His breath came short.

Earley was speaking, telling him things that he had never known.

"I want to tell you why I chose you. Why I think you'll do this. It's a hard thing to do—he's your son—but I think you'll do this. My reason might not ... I hope it makes sense to you. You don't realize how ... powerful you seemed to me, back then, how White you seemed to me back then, but you don't any more. That's why. That's why."

Harry said nothing, peering at him. Time was a flood, he was thinking, it stalls and goes backward, just like the water, and then it floods. Earley looked so much like Geneva.

Earley licked his lips and continued.

"That night long ago, with the fire: you never became a Negro, but you stopped being White." He nodded as if he'd asked a question and Harry nodded back. "Okay, you stopped being White—that was from your position, and all those White folks in the crowd. But you see, from my position, you were never more White." He laid his hand on Harry's knee, just a touch, and ran his tongue over his lips again. "Okay, before, you were White enough, because you could have my mamma, and I was old enough to know that it didn't matter how she felt, or even that she was married, none of that mattered because you were a White man so you could have my mamma. But on that night, it wasn't that you saved our lives. That was all too fast for me, and too confusing. All I remembered was suddenly we were outside that fire and then you changed my life forever. You took us. You just upped and took us away. And thinking about that, it came to me, that only a White man could do that, just change our lives like that. So, for a long time you were the Whitest man I ever thought could be. And all that time you were failing at being a Negro—and now I know how adrift you must've been—but all I was thinking was how White you were. You ruled my life. You'd changed it in just one stroke. I was afraid you'd do it again. One shoe dropped, I was waiting for the other."

He stopped and shrugged his shoulders, a slight movement, and Harry nodded his head. "I remember that night driving to Chattanooga, and you kicking the back of my seat."

"Yeah, that's right. I told you about my father. Because you didn't know and I thought you'd as good as killed my father that night. You took us up and made us go." Again he reached and touched Harry. "I'm getting ahead of myself here, but later, much later, after I'd grown, I realized something. My father was in the crowd that night. He had to be. Nobody missed a fire. So he watched it all, and he didn't do nothing while you— And you remember ... what my momma said to you?"

" 'Come on baby. Let's go.' "

"Yeah, that's it. She looked that crowd over and then she called you 'baby.' What would you have done if she hadn't called you 'baby'?"

Harry shook his head. "I don't know—"

"She said 'Baby, let's go' and so you took us, or rather, *she took you*, she took all of us. She took us home. She took us to our family." Earley licked his lips. "My mamma saw my father in that crowd. And then she turned to you and said, 'Come on, baby. Let's go.' That's what I now believe. She's the one who changed our lives. You weren't so White. You were just a natural man—a scared and confused man.

"I'm telling you now, what I would've told you if I'd written to you. That's why I hardly ever did, so I wouldn't tell you this. But if I'm going to ask you to betray your child, you deserve to hear this."

Harry could picture Geneva's brave face, held high, scanning the crowd in the orange light. *One flesh, made from our flesh, and look what I've done—our son is a killer.*

Earley was speaking. "But before that, when I was a child, I believed in childish things. I thought you were so White. And when my momma died, there was the other shoe. And then, after you left, my grandmother, Mama Lou, she took sick."

Harry nodded his head. "Geneva's mother, Mama Lou—I remember her. She and your Big Mama Darling—Big Mama Darling had your home house—you see, I remember it all.

They were the ones who'd decided I could stay. They sided with your mother—"

"—against my grandfather, yeah, he told me that, after you'd gone. He told us he knew you'd never stick." Earley took out a handkerchief and wiped his face. Lilly missed you ... really missed you. She couldn't understand why you left us."

Harry peered into the darkness beyond Earley's face. *Oh baby, baby, just look at our child.* He blinked his eyes. "I ... I had to leave. I had no time left. I couldn't wait."

Earley held up his hand. "Now let me finish. I said these were childish things, but not all of them. Not all. This is something you don't know—

"When Mama Lou got sick, she got so she couldn't leave her room. Lilly and I would visit her every day. I remember: the house seemed to smell different to me than it did before. That, I believe was my Mama Lou. And it was darker. Grandpa would draw the curtains closed, but in my mind the curtains weren't it—it'd just become a dark place to be in. Later on, I'd think about how dark whiteness was. You see, Grandpa had worked so hard to keep all that whiteness at bay. But ... our family doctor had died. He was Colored. The Klan had run the other one out of town. Grandpa had no choice but to get my Mama Lou a White doctor. Anyway, Lilly and I would walk very slowly to our Mama Lou's room; I'd run a hand along the wall; it was so dark only the feeling on my fingertips told me where I was. Lilly held my other hand.

"We'd sit with her. She had this wild look on her face. She'd cry the pain was so bad she couldn't take it. She couldn't walk with this pain, she couldn't work with this pain. The doctor, she said, he didn't care about how an old Colored woman felt, or whether she lived or died, so he wouldn't do anything about this pain. Lilly would stroke her hair, her cheek, and Mama Lou … she'd take hold of my shoulder, she'd grab on to my upper arm, and she'd squeeze so tight it hurt. 'You've got to do something for me. You've got to do something about this pain.' Crying while Lilly stroked her hair.

"And I was only a child, you understand. I'd look at her face and into her eyes, and I could understand her words. I could see her panic. And I knew what the word 'pain' meant. I'd felt pain. But I couldn't feel hers, I couldn't feel how bad it was, or what kind it was, and as we sat there I wished I could take it and feel it and howl and scream from it, and then she would know that I knew what it was. How she felt. And that scared me. I was just a boy.

"Her holding on to my arm, I told her, 'Mama Lou, Lilly's here. She's stroking your hair.' And Lilly'd put her finger to her lips, telling me to hush. And she kept on stroking her hair and face, and she whispered low, 'Mama Lou. Mama Lou.' And after a while, Mama Lou would reach with her other hand to take hold of mine.

"But I couldn't take it. I couldn't share her pain. And how she looked at me and her voice, that scared me too. It was all too much for me.

"She'd say to me, 'You got to do something.'

"She'd say, 'You got to stop this.'

"And I'd start crying. 'Please don't, Mama Lou.' And then there was another hand on my shoulder. It was my grandpa's hand. He took Lilly and me from the bedroom and then he went back and I could hear his voice, murmuring, and hers, pleading, and finally only his and then he was out there with us in the hallway, and he looked at us careful, real careful, back and forth from one face to the other, and then he told Lilly to go back in. 'Your Mama Lou loves you to stroke her hair.' Then he turned to me and said, 'It's a shame, boy, to see her and be stuck inside your skin.' So, he knew how I was feeling, because he felt it too."

Earley paused. He ran his tongue across his lips again. "Here's the point. That's what I thought was wrong with you. You were always content to be stuck inside your skin. I mean, you never thought you could escape it. And that didn't bother you. Not so much. Not enough. Back then I thought you didn't need to worry about it because you were White. I don't think that anymore."

Harry shook his head. "This isn't fair. How do you know what I think? You think I don't care? You think that's why I won't say 'yes' to you now?" He was leaning in, up close. "When I told Timothy the truth he left and I've never seen him again. He left and now you tell me he's joined the Klan. When I told him the truth, I turned him into a murderer."

Harry stopped and shook his head again, violently. "No, no, no. I did that when I took him away from you, and Lilly. His family. I turned him into nothing; just an empty house, for seven—" Harry stopped, looking at Earley.

He was looking off somewhere, maybe trying to see to the street out front. "When my grandpa told me and my sister you'd gone, he said it was good riddance. My sister was bawling, and all of a sudden I was on him, beating at his chest with my fists. He was getting old by then, and I must've done some damage, he almost fell backwards and he couldn't get hold of my fists. Uncle Pete had to pull me off. And I probably knew, even then, that I really was trying to hit you and maybe my real father too. And now I figure I was trying to hit myself as well— And I think my grandfather knew. He was never a gentle man, but he was gentle with me then."

Harry didn't say anything. He'd let Earley say his piece. But he wondered how long this would be his life now, meeting here at night, in his house or here in the yard. He already was waiting for it, waiting through the day. Would he one day look forward to it? It was folly. These meetings couldn't last. He looked back behind him to the street as well. He knew he was flirting with disaster.

"Mr. Harry, here, let me finish now. That's what I thought about you when I was growing—you were the Whitest man I could ever know. You'd changed my life two times over. You had that power. It would make me angry. But that faded as I grew. And then I got your letter."

Earley chuckled softly. "You were smart to send it to the home house. It was Lillie's house by then. I'd moved on to New York City. She sent it to me. You remember what you wrote in it?"

"I sure do. Half of it was me apologizing for writing."

"And the other half was explaining how I'd likely never get it. And I wrote back saying you could write to me, and I'd tell you if ever my address changed, but I wasn't likely to reciprocate your letters." Early glanced toward the street, and then back at Harry. "And I didn't. Not much ... a time or two."

Harry said, "I looked at that envelope a long time before I dropped it in the box. I figured I could've rolled that letter into a bottle, and dropped it in a river, and it would've had just as much a chance of getting to you. I think that's how I got the nerve to send it—I figured it'd just get lost."

"You never apologized to me for leaving—never to me or to my sister—just for writing. I waited for that apology for a long time. But your letters calmed me. They jolted something loose inside and then they calmed me. You just wrote about what happened to you. And reading them I saw that here was just a man, set upon by circumstance, unasked for—just like me, just like me."

Earley paused, and then he repeated it, "—just like me. You're not a White man to me anymore. You're just a natural man. That's how I can ask you what I'm asking—to put a stop to evil. I wouldn't ask you if you were White. It's what you'd ask a natural man."

Harry sighed and shook his head. "You think because I won't, that I don't care. You talk about evil." He pointed back to the house. "Inside there's a boy. I married his mother to protect him from evil. I don't think I've done anything since then to help him. But if I do as you ask it would destroy his life."

Earley looked at the house—all its windows dark. "I believe you think that. But you don't know." He looked back at Harry. "I'll be coming back."

Harry smiled a faint, wan smile. "I know you will."

"I want you to tell your story to somebody I met here. He's a SNCC worker. I want him to break the news. I want it to come from the Movement."

"He knows about it? You've told him?"

"Yeah, but you're the only one with proof, all those letters. You've got to give them to him."

"I won't have a word to tell him."

"Yes you will. I'll be back."

That was it. They stood there for a moment longer. Then Earley nodded, and then he left.

Harry watched him go. *Oh baby, baby, how did my life get so big?*

The couch, the folded sheets upon it, waited for Harry. Back in the house, he wished he could squeeze his life down to size and stuff it in the pillow there. He'd lay his head down on it, and sleep and dream—as small a life as possible.

36 • The Drowned Man

Harry was in his office. He usually left at five but it was well past six. He had telephoned Emily to hold his supper and it had been an awkward conversation. That day at dinner she'd complained that she'd be alone all day, that Callie had taken the day—"very urgent business" not specified. Now, on the telephone, she told him she'd had nobody but Evy to talk to—no adult all day, and now he'd be home late. "I'm about ready to tear down the walls, Harry." He suggested she call Miss Marley, the widow from across the street. "You can watch the television together. She'd like that. She doesn't have one. I'll be home before dark."

Emily was silent for a moment. "Maybe you're right. I need to see more people." The line went quiet again. "And when you come home, you needn't sleep in the guest room." Harry told her that would be fine. "I didn't sleep well at all last night. I sleep better with you."

He tried to finish up his work but it was hard for him to concentrate. He looked at the clock. He looked at the sky. It was almost seven when Miss Marley called.

"Harry! Come quick! Come home!"

"What? What's wrong?"

"It's an emergency!"

Harry heard the phone click. She'd hung up. He drove as fast as he could.

A police car was parked in front of his house. And Miss Ester's car. An ambulance was backed in his drive. Harry parked in the street and ran up to his door. It was open. He saw the stretcher coming out; he had to step aside to let it pass. It was Emily, her eyes closed, out like a light and a sheet up to her chin; and standing behind her was Miss Ester, severe, gripping Evy's hand, and Evy's eyes bewildered and scared, glued to his mother.

Harry gasped. "What happened?" A policeman stepped up to his side.

Miss Ester faced him and pulled Evy behind her. "You're as much to blame as anybody. Look at her!" She didn't wait for a reply. She turned and followed the stretcher to the ambulance.

"What happened?" Harry followed Miss Ester, Evy; he tried to reach for the boy. "What happened to her?"

"She's had a nervous breakdown. Look in there," Miss Ester pointed back to the open front door, "dishes and things thrown against the walls. She's a danger to herself and to my grandchild. I'm going to have her committed to a sanitarium. I'm taking Evers."

Harry couldn't speak. He turned and looked back through the door. She was right. The television, the photographs, the painted plate, the porcelain doll, everything upended. Then he heard Evy's voice behind him, in the driveway. Harry looked at the boy. "Why'd that—," Evy looked up at his grandmother and she nodded, and then he finished his question, "—why'd that nigger hurt my momma?"

"What?" Harry looked at Miss Ester. "You can't do—"

"Stay back. You were no protection to my daughter. You brought this evil to this town."

Evy was looking into Harry's eyes, "Why'd that nigger hurt my momma?" He said it without faltering this time, but Harry could see the boy was confused. What could he mean?

"Who did this, Evy?"

They were loading Emily into the ambulance. Miss Ester was pulling Evy away. He was looking back at Harry. He was saying something. Harry could hardly hear him— Miss Ester was jerking him to her side, talking over his voice: "He's living with me now."

Harry reached for Evy. Wide-eyed, trembling, and crying, Evy stretched out his hand. Harry caught it, but the policeman grabbed Harry's wrist and twisted it, sharp and hard, and Harry had to let the boy go. The policeman pulled Harry around to face him, and put his hand on Harry's chest. Harry stared at the cop, started to push his hand away, saw the hatred in the policeman's eyes, and slowly stepped back instead.

Harry looked over the cop's shoulder at the ambulance, at Evy. What had he said? It sounded like 'Callie.'

Harry watched Miss Ester load her grandson into the backseat of her car and get in after and strike her umbrella on the front seat before her, her way of signaling her driver, and then Harry watched the car glide away, taking Evy to her house. He watched the ambulance leave. The policeman gave Harry a shove, sharp, but not enough to knock him down; then he sauntered to his car and left.

Harry looked around. The front door of his car stood open, jutting into the street. He walked around the car to close it. And in each house people were watching him. There was nobody in the windows, there was nobody at the doors, but he knew he was being watched just the same. He was pinned to the middle of the street, exposed—this, his last betrayal—he didn't even know what he had done—but he was burning, burning, from the inside out. There was everything to see, there was nothing left to see. He hunched his shoulders and put the heels of his hands up to his eyes.

37 • The Drowned Man

Lloyd made some phone calls while Harry sat slumped in Lloyd's parlor. Harry had been turned away at the hospital. He didn't even know if Emily was there. Lloyd was his last resort. Harry didn't bother to put on the light, he just let the daylight drain. There was nothing much to see here anyway: some magazines, the couch he was sitting on, the table before it, the window across. His son—Evy was certainly his son now, made kin by his betrayal—gone to that evil house. He thought Callie'd hurt his momma. Callie? Harry couldn't believe it. There had been no bruises on Emily that he could see. But under the sheet—? Maybe. Harry knew nothing. Just his boy's words—what he'd called Callie. Evy had never used that word before. And his last look, being pulled away, he was pleading—what's happening? And that house, taken to that crazy, evil house.

Lloyd walked in, sat across from Harry, and got down to business. "Emily had Miss Marley over—she didn't care to eat her supper alone, with you working late, so she'd invited her over." Harry knew this, but he sat, silent, and listened to Lloyd.

Lloyd leaned forward, his arms on his thighs, his hands between his knees. "They were watching the six o'clock news and there she was, Callie, on the television, in the footage from today's march. Miss Marley said Emily dropped her tea. She stood up, she was transfixed. 'That's Callie ... how could she?'— Miss Marley said Callie was standing in the line to register to vote, and somebody from the crowd had thrown a rock. Callie turned, she raised her fist, she was looking at the faces cursing her, and then she took a step. A policeman appeared; he put his hands on her. She pushed at him, they grappled, and then another cop came, he had his billy club out, and then she got wild. The camera joggled; it went askew. But you could still see the policemen, their backs, as they closed down on her." Lloyd leaned back and put his hands on the armrests of his chair. "And then they dragged her away. Her whole body was limp."

Lloyd told him all this in a monotone, droning like a fan, steady, as if every day is just like the next; and that was a lie—that's what Harry would remember thinking, that and a minor sense of aggravation at the manner of Lloyd's speaking. Harry stood, but suddenly felt so weary he plopped back down again.

Lloyd finished: "Miss Marley said Emily started screaming. She started screaming Callie's name. She knocked the television down. She started throwing things. And Evy saw it all. The little boy was terrified. Miss Marley scooped him up and carried him out and called Miss Ester from her house."

Harry murmured, "Marley Breecher, she called me … later." They both sat silent for a moment. "Was Emily hurt? I couldn't see."

"No, but they gave her a sedative. That's why she was out when you got there."

Lloyd paused, but Harry said nothing so Lloyd continued. "First off, they took her to the hospital. But then Miss Ester had her moved."

"Where has she taken her?"

Lloyd named a sanitarium in Memphis. "They're good. They'll calm her down. Keep a good watch until she's better."

"I'll go see her."

Lloyd looked over to the side, away from Harry, and rubbed the back of his neck. "You'll have to ask Miss Ester to do that. She's had her declared incompetent. She's taken power of attorney."

Harry said nothing. For a moment he was lost. He'd been looking down, but now he looked up at Lloyd. "She can't keep him. I've got to get him back."

Lloyd leaned forward, frowned. "Do you mean Evy?"

"Yes, of course I mean Evy. He's my boy. She can't have him."

"So he's your boy now." Lloyd leaned back. "When did he become …?"

"You've got to do something, Lloyd. You've got to get a court order. You've got …"

"*I* don't have to do anything, Harry. More to the point, I *can't* do anything—because you don't have a legal leg to stand on. And that's your fault, Stranger. You never adopted that boy, and I begged you to." Lloyd lowered his head and shook it, a small, slight motion. When he looked back at Harry his face was placid. "Miss Ester's the only person who's got a legal claim on that boy."

"But his mother."

"His mother's in a sanitarium. Her mother put her there."

"But she has no right to. I'm her nearest kin, I'm her husband. You can get a court order for that."

"But you're nobody, Stranger. And that's your fault too."

"What do you mean? Are you talking about that goddamned newspaper picture?"

Lloyd looked down at his hands, clasped in his lap, his chin tucked down against his neck. "Well, that picture, yes. But … well, we—the good people here in town—we didn't like that picture. We wanted to forget about it." He looked up at Harry. "And we would've, but for all your years here, Stranger, there's been nothing—you've done nothing that you or anybody else here can talk about. Not one story."

He settled back in his chair. "Miss Ester, now, she's not blood either, like you aren't, and she married in, like you did, and that was Del Ray's house and his uncle's before him, but she's made it her own. When people talk about that house, they talk about Miss Ester. It's her story now." He waved Harry quiet. "And it doesn't matter if it's a crazy house. And it doesn't even matter if it's evil. It's her house, and it's her story—one of *our* stories. Don't you get that? She's cleared the ground she stands on. She belongs. We take care of our own. Don't you see?"

Harry blurted out a laugh. "I can't believe ..."

"Just who are you Harry? Where did you come from? Where were you born? Who are your people? Really, Stranger, you've never given us an accounting of yourself."

Lloyd waited. Finally, Harry spoke. "You'd help me if I told you?"

"Maybe. It depends on what you say."

Harry gripped the arms of his chair. He wanted to flee. "But the boy ..."

"... is with his nearest blood relative, his grandmother."

"But she's crazy. And her house *is* evil."

"Don't change the subject Harry."

"All those stories about Del Ray killing Negroes—he filled a whole room full of his trophies, ears in jars—like people did after lynchings. And she's still got them." Harry rose out of his chair. He stood over Lloyd, leaned down, put his face up close.

"Look, you once told me it doesn't matter about the law. It's just the people who enforce it."

"Harry ..."

"Everybody knows what that house is like. They know what Del Ray was like."

"Harry ..."

"That's no place to raise a child. Everybody knows that. You can ..."

"Harry!" Lloyd stood. "First off, get out of my face and sit down. You haven't listened to a word I said. And I asked you a question. Are you going to answer it? And answer me another one—it's really the same one—how come you never adopted that boy?"

Harry said nothing. He took a step back, felt his body pulsating; maybe it was just him, or maybe his body was bulging and ebbing, like a figure in a fun-house mirror or a body underwater.

Lloyd, still standing, scowled. "Was it the background check? What are you afraid of?"

"I'm a good man, Lloyd."

Lloyd turned away, was looking elsewhere, at something—Harry didn't know what—through his darkened window. "That's not good enough Harry."

Harry looked to the door. He had to get out of this room.

Lloyd waved his hand—a dismissal. "It doesn't matter. The boy is with his own. He's with us." He walked over to the door. This was goodbye. He was looking at Harry and Harry could see it in Lloyd's eyes; he didn't even have to hear the words. "I'm sorry Harry, I really am, but there's nothing I can do."

Harry drove out of town. He drove to the old ruined dock he'd visited his first day here. Down a dirt road, past a torn-down building, right to the river's edge— Harry left the keys in his car. He walked, slowly, into the river, up to his knees. The water was warm in the night. That still noise he'd heard here before, when he decided he would stay, it hadn't changed. The water, the insect drone, the green smells of flowers and algae and fish—he paused, becalmed, and turned to the west, to the treetops, to the glare of the lights of the town. This abandoned place: he'd learned this was the first landing built on the river, it was to have been the center of town—that was eighty years ago. Was that so long a time? This river so still, but he could feel its currents at his feet. The whole world was turning, going about its business, but he was standing still. His breathing came deeper. The night of the fire, the day here at the demonstration, the day he told Timothy the truth: he had always told himself he had never meant to take on the world, he had only done what a decent man would do. This was what it got him. You've got nothing left to lose, and then you lose some more, until you have nothing, and still you lose some more.

He had nothing left to lose. And none of this—why Evy was gone, the why of that evil house, the why of his lies to Timothy, of the fire—none of that could stand.

He slowly turned; the mud pulled on his ruined shoes. On the bank he took them off, his socks too, and threw them in the river. Barefoot, he got back in his car. He was going to drive home and wait for his last son left—Earley.

Earley was waiting for him. He emerged from behind the willow and the lilac—Harry could smell the blossoms on his clothes. Harry told him, "Get your friend. Bring him here tomorrow night. They've taken my boy away. This will always happen, and it cannot stand. It must be stopped. Whatever I can do, this cannot stand."

The next day Harry took the box out of his safe. All the pictures, all the letters, he stuffed them in his pockets. Before that, he withdrew a sum of money from his bank. Not all of it. That could draw attention. Nobody could know what he was going to do.

And the first thing he did was buy new clothes for Evy.

38 • The Wounded Man

They pick me off that bench and drag me to that jail. I'm barely alive. I'm on my stomach on the floor. I can feel every mote in the air—everything in the world hangs just above me, poised inches off my back. Any second now, it's all going to fall. I pass out.

I'm in a hospital. I'm back in jail. I'm nothing but my stories. I'm nothing but my back. The whole world's falling on it.

Out there, kneeling back down to that bench, somebody stole my voice from me. So ... okay; from here on out, I'm not going to say a mumbling word. Besides, some things are too hard to hear, to say.

But my stories won't leave me be. They're rolling and a tumbling, way inside my head; one comes up top and then another, and another. Two in particular: Our first freedom meeting; that was months ago. And now, here in jail, laid out on the floor, is another story too. They come and go, one and then the other, over and over, and again and again.

◆━━◆━━◆

You get to the Negro Elks Hall at the edge of Williams Point, near its southeastern corner, at the end of a dead-end street that points, like an aspiration, to the highway going west. Everything new in this town has been built along that highway. There's the Holiday Inn. There's the industrial park, built sometime back in the 'fifties. It's got only one factory—they make pianos—it's the only building there. Beyond it are the cotton fields, brownish black in the winter's night.

The Elks Hall was built as big as a church. It stands off by itself from the few houses on the street. It's surrounded by a lawn of hard, broad-bladed grass that's trampled flat and slick with decay where the Elks park their cars. Even with the building's size, I wonder: do all the good White people driving on that highway ever look its way? Do they ever consider the life inside it? I think they're missing history. We held our first freedom meeting there, in January, in 1963. Everybody who'd signed up for our food was there.

They didn't know what to expect. They found their way through the rows of folding chairs, murmuring and nodding. For most, this was their first time here. They took it all in, looking this way and that. The radiators against the walls, so many of them and all turned on; people pointed and took off their coats. They looked at the polished, wooden walls with their yellow, orange, and reddish hues. In the dim light, amber skin looked brown and brown skin looked Black. We passed out fans at the door—flat sticks like large tongue depressors stabled to cardboard ovals with the printed words "Freedom Now." The hall grew crowded. Some people already were fanning themselves. Most were dressed for church.

Aunt Ertharin stood up and began to sing. She didn't announce the song, she just sang the first line, "This little light of mine," and the crowd sang back, "I'm gonna let it shine."

She sang the second verse. "Hide it under a bushel? No!" And the crowd sang back, "Let it shine, let it shine, let it shine!"

It was our gospel voice, the spread harmonies, the moan wrapped in joy.

People stood and swayed in time: sideways, slowing to a pause, then snapping back the other way, and slowing to a pause again. Aunt Ertharin sang the new words, "I've got the light of freedom," and the crowd sang back, "I'm gonna let it shine." Women sang wordlessly in rippling moans, and a soprano voice reached way up. The Rev. Lispcomb walked to the front and joined Aunt Ertharin. They made up new lyrics, right on the spot. The crowd sang them back and then sang entire verses with them, "I'm marching with the light of freedom, I'm gonna let it shine!" "We've got the light inside us, we're gonna let it shine." The people pressed forward. They worked their fans. "Freedom's gonna light the world, we're gonna let it shine." Then another song, and another; swapping out old words with new. "Ain't nobody gonna turn me round, turn me round, turn me round ... Mayor Lott ain't gonna turn me round, turn me round, turn me round ... Ku Klux Klan ain't gonna turn me round." People shouted and laughed, they pointed their fans and waved their hands. They wiped the sweat off from their faces while they sang.

Then Morgan walked up to the podium and raised his hands for quiet. Somebody said amen.

Morgan looked over the crowd before he spoke. He took a deep breath. "I come from Drew. You know where that is, and some of you even knew my father. But most of y'all didn't. You didn't know him and you don't know me. So I'm going to tell you a little bit about myself so y'all will know who I am.

"I grew up in Drew, right here in the Delta. That was the spot my father chose. His family came from some place in Georgia: a place we never went back to, with a name we never mentioned. I couldn't call it now to save my soul. The year they left—it was my grandfather and grandmother, and my father and my mother, and I was just a baby, and two uncles and an aunt—we all came. There were more of us we left behind. I couldn't call them to you now. We followed a White man who we'd worked for on that Georgia place. It was never spoken: why *we* left. But the Delta was someplace to go to, and Georgia was someplace to leave. That White man, Mr. Henry ... he could've been worse, easily worse.

"That Mr. Henry, living way out in Georgia, had managed to marry a Delta planter's daughter, so he came West to settle on her father's place, just outside of Drew. That was White folks' mess. My growing up in a foreign place, for no reason that I understood, with little knowledge of the people we left behind—that was Black folks' mess."

He put his hands on the podium, fluttering his fingers on the edge of the wood.

"I have one memory of Mr. Henry's place in Drew. It wasn't a single thing. It was a repeated thing. Every fall, after the cotton was in and Mr. Henry had figured each family's share and the deductions for food and clothing, for the mule and the plow and the harness, for the doctor and whatever else Mr. Henry figured, and here's what you got left; and then my elders would stay up late into the night if they'd broke above even, and they'd figure the cost of a house and a store, and every fall they'd curse the shares and they'd promise themselves to be gone for sure if they ever made enough. And then there came that one holy year, when the weather was right and the market was high, and because Mr. Henry was mostly an honest man, they finally made enough money to leave." Morgan smiled. "I always have a chuckle about that: that Negroes on shares couldn't leave a cheating planter—not straight up during the day. From those you had to sneak away at midnight. You know what I'm talking about. Only an honest planter, like Mr. Henry, who figured your shares right and didn't overcharge your deductions, it was only one of those that a Negro could leave straight up in the light of day. Only the good Whites had to face our good riddance.

"All those years, cropping for an honest White man; that place was never my home."

<hr>

It's nighttime in this jail. It's my first night here, but I don't know what day it is. Somebody cuts off the one light bulb we've got. There, in the dark, everybody sings a freedom song:

Now, we've been 'buked, and we've been scorned.
We've been talked about, sure as you're born.
We have served our time in jail
With no money to go our bail.
But we'll never turn back. No, we'll never turn back
Until we've all been freed.

The words pour slow, draw long. I'm on my stomach, on the floor. I can't sing a word. I can feel an itch, all over my back. Just below it, a dull pain seeps down from my skin to my muscles.

My head is turned to one side. Somebody comes over and kneels down behind me, at my ear. It's Morgan—I can't turn my head but I know his voice. He's whispering so only I can hear.

"That song takes me way back. 'Never turn back, never turn back.' My grandmother sang it to me. It's a nighttime song. It keeps you alive until you wake up next morning."

I don't say a word.

Morgan goes on. "My grandmother told me that Jesus holds all the souls to his bosom. But he can only hold so many of them, so every time a baby's born, Jesus drops a soul down from heaven and that becomes the baby's soul. And Jesus is careful to only drop a soul from the same family. So, you see, we're all our ancestors. That's what my grandmother believed, and that's what she taught me. And I do honor for her, and for all my elders."

A clock is tolling somewhere outside. Inside there's footsteps somewhere and a cough, and something else: I can't tell if it's laughing or crying—but it's the most wretched sound I have ever heard. Somebody—I think he's in another cell—is tossing on his mattress. He's lucky he has one.

"Aleck, I'm going tell you something I've told nobody else—not even my own people. Even with my grandmother's, and my own mamma's teaching, as I grew older I couldn't find it to believe in a Jesus that White folks worshipped. I only could see that he was the White man's god. So I stepped aside from their teaching. But there was one thing I could believe from the Bible—from the Old Testament—'dust to dust.' Now, you know, when you're out by a river or a creek, and you stoop down and look at the soil—it's black.

"Now here's what I believe; that color comes from us, from our ancestors' bodies buried here. We worked this earth. When we Negroes die we become this earth. Not just our blood and muscle and bone, but our souls too. We don't fly up to Jesus' arms. No, our souls seep down into this earth right here, the earth our descendants one day will walk on. And we walk on our ancestors now."

The dull pain is growing sharper. The itch is turning to fire.

"That's why it's such a sin, what's been done to us. I don't care about segregation, but we were kept from our rightful ownership of this soil, our ancestors' souls. We've been driven out, it doesn't matter where we've gone—to Florida or Georgia, or Memphis or Chicago, or even little stores in Drew. We should've been able to stay on the land. Work the land. And reap whatever we sow. When we eat what we sow, when we walk on our land, our ancestors nurture us. That's what I believe. And that's why I'll never go up North, no matter how bad it gets down here. A man shouldn't walk on another man's ancestors."

―◆―◆―

In the Elks Hall, at the freedom meeting, Morgan gripped each side of the podium with both hands. He had the crowd with him, hanging on his every word. "When we moved to Drew we bought a dog-trot house and rented a storefront that we tended. My father also worked in the cotton seed mill. We'd often pass by the road that led to Mr. Henry's place, but we never turned in. Just like Georgia, we had no need to go back and we had no desire. One uncle still cropped shares, but no longer there. He bounced around. The other uncle moved to Memphis and then to Chicago. Every summer he'd send his children back to Drew—that dog-trot house became the family's home house. And it surely was home, in a way Mr. Henry's place could never be. It was the spot my father chose.

"Georgia, Mr. Henry's place: neither one was home. And there were so few memories, just the years, too many years. So much of your life really isn't yours. So much of your life is passed in places that you and your kin don't choose. And life there is paltry—not just money poor, but paltry. From first light to last, plowing and planting and chopping and picking, the heat and the sweat, the bits of cotton plant under your clothes, your fingers cramped by noon; everything's tiring and mindless, because none of its yours. None of the work is yours. It's just your body aching."

That night in jail, Morgan touches my arm, gingerly. He whispers, asks me if I'm alright. Are my bandages okay? I think I nod my head, but I'm not sure it moves. I feel pinned to the floor. He tells me I'd have a cot or a bed, but the police took them all from the cell. I try to catch every word he says, words my pain tries to push aside. He tells me, still whispering, his voice closer to my ear, "This land can speak. The ancestors buried in it, they would speak to us if we worked this land as *our* land—they would tell us what to plant, and where and when. *We would just know.* But the White folk came between us. They decided what we'd plant, how much and where and when. So our land's been denied to us."

He pauses. I wonder if he's finished, if he's gone. But he's still there beside me.

"Now you listen to me carefully, Aleck. Now, you understand me. I don't trust Isaac. You mustn't listen to a word he says. He's a Jew. His people, they should understand this, our displacement. They're displaced too. But he doesn't seem to care. None of them seem to care. You got this Aleck?" He pauses. I don't say a word. "I asked him this when I first met him, and he never did answer me: 'Why aren't you agitating up in New York City? I know your people have problems up there. That's where you live.' That's the problem I have with him and his kind: just his being here says to me he doesn't care about being from any particular place. He's always talking about the 'universal brotherhood of man.' His kind all stick together, and I'd say that's a good thing, but he won't even admit to that. *His* kind, his 'spiritual' kind he calls them, he says they're from all over; they're from everywhere. That's the way Jews are: everywhere, and no roots. Now, if you look at a map you'll find all sorts of places, real places, but you won't find any 'everywhere.' That's just something people like him think up. But it doesn't exist! It isn't real. It's nowhere. And that's my problem with his kind; he denies his heart, his core. He preaches an idea about people, but he doesn't preach real people."

The pain grows. It seeps further down into my body. I don't say a mumbling word.

◆—◆—◆

In the freedom meeting, Morgan raised his hands. He held all those people up in them. The Elks Club was his own personal church. "How can a man work, how can he stand, when he has no ground that's his? Your memory is belittled by shame, it turns fitful, it's full of holes and places worn thin like second-hand clothes. Whole clumps of your life are best forgotten and gone. So I say blessed is the man who can stand because that man can place himself *in a place*. The storefront in Drew, the home house—those were my father's life-sermons.

"Our home house, that was my father's home, but sometimes I'd wonder if it ever was mine." Morgan hesitated and put his hand on his heart. "Understand me, I loved my father and he loved me. Of course it was my home. But sometimes I wondered. Sometimes I was afraid that I never, really, ever owned my past. Not all of it. Parts were always held beyond me. And if you don't own your own past, how can you own where you lived it?" He paused again; the people were quiet, nobody moved.

"How can you own your past when so much is done to you, by White folks? I'd ask myself that, many times. And how can you be home, when it's White folks who're in charge? Those thoughts troubled me. They've troubled me all my years."

Somebody said "Amen." That stirred people. Voices raised—affirmation, exclamation. Morgan reached out his hand for quiet.

"I understood you've got to stand up right where you live. I understood you've got to stand up and take what's yours and you can't let your fear rule you. I understood, because that's what my father taught me. That's what freedom is! If you want to be free you've got to stand up and claim this spot your home! I knew what should be done." He paused again and looked down at the podium. Then as he spoke he slowly raised his head. "What I didn't understand was that *I'd* never done that before, myself; done what my father did, not until now, here in Williams Point. I'd never stood up to those who would own my past and deny me my home and tell them NO!" His arm swept wide. "So this is my home, this is my home, this is my home. And I own my home! Because it doesn't matter how poor y'all are, what kind of money y'all don't have; the only thing y'all need to own your own home is to claim it! It don't matter what the deed says! And when y'all claim it, y'all are free!"

I'm looking off to a corner in the jail. Morgan stays behind me. Maybe he's sitting on the floor, maybe he's on all fours, leaning to my ear. I don't know.

"Aleck, you've known me just about all your life, just about as long you've known your own mother and father. You know how much I loved my Emma, how I mourned her when she died. She never gave me children, you know that, and I don't know the fault of that, I don't suppose it matters. But all those years when I had all you boys under my wing, I'd look at each one of you and wonder, which of you, if any of you, could've been as good as any boy of mine. Because mine would've been a special boy, a comfort to his parents and a light to his people. And I've sorely missed that, the pride of being a father to a boy like that.

"That boy is you, Aleck. No other one comes close. That's why I chose you to join me here. It shouldn't be any surprise that I love you like a son. I'd like you to consider ... that you'd see me as your father.

"Aleck, I told you—I told all you boys coming up in Drew, your fathers beat y'all the way they did because they were afraid of what the White man would do if y'all ever misstepped. But Aleck, your father never beat you. He ignored you. He put you at risk, without that proper disciple. Your father was never afraid of any White man ... but he ignored you because he was afraid of his own heart."

I concentrate to hear. I also try to think ... a memory from home. With the pain, I can't quite focus—

"You need more from a father than that, Aleck. He's got to keep you at arm's length, because a man can't touch his own without touching his heart."

I'm trying to catch that memory, but I'm afraid if I let go of Morgan's words I'll drift away ... from ... me on my back, my head turned to the side, the sticky, rough concrete beneath my cheek, the humid hot air on me, the bandages burning, the pain seeping—me.

His hand is on my arm again.

"He's afraid of where his heart will take him, Aleck. He's got good reason, too. He killed a man, Aleck, that's where his heart took him. That one time. If his heart ever ruled him again, he'd be like a locomotive out of control. So he'll never change. He's a strong man that way—I'll give his due—but he can't be the father you need." He's patting my arm. He's stroking it. "You think about it Aleck. I'd be a good father to you."

And then he's gone.

And somewhere I see—remember—my Papa Joe. He's looking at me so kindly, because I'm upset, and he's telling me my father's a good man, that my mother wouldn't have married him if he wasn't. "And I wouldn't've let her." And I'm disappointed because my grandfather didn't give any credence to my complaint, whatever it had been. And that's it, or all that I recall; just a scrap—his face and words. This is the first time I've even remembered it.

So I'm thinking, how many other memories are missing and how can I know who I really am, or who my father is, with all that I've forgotten. I want to hear my father's story. Not from Morgan. From him. I want to tell him mine. Everything I know. I want to write a letter home. To my daddy, home.

I wince. I'm sweating. The pain is growing. The heavy air above, the bandages' fire, the pain spreading, and the anguish in my chest. The anguish in my head. It that where my soul is? My chest and my head? *Hold me in your arms, Daddy. I'll hold you in mine. Tell me your heart, Daddy; I'll tell you mine.*

To Morgan, I don't say a mumbling word.

Morgan stepped away from the podium. Folks were shouting praise and encouragement. He raised his hands for quiet. "I've always feared that this feeling I've got about not owning my past, not completely as a White man must, might be something common among our race; that maybe we've wandered in the wilderness too many days too long, and me a life too long; and that we're doomed always to be sojourners. But now I know my fears are wrong."

He stepped back up to the podium. "Now I know my father owned more than just a house. Now I know he owned his past and his freedom too! He was as free as he could be. And he had nothing to be ashamed of. I'll repeat that. Whatever he did, to Negro or White, he had nothing to be ashamed of. And neither do any of you. Y'all have nothing to be ashamed of. No matter how poor y'all might be. No matter what y'all might've done. Because today, this Day of the Lord, we've stood up to our fear and we've claimed our pasts, all of us. We all own our pasts now, and with every note we've sung tonight we've shared them with each other. So y'all have nothing to be ashamed of, and y'all never had. Never had, never had. Don't let anybody say you've ever had anything to be ashamed of.

"This is something new, what we're asking y'all to do. When y'all come with us to the courthouse, past all the White men's stores, and ask to register to vote—no, no, *demand* that you be registered—y'all will be doing something never done before. When y'all go in, in one big group, with the White folks watching, and demand to be registered, y'all will be doing something never done before. It's going to be a new way from here on out. We're not whispering any more. We're not patient any more. We want our freedom now, and we'll shout it from the rooftops. So don't any of you ever be ashamed of what you were before. Be proud of who you are now, and be proud of the ways that brought you here. That is very important. When the policemen try to scare you, when they bring out those police dogs, be proud of who you are and of your ways, and then your fear won't rule you.

"Whatever the White man holds of our pasts—that just don't matter anymore. You know what we once were? Kings and queens in Africa! Kings and queens! We've just got to claim that for ourselves. And without delay! 'The only thing that I did wrong was stay in the wilderness a day too long.' But that was yesterday. Today is the Day of the Lord, and tomorrow too, and the day after. Come the day, we'll show every White man in Williams Point just who owns the streets of this town—because we'll claim them! Everybody here, when y'all wake up tomorrow, and the day after that, and after and after, forever after, your mind's going to stay on freedom!"

———

It must be days later because I'm in Morgan's bed. Somebody's in the room with me. I could speak. I just don't care to.

There's a preacher here, the Rev. Coleman, who has the biggest Baptist church for Negroes in this town. He won't make our announcements in his church. He won't march. He's already registered, but he won't tell us how he did it, or help us in any way. He's not with us. But he's taken an interest in me. I've seen him several times watching me talk to people on the street, or outside his church—intently, like he was weighing me in a balance. He wants me in his church, he tells me, but more than that—I can tell—he wants me away from the Movement; he wants me away from Morgan. He invited me to a church picnic for the young people. The young men buy the baskets that the young ladies bring. It's an auction. Your bid wins the basket; you share it with the girl. I've been to those in Drew. It's a pleasant afternoon, on a blanket on the grass in front of the church. But I didn't have the money for a bid. Rev. Coleman told me not to worry. It'll be his treat.

And I'm so tired all the time. I needed a vacation, if only for an hour.

He bought me a basket and, for an afternoon at least, I had myself a girl. I'd seen her around. Her name's Lynette. She was perched on her blanket like she was riding it sidesaddle, her skirt spread outward like an open fan, her knees forward and together and her feet tucked under her dress and to her side. And her balance was perfect; she held her back straight but nothing about her was stiff. She served the food and passed me my plate. Each movement was graceful and only what was needed—each one unadorned and simply and purely hers. And her food was delicious. Fool that I was, I asked her if her mother had made it. She took it as a joke. But no, she said, she did. We didn't talk about the Movement. She told me she was going to Spelman in the fall. She asked me about the campus and the town, and about my teachers and what I studied. And when I answered she listened with a pensive smile, leaning on her right arm propped into the grass and her head slightly tilted to the left. Her eyes were intelligent and direct. She said she wanted to be a lawyer. A woman! I snickered and she threw a bone at me. She laughed at my surprise. Then I laughed and we laughed together. And then, all I could think of was us, and a drawn shade and a closed door, and a room golden, dim in the afternoon glow, and a ceiling fan lazy, and sheets damp and warm and wrinkled and pushed to the foot of a bed—an eternity perched on the cusp of each lolling second. And I had no need for anything else, nothing else in the whole, wide world.

There was no 'Freedom Now' here, no three days and risen through that goddamned window—just me and this girl. I wanted to lie face down in her lap and everything would just be the cool feel of her skirt, and the clean smell of it, and of her skin just underneath, and the various sounds—voices, breezes, birds—all cancelled into silence and the brown darkness of the starched fabric against my shut, still eyes. She would've played her fingers in my hair. And I would've remembered only that, and not our getting up, or our clearing up the napkins and the plates, or my saying 'I'll see you.' I wouldn't have needed to remember any of that, but just myself, serene, and her and the hollow of her lap.

Afterwards Rev. Coleman took me aside. Me and Lynette—he said that's what life is all about. He said I should attend to my youth, to my living, and I should look for the good to be found, properly, in God's creation. But what I was doing, he said, was trying to shake the leaves off the world, here during the summer, when the time wasn't ripe—I was striking out for the territories, and outside of life—that's what was wrong with this protesting, he said; it would rush history and history is not to be rushed—it keeps its own pace and, in time, it always overtakes those who run too far ahead. SNCC, he said, was an army stretched too far and thin, and we'd be cut off and cut down. He told me, when our last abstract dream of justice dissipates in the morning's sun, like the dew that fancies itself a river, then history will come, impersonal, unforgiving. It will choose its own course. It may go this way or it may go that, but it will be as steady and implacable as a train howling and whistling to its station.

We were in his church, the sanctuary. It was cool there and the pied light spread like a quilt over honeyed-oak pews. I traced my hand over the broad, honest grain—my grandfather's hands; the grain in oak always reminded me of my grandfather's hands. My mother's father, tall in his straight-backed deacon's chair, taller than any man I'd ever known, taller even than my father.

He was my first image of God. He'd grown his hair long, it was a salty gray and wiry and stiff, and he also had a beard. My mother would tell me in church, "Look up. Look up. You can see Jesus right there." She meant a picture, behind my grandfather on the wall. But I saw my grandfather. He looked like Jesus—he was Jesus and Jesus' friend. Once I drew a picture of my grandfather walking with Jesus, holding hands. I couldn't decide who was the taller so I did my best to make them exact. I wasn't satisfied with the result. And the paper was too small.

I don't remember exactly when it was, when I understood my mother was pointing at a picture, and my grandfather wasn't Jesus and had no special relationship with God, none that nobody else could have. But I was disappointed. And when my grandfather was laid to rest ... I didn't think too much about church after that.

I didn't tell Rev. Coleman any of this. I looked up from the pews, my grandfather still with me. The air seemed to float and I seemed to sway. I closed my eyes and opened them, and something clicked in my mind—this Rev. Coleman, showing me his church, he wants me to be his son. (He's childless.) I wanted to cry out, "Let go of me, I'm not your son. Let go."

(Every Negro man wants a son. I get that. He wants to see himself in what he's created. He wants to feel the fullness of his being. But these men wanting me to become their son? No. Aren't I already a grown man? And besides, how can any man be a father when he can't protect his children? When your daughter's raped? When you can't feed them when they're hungry? And when every man-child's gone up North, *who can be a father here?* And my father, I remember how Morgan would always take his side. Now I wonder how much better a father I could be.)

But I had my own question for Rev. Coleman. "How tall is God? Is a man as tall as God?"

"That doesn't make sense, Aleck."

"I know. That's the point. God can't fit in here."

I turned away. I made my escape. But that girl, Lynette—I told myself I'd remember her.

Later, I saw her off to college at the bus station. Her people were there with her and I didn't intrude. I stood away, over at a street corner, against the post of a street sign not too far away, and as she took her first step up and on to the bus she glanced my way, over the heads of the people in between, then to her family and quickly back to me. She smiled, and then, another step up—she was gone. And for a moment I panicked. I wanted to push my way to the bus. I wanted to get in and find the empty seat beside her, and sit side-by-side all the way back to college. But I couldn't do it. Instead, I searched the windows for the image of her face. In the cheap window's glare her face would look distorted and gray, like it was under water, but I didn't care. I wanted that moment to last, before she'd be gone.

But I couldn't see her. I waved anyway as the bus pulled away and down the street. Maybe she saw me. Maybe she turned to look at me as the bus drove away. And what, I wondered, what kind of story should I make of that? Me not getting on that bus, me letting her go, me staying here. Was I damned or was I saved? I still don't know.

(At the end of our picnic—she was standing up to go—she took my arm and drew me close and told me, her voice kept low, "What you're doing here, you're the bravest man I know." And then she kissed my cheek and walked away, much too quick, and left me flat-footed and without a word to say.)

Just days before we went to jail, I got a letter from my father. That was a first. I didn't recognize the handwriting. It wasn't my mother's, it was masculine so it had to be his, and there at the end was his name. When I took the letter out the paper was wrinkled, like somebody had crumpled it up. A tear was taped.

It starts out stiff. How was I doing? I should write back, tell him about my typical day. Was I safe? He hopes I'll be returning to school without too much time lost. Then the handwriting starts to change. The same hand, but less practiced, like he's writing faster. He fears—with so much money spent, the whole family had paid so much, was hoping for so much—he wants me safe and back in school—and he can't understand why I'm doing what I'm doing. And yet ... he's proud of me. I took that shotgun's blast and I didn't back down. That took real courage. Then he repeats it—he's proud of me, Aleck, his son. "That was your mother's raising, not mine." But just come home Aleck. Just come home.

The letter ends right there, abrupt; no "yours truly" just "your father, Chester." I thought about the crumpled paper. Somebody smoothed it out before it was mailed. I looked at the envelope again—it was the same handwriting—and thought about my father wadding the letter up and throwing it away, then fishing it out and smoothing it and taping the tear— maybe that's when he wrote his name—and then mailing it to me. I laid my hands on the paper and felt every wrinkle. And I remembered all the rumors about him. And that he never beat me. I'd tell my friends he did. Their fathers all beat them, so I'd say, "Yeah, he really turned me out." It wasn't that he wasn't ever mad; he could be terrible mad. But he always had my mother whip me. And she could barely lift her hand to do it. She had to force herself. She finally admitted, yes, your father was in jail, but just once, and that was long before you were born. She never told me what he did. She'd just say it wasn't important. The rumor was he'd killed a man, up close, with a knife or even with his hands. But he never touched me—not once, not in any way.

So this letter, his first to me: I can imagine the blood flowing from his veins and into his pen and onto the paper, forming the letters, drying black, and him seething, and afraid, and wadding it up. And maybe other letters, in the past, tearing those up too. But this one he sent.

Growing up, I felt just inches from my father's violence. I feared it and craved it. All those years—I was wrong about him. There was no violence to be near. None expressed. Only his enormous self-control. I thought he didn't care. But he did. For all that time, he did.

I thought about the telephone in our office, and Deborah, and what it hurts me to hear. Well, what hurts my father to hear? Prison? What the White man did to him there? Or that engine he thinks is inside him, always idling; and he dare not give it any gas, it'll jump— Does that hurt to hear? Rev up that engine, he might kill somebody. He might kill someone he loves.

His heart: Can he hear his heart? Does it hurt him to hear it?

All those years—I'll never get back what I lost. Was it ever mine to lose? My breath comes short—yes, it was; it was mine to lose. It was my right as it is any man's son. But now I think I know, just a little, the cost my father pays for being the man he once was, if only for a moment; and now, for being the man he is.

⊷⊶

That cop, outside the jail, he's screaming at me. "You call me sir! You want another beating?" I had told him I only call my father sir. And for that, all my talk had been beaten from me.

I look down and around, and my body wobbles. Ah, there's the bench. The pain feels eternal. I step to the bench, careful not to fall, and I bend to lay myself back down.

Then I hear a voice. It's mine.

"You'd do the same for your father."

Now I'm lying down. I wait for the strop. I wonder if I'll even feel it, my pain is so bad. But nothing happens. Voices roil above me. I hear that red-faced, scrawny cop; he's cursing me. Hands grab my arms at my shoulders. I'm being carried; my feet drag on the concrete. I'm dropped to the ground. I'm lifted to a mattress. I must be in the jail. I pass out and then I'm in the hospital.

"You'd do the same for your father." I heard the voice. It was mine. But I never said those words.

If I had a mirror, I'd see my father in it. I'd tell myself, don't hold on so tight. Let go, Daddy, even if it hurts. Let go and listen.

Tell me your story, Daddy, and I'll tell you mine.

At the freedom meeting, Aunt Ertharin began the new-old song, the freedom song, "Well I woke up this morning with my mind stayed on freedom," and the crowd joined in, drawing the syllables out, with hushed voices and moans. "I walked and talked, talked and walked, and my mind stayed on freedom." Then they slowly built to their full voices—"Hallelu, hallelu, hallelujah"—ecstatic and clapping.

And when the people left, sated and exhausted, just outside the door was a line of White men with flashlights, shining them in the faces of the people as they walked by. A White man asked, "Who are you? What's your name?" Morgan and I walked up to him, the one in front. He shined his light in our faces and made us shield our eyes. Morgan asked him, "Who are you? Are y'all the police?"

His only response was, "What's your name?"

Morgan didn't answer. I didn't either. Even if they're police, they're not telling us to stop. Morgan turned back to his people and told them to keep walking—don't answer and don't stop walking. "Sing, everybody sing." Aunt Ertharin began. "Ain't nobody gonna turn us around." Voices joined, hushed at first, as the people filed by, shielding their eyes from the flashlights, then singing louder, and nobody spoke their name to the repeated question. And we passed out of those men's sight and were still singing when we reached the Pilgrims' Chapel Church a few streets away. There we stood together and finished our song. "Ain't no flashlights gonna turn us around." And everybody went their way, through the dark, spreading out to all the Negro parts of town, like water seeking cracks in the hard-packed ground.

This bed's nice. Deborah's here. How long has she been sitting here beside me? How many days? I slowly turn from my stomach to my side—I'm so stiff, and it still hurts—I turn to face her. She doesn't say a mumbling word.

So I smile. "Hey, Deborah. How're you doing? If you've got something to say to me, I can listen now."

She looks at me and frowns. She gets up and leaves.

39 • The Wounded Man

I go to Deborah's door. I want to talk to her. Dammit, I want *her* to talk to me. So I'm giving it one more try. Her mother answers. "It's good to see you up and about Aleck. I've been hearing from the neighborhood, how you've been."

I give her my thank-yous and then I ask for Deborah.

"She's not here."

"When will she be back?"

"She's—" Miss Eunice ducks her head. She speaks slow and very softly. "She's not here ... anymore."

"Where is she?"

Miss Eunice is closing the door. "You'll find her."

I stand there for a moment, looking at the closed door. Then I turn around. Aunt Ertharin's house is just down the street. She'll know.

Deborah answers the door. Her face doesn't show a thing.

"Come in. Sit down. I'll tell Aunt Ertharin you're here."

"But ... I was looking for you."

I try to look her in the eye, but she won't let me. I edge past her through the doorway. She just stands there, her hand still on the door. It slowly closes.

"What do you want me for?"

"To talk." I look at her. She still shows me nothing. "For one thing, to thank you for sitting by my bedside."

"You were awake. I could tell that. You were awake for a long time."

"I couldn't talk."

"Couldn't talk ... or wouldn't?"

"Does it matter?"

"Yes. It does matter. It makes a big difference."

I'm sitting down. She's still standing. I point to a chair. "Make yourself comfortable. What are you doing here? Are you living here now?"

Deborah hesitates. Then she sits down.

"Are you helping Aunt Ertharin?"

"She's—" Deborah looks back to the rest of the house. "I was going to say she's fine. But her back's hurt, bad. She still walks with a limp. She'll have that beating forever. So I decided to stay with her for a while."

"How are you doing? You were beat up pretty bad too."

"I'm okay. Not as bad as Aunt Ertharin. I don't need any doctors."

"And after you've helped her, will you go back home?"

Deborah's still looking toward the rear of the house. The kitchen, the bedroom. This way and that. Anywhere but me. She doesn't answer my question, but then she shakes her head no.

"So ... taking care of Aunt Ertharin wasn't the only reason you left home?"

Now she looks at me. "It's good enough."

I nod that it is. "Does she listen to you? I don't think enough people do. I didn't. And I don't think your mother does. I think that's another reason why you left. Have you told Aunt Ertharin your story?

"I don't have to. She's known all about it for years. But yeah, she listens to me ... and I take care of her."

I look down at the floor. "You could tell it to me now. All of it. All that time you were watching over me and I wasn't talking ... I was thinking. I thought about a lot of things. So ... you could tell me your story now."

I wait in her silence. "Do you want to?"

"Not especially."

I nod my head. I don't say a thing, because there's nothing for me to say. I get up. Deborah stays seated. I go out and back up the street to Miss Eunice's house. I'm telling myself, this isn't over.

I knock. She answers and I stand there trying to think what I should say. I keep my tone civil. "Can I come in Miss Eunice?" She stands aside, just barely, and I walk in. I'm careful not to brush against her. Now I'm facing her in her front room. Her head comes up to about my shoulders. She's watching me like I'm a junkyard dog and I almost bend backwards to keep from frightening her. She's waiting for me to speak.

I get right to it. "Ma'am, you've got to let her tell you how she feels. You've got to let her have it out with you. You owe her—"

"What are you talking about?" She starts crying.

I take a step backwards. "Your daughter. Deborah. You know what's happened to her. Have you ever let her tell you how she feels?"

She's got her hands up over her eyes and she's bawling. Her shoulders heave. I don't think she realizes I'm here in front of her anymore. In her mind she's all alone, just her and her misery.

I reach out and touch her, very lightly, very briefly, on her elbow. "You're losing her. Do you know that, ma'am? You could lose her." I say it as kindly as I can.

She pulls her hands down from her eyes and looks up at me. "I tried to protect my daughter."

"With all due respect, ma'am, that's not good enough. She's never asked for that. That's not what she needs. She needs to tell you her story. She needs ... so much ... to do that." I don't go into why I know this. "You're her mother."

She looks up at me. Her face is shiny with her tears. Her mouth drops open.

"Her story? *Her* story?" She works her mouth, her jaws. She clinches her fists. "What about—?"

I'm really in it now. This woman, standing here, her face stuck out, her neck about to snap. I'm thinking that maybe she'll try to hit me. How do I get out?

She shakes her head. She stops and glares and trembles. "You ask for too much. Y'all are asking too much. What right do y'all have to come here? Everything was fine ... before ... before—" Miss Eunice gathers herself. "Just who're you working for? That's all I want to know." She's almost screaming now. "Who're you working for?"

She can't say another word. I'm looking at her tears, her open mouth, her working jaw.

I've been in this house before. The threadbare rug, bigger than the floor and rolled up against the walls; the sagging wallpaper; the sofa and the chair, each under a blanket. I've seen this all before. I could rip this room apart, but that isn't my intention. Because, if I did, where would she live?

Where would Deborah live?

Some stories have no ending. Some efforts fall short. Some puzzles can't be solved.

Her question? I work ... for her. I work for all our people.

I take a good look at her—Miss Eunice—to study her contorted face. I wonder what her stories are. Still I tell myself, this isn't over.

Later, I go back to our place. Morgan's there. He's been waiting for me. He knows what happened, I can tell.

"What the hell were you doing?"

" 'Freedom Now,' Morgan. 'Freedom Now.' "

"You call what you did freedom? Do you know how upset she is?"

"Who, Morgan, who's upset? Miss Eunice or Deborah?"

"Yeah, Deborah's upset, they're both upset, and you're upset and I'm upset. Everybody's upset. And do you know why? Because a White man raped a little girl and she wasn't his first one and she wasn't his last. And the Christian White folks here know all about it, and they could've put a stop to it, or at least not elected him their goddamned mayor." He punches a finger in my chest. "Just you remember who the real villains are. It's none of us. It's not our people. You got that? What could a Colored man do? Tell me, Aleck, what could a Colored man do that wouldn't have gotten him lynched or run out of town? And what could Miss Eunice have done? You're lecturing her, about her business, in her own house—so what should she have done, Aleck?"

"All she has to do is listen—just listen to her own daughter. Not another goddamn thing. All she has to do is let her daughter tell her how she feels."

"That's family business, Aleck. That's none of yours. And no little girl bosses her family, Aleck."

"You hear yourself, Morgan? Do you hear yourself?"

"Yeah, I hear myself loud and clear. I'm just saying what I've always said to you, ever since you were a little boy—and you never got it then. Respect your elders, Aleck. You don't understand what they had to go through. Even though you got your own taste of it—more than your share, yes, too much and more—that doesn't make you special. That's what our people have been up against ever since they first set foot in this goddamned country. What you got and more. And you still don't understand.

"They've got nothing, Aleck, nothing to be ashamed of and nothing done wrong. Respect your elders, Aleck. Don't you tell them what to do!"

We're standing face to face, close, the dim light squeezed red between us, we're not speaking; we're both breathing heavily. Morgan steps away. "You go and apologize to that woman."

I hesitate. Then I turn and leave.

Morgan follows me out, but I don't go back to Miss Eunice's house. Maybe I would've, but with Morgan right behind me I go to our office instead. Morgan follows me in. I glance back at him and bite my tongue. Neither of us speaks.

By now it's night. I wanted to be alone, to sit in the dark and stew. Well, I can stew in the light with Morgan here. I try to read a magazine. Morgan opens his chess board and arranges the pieces to a problem. I glance over. I've seen him do that one before. He still hasn't solved it. He looks over from the desk. He won't leave and, dammit, I won't either. If one of us leaves, the other will surely stay behind. And whoever leaves will go on home because there's no place else to go. And when he does he'll open our door and look out our window, and later he'll cut out the light and go to bed. But he will not sleep.

So, neither of us leaves, and neither of us speaks, and neither of us sleeps.

Days later, when it's just the two of us in the office, Morgan shoves a piece of paper at me. "Here, you need to read this. It's from Atlanta. It's about our freedom election and all those volunteers we're going to get from Stanford and Yale."

I hold it in front of me. "What happened to our grassroots Movement?"

"You don't like it, you can quit."

I look up. "You don't like it either."

"But I'm not asking the whole world to step to my music."

I throw the paper down. "No, you aren't. Some people can just drown in their own shit, is that what you say? So long as it's Deborah and not one of your elders?"

Morgan's at his desk and I'm at mine. I stand up. "You remember that night in jail? You were talking all that shit about my father. Maybe you didn't think I heard, but I did. What happened to staying out of other people's business?"

Morgan looks up at me. "What do you want from me, Morgan? What hole am I supposed to fill? You stick up for Miss Eunice, you talk about all that she can't do, but after all these years now you talk shit about my father."

Morgan looks down at his desk. "I can't be everybody's son, Morgan. I'm just ... look, Deborah came to me and I let her down. And I know the feeling. I've been let down like that before. So now I'm trying not to be like my father was. But I'm still his son. I ... I got a letter."

Morgan doesn't let me finish. He doesn't say a thing, he just stands up. This is the first time he hasn't had an answer for me. I'm trying to look into his eyes, but he's not letting me. He's moving to the door, and he looks, for the first time that I can remember, like an old man. And I know that I've hurt him—more than I ever thought I could.

He walks out, and I don't follow.

✦ ✦ ✦

The work goes on. But Morgan and I, we're like two trains running. We're on parallel tracks, going in opposite directions. Every day: two trains walking, two trains talking, we're working side-by-side, but we're both on our own set of tracks, neither one of us are really connecting with the other, we're each caught in our own … logic, imperatives, preoccupations? Each one to our own destination.

If anybody notices, they don't say a word. And Deborah is back. You can tell she still moves in pain. She does her rounds, but she hardly says a word. The look on her face: it's like she's thinking we can all go to hell.

But one day she's following me as I walk out the door, the day's work done. I'm not walking to her neighborhood, but she's right behind me. I stop and look back at her and she catches up.

"I heard what you told my mother."

I don't say anything to that. I gesture to a sundry store we're passing.

"Do you want a soda?"

Deborah scuffs her toe in the dust. You can smell the dirt. It's not a loamy smell. It smells bitter and dry. She looks at me. "NEHI. Grape."

We sit beneath a tree, each with a bottle. The sun comes down between the leaves. Deborah takes a swig and so do I. We're looking at the sundry store and down the street. The street's dirt, clay—rutted and dry, a tawny pink—and the store front's weathered, pale and squat; and everything seems too still, too quiet to be real, like an old, yellowed photograph. The dust prickles at my nose. Only a handful of people are out. I've had this feeling before: this is what a railroad station is like after the train is gone—not quite empty, there're people left behind; but it's used up and yet somehow incomplete. Everything looks ... belittled: belittled by dust, belittled by heat, by time and neglect, by poverty and venality and despair. This is her hometown. She was beaten for these people. Surely that must mean something—what she thinks of them, how they're worth it.

One day I'll be leaving, not as soon as Isaac and Johanna, but one day I'll go back to Morehouse. I'll be one of the Talented Tenth, a doctor or a lawyer or an Indian chief. When I leave—and when Morgan leaves—we'll be leaving Deborah behind. I ask her, "Will you ever leave?"

She was about to take a drink. The bottle stops halfway to her mouth and she brings it back down to her lap. She looks right at me. "I don't know. The real question is, if I do, will I ever come back. Maybe I'll have to." She considers that. Now she's looking past me, down the street. "Yes. I'll have to. These are my people." She looks back at me. "If they weren't, why would I be so angry with them?"

She shakes her head, like she's shaking off that thought. "All my life I've lived in the back of the bus: 'Mind you other people's feelings.' Well, what about my feelings? When can I speak up? When's my turn?"

"You can tell me. Right now, you can tell me anything at all. Whatever you want."

She doesn't say a word. She looks up through the tree, squinting.

She starts talking about Morgan.

"You hear him, in the freedom meetings. We're all righteous and blameless and this is God's time and we're all God's saints. I can't help but roll my eyes. How would he know? He just says it to make people feel good." She tilts her head back and closes her eyes. "I'd follow him to hell and back. He's a real hero; he's a Race Man right down to the bone. But ... he's lived so much and seen so much, and I'm just a kid, but sometimes I think he's the innocent and I'm the jaded one. Sometimes my head feels so old." She rubs her brow and looks at me. "Don't laugh. You know it. He thinks Negroes are special, like we've got some special grace, like whatever god he believes in is just waiting for the right moment to reset the balance, and we'll all be back in Africa or something, and we'll all be kings." Now she laughs, a short and bitter burst. "—or queens." She takes a drink.

"He's a hero," she says. "I believe that. But who's he giving all his heroism to? People have to earn that. He talks about how much we've suffered, and he's right, but then he says that's the reason why it's our time now. Well, to do what? To be what? Look what happened to me. My family couldn't look at me. My mother still won't. My father ... he wants us in Chicago. But I can't help but think, what happened to me ... he's ashamed. Everybody's ashamed, and I've got to pay for it." Deborah pauses. I'm looking at her and she's frowning.

"I don't think suffering is enough." Deborah tilts her head down and I have to lean over to hear her. "It's not been enough for me. I'm no queen." She looks up at me. "And you're no king. Nobody's a king, not even kings. We're just ordinary people. There's no special grace. Morgan always says you've got to be from someplace, and be from a people, to be something more than just who you are, but if you don't ask for more than that, isn't that all we'll ever be, just who we are? And Morgan does ask for more, the Movement does—he asks, but somehow, he doesn't. Sometimes I'm afraid—you give your heroism to people who don't deserve it—it could be like you were no hero at all."

Now she turns, sitting there beside me, and looks right at me. "Do you think we deserve it? Your heroism? Morgan's?"

At first I don't say anything. I'm holding my bottle up against my temple. "You've got to take people as they are."

"No I don't. I'm sick of everybody. They can all go to hell."

I hold my bottle up and look through it. It glistens in my hand. "Our people, just to live right, with all the White folk's shit we have to deal with? You have to be so heroic to do that, and lots of folks just can't. It's not fair to ask them."

Her voice is dead cold. "Nobody cares about me. Why should I care about them?"

I squint at the light refracted through my bottle. I'm trying to think of what to say.

I look at her. "But you do care. You just said so yourself. That's why you volunteered." She's got her face down. Then I tell Deborah what happened to me outside that jail, me being beaten by that cop and why he stopped.

"Oh god. Not you too." She smiles like she's holding back a laugh. "So God spoke and saved you? You know my minister came to see me, after I got beaten. He told me affliction is a great spiritual teacher." Now she laughs, another short burst. "Well, there weren't any teachers in that cell when they beat me, and that wasn't any classroom. I didn't learn a damn thing in there except this: this world is small and cheap, and it's not worth the god that created it, unless that god is small and cheap too."

Deborah has a paper napkin from the store. She uses it to wipe her eyes and nose. "I wish it was a big world. I wish it was big and simple. I wish everybody descended from kings and queens. I wish nobody ever did anything wrong."

She looks right at me. "You know, sometimes I still feel dirty. And I never did a single thing wrong. But look at how I am. Everybody disappoints me. You're right, that's the way people are. It just is. People say I've got to accept that. But I don't. I won't. And I pay for that every day. I feel so alone. But I won't— There should be heroes, but you're right, there aren't—not nearly enough. I wish we didn't live in a world like this. If we didn't, I wouldn't be the way I am, would I?"

"No, you wouldn't." I say it as gently as I can.

"You sound like I'm better off this way."

"No, I'm just saying it's not a simple world and you're not a simple person. You're not just one thing. And that's to your credit." I pause for a second. "And you don't always have to be at war."

"Yes I do. I've had to be, ever since ..." she looks away, down the street. "Why not? What's so different now?"

I tell her something more. She listens. She finishes her soda.

"You're right. I wouldn't like a god like that." Deborah gets up and walks away. She leaves her bottle, empty, under the tree.

40 • The Wounded Man

"Killed by the Klan." They say Isaac was killed by the Klan Here's what I know about him.

I'm driving and Isaac's sitting beside me. It's the late afternoon. We're heading north, toward home, from a settlement called Pal's Landing—Negro farmers, landowners, just like at Brown's Haven; there's not too many left, but they're with us—and we're passing Yazoo City, right on the edge of the Delta, right under the Hills. A car comes toward us and slows as it passes. I tell Isaac, "Keep an eye on that one. See if it stops and turns around."

"Yeah, it's turning."

I floor it, but our car tops out at under a hundred and the car behind us is gaining. It swings to the left lane beside us. The man driving motions me to pull over, like he's a cop. But it isn't a police car and he isn't in uniform. I pull over anyway because he could cut me off, but I don't pull off on the shoulder. I stay on the road. He pulls over in front; then he's at my door, tapping on my window with a pistol.

"Get out of the car, nigger."

I have the car in reverse, my clutch in, and the engine running. I glance at the rearview mirror. Nobody's coming. I stomp on the gas and pop the clutch and pull hard on the wheel to the right. The man goes sprawling. We lurch onto the shoulder, perpendicular to the road. Then I turn back to Yazoo City. The man with the pistol scrambles to his car. I fishtail on purpose, I hear gunshots; they're trying to shoot out my tires. But even if they miss, I know they can outrace us.

I run a stop sign at an empty intersection. "What're they doing, Isaac?"

"They're gaining on us."

I turn right.

"Why are we going this way? We're going into town. There's traffic this way."

The engine's so loud, I shout. "That's right."

Up ahead, a car is stopped at a stop sign. Facing us, another one's stopped in the other lane. The cross street has no stop, and a car is coming. "Hold on." I pull into the left lane and pound my horn and run the stop sign. Brakes are squealing all around me. I swerve back to the right. "What are they doing Isaac?"

"It worked. The intersection's blocked. We lost them."

I look ahead. We're gaining on a car, and nobody's in the left lane. I pass the car, and then another. There should be a country road here that goes up into the Hills. I take it—it's like a roller-coaster. Then I take another one. I keep asking Isaac if he sees anybody behind us. He doesn't. Finally, I slow down and head northeast through Holmes County, driving away from home, deep into the Hills. I stay on the country roads.

Isaac slumps down in his seat, bug-eyed. "What are we doing way out here?"

"We're going to take our time getting back. I'm going to take the long way home and come in from the east." I drive into Carroll County, and then turn west to Horatio County and Williams Point.

Driving steady, under the speed limit, I let go of the steering wheel, one hand at a time. I didn't realize how tightly I'd been holding it. I wiggle my fingers, one hand at a time.

I don't say much. Neither does Isaac. The evening draws down. The low sky's translucent. There's a milky scrim just above the trees, that, upward, changes to lavender, then changes to purple, and up high the clouds are combed thin, and as I keep driving the purple darkens to black and the milky scrim thins to a line on the horizon, and then, finally, it's gone, and the moon swells and pushes the stars away from the sky. The earth flattens. We're back in the Delta.

Headlights pop up behind. I slow down and sped up and the lights stay the same distance. We're just east of town and close by the river. I'm thinking there'll be a car in front of us soon to block us. Somewhere there's a turnoff, a dirt road. I look for it. But when I see it, it's almost too late, and I have to turn hard. We bounce along a rutted road to a fork, I take the left and clear a low ridge down to a clearing—there's a broken-down shack here, and no other road; there're trees all around, and the smell of the river that's just beyond. I've never been here, but suddenly I realize where we must be, where long ago a Negro died. He was lynched. In the middle of the clearing I turn the car around to face the only road. I can see it in the moonlight, one car, in profile at the top of the ridge, blocking our way to the dirt road and the highway beyond.

I call Morgan on our CB radio. He'll call the FBI. Minutes later he calls me back. "They'll telephone the police. That's the best we can do. Now that the FBI knows what's going on, nothing should happen. Let's just hope so. Just lay low till somebody comes." And then, too casually, he says, "You've got that gun with you, don't you?"

I tell him I do. It's in the glove compartment of the car.

We roll down our windows. The moist air oozes in. I think of summer nights like this, on a front porch, my people and our friends gathered—and the air lulls you; everything and everybody blurs into a warm, moist wash, and your world is one broad watercolor stroke. And I feel an immense nostalgia for those slow, steeped evenings, because now, even with the oozing air that settles here, I feel very hard and brittle and separate. I feel like a beetle: I'm bedded in gauze and set out on a table. I'm lit and exposed. And next to me—I'm supposed to know this man somehow. For all our working together, he's a stranger to me, but he's who I'm waiting with, here, alone, for the White Mississippi police to save us.

"You think we should run for it?"

"No, I don't." I can see Isaac's eyes, wide in the moonlight. I tell him, "I think I know what this place is, but I'm not familiar with it. How would we get back? I don't know. You want to walk on these roads, here at night? Besides, Morgan said the FBI would call the police."

"You trust them—after everything, so far?"

"They're the least of our worries. They'll have to answer to the FBI. But until they come, we don't know what those people are going to do." I point to the car in profile, blocking our way.

"I don't mean the police. I mean the FBI. You trust them?"

"To do right, tonight?"

"To do right anytime. My father hates them, because of what they did to his brother. My uncle, Uncle Lenard, he was a communist—he said he was always being watched and followed, and his telephone was tapped. I was just a boy. I didn't believe it, but my father set me straight. He told me about men coming into our neighborhood and asking questions about him and his brother. And he'd been questioned himself, many times he said; it was harassment and it was all about my Uncle Lenard.

"My uncle was harmless. He was an idealist. He was a smart man, a scientist, but he never could hold a job. That wasn't his fault. They ruined him, and he never hurt anybody." Isaac's voice shriveled to a whisper. "It took me a while to put two and two together.

"Anyway, you trust them too much—you and Morgan Wright. The whole Movement trusts them too much."

I must've been staring at him. He stopped talking and edged just a bit toward the car door. "You've ever known any communists?"

I glanced up at the road. "No. Never have. Don't tell me you're one?"

"No. And my father isn't one either—only my uncle." Isaac smiled, weakly. "My father's an atheist. He says you can't be an atheist and a communist too. He says communists have just as much faith as Christians. God, the masses, history, he says it's all the same to him. He calls himself the ultimate cynic—but I don't think he is."

I don't reply. All this talk. It registers in the back of my mind while I'm concentrating on that car blocking the road and listening for another car to come—friend or foe I just don't know.

Isaac manages another smile. "You know my father's rich. Sometimes it's hard to believe he still is—he gives away so much: union organizers, unpublished poets, autodidacts that don't have a dime. Synagogues and schuls and socialists."

"Synagogues? I thought you said he's an atheist."

"Oh, none of it makes any sense—he'll tell you that himself. He says, to act consistently is to betray reality—because it's bigger than any philosophy. He'll give money to anybody who needs it. Most philanthropists, he says, only give to those who already have it."

I look away, out my door window. I don't care about his father. But I let him talk. What else are we going to do?

"When I told him I was leaving Columbia to work with SNCC, he took me in his arms, and he cried and he hugged me. He told me he was proud of me. But I knew something else. He was afraid I was going to die, and still he blessed me. And I went. I went because my father would not abide himself if he thought he had kept me from going. He has a lot of opinions, but hardly any beliefs." Here Isaac pauses. Maybe he's smiling, but I'm still looking out my window. "One belief he does have is the innocence and perfection of his son. I would never forgive myself if I were to cause my father to change. I don't want him changed. He's a ... he's a rich man of the people; he's a holy, unholy fool; and he's—he's proudest of this—he's a traitor. That's his word. He's the enemy of everything predictable and defined. And he always makes me smile."

I can hear a quaver in his voice. I don't know if it's from love or fear. Maybe it's both. Maybe he thinks this is his last chance to praise him.

I look at him, but I don't reply, and he falls silent.

We sit for a while. I can hear the insects and even the trees around us, their leaves stirred by a wind you can't feel, like a slow river's current you can't see. The sound's faint and distant, and it's incessant, like strings bowed impossibly long, and it's discordant and unresolved. And below that sound, beyond our little clearing, are the cotton fields—I don't have to see them to know—they're like dry fog in the moonlight, and they stretch ... to gray, to black, to invisibility— Even in that clearing I can feel their bitter dust in my nostrils.

Every once in a while, there's another sound, altogether different, in the distance—an automobile on the highway driving by. I can't help but ask myself: Is it coming here? Will it slow and take the turn? And who will it bring?

I look down at my skin, hard and brittle. I tell myself I have to remember this, every sound and feeling, it'll be my story and I'll have to tell it well.

If I'm still alive.

That car on top of the ridge, it hasn't moved. I guess that's something.

Isaac breaks the silence. He asks me if I've ever feared for my life before. I tell him no. I tell him about the time I was shot. That was over too fast and the next thing I knew I was in a hospital bed. And that other time, my third night here, when Morgan and I had to flee through that window, there was no time to be scared until we'd hid ourselves. And then, we weren't exposed like now, so no, I was scared but I didn't fear for my life, not then. And then I tell him what I know about this clearing. "They lynched a Negro here, back in the 'forties right after the war. He was a veteran." Isaac doesn't say a word.

But I don't tell him about that time outside the jail when I was beaten. But, then, I didn't fear for my life—I despaired for it.

Isaac looks at the car blocking our way out. "The closest I've been was during the sit-ins at Woolworth."

I turn to him. "You never told us about that."

337

"No. I was afraid you wouldn't take me. I thought if Morgan knew about it he'd think that's what I'd want to do here, instead of the voting drive."

I nod. He's right.

Isaac tells me, "There were four of us, two Negroes and two Whites. We sat at that lunch counter for three hours. We ordered, we were told to leave, and we sat there. We ordered again. Word must have spread fast; there was a crowd behind us in minutes. That was three hours of hate. People came and went, but there were always about a hundred people there behind us. The police stayed outside. Toward the end, I noticed some men in sunglasses and suits and ties lined up along the wall right next to the door. Later I heard they were FBI, but I don't know if they were. They were somebody official. Anyway, they saw everything and did nothing. People pressed up behind us and screamed in our ears. They spit on us. They poured sugar, salt, ketchup, and mustard on our heads and clothes. Most of them were teenagers but there were a lot of adults there too. Somebody hit me in the back of my head with a glass sugar dispenser, then they smashed it against the counter next to me, over and over until it broke, then they raked the broken edge across my neck. My blood was all over. Somebody else hit me behind my ear. He must've used brass knuckles. I nearly blacked out. I was so scared. I couldn't have moved if I'd wanted to.

"But then I felt something—it was me, my soul—that's the only way I can explain it; I ... it seemed to shift back up and over me, behind me, protecting me somehow. I was watching me and telling me everything was going to be okay. Somehow it would be okay. And that kept me ... composed. I got through it. When they cut and hit me, I nearly panicked I was so scared, and that's when it happened. That's when my soul rose."

Another car passes by on the highway. You can barely hear it.

Isaac looks again at the car on the ridge. Its chrome and its windshield—you can see the moonlight's glint. "We were right there for everybody to see; we were Negroes and Whites together, the four of us, we had a real brotherhood, a universal brotherhood of suffering, redeeming everybody in that crowd, all of them, even the FBI, if they'd have just stopped to look and see."

I don't want to see, so I look at the car. I turn to Isaac. Anything to pass the time.

I ask him, "Do you believe in God?"

"Well, when I was twelve I told my father I was an atheist just like him. I was so proud to say it. He scolded me. I should never be anything just to be like anybody else—even him. He said he'd give me a book to read on my birthday when I was old enough and I wasn't to say I was an atheist or anything else until I'd read that book.

"So I asked him every year for that book, to be old enough to get it you see, but he never gave it to me. Finally, I stopped asking, and that's the year I got it. It was a book of essays by Simone Weil. My father said, 'Here, this woman was a Jew and an intellectual. She hated religion, she hated institutions. She hated fairy tales. She should have been an atheist just like me. But she believed in affliction, so she decided she was a Christian, only one without a church.' He said she was the perfect individual, a traitor to the atheists *and* the church. But she was the outsider who looks in and says, here everybody, here's the way out. He said, 'You read this book and then think about whether you should be an atheist.'"

I look at Isaac and smile. He looks so earnest. I say, "A book—? You can't get belief out of a book. What about life?"

Isaac smiles back. "I'm not as cloistered as you might think. Anyway, I wrote to my father about what happened at the sit-in and asked him about it. He wrote back that he'd explain it psychologically, like some kind of displacement of the self away from danger. But that's not important, he said. 'It happened to you, so how do *you* explain it?'"

Isaac pauses. I wonder if he's considering his answer or thinking about his father.

"I don't know—maybe it was my soul." He smiles. "At least that's more poetic than displacement." Isaac takes hold of my arm. Instinctively, I stiffen. "But now, right now," he says, "I'm afraid for my life because of my father. If I'm gone ... I'm all he's got left."

He's looking at that car.

I tell him, "Don't look that way. Look over at the trees."

He does what I say. We sit silently for a while. I'm wondering, will his face be the last one I see?

There's a low haze of light to the west—Williams Point. We were so close to home. There's the moon and a few stars; the sound of another car on the highway. How long does it take for a policeman to come out here? What will happen when he comes?

Isaac asks me why they're waiting. He means the men in that car.

"I don't know. Maybe they're waiting for somebody."

"You think they're out there, out in the trees, surrounding us?"

I nod my head. "Could be. We should keep watch." Now I'm thinking about the gun in the glove compartment. There're several yards of clearing between us and the trees. I'm thinking, how many shots? How close to the car before I fire? Will I aim well in the night?

❖

Isaac asks me, "What about your father?"

He has himself turned around in his seat, his back to the glove compartment; he's scanning the trees. I don't reply. "What about your father? How do you two get along?" I don't reply, but Isaac won't stop. "We've been working together. We were jailed together. We might die here together. And we hardly know each other. I've told you about mine. What about your father?"

I say his name—Chester—and say there isn't much to tell. My father never says much. He's never showed much. He loves me, but every father loves his son, it's not remarkable.

I don't tell Isaac I'm afraid my father believes that I don't respect him because I left college for this. Coming here and joining SNCC is the best thing I've done in my life—and my father can't understand. I don't tell Isaac about that cop, how I wouldn't call him "sir"—and how I can only call my father "sir" because that's the least I can do for him, who confessed his shortcomings in a letter and told me how proud he was of me; who I've judged so harshly; and I'm afraid I'll keep disappointing him for as long as I stay here, and maybe for the rest of his life.

And I don't tell Isaac what I said to that cop—*you'd do the same for your father*—and that it wasn't me who said it.

We're both looking at the trees, me out the front and Isaac out the rear, but it's too dark to see if anybody's there. That car's still there. And my gun, my gun's here. This moonlight—you think you can see more than you really do. And your depth perception's shot. I'd have to wait until they were right on top of us before I shoot. Could I do that?

I tell Isaac to turn around and open the glove compartment. "I've got a gun in there. Get it for me."

Isaac stares at me, eyes wide and his mouth open. Then he fumbles for the gun and puts it in my hand.

I notice for the first time, he's sweating. And he's breathing heavy now. He's looking back out the rear again, anywhere but me and my gun. "Okay. So much for your father. What about your mother? What's her name?"

I shrug. I check to see the gun's loaded. "Nellie. She'd give me anything I wanted that was in her power to give. And she's got no problem with me being here." I stop. I've said too much. I don't say any more. I knew the gun was loaded. Checking it was just a reflex. It's what you're taught to do. I put it down beside me.

Isaac is trembling now, but he's keeping his arms close to him, he's not moving at all except for his trembling. "God? Do you believe in God? You asked me."

I think for a moment. Then I tell Isaac about when I was a child, about the church choir, and about our congregation's singing, about how the people walked with a certain sway when they walked to the alter to give their offerings; and how everywhere the colors were warm and old and primary and steeped in a darkened yellow of polish and veneer on the pews and on the pulpit; and the air smelled of flowers and varnish, and soap and perfume and pomade.

And I tell him about the sermons: one in particular I remember, "Jesus in the Garden," about how Jesus prayed and wept the night of his betrayal, and how our preacher returned to the phrase "Jesus wept—in the Garden" throughout the sermon, over and over, until that was all he said, repeating "Jesus wept—in the Garden," and nothing else. For the first two words he'd chant the three syllables, sharply, and then he'd pause. And for "in the Garden" he'd draw the words out, making them a melody, descending, but with an upturn at the end. Over and over, those five words, and then the piano player began to play. The preacher chanted "Jesus wept," and then the piano played the melody for "in the Garden," and it was all music then. The preacher sang "Jesus wept," he sang it and repeated it, and the piano would rise to match his voice in response, playing "in the Garden," and both soared in a duet, louder and louder, over the growing shouts and amens from the congregation and their staccato clapping and the women wailing, and suddenly the preacher raised both hands, stretched them upward and out to us, and he stopped us all and shouted, "You think you're up? God will strike you down! You think you're full? He'll burn you hollow! Ohhh, Jesus wept!" And with those last three words—sounds really, guttural, the most terrible sounds I've ever heard—right behind them came the piano's chords, pounding, and the words for those chords were on everybody's lips though nobody said them loud, "—in the Garden," and throughout it all we sweated and shouted and our hands rose with the preacher's voice.

And sitting in the car with Isaac, with our sweat and the heat and that car on the ridge, all of these memories are gathered, they're forward out in front of me, and they're rushing away from me up into the night, faster and farther; and the moon and the stars too, they're shooting away from me, leaving me in the dark alone with Isaac. And I don't want to lose those memories. I want to reach out my hands and catch on to them and hold them. I want to ride them all, away from here. That church, that Eden; those few hours of worship and communion, when we were better people than we really are—Right now I want to believe, like Morgan does, that we really are that way: kings and queens in Eden. "This Eden ... Jesus wept ... in the Garden ... this Eden"—the words merry-go-round inside my head, nostalgic and mocking.

And I can't, I can't believe like Morgan does ... because Jesus wept, in the Garden.

The moonlight returns, and the oozing air, and the obscurity of cotton in the night, and our flesh and our sweat, and nothing looks like it does during the day, you can't aim a gun at night, and all I hear is the impossibly long drone of the insects and the trees, like they're asking a single, long, incessant question—

Isaac turns back and looks out at the car again. "Tell me about college. What was college like for you?"

Oh god. I take hold of Isaac's arm. "I don't want to talk anymore. I don't want to answer your questions anymore. I'm scared. It's too late to get to know each other. Even if it wasn't—you're not like me." I put my forearm next to Isaac's. "See, we're different."

"That's bunk."

"No it isn't. Does that bother you—that I think we're different? Look, I know, ever since you got here, you've wanted to be my friend. And that's fine, but ... I knew you wouldn't understand, and you wouldn't think much of my reasons even if you did, but you came here, here where I live in Mississippi, and you'll leave here too, because you can, because you should, but I can't—there's something here I have to face every damn day in my life, whether I'm back at Morehouse, or home, or here, that you'll be able to walk away from—and that's no fault of yours, it's because your skin is different from mine—but at least you could acknowledge it, but you won't. And I knew you wouldn't."

By now I can hardly see him. Just his silhouette, and he's breathing hard. "Okay, maybe. But when you put your arm next to mine, you think you're only one thing, and I'm a different thing. But nobody's just one thing. There's some level where you can know the most different person from you in the world. You can know them because they're you, because nobody's just one thing."

I don't want to hear this. I'd said something like it myself, not too long ago, but I don't want to hear it now. "That sounds like more books."

"It's not just books. I can prove it. Or I will ... if we ever get out of here. If I get a chance to prove it. All this bunk about race just keeps people apart. But I've been looking into something and it's going to blow all that crap to hell."

"What do you mean?"

"I can't tell you now, but I will later, at least I hope so. I still need the proof."

I don't believe him. And he can tell that.

"Look, Aleck, this is going to be a bombshell. If you knew me you'd know I don't— Look, I've got to do this right. Ever since that sit-in I've been restless, like I'm perched on the cusp of something. Well, I found it, right here in Williams Point, something that everybody needs to know about so they can see we're not so very different after all. I just need the proof."

He stops for a moment. He takes a deep breath, anything to keep himself calm. Then he starts babbling.

"Anyway ... anyway ... you can hold your arm next to mine all you want, but we're all in the same shit—you, me, and those people in that damn car out there. Look," he pauses, breathing hard, he's looking out the car windows, searching for people under the trees, "there're things, social things, cultural things ... you know, your church or where you grew up, your neighborhood and your family and your friends, and each one's a bridge ... they're supposed to be bridges," he's lowered his voice, as if there were somebody near who could overhear, "to God, bridges to God. But instead—" He stops, we both look at that car—behind it, we heard another car, closer than the highway, didn't we? We listen. There's nothing. Isaac's breathing through his mouth like a fish in a boat. "Instead ... instead ... we build houses on them; we don't know they're bridges ... we're lost ... we've forgotten ... we're supposed—" He stops again. We listen. "Was that a car door?"

We can't take our eyes off that car. I lay my hand on the gun. Isaac's voice wavers. "We're supposed to go toward God. We're supposed to cross the bridges to God. So it's the same shit ... that we're all in. It doesn't matter if you're White or Negro. Those Whites up there," he points at the car, "they don't want to cross over; they think they'll lose everything. Is somebody there?" We listen. "But we have to ... we have to be willing to leave everything we love—"

He pauses as if he's finished. We listen some more, but there's only silence, or rather, the insects, the leaves—

Isaac is pointing at the car on the ridge. "It's because of fear they do this. They think they'll lose everything to the likes of you. They fear you because they think you're different. But you're not. I'm not. So there's nothing to be afraid of."

"But I am different."

"No. Not that way."

I don't answer. All I'm thinking about is the gun. It's the only thing that makes sense to me now.

◆——◆

Sudden headlights sweep up into the sky. There is another car, behind the first one. The headlights pause, at a standstill, pointed at the sky. The car blocking our way backs up and then the other car pulls forward, over the ridge, and bumps down towards us, and the air behind it billows with dust. Its headlights glare. We have to lean out our windows to see, and all we can see are those headlights. I turn on the ignition and switch on ours. There's only one man in this car. It doesn't have a siren. It isn't a police car. It stops in front of us. The driver leaves his lights on and gets out, he's short and thin, and while his left hand is swinging naturally, his right is hovering at his hip. He's carrying a holster.

I pick up my gun, but keep it low at my hip. "Isaac, you duck down if I shoot. And after I do, maybe you should run for it."

I lean my head out my window. The man stops. He's half way here. He puts his right hand up to shield his eyes. Then he slowly lowers it and I get a good look. It's the cop who kicked me on the street and had me beaten outside the jail—the scrawny one, the one I wanted to kill. He's not in uniform, but he has his gun.

I cock mine and bring it from my hip up to my belt buckle. I'm trying to stay cool. He's got to draw first. He thinks I'm unarmed. Damn cocky bastard. If he gets careless …

The cop steps to the side away from my headlights. He's close enough to see me now and he stops. We're looking right at each other and I can tell he recognizes me. He reaches into his shirt pocket and pulls out his dark glasses and puts them on. Baynard James. I remember his name is Baynard James. He starts walking again, coming right up to my car door.

I uncock the gun and thrust it back at Isaac. "Put it back. Quick."

I don't take my eyes off the cop, he's walking right to me, but I can hear Isaac fumbling with the gun, shoving it into the glove compartment, and, finally, the click as it shuts. He's just in time. Baynard James leans forward and looks through my open window. "What fool thing's going on here?"

I ask him, "Did the FBI call you?"

His dark glasses look bigger than any I've ever seen. We're inches apart, eye to eye.

"Get the hell out of here."

"Did the FBI call?"

"Yeah, they did. The station. I was going home. I said I'd handle it. Now get the hell out." His arm's out pointing to the ridge and the highway, but his face is right on mine.

"What about the others up there?"

"They're gone. I said I'd handle it."

"Did you know it was me here?"

He doesn't answer. He stands straight.

"Did you know it was me?"

He steps back from my car. When he speaks, it's to the air or the dust up in it. "When you get to the bypass, turn east.

Don't turn west." He walks back to his car and drives away. I start the engine. At the ridge, nobody's there. We get to the bypass and the highway's deserted.

Isaac asks, "Are you going to turn west?"

West is the quickest way back. "No, I'm going to do what the man said."

"Why?"

I pause. "We've had dealings."

"What dealings?"

"I ... I believe I annihilated his world. For that, I figured he'd either kill me or save me. It was a fifty-fifty chance, and when I saw him I took it. Well, so far so good. There's no reason to stop now."

"What? Annihilated what?"

"Forget it." I glance over at Isaac. "To be honest, I really don't know."

We drive east, turn south, and then we loop back to town. We don't talk again until we're a couple of blocks from our office. Then Isaac tells me, "What I said back there, about crossing bridges. My father would say it's all a pipe dream. I say you have to leave everything you love behind, leave it all behind. And all for a pipe dream, my father would say." I can barely hear him, he's speaking so softly. "When you wanted that gun ... I've never even held one before ... I just never believed ... but I gave it to you for my father." Then I feel his hand on my arm. I glance over and he's looking right at me. "I was willing to kill so he wouldn't lose me. I couldn't even live up to my own pipe dream."

Later that night—it's a long time before I can sleep, before the fear leaves—I keep getting stuck on what I'd just done, betting on that Baynard James. I mean, it turned out okay, but

I can't shake the feeling I was a damn fool to do it. I try to remember what it was I saw in his face to make me put that gun away. He recognized me, but it was more than that. The more I try to remember, the more I want to forget it. I just want him out of my mind.

So I think about what Isaac said: that we're not different. But I am different. I'm thinking maybe I'm not even like my father. He feared whatever it was inside him that made him kill a man. And he's controlled it ever since. I don't know if I could do that. I've just grown weary of it—everybody's violence. I've never even had any of my own. Just that one time I kicked that White man. Maybe I'm not up to it.

I smile. I should've kicked him in the nuts.

And now I'm beginning to think I know Isaac: his idea of himself, the logic of whom he thinks himself to be. He wants everybody to be saved and to be worth saving, so they all have to have bridges. He wants to believe the best of people, so love is why they fear, and fear is why they kill.

But—maybe I'm not so churched anymore—but I still remember my Bible. Most people don't take the narrow way. Most people aren't saved. Maybe what they'd fear the most would be their own salvation, what that would require them to do. You believe in the best of them at your own peril.

Anyway, I'd tell Isaac this: "You believe in innocence. You believe that suffering brings redemption." Suddenly I realize: Morgan believes in those things too. So, I would tell them both, "I don't believe in either of those things."

Isaac never did tell us what his "bombshell" was. A few days later he was dead. "Killed by the Klan." The TV, the radio, even his father—they all said he was killed by the Klan.

41 • The Drowned Man

Harry had Evy's new clothes folded in his car. It was late at night. He had this last piece of business to attend to. Then he'd rescue his boy.

Earley and Isaac sat with Harry in his kitchen. He'd pulled the shades and drawn the curtains. Around the table, Harry told his story, and showed his pictures and read Catherine's letters. "Here, here's Timothy's birth certificate, here're the photographs." He put them in Isaac's hands. "You take them. The letters, you take it all. You've got to stop him. You've got to stop them all."

Harry paused, and took hold of Isaac's arm. "But you have to understand how I feel about my son. I have to live everyday knowing he's a murderer. That's what the Klan does. They burn crosses. They terrorize people. People like … me once, and him too, Coloreds, though he'll never admit it— But that's what he is. You can't know what it's like to have raised your boy to be a murderer. Nobody should know what that's like. At first I said, 'That's not Timothy, that's somebody else.' But that didn't … I couldn't …. I lay it at my own feet, for the choices I made. Tell people that, that I'm the one to blame.

"After Timothy left, I tried to think about the ordinary— my errands to run, the news in the newspapers … local news, automobile crashes, fires. Things you can cluck you tongue about and say, 'why that's just too bad.' But life burns all that away.

"That feeling just sticks with me—the burning that's inside me. Ever since I rescued Geneva and her children and changed our lives forever, life has burned me to my core, and it's just as I feared, there's so little of me left. When you strip yourself of family and place there's not much left of you, not much else that matters. I'm not a great man who can rise above his raising. I don't think many people are." Harry gestured at Earley. "That's why I wrote to him after all those years. I didn't want his forgiveness—I didn't think I deserved it—and I didn't do it for his understanding. I wrote to him simply because he was all I had left."

"And Timothy hasn't even that. There's not one person he can claim as kin. And I'm the one to blame."

Isaac stared at the pictures of Harry's granddaughter. "She looks just like—who is this?"

"You might know her. She's older now, of course." Harry pointed at the picture. "Her mother wrote that she's joined the Movement. But she's in Atlanta."

"You said her name is Johanna? Is it Johanna Burnham?"

"Yes, it is."

Isaac was gathering up the pictures. "She's here in Williams Point. I've got to show her these. I've got to tell her this. She should be the one to tell the story."

Harry took one of the pictures: a beautiful child posed, a proud mother kneeling at her side, a father standing behind, smiling. "Her mother used to write to me that Johanna would redeem us all. Everything that had gone wrong between her and Timothy, somehow that little girl would make it right. That was her daydream." He stared at the picture. *Now it's going to be her nightmare.* Harry put the picture down. *I can't— I can't save them.* He picked up the picture again. He muttered, "Evy ... Evy depends on me—"

He couldn't look at Isaac and he couldn't finish.

Isaac put everything in a shoebox. "Johanna will want to see this." He turned to Harry. "She *will* redeem you all. She'll redeem us all now. And people will finally see. There's no 'race,' and there're no boundaries. Everything we fear in our so-called 'enemies'—they're no different than us. Everyone's a multitude, and every multitude is one."

When they were finished, Isaac stood to go. He was holding the shoebox filled with the pictures, the letters, and Timothy's birth certificate. He paused and looked at Harry. "You're doing a brave thing, sir. You've lived quite a life. *You*'re a multitude."

Harry, embarrassed, smiled; he shook his head. "No I'm not." He got up and opened the door. "I don't regret losing my Whiteness. I don't regret not being Negro. But I do regret not having any family anymore. I have no history. I have no place. Without a race, you can't have any of those things. And this country ... it will punish you for that."

Isaac nodded. He pursed his lips and looked down at the box. "Not anymore. That's what we're going to change."

Harry said nothing to that. He watched as the two men left and disappeared into the night, to whatever course that Earley used to find this house and return to it, night after night—just like a night creature, whose sound you sleep through, or if awake, the sound that you ignore. Harry wished them well. And he wished he could believe like Isaac did.

That boy Isaac, he hasn't lived long enough to know. Harry was afraid that life would burn them all, Negro and White, gentile and Jew, that it would burn them all down to their cores. There was so little left of him now, and Timothy ... Timothy would still bear the burden of his, Harry's, choices. Standing at the door, he was telling Isaac in his mind: *I'm old now—I've been old since the night of that fire—and here you are, a young man determined to save the world. I was never so inclined, but I was young once. Handsome and tall ... and as innocent as you.*

Harry waited until midnight, and everybody certainly asleep, before he drove to Miss Ester's house. The windows were dark, still he waited. He listened for a long time, but he couldn't hear a sound.

Satisfied, he walked from his car to the door. It was unlocked. He opened it just far enough to creep on in and he paused to let his eyes adjust. It must be just as he'd last seen it. He couldn't imagine it changed. The looming newspapers, the old-style furniture, the dust, the dark, Del Ray's trophies: all of these were obstacles on his way to Evy's room.

He crept up the stairs, and then he paused to remember which way to turn. He reached the room where Emily had slept. He turned the door knob slowly. The boy was asleep. Harry knelt by the bed and slowly, gently, placed his hand over Evy's mouth. He did nothing else. The boy woke, his head jerking upward against the palm of Harry's hand.

"Shhhh—it's me. I've come to get you. I'm going to take my hand off your mouth now, but you mustn't make a sound." Harry raised his hand. "Your mother's going to be okay. Some doctors are helping her. She's going to get better. We're going to get away from here and when your mother gets better we'll go get her as well. Would you like that?"

Evy nodded yes.

"Good. Do you want to leave with me?"

Evy nodded yes.

"Good, good. Your mother will be okay. Callie didn't do anything to her. Don't you worry. Here, just slide out of bed.

Don't worry about your clothes. I've got some new ones in the car. You can come with me in your PJs. You can leave everything else behind. You're never coming back. Do you understand?"

Evy nodded.

In the car, Harry drove south to the outskirts of town. Evy changed in the back seat. He handed his pajamas up to Harry. He rolled down the window and threw them out, his right hand still on the wheel. He never stopped or even slowed.

Evy clambered up to the front seat. Harry glanced at him. He was quiet, slouched in the seat, but he was looking up and out the side window, at the murky, starless sky above.

Harry turned west, to the Holiday Inn. "Do you want to lie down and sleep? There's room in the back."

"No sir. I'm okay. I'm not sleepy."

Harry told Evy, when Emily was well they'd get word to her. "I'm good at that. I'll find her. It'll be easy because she'll come right back home to Williams Point. And as soon as she hears from us, she'll come join us, and we'll be together and never be bothered again."

Harry smiled in the dark. "Where would you like to live, Evy: In California? In Hawaii?"

Evy giggled at the thought. It was the only time he smiled.

—◆— —◆—

Harry pulled into the parking lot of the Holiday Inn. He could see his car's reflection, squat and dim in the lobby's glass façade. He sat for a moment, breathing heavily. He didn't even know if Timothy was there. He was throwing dice in the dark. He braced himself.

Evy turned stiffly in his seat, his eyes wide, and looked around. "Why're we here?"

Harry turned to him. "I'm not going to be but a few minutes. Then I'll be back and we'll go someplace. Would you like to go to California? We could keep driving till we get to California."

The boy nodded and stared at the motel's neon sign perched above the lobby's door.

"Good. Now you get in the back seat and lie down on the floor. You must be very quiet and very still. I'll be back real soon. I promise."

In the hotel, Harry told the clerk he wanted to speak to Thomas Wilbur. The clerk dialed a number, spoke a few words on the telephone and hung up.

"He's not in."

Harry shook his head. "That's too bad." He looked up at the rows of key hooks. Most had their room keys. But one line of six was empty—on the second floor. "Can I use your pay phone?"

"It's over there."

Harry walked to the far end of the lobby, past the pay phone, and took the stairs to the second floor. Two-oh-four to two-ten—he knocked on a door, and kept knocking until he heard somebody stirring inside.

"I'm looking for Tom Wilbur." The man stood still, silent, his hand on the edge of the door. Harry persisted. "I'm his father. I've got to see him."

The man looked closely at Harry's face. "Okay, two doors down."

When Harry knocked and the door opened he was face-to-face with his son. Harry edged in before Timothy could react.

Harry closed the door behind him. "Are you alone?" He looked past his son into the room. Timothy hissed at him.

"What's going on? What're you doing here?"

"Is anybody here?"

"No. Get away. Leave me alone. I've left you alone. What're you doing here?"

"You're in danger. You've got to leave—at once. Go to Mexico. Go to Canada. You've got to leave this country—"

"What the hell are you—?"

Harry put his hands up to touch his son. "I've told them all about you: who you are; who I am; who your mother was. I told them you're a Negro."

"What the hell! What the hell! Who did you tell?"

"It doesn't matter who I told. What matters is that tomorrow everybody in this country will know. Harry gestured at the door behind him. "Your friends will know. You've got to leave here now." Harry reached for him but Timothy stepped back. "You've got to stop what you're doing. You've got to stop this killing."

Timothy grabbed Harry's lapels and pushed him back against the door. "I'm no nigger! It's a lie goddamnit! What did you do to me? Why? I left you alone. You gotta tell me who you told this to."

"I can't." Harry tried to twist away. Timothy grabbed him by his throat. Harry couldn't breathe. His knees were giving way. He was sinking to the floor. Timothy loosened his grip. Harry could barely speak. "You've got to go."

Timothy gripped him tighter.

"You better tell me, old man!"

Harry was gasping. His vision was blurring.

"I'm gonna kill you, old man!"

Timothy tightened his grip and slapped his father, twice, across his cheeks.

Harry gurgled. "SNCC. I told SNCC."

"Was it a nigger?"

Harry slid downward until he was almost sitting on the floor. Timothy still had him by his neck.

"No ... a White man."

Timothy pulled him forward and slammed him back against the door. Harry's head hit the door knob. He slumped to the floor.

―◆― ―◆―

Fifteen minutes later Evy wandered into the lobby of the Holiday Inn. He asked for his daddy. "He came in here looking for a man."

The clerk called the police. They found Harry behind the dumpster out back. He was unconscious. Someone put something under his nose—sharp, acrid, his head snapped back—then there were men all around him. He rose. He fell.

―◆― ―◆―

Was he moving? Was he floating? Harry didn't know. Those men all around him, looming, drawing near and then receding, back and forth, back and forth like waves: they disappeared.

Harry came to in a hospital. By his bed was a policeman, seated, pitching side to side. The policeman stood—his body wavered like in a fun-house mirror—and he leaned over Harry and told him he was under arrest, for kidnapping, and that Evy was safe back home. Harry only stared. He didn't say a word. The policeman shook his head, and his body wavered and ebbed and flowed.

42 • The Hanged Man

It had to be the Jew. Timothy knew where he lived. A separate room behind a deacon's house. He drove there alone.

He crept through an alley into the backyard. He had a switchblade in his hand. He saw the light from under the door. He put his hand to the knob and opened it.

He was too late. Isaac lay on his back on the floor of his room. Above him Johanna was holding a scissors in her hand. The blades dripped blood on the body. At her feet, behind her, was a shoe box, its contents splayed.

She looked up with a start. Timothy put away his knife. He reached out his hand, his palm up.

She stared at him; looked down at the body. She backed away. "He said I'm a Negro. He said he had proof. He was going to tell—"

"Shhh. It's okay. I know. I know all about it."

"How could he have thought …? This would've ruined my mother. My father would've divorced her. He'd have had to."

She looked up at Timothy. "My father is a very important man. People *listen* to him. They do what he says. This … this would've destroyed him. My whole family would've been destroyed."

"It's okay. Here, give me your hand."

"And me … I was meant to do great things in this world."

"Shhh. You don't have to explain. Give me the scissors."
He stepped over the body to her.

"—great, good things. I couldn't do that if ..." She looked around the room. Her eyes widened.

He put his palm out. "Shhh. It's okay."

She let him take the scissors from her hand.

"I didn't mean to. I just ..."

"It's okay. Here," he gestured to a basin of water. "Wash your hands."

She did as she was told. He was watching her, and she couldn't keep her eyes off him, this man who'd burst in upon her. He wondered, did she recognize him from that night in her room?

He looked down at the shoe box, at the letters and the photographs. Had she read them? Seen them? Did she know who he was? Did she even care? She hadn't said a word about her real father. He pointed at the pictures and the letters. "Leave those here. I'll take care of them."

She nodded. She gave the body another look and sobbed. Once. "When he first told me, he was ecstatic. He thought he had good news. He thought I'd want to tell ..."

He put his finger to his lips. "Go. Don't tell anybody. I'll fix this for you."

She hesitated, and then she obeyed. With the scissors, Timothy scratched the letters KKK in Isaac's chest. He looked around for a towel and found one. He dipped it in the basin, the scissors in his hand.

And then he wiped them clean.

43 · EPILOGUE
THE WOUNDED MAN

"Killed by the Klan." Everybody says Isaac was killed by the Klan. Who am I to swim against the stream?

The college volunteers came and we had our freedom vote that fall. Morgan worked it hard. But he's been talking about his store in Drew. He says he should be tending it. This movement is no longer his—it's not his color and it's not his kind. I think that's what he believes. He's still exhausted from the effort and the constant worry. He doesn't sleep too well. When the college volunteers were here he was always on edge; there were too many White people around, even though they were young and sympathetic. It's how he was raised and all the crap he's seen over the course of his fifty years; he was watching his back just out of habit. And that will wear on you. And they didn't even notice that anything was wrong. There's talk now about bringing in even more White volunteers next summer, for the whole summer, and all over the state. I don't expect Morgan to be here when they come.

You really couldn't say a word against our volunteers this fall. They worked with sincerity and dedication—in the face of Isaac's death. Then they left, and we were left here with our lives. One played the guitar. He'd sing a song, "Wasn't That a Time."

Our fathers bled at Valley Forge,
The fields were red with blood.
Wasn't that a time, wasn't that a time,

To try the soul of man.
Wasn't that a terrible time.

 He said that song was about them, the volunteers now, and that the history books would write about what they did. I don't doubt it. After all, America will have its story. And I'll have mine.

<hr />

The last time I saw Isaac, his last night, I was over at Mr. Courtland's café. Mr. Courtland had some money he wanted to give to the Movement. He'd always insist on it being just us two, alone in his kitchen, and always at night. It was very hush-hush; he didn't want anybody knowing his business. When I came, the place was closed, but Isaac was there with Johanna; they were huddled at a table. I nodded to them and went on back. Mr. Courtland was giving me the money, counting it into my hand, when we heard Isaac at the top of his voice. "You can't avoid this. You've got to deal with it."

 I turned around but I couldn't see a thing. I was too far back in the kitchen. Then I heard the screen door slam, and when I came back out there was only Isaac. He had his back to me; he was in the doorway, his fist against the frame, and then he pushed the screen door open and was gone. I didn't give it much thought—just something between them. But in a couple of hours he was dead. Now I remember that night with the two of us together, sitting in the car, and why I don't agree with him, because the way is narrow—and there he was with his fist pressed against the doorframe, his head sagging, and— and now, still, at any moment, I catch myself looking at a door, thinking he could come in through it and apologize for missing the morning's canvass.

Johanna had stayed in her room for three days after he'd died. And then she left a note, and left, and went back home. She said she needed time with her family. She never came back.

I don't know what happened in Isaac's room that night—only that his killer didn't bring a weapon; Isaac was killed with his own scissors—but when people ask I just say yes, he was killed by the Klan.

⸻

I saw that cop the other day, that Baynard James. I see him once in a while; it's hard not to in a town this size. It's like nothing ever happened, no beating, no voice—there's no ground between us that we could walk on to approach each other even if we wanted to. And I don't.

Whatever happened on *that* day, all I know is what I remember. Maybe it's what I choose to remember. The event has passed and now commentary is all that's left. I can draw this lesson or that, whatever story I want to tell.

("Killed by the Klan": is that Isaac's only story?)

Stooping to that bench outside that jail, I heard my voice, but I hadn't said a mumbling word. That's the story I want to tell.

It's what I told Deborah, sitting under that tree, drinking our sodas: I'd already been beaten, and that Baynard James expected me to call him "sir." And I didn't. When I knelt back down on that bench, it didn't matter anymore whether I'd be beaten or not. For those few seconds, it just didn't matter. And what my voice—*that* voice—did say was what I needed right at that moment, because my being beaten didn't cause it—not my pain, nor the danger I was in—that voice came from a source independent of myself and the world around me. For that one moment, I was truly free.

And I told Deborah, you can't live like that—not for more than a few seconds.

I told her she wouldn't want any part of this God. I told her there's no way to describe this God. I don't think anybody can really believe in Him for very long—only for as long as He holds you. And if He holds you too long, He'll annihilate you. He's not a God you can teach to children in Sunday School.

That's what I told her.

Look, I'm just a normal guy. When I wake up in the morning I wash my face and brush my teeth, and I'm just thinking how I can survive the day and do some work. I'm just here in the world, going from day to day, and I don't see beyond that. I don't believe in much. But I believe this: on that bench that was my voice speaking but it wasn't me.

You'd do the same for your father.

I told Deborah I couldn't have said those words, because, behind them is this: I could understand that cop and he could understand me, right down to my bottom, through and through, because that's the only way those words could've stopped him. Him understanding me—that's the worst of it: I couldn't accept that. I still can't. This universal brotherhood that Isaac talked about—it's a terrible idea. It has no standards, no boundaries. It means we all blend together. That racist cop: I should be off limits to people like him. There's no honor in a God who would have that racist cop know and understand me. Where's the good? Where's the evil? What separates them? What separates us?

So here's my story now: you can only live your life if you put aside the eternal. Just suppose that Isaac's right, that the world is a bridge to God. Isaac wanted us to cross that bridge. But once we do that—if we even can—we'll leave this world behind. And I'm not ready to do that yet. I'm not ready to trade this world for God.

("Killed by the Klan?" His story should be better than that.)

I've taken to reading the Bible. I'm looking for loopholes. Here's one: What did Jesus say to those who saw his miracles? He told them not to tell. He wanted nothing known. He had too much respect for us—for our humanness, for our dreams and for our lives. He found us good—not like the Creator did, perfect on the sixth day—but here and now. Fallen, but still good. Good enough for grace. The eternal could wait. He was giving us a chance to live in our world.

I don't believe in progress. Maybe I never did. Now I don't know what I believe, but there's no unbroken line tilted upward, running triumphant through history. Maybe there's revelation. Maybe there's a lightning burst in the night, but then it's dark again, and we're left to stumble through. Our words, our lives—we might onetime fly up into the sky, we might even touch the eternal, but we'll fall down just as fast, earthbound and crippled. I don't want to fly. Right now, I just want to attend to my people, to my race, and not be responsible for anybody else. I'll feed the children their bread and let the dogs take whatever crumbs they find. That's in the Gospel. Those are Jesus' very words. And that's what I told Deborah.

At every freedom meeting I stand before my people and tell them my stories—three days and I'm risen, right through that window with Morgan right behind. I pretend to courage when all I have are words. Every day I rise with the morning's light.

I walk the streets and knock on doors. The houses are still ramshackle. But this is where Aunt Ertharin lives and Deborah with her. And two streets over, Rev. Coleman still isn't with us, but he sees to this: on every Picnic Sunday, every young man in his church will have four bits to bid on the young ladies' lunches. Come next summer, I'll be ready with mine. It's a calming joy for a man to watch a woman smile as he eats her food on a slow Sunday afternoon. And Rev. Coleman says nobody will go wanting; not in his church, no sir.

Last month we walked together around the back of his church. There're trees there, grown tall, that he said his father helped to plant—oak and maple, walnut and pecan. He said it's a beautiful state—Mississippi. I agreed. Oh, yes indeed. I told him that after I've gone back to college I would return one day, to this very town. And then I'll never leave. I told him he might think he's not with us, but he really is—he just doesn't know it yet—because we're with him. He smiled at that and he didn't disagree.

This spring those trees will cool the air and make it sweet. Standing there ... there are some things—little human things like laughing at yourself, like eating barbecue and sweet potato pie with a pretty young woman (she's so sweet, you'd marry her on the spot!), like a spring day and a tall blue sky—and you can find them right here, even in Mississippi—especially in Mississippi. These things keep you in mind of, well, a fullness of being—maybe even a godliness—while we stumble here on the ground.

Aunt Ertharin and Rev. Coleman—each in their own way, they keep their faith with this community. There's something resilient here as well as damaged, which means there's something human. So, I'll keep on working. And I'll try not to be afraid. Tomorrow I'll find my way to Eunice Donaldson's house and shell peas with her, and to Aunt Ertharin's house and Deborah. I'll listen to them all. Aunt Ertharin will tell Deborah that what you get out of life doesn't have to be what life gives you. She'll tell her she doesn't know her own righteousness and she doesn't know her own faith. And I'll nod my head, yes, yes, and listen to their stories—as I've begun to do.

Listening, I've realized something about home: my home, where it is and how I make it mine. I can tell my stories anywhere. Those don't bring me home. But Aunt Ertharin, Miss Eunice, her daughter Deborah, even Rev. Coleman: their stories, when I listen, when I really hear them, I find myself at home. They've become my kin. Sad stories, funny stories, victories and defeats, endurance and death. Maybe it's the sharing—but for me, hearing others' stories makes that place my home.

I wrote my father a letter. And after the freedom vote I went back to Drew. My father asked me for how long. I said for a day, maybe two. I smiled, a little nervous, and said we'd see how it'd go, and he nodded he understood. "You have to go back, I suppose." We were standing in the front room, facing each other. He had an uncertain look in his eyes and I supposed I did too. Seeing him surrounded by the old familiar furniture, the worn and faded rug, the sofa and stuffed chair pristine beneath their plastic covers, the patterned paper on the walls, the pictures all around, and the sound of my mother fixing supper in the kitchen—I marveled at how I didn't know this man. Not like I should. Did he know me any better than I knew him? I thought maybe he did. And that calmed me. My father gestured to the sofa and, as I stepped to it, he sat down in the chair. If my mom had come out, she'd have sat down beside me.

Mom fixed us her best supper. And afterwards we sat together on our front porch, my father and me and my mother in between. It was dusk. We wrapped our coats against the cold. My father shared a jar with me, and I told some of my stories. And my mother told us hers, about Papa Joe and Mama Sal. Stories I'd heard so many times before, and, God willing, I'll hear again; and one day I'll tell them to my children, those and others about their Grandma Nel and Grandpa Ches. Back and forth, my mother and I told our stories, and my father listened while he cradled his shotgun in his lap.

A couple of times, what looked like a strange car down the road had my father and me rise from our chairs, and peer through the twilight to see if the driver was Colored or White. Rising up and sitting down, that edge stayed with us all through the night. And then a third time, long after sunset, a pair of headlights on the bend before our house, swept our porch and, for a second, blinded us, but as my father rose I could see a dusky arm wave from the driver's open window. We all relaxed. Most likely someone we knew. Maybe even loved.

We settled back down, and my mother and I continued swapping stories. Once we'd talked ourselves out, an easy country silence settled in, and my father leaned back and looked up at the night above our neighbors' homes, as if he were counting stars. I could tell by the tilt of his head, but I couldn't make out his features in the dark. My mother and I stayed in our chairs. We wouldn't go in before he did, and he seemed content to stay. I listened to the quiet night sounds and wondered what might be the expression on his face. He must've been at peace, I suppose. Comfortable, at least. But watching, always watching, for any cars coming down the street. Again, I could only tell that by the tilt of his head.

We could've stayed inside that night, safer in a back room, with the lights off in the front. But we didn't. What we did made no sense, but we claimed what we knew should be ours. Look here, we said, we're home. Again. Again, and again. We're home.

◆—◆ ◆—◆

Here's another thing I told Deborah: I'd wanted to kill that man, that Baynard James, when he had me outside that jail. She asked me why I didn't. I told her I saw the last of y'all going into that jail, and only harm would come if I killed him, to every single one of y'all in that jail. And I also remembered something my grandfather told me, of living your life to be commended. Killing that cop: would I be commended for that? I shook my head no. Those were my reasons. She nodded her head. They seemed good enough for her.

But I can't help but wonder: what was God's reason? After all, He was there. That whole time. No matter what reasons I had for not killing Baynard James—maybe He had reasons of His own.

Anyway, I'm going to tend to my garden, in my people's own backyard. But while I do, I'll be mindful of that single weed of truth—that bending to that bench I didn't speak those words. That weed—maybe, one day, I'll be reconciled to it. A scant few seconds and something I heard my own voice say; if it weren't for its scandal I wouldn't be alive today.

"Killed by the Klan?" Here's a better story for Isaac. (I feel he should have one, and he can't tell it for himself.) "If any man have ears to hear, let him hear." Just those words.

There's no loophole there. They exasperate me because I tell myself—and on this, I must insist—I will only tell the stories that are mine, and only to my people, and I will listen only to the stories that are theirs. But every time we speak, our words escape into the air. And spread. Like music. Once there, strangers too can hear them, and even profit if they dare.

Acknowledgments

I would like to thank the following people for their comments and suggestions on my manuscript through its various stages of completion: Mary M. Walters, Cynthis Childes, Aubrey Schultz, Shiela Pardee, Anna Willman, and Stephen Woodfin.

I also would like to recognize the community support provided by the Maryland Writers' Association, the Willamette Writers' Association, and the Creative Writers' Critique Group of the Osher Lifelong Learning Institute in Eugene, Oregon.

Finally, I want to give my special thanks to Isabella Felix and Dante Zuniga-West for their insightful comments and suggestions.

About the Author

Born in the baby boom, educated and loosed upon the world, I've tried to make an impression upon it. I got myself a degree in cultural anthropology and did field work in the Mississippi Delta. I saw the first Black man elected in his county since Reconstruction. Later, I worked for private aid organizations that gave medical materials to doctors in hospitals and clinics in developing countries. I saw famine in Africa. I saw bombs fall in Eritrea. There, I met goat herders who would rather starve than eat their goats, and visited hospitals hidden in caves. The doctors fashioned light switches from used syringes.

Then I married, and I helped my wife raise two fine boys. Truly, my wife and sons don't know their own righteousness, and that is the one of the best things you can say about anybody. For a while, I worked for a homeless shelter. I taught college students anthropology. Then I worked for a law firm and began to write at night. Now I'm retired. So far, two novels bear my name—*Motherless Children* and *Smokestack Lightning*.

If I could be British, I'd be Graham Greene. If I could sing, I'd be Bob Dylan.

Looking back, I can't say I've made much of an impression, but I'm betting on God's grace. Someday, I hope to be a witness.